Books by L.M. Brown

I0607491

Falling into Darkness

ISBN # 978-1-78686-093-4

©Copyright L.M. Brown 2016

Cover Art by Posh Gosh ©Copyright 2016

Interior text design by Claire Siemaszkiewicz

Pride Publishing

Published in 2016 by Pride Publishing, Newland House, The Point, Weaver Road, Lincoln, LN6 3QN, United Kingdom.

FALLING INTO DARKNESS

L.M. BROWN

Dedication

For Lee Rey.
Thank you for all your encouragement in writing this story.
Without you, Michael and Lucifer's story would never have been finished.
I hope you enjoy their journey.

Chapter One

He was breathtaking. The archangel Michael could think of no other word to describe him. His long, blond hair fell down his back in luxuriant waves, stopping just above the perfectly rounded buttocks. The strength in his muscular arms carried him up the cliff side with ease, his feet never missing a step. His pure white wings didn't have a hint of gray in them, showing all who saw him he was completely at peace in his emotions.

Even though all angels were beautiful, in Michael's eyes, Lucifer outshone them all.

It had become a habit of Michael's to wander to the reflection pool at the same time of day Lucifer liked to visit.

Lucifer enjoyed searching for gems embedded in the stones, always striving to find the most perfect pieces for the jewelry he crafted. The best time to see the hidden stones was at dawn, when the rays of the morning sun hit the area at just the right angle.

Michael had discovered Lucifer's habit of visiting the pool by chance, but now he made sure his morning walk coincided with Lucifer's swim as often as possible. He loved nothing better than beginning his day by watching Lucifer at his work.

He had every intention of introducing himself one day, but until then he was content to observe.

Michael took a bite of one of the peaches he had picked on his walk from his home on the beach. He had gathered a few, just in case he found the courage to speak to Lucifer this morning. He sighed as he admitted to himself he wouldn't say anything today, just as he had held his silence yesterday, and all the days before.

He didn't even know how long he had been watching Lucifer. It must have been several weeks now, if not months. He wished he could think of a single word to say to the aloof son of the morning, who outranked even the archangels.

Michael didn't think Lucifer had seen him, yet something must have given his position away, because the angel peered over his shoulder from the cliff wall and stared directly at him.

He opened his mouth, willing the right words to come from his lips, even as he suspected he would probably say something monumentally foolish. Before he could utter a word, Lucifer let go of his grip on the rocks and dived gracefully into the deep, clear blue waters below.

Michael toyed with the edge of his robe, wondering whether he should join Lucifer in the pool. Had Lucifer's piercing stare been an invitation?

While Michael deliberated, Lucifer surfaced and drew in a long breath. He ran his hands through his wet hair, the move drawing attention to his perfectly defined pectoral muscles.

Michael *had* to say something. Lucifer had seen him and it would be rude not to acknowledge him now.

"Good morning," Michael called. His voice came out as something of a squeak and he cringed at the embarrassingly juvenile sound. He could have communicated his thoughts telepathically, as all angels could, but he had never enjoyed hearing someone else's voice in his head. His fellow angels considered him a little odd for this particular quirk, but they respected his foible and spoke out loud unless absolutely necessary. Now Michael wished he had sent his greeting to Lucifer's mind — at least then he wouldn't have sounded so childish.

Lucifer inclined his head in response and dove under the water again.

Michael hung his head in disappointment. He had a

feeling he had committed some kind of *faux pas*. Not only had Lucifer failed to reply to his greeting, he hadn't even offered the smallest of smiles.

Now he thought about it, Michael didn't recall ever seeing Lucifer smile. Even when he had struggled to reach a particular jewel and had, at last, been successful, he hadn't smiled at the accomplishment. Michael suspected if Lucifer ever did smile directly at him, he would be entirely lost to the angel.

Lucifer continued to swim, diving under the water before returning to the surface, sometimes with a gem from the bottom, sometimes without. He didn't look in Michael's direction again.

Michael ate the final peach, knowing he had no intention of offering the fruit to Lucifer today. When he had eaten the last bite he rose from his place on the grass, intending to head to the communal conclave, where the rest of the archangels would be congregating and monitoring the earth, enjoying the new day.

"Did you enjoy watching me?"

Michael stumbled into a bush, nearly losing his balance entirely. When he faced Lucifer, the angel had exited the pool and stood near the robes he had discarded earlier. Lucifer didn't seem in any hurry to pick up his clothing. He stood naked and unashamed before Michael, who couldn't keep his eyes from straying downward.

"Or should I have asked *are* you enjoying watching me?" Lucifer amended.

Michael's face burned as he met Lucifer's gaze. He half expected to see a teasing smile on the angel's lips, but his customary scowl remained in place.

"I..."

Lucifer laughed without humor. "Archangels," he muttered, just loud enough for Michael to hear. "Spare me from ogling archangels who can't string a sentence together."

Michael wished the ground would open up and swallow

him. He never had trouble speaking when he talked to anyone else. Why had he become tongue-tied at precisely the wrong moment?

Humiliated and dejected, Michael hurried away, leaving Lucifer at the side of the pool.

Michael knew in his heart he wouldn't go back tomorrow. His one chance to speak to Lucifer, to secure his attention, had slipped past him, never to return.

* * * *

"What brings you here so early?" Gabriel asked as Michael took a seat at the breakfast table two mornings after his humiliating episode with Lucifer.

He hadn't been back to the pool, following their embarrassing exchange, and Michael's path had not crossed that of Lucifer's, much to his relief. He couldn't believe he had been so foolish as to get caught spying on the son of the morning. What must Lucifer think of him?

"Two mornings together," Raphael added with a teasing smile.

Michael sniffed haughtily. "Just because I'm choosing to keep you company instead of dining alone at home."

"Oh, is *that* what you're doing?" Gabriel asked. "Because your body might be here, but your mind is clearly elsewhere."

Raphael laughed. "His mind is probably lingering wherever it is he usually spends these hours, which certainly isn't in his home."

"What do you mean?" Gabriel questioned.

"I've been to Michael's house most mornings these last few weeks to invite him to join us, and the place has been surprisingly empty."

Michael studied his plate of food. He hadn't realized his presence had been missed. Normally a late riser, he had gone to a great deal of effort to wake early enough to see Lucifer at the pool. He hadn't imagined Raphael had attended at his home so early.

Any hope Michael had that Gabriel would let Raphael's comment pass vanished along with his plate.

"Give that back," Michael demanded.

Gabriel shook his head. "Not until you tell us where you've been going so early in the mornings. It must be something important to encourage you to stir out of your bed before the sun is at its zenith."

Michael rolled his eyes. "I've just been walking the heavens, enjoying the birth of each new day."

Raphael snorted. "This is the same archangel who couldn't even wake to watch the sunrise from his own private beach, no matter how often we told him the sight would be spectacular."

Gabriel laughed. "I don't believe him either. I think our Michael is hiding something."

"I'm sure he is," Raphael agreed. "The question is what?"

Michael didn't want to rise to the bait, but they didn't need any encouragement. The life of an archangel rarely contained intrigue or mystery and a small part of each of them seemed to relish the same whenever the chance arose. Michael accepted their teasing with good humor, just as he knew they would treat his friendly jibes in the same manner.

"Or maybe it's who," Gabriel suggested. "Metatron has appeared rather lonely since he parted company with Sandalphon. Perhaps Michael has been warming Metatron's bed instead of his own."

This time Michael laughed along with the others. "No, I promise I've not been sleeping in any bed save my own."

Raphael waggled his eyebrows. "Who said anything about sleeping?"

Michael groaned at the poor quip, but before he could deliver his retort, a hush came over the room. Across the table from him, Gabriel's jaw dropped in apparent surprise as he stared at something over Michael's shoulder.

Next to him, Raphael twisted in his seat and his expression

morphed into one of shock too.

Michael wondered what might be happening behind him, yet he couldn't move a muscle to see for himself. His spine tingled and he had the strangest sensation someone was staring straight at him.

"What is it?" he whispered, and in the silence of the room even his quiet question seemed obnoxiously loud.

"The son of the morning," Gabriel murmured as he set Michael's plate back in front of him with a shaky hand. "Lucifer."

Michael must have misheard. Lucifer never came into the communal areas of Heaven. He, along with the other favorites, remained solitary, rarely associating with the rest of the angels, and never in a crowded setting such as this.

Slowly, barely able to draw breath, Michael faced the entrance.

Lucifer stood in the archway, the morning sun behind him. There could be no mistaking his silhouette for that of another.

In the brightness of the light, Michael couldn't tell what Lucifer searched for, at least not for sure. Only his instincts told him Lucifer had eyes for him, and him alone.

Slowly, Lucifer strolled into the room. Every angel in his path stepped aside to let him pass. Some bowed their heads respectfully, but he didn't acknowledge their deference in any way.

Finally he arrived at Michael's table and came to a halt.

"Good morning," Lucifer said.

"I..." Michael mumbled, once again silently cursing his ineptitude.

"I see you still have trouble forming sentences," Lucifer commented. "Let us hope you can manage more than a single word by this evening."

"Er..."

Raphael gathered his wits together first and rose to make a sweeping bow. "Great angel, welcome to our table. Won't you join us and partake of the fruits?"

Lucifer spared the archangel a momentary glance. "I have already eaten this morning."

Raphael didn't seem to know what to say, so he sat back down with a bump.

Lucifer returned his attention to Michael. "This evening, at sunset."

"Where?" Michael asked, his voice croaking embarrassingly.

"Rumor has it your beach is quite pleasant."

Michael nodded, not trusting his voice enough to try speaking again.

"Tonight then, Michael," Lucifer said, before sweeping away in a flurry of robes, everyone once again stepping aside to make way for him.

"The son of the morning knows your name?" Gabriel asked as soon as Lucifer had gone. "Is he the one you've been meeting each dawn?"

Michael ducked his head. "I wouldn't say I was *meeting* him, exactly."

"But you *have* been with him in the mornings?" Raphael pressed. "You kept that quiet."

There would be no escaping the interrogation and Michael accepted he had to come clean.

"I couldn't sleep one night and ended up walking through the lands to the north of here. I chanced upon Lucifer coming to the pool of jewels one dawn. It seems he visits there most mornings."

"And you've been at the pool with him," Gabriel concluded.

"I wouldn't say *with* him," Michael mumbled. "I just happen to be in the area at the same time."

"Just happen?" Raphael chuckled and leaned in to whisper. "I heard a rumor that when Lucifer is diving for jewels he disrobes completely."

Michael's face heated again.

Gabriel roared with laughter. "You've been spying on Lucifer?"

"I wouldn't call it *spying*," Michael replied.

"But everyone else would," Raphael teased. "Oh, Michael, what would we do without you to keep us entertained?"

Raphael and Gabriel laughed and teased him for a little while longer, until Gabriel asked the question that had been bothering Michael ever since Lucifer's appearance.

"If all you've been doing is ogling him, how did Lucifer know your name?"

Michael shrugged. "I don't know. Maybe I projected it telepathically without realizing."

"Or maybe he's been watching you too?" Raphael suggested.

Michael laughed loudly and shook his head. The idea was too preposterous to take seriously. Lucifer hadn't even seen him until two days ago, and the impression Michael had made was hardly one of note. The far more likely explanation was that Michael had accidentally revealed his name without being aware he had done so.

He supposed it didn't matter. All that did was that Lucifer would be coming to his beach tonight. Michael didn't let his thoughts linger on how Lucifer knew where he lived too.

* * * *

Michael sat on the sandy dunes waiting for Lucifer to appear. Sunset wasn't for at least another hour, but he either sat here or paced the small beach hut until then.

He had already changed his robes four times, before finally deciding on the cream set with the golden trim and sash. If he returned to the hut once more he would, no doubt, change clothes again and still be debating what to wear when Lucifer finally appeared. No, it was better he sit still and wait as patiently as he could for his guest to arrive.

He had spent most of the day wondering what Lucifer could possibly want with him. Had Michael offended him by watching him at the pool? The angel certainly hadn't seemed too happy to find Michael spying on him. Lucifer's reaction, combined with Michael's embarrassment, was why Michael had chosen to stay away after he had been caught.

Lost in his thoughts, Michael didn't notice the minutes slipping away until he saw the shadow of an angel in flight on the sand. Lucifer landed gracefully, several feet away, his back to the sea.

"Good evening," Lucifer said as he drew closer.

Michael wondered whether he could trust his voice not to betray him again, decided not to tempt fate, and offered a smile to the angel as he gestured to the spot on the sand beside him.

Lucifer sat and stretched out his long legs next to Michael's. "Why haven't you been to the pool the last two days?" he asked.

Michael couldn't meet his eyes. "I don't go there every day," he said. He spoke the truth, in so far as it went. Occasionally he missed a morning when he overslept, or when his duties kept him away.

"You've never been absent two days in a row before," Lucifer replied. "Not once, in all the time you've been watching me."

Michael gaped at Lucifer.

"Did you think I didn't know you were there?" Lucifer asked, and the smallest of smiles appeared on his lips.

"Yes."

Lucifer rolled his eyes. "Foolish archangel, of course I knew. I sensed your presence weeks ago. The first time I could feel your surprise, I don't think you knew I would be there. After that first dawn you came for me, didn't you?"

Michael nodded. He had heard rumors the son of the morning was a powerful empath, and Lucifer's words confirmed the stories.

"Did you never wonder why I kept returning to the pool when there are so many places in this wonderful realm where I can find what I need?"

"No, I guess I didn't."

"I enjoyed you watching me. Couldn't you tell?"

Michael's gaze drifted down to Lucifer's lap, where his robes tented ever so slightly. It could simply have been the way the fabric had fallen, yet now the idea had been put into his head, Michael wondered if Lucifer might be aroused.

"Your thoughts are written all over your face," Lucifer said. "You can hide nothing from me. Why don't you ask what you want to know so badly?"

"Am I projecting my thoughts?" Michael asked.

"No, but they're clear to me just the same. Ask the question."

"I..."

Lucifer gave him another small smile and Michael's heart leaped to his throat. "And you were doing so well at constructing those difficult sentences." Lucifer leaned in to whisper. "Ask me, Michael."

Michael stared into Lucifer's sapphire-blue eyes and finally found his tongue. "Are you aroused?"

Lucifer's smile widened, revealing perfect, pearly white teeth. "Give me your hand."

Michael didn't hesitate. He placed his hand into Lucifer's open palm and let the angel guide him. He didn't break their gaze as Lucifer placed Michael's hand over his groin and encouraged him to touch the hardness.

"Have you ever done this before?" asked Lucifer, his voice breathless.

"Yes."

"Who with?"

Michael frowned. The hardness in Lucifer's voice when he asked the question took him by surprise. "It doesn't matter. My last relationship ended centuries ago."

Lucifer didn't seem pacified, so Michael concentrated on stroking him firmly through the soft fabric of his robes.

"What about you?" Michael asked, not because he desperately wanted to know, but because he wanted to hear in Lucifer's voice how close he was to losing control.

"No one," Lucifer gasped. "Oh, Michael, that feels so good. Don't stop."

Michael laughed. "I have no intention of stopping until you're so far gone *you* can't form a simple sentence."

Lucifer sank back on the sand, his wings vanishing from sight, just as Michael's did when their physical presence wasn't required. Lucifer closed his eyes and Michael took the opportunity to ease aside his robes. By now there could be no mistaking his erection for anything else. The hard flesh rose from a nest of blond curls and Michael licked his lips at the thought of taking the length into his mouth. Not tonight, though. If Lucifer truly hadn't felt the touch of another man's hand on his cock, then Michael intended to take his time and let Lucifer enjoy one sensation before moving on to another.

Michael watched the emotions flit across Lucifer's face as he played with his dick and fondled his balls. He suspected his own face held an equally stunned expression. If anyone had told him when he woke up this morning he would be doing this tonight, he would never have believed them.

Lucifer groaned and raised his hips a little. "Ah, Michael, Michael."

Michael loved the sound of his name on Lucifer's lips, especially spoken so breathlessly, almost a plea.

"Let go," Michael said. "Come for me."

He could tell Lucifer wouldn't last much longer. A man could only take so much, and for one who had never done this before, keeping control would be almost impossible.

When Lucifer finally came, spilling over Michael's hand a few moments later, Michael couldn't take his eyes off him. Since the first day he had seen him, Michael had considered that Lucifer might be the most beautiful of all the angels. Now, watching him come apart at Michael's touch, he knew he had been right. The expression of bliss on Lucifer's face would forever remain in Michael's mind as the most wondrous sight ever.

Michael reluctantly released Lucifer's cock and stretched

out beside him, resting his head on his clean hand, watching the angel come down from his orgasmic high.

Lucifer blinked at him and the smile spreading across his face was truly stunning. Michael's breath caught in his throat at the vision before him.

"Come to the pool with me tomorrow," Lucifer asked.

Michael nodded and Lucifer raised his hand to brush his fingers through Michael's hair. He leaned up and pressed his lips to Michael's, the kiss almost tentative and unsure, and such a contrast to the seemingly confident angel.

It was on the tip of Michael's tongue to invite Lucifer to spend the night in his beach hut. Before he could ask, Lucifer stood and gathered his robes together, covering his nakedness.

"I'll see you at dawn," Lucifer said.

He didn't give Michael a chance to reply before his wings reappeared and carried him into the air.

Michael watched him until he had flown away, into the mountains. He had a feeling he wouldn't be sleeping much tonight.

* * * *

The next morning Michael walked to the pool even earlier than usual. He wasn't surprised to find Lucifer already there before him. The son of the morning sat on the edge of the pool, his feet in the water and his robes on the ground beside him.

"How long have you been here?" Michael asked.

"All night," Lucifer replied.

"You could have stayed with me, if you'd asked," Michael told him.

Lucifer glanced at him. "I didn't want to. I was curious to know if you'd come here this morning, and if you did, how early you would be."

"Am I so predictable?"

"No."

"You *knew* I would be early."

Lucifer shook his head. "I knew you'd be early *if* you came. I found myself unsure as to whether you would."

Michael shucked off his robe and placed it on top of Lucifer's. "You owe me for last night," he said. "Of course I would come here this morning."

Lucifer blushed as Michael stepped closer. "I'm sorry."

"What for?" Michael asked as he sat beside him.

"For taking my pleasure while you didn't," Lucifer explained.

Michael smiled and gave his cock a rueful glance. "I didn't spend the night hard and aching, if that's what you're thinking."

"You didn't?"

There was something in Lucifer's tone Michael couldn't quite place.

"No, of course not." He mimed a crude gesture with his hand and knew his meaning had not been lost on Lucifer when the angel smiled at him brightly.

"You pleasured yourself," Lucifer said.

"Yes." Michael choked back a laugh. "Did you imagine I found someone else after you left?"

"The thought might have crossed my mind," Lucifer muttered.

Michael could hear the jealousy in his voice and sought to reassure him. He gave him a nudge with his elbow. "No, just my own right hand."

"Tell me about it," Lucifer said. "Describe to me what you did."

Lucifer's words alone sent shivers down Michael's spine. "I..."

"Close your eyes and just say the words," Lucifer encouraged.

Michael took his advice, hoping it would work. He shouldn't be this nervous around Lucifer now, not after what they had done last night.

"I stayed on the beach a while after you left. The tide came in so I had to go inside eventually. I sleep on a comfortable cot, one you just sink into. I ached for your touch."

"Go on," Lucifer said when Michael stopped talking. "Tell me everything."

"I lay in my cot, naked and aroused, and I took my cock in my hand. I stroked myself, over and over again."

As Michael spoke, the words began to come easier, tumbling out one after the other as he described the exploration of the most intimate parts of his body.

"I rolled my testicles in one hand while tugging myself with the other. I was hard and leaking and I ached so badly. I wanted you to be the one touching me, but you'd flown away, so I had to settle for my imagination. I tasted my own seed as I wondered whether I would ever have the opportunity to taste yours."

Michael could almost feel the featherlight touch of fingers stroking his erection and he stumbled over his words once again.

"Is that all you did?" Lucifer asked. "Or did you touch yourself anywhere else?"

"How did you know?" Michael whispered, opening his eyes for the first time. Lucifer had moved closer and Michael realized he hadn't imagined the touch on his cock. Lucifer was running a single finger along his length with casual ease.

Lucifer moved his hand between Michael's thighs and Michael spread his legs wider in response.

"No, no, no," Lucifer chided. "You need to tell me first."

Michael didn't need to ask what Lucifer meant, nor did he need any further encouragement. This time he didn't have to close his eyes to speak.

"I fingered myself," he said, his voice stronger now. "I pushed my index finger into my arse and imagined what it would be like to feel you inside me."

"Just one finger?" Lucifer asked as he eased Michael back onto the bank and into a position where he could easily access his arsehole.

"At first," Michael replied. He moaned when Lucifer inserted his finger.

"And then?"

"Then I used two fingers," Michael said. Lucifer's actions matched Michael's words, his second finger stretching him nicely. "I need more, so much more. Oh, Lucifer, right there, please don't stop."

"How much more?" Lucifer asked. "Did you use three fingers?"

Michael shook his head. "I was too close already. Two were enough last night."

"And now?"

Michael growled with frustration. "More, Lucifer, give me everything."

Lucifer withdrew his fingers and lined up his cock, ready to take their place. "Is this what you need?"

"Yes, oh Lucifer, yes, give it to me." Lucifer laughed and Michael glared at him. "What's so amusing?"

"This time three days ago you ran from me, barely able to string a sentence together. Now look at you. Wanton and desperately begging for my cock."

Michael raised his knees, displaying himself for Lucifer.

Lucifer made a sound of approval and pushed his hardness into Michael's willing arse.

Michael tensed at the burning pain for only a moment or two. Lucifer brushed his fingers against Michael's flesh, right where their bodies joined and the discomfort and pain instantly vanished at the angel's touch.

"You feel so tight," Lucifer said as he slowly thrust the rest of the way inside. "I've never felt anything like this before."

"Good?" Michael asked, though, from the expression of wonder on Lucifer's face, he already knew the answer to his question.

"Yes, oh yes." Lucifer pulled out a little before easing his way back inside.

Michael canted his hips in encouragement, his movements

drawing Lucifer deeper inside him.

He closed his eyes and threw back his head as Lucifer quickened his thrusts.

Angels had what could sometimes seem to be endless stamina and this was never more obvious than right now.

Michael's breath grew short when Lucifer increased his pace even more. Michael's cock ached and he yearned to take himself in hand.

"Take my legs," he ordered Lucifer, encouraging him to place them over his shoulders, freeing Michael's hands to touch himself.

Lucifer did as Michael asked, and once he had his hands free, he took hold of his erection and rapidly tugged at it, matching Lucifer's fast-paced thrusts.

He wouldn't last long. Pre-cum appeared at the tip of his cock head and he gathered the semen onto his fingers.

Lucifer watched his every move and, when Michael held his sticky fingers up, Lucifer didn't need any encouragement to take them into his mouth. He sucked them eagerly and Michael couldn't help wondering how those lips would feel wrapped around his shaft, sucking on his length.

Michael didn't realize he had projected the image until Lucifer spoke.

"One day soon, I'll suck your cock dry," Lucifer promised. "Then you won't need to imagine what it would be like."

Any fleeting embarrassment at Lucifer hearing his private thoughts vanished when Michael saw the eager anticipation on his lover's face.

In the meantime, Michael enjoyed the new feeling of being taken by the angel he had been fantasizing about for so long. The realm of angels had never felt quite as heavenly as it did the moment the heat of Lucifer's orgasm filled him.

Afterwards, when Lucifer had reluctantly withdrawn, the two of them swam in the pool, cleaning themselves and each other. They touched and kissed as the first rays of the sun hit the water around them.

When they had sufficiently recovered, they swam back to

the bank, where they took each other in hand and slowly drew out their pleasure once more.

They didn't talk much, though Michael burned with curiosity to discover whether Lucifer was truly as untouched as he appeared. He had admitted no one had ever touched his cock, but that didn't mean he had no experience at all. There were any number of ways he could have been intimate with another, without feeling another angel's fingers wrapped around his dick. As curious as he was, Michael didn't wish to raise the subject. He found himself reluctant to start a discussion that might lead to how much experience he had, and fan the spark of jealousy he had already seen in Lucifer's eyes.

Michael didn't consider himself to have been promiscuous during the centuries of his existence. He had taken a few lovers into his bed, though none for at least a century. Unfortunately, compared to Lucifer, he had a vast amount of experience and a sexual history he wasn't comfortable sharing just yet. Maybe later, when they were more settled in their relationship, Michael would be able to raise the subject of their pasts. Of course, this was assuming they were even in a relationship. Maybe Lucifer didn't want a long-term lover.

"What are you thinking about?" Lucifer asked, breaking into Michael's morose thoughts. "Why the sudden frown?"

Michael guessed he would never know unless he asked, so he plunged right in. "What does this mean to you?"

"This?"

"Last night on the beach and this morning. What we've done together."

"I found it enjoyable," Lucifer replied. "More so than I imagined it would be."

"But do you want more?" Michael pressed, even as his heart lifted a little at Lucifer's second declaration of his inexperience.

"Of course," Lucifer said. "I still haven't tasted your seed, have I?"

"And when you have?" Michael asked. "Will that be the end of our time together?"

Lucifer sat up and turned away from Michael. "I don't know."

"Maybe you should suck me now and we'll find out."

Lucifer glanced over his shoulder and gave Michael's soft cock a pointed stare. "I don't think you're in a position to offer me a taste right now, do you? Even if I can get you hard again, I doubt there's much left for me to taste when you come."

Michael suspected Lucifer was correct, but disappointment swept through him at the knowledge they weren't going to continue their exploration right away.

Lucifer stood and held his hand out to Michael. "Come with me."

"Where to?"

Lucifer smiled. "No questions, just come."

Michael took Lucifer's hand and let the angel pull him to his feet. They gathered their robes and covered themselves and Lucifer spread his wings wide. Michael began to do likewise, but Lucifer shook his head and drew him into his arms.

"Let me carry you."

"I'm perfectly capable of flying under my own power," Michael pointed out.

"I know, but I want to, just this once."

Lucifer offered him a sweet smile and Michael could refuse him nothing. He wound his arms around Lucifer's waist, tucking them inside his robes, and let the powerful angel carry them into the air.

While Michael had flown many times before, he had never been carried by another angel. Even when he had first learned how to control his wings, he had always flown or fallen entirely by himself. To let another angel carry him required a degree of trust, despite the fact he had wings of his own if Lucifer should let him fall. Not that Michael thought he would. Lucifer held Michael as though he were the most precious thing in the world to him, carrying him high into the clouds and far away from the main residential area of the archangels.

The area Lucifer landed in was completely unfamiliar. In all his years as an angel, Michael had never seen this place. Yet as soon as he saw the structure they had landed in front of, Michael could tell this was Lucifer's home. The building had been crafted entirely from jewels, some larger, others small, and in such a vast array of gems, the entire place shone like a thousand sparkling rainbows. The house was a little larger than Michael's beach hut, and when Lucifer guided him in through the entrance, Michael stood in awe of the opulence. Soft pillows had been scattered around the room, and platters of the best fruits the realm had to offer were set out ready for guests.

Lucifer picked up one of the dishes and held it out to Michael. "Hungry?"

Michael nodded and took a piece of pineapple. He had barely eaten a thing before going to the pool and their activities there had worked up quite an appetite. The sweet juice of the fruit was without a doubt the best he had ever tasted. When Lucifer picked out a second piece and brought the fruit to Michael's lips, he took the segment from his fingers with his teeth. He held Lucifer's gaze as he ate the second portion. He licked the juice from his lips and Lucifer's blue eyes darkened with lust.

Lucifer walked Michael backward to the nearest pillows and they sank to the floor next to the main table.

Michael chose a purple grape and pressed it against Lucifer's lips. The angel opened his mouth and let Michael place the fruit on his tongue. He closed his lips on Michael's fingers and sucked them lightly. Michael's cock hardened again, and he had a feeling he could become quite addicted to Lucifer's mouth on various parts of his body.

They fed each other grapes, slices of apple, segments of nectarines, and more, and each time they offered a piece of food to the other, the exchange was accompanied by licks and sucks to the fingers of the hand holding the fruit. They moved closer to each other, until Michael practically perched on Lucifer's lap. They couldn't get close enough. Pushing their robes aside they sat flesh to flesh.

Lucifer pulled Michael against him, setting him so Michael straddled Lucifer's thick thighs. Their cocks brushed together, each of them as aroused as the other.

Michael reached behind him to the table, blindly searching for the half orange they had not yet eaten. He found the fruit after a few moments and brought it between them. With a wicked grin at Lucifer, he squeezed the orange and let the juice run down Lucifer's chest. He watched the liquid dribble over his stomach before reaching his erection. Without a word Michael licked at Lucifer's chest, following the route the juice had taken. He eased back just enough to continue his mission to lap up every last drop. He arrived at Lucifer's cock, making sure he covered every inch of his length, as well as his balls, until not a trace of orange juice remained.

Lucifer's cock stood erect and a drop of pre-cum gathered at the tip. Michael licked it up, then teased Lucifer's slit with his tongue. Lucifer cried out above him as he spilled his seed over his stomach. Michael didn't hesitate setting to work lapping up the cum, reveling in the taste.

After he had finished, Michael sat back and saw Lucifer gazing at him with something akin to wonder on his face.

"What?" he asked.

Lucifer smiled. "Your turn now."

Michael shifted so Lucifer could get another half of orange from the table. Lucifer, fruit in hand, eased Michael onto his back and held the orange directly over his groin.

"Going straight for that, are you?" Michael teased.

Lucifer squeezed the orange. The juice hit Michael's sensitive cock and he bucked his hips.

"Shout if you want to," Lucifer said. "I want to hear how much I please you."

"Oh you do," Michael replied, his breath already coming

in short gasps.

Lucifer eased a cushion under Michael's buttocks, raising his groin enough for Lucifer to bend over him easily. He stroked Michael's length with his tongue and Michael crooned and moaned with every swipe of the damp muscle along his member.

"Suck me," Michael begged. "Please suck me. Take me in your mouth, Lucifer, please."

Unfortunately Lucifer didn't appear to have any intention of doing as Michael asked. He licked and teased for what seemed like forever, yet he didn't take him into his mouth, not even when Michael began to come. Lucifer lapped up Michael's cum as eagerly as he did the orange juice, but he didn't seem to want to take things any further.

Thankfully for Michael, he didn't need Lucifer to suck him to push him over the brink. He was too close already. Just the sensation of Lucifer tonguing him intimately was enough, and he came with a shout of joy, his semen splashing his stomach and Lucifer's chin and lips.

Seeing the evidence of his pleasure on Lucifer's face, Michael almost came a second time. He pulled Lucifer's head toward him, bringing their mouths together in a fierce kiss. He poured everything he felt for Lucifer into the kiss, feeding on the returned passion.

Lucifer pressed down on top of him and Michael spread his legs instinctively. Even though he had taken Lucifer inside him not too long ago, he yearned to do so again. Something in him needed Lucifer close for as long as he could keep him.

In the back of his mind, where he barely acknowledged the thought, Michael couldn't help wondering how long he would able to keep Lucifer in his arms. There seemed to be something almost ethereal about him, even more so than the rest of the archangels.

Lucifer nudged Michael's hole with his stiff cock, and Michael moaned in anticipation.

"Take me, Lucifer," he begged.

Lucifer grabbed a vial of oil from the table and dribbled it onto his cock and round Michael's hole. It helped to ease his way inside Michael's already stretched arse, and this time Michael knew Lucifer wouldn't need to use his powers to take away the pain.

Michael relaxed his muscles as Lucifer pushed inside him, and he relished the feeling of being filled by Lucifer once more. He brushed away the unsettling thoughts of how fleeting this relationship might be and concentrated on the here and now. He met Lucifer's thrusts with eagerness, shouting out encouragement and almost screaming his pleasure.

It could have been minutes, or possibly hours — time in the realm of angels could be difficult to monitor — yet for Michael it seemed as if Lucifer had been inside him forever. They lay in a sticky, sweaty mess, in the mass of pillows and cushions. Michael rested his head on Lucifer's chest, the scent of orange juice still lingering on his skin. They would have to clean up soon but not yet. They had all the time in the world. The life of an archangel could last an eternity and Michael hoped Lucifer would be in his for many years to come.

Chapter Two

Any lingering doubts Michael harbored about whether he and Lucifer were in a relationship swiftly vanished when, following Michael's visit to Lucifer's home, Lucifer flew to his beach the very next day, and the ones following.

"Where are we going?" Michael asked.

He had been following Lucifer as they flew over the mountains for nearly an hour. His lover insisted on remaining tight-lipped, telling him it was a surprise.

They were many miles from Michael's home when Lucifer finally pointed at the ground.

Michael followed Lucifer down to the edge of a large lake, landing lightly on his feet.

"What do you think?" Lucifer asked as he waved his hand to encompass the world around him.

"It's beautiful," Michael replied. "So quiet and peaceful. It's almost as if no one else has ever been here."

"They haven't," Lucifer said. "This is newly created."

Michael frowned. Only He could create places in this realm and it had been many years since He had last done so. Angels could create and alter things within their personal homes, but nothing like this.

"Do you truly like it?" Lucifer asked.

"Yes, I do."

"Good, because it's yours."

"What?"

"I've built this place for you to come to when you wish to be alone."

Michael stepped back from Lucifer, shaking his head. "How did you do this?"

"The same way you could, if you were taught how."

"Only He is allowed to create."

"If He didn't wish us to do this, why give us the power to do so?"

"Just because you have the power, it doesn't mean you should use it."

"*We*," Lucifer amended. "You have the ability, just as I do."

"I would never presume to wield such power, and you shouldn't either."

Lucifer smiled. "You need more imagination, Michael. The possibilities are endless."

"Does He know you've made this?" Michael asked.

"I don't know. Does it matter?"

Michael guessed not. What mattered was that Lucifer had done something no angel was supposed to have been capable of. "I think we should go back. We can eat with the others. I'd like to introduce you to my friends."

"I've already met them," Lucifer pointed out. "And I'd rather eat alone with you."

Michael didn't have an opportunity to argue. Lucifer waved his hand and a table with two cushioned chairs appeared beside them. All Michael's favorite foods were spread out before him and his mouth watered at the sight.

"Won't you join me?" Lucifer said as he pulled out one of the chairs for Michael to sit on.

Michael smiled and took his seat. There would be other opportunities for Lucifer to get to know his friends.

They ate their meal in pleasant solitude. Michael nudged Lucifer's leg beneath the table and Lucifer responded by rubbing Michael's shin with the sole of his foot. The temptation to tease Lucifer's groin was almost irresistible but Michael held back. They had done little talking the last few days, and now seemed to be the perfect time to remedy that.

"Can I ask you a question?" Michael said.

"Of course. What is it?"

"Why have you taken no lovers before me?"

Lucifer took a drink of his grape juice before answering. "Why do you want to know?"

"Just curiosity, I guess. You're the most beautiful angel I've ever seen. I know others think so too. It makes me wonder how you could remain untouched."

"I don't care whether other angels like my form," Lucifer said. "All angels are beautiful."

"Then how is it you were still a virgin before me?"

Lucifer continued to sip on his juice for so long Michael became uncomfortable. Had he overstepped the mark with his question?

"Most angels avoid me," Lucifer finally said. "They avoid all the favored ones, but me most of all. You didn't."

"Surely I'm not the first to…er…"

"Spy on me?" Lucifer suggested. "Yes, you are."

Michael flushed. "I was going to say that I can't be the first angel to get your attention."

"You're that too," Lucifer replied. "Others may watch me from afar, but they hold no interest for me. You, however, were so bold in the way you observed me from the edge of the pool. I felt perhaps you might be my equal."

"Even after I stammered and ran?"

"Even then. In fact, your obvious adoration of me is what made me decide to pursue you. I knew, if you were that enamored of me, you would be the perfect angel to teach me of the pleasures to be found between two men."

"There are many who could guide you in such things."

"Maybe there are, but I find myself content to learn from you. I can envisage no finer tutor in such matters."

Michael ducked his head as his face heated at the compliment.

"Do not hide from me," Lucifer said. "I would rather gaze into those beautiful blue eyes than view the top of your head."

Michael met Lucifer's eyes and returned his smile with one of his own.

They continued to talk, long after the sun had gone down, and the stars twinkled in the clear sky above them.

Lucifer vanished the table and chairs with a wave of his palm. He took Michael's hand and linked their arms together as they walked around the edge of the lake.

Michael looked out over the water. In the moonlight, the lake appeared even more beautiful than it had in the sunshine. Lucifer's craftsmanship was unsurpassed. Michael couldn't deny the skill it had taken to create the lake and surrounding area, even though Lucifer should not have done this.

"You really shouldn't have made this place," Michael said.

"I built it for you. Would you have preferred something else? Whatever you desire, all you have to do is say."

Michael embraced Lucifer and kissed him lightly on the lips. "I have everything I could ever wish for, right here in my arms."

"Then you do not like my gift?" Lucifer stuck out his lower lip in a pout.

"It's beautiful and perfect, but it's too much. Please, Lucifer, return this place to what it once was."

He didn't look happy about it, but Lucifer did as Michael asked. The lake dried and filled, replaced with stone and rock. The idyllic haven returned to the desolate wasteland it had once been. One day, it would be transformed once more, but this time by Him.

Michael kissed Lucifer again. "Thank you."

They flew, hand in hand, back to Lucifer's home in the mountains. Michael glanced behind them only once, remembering the lake and the pleasant evening they had spent there. He pushed aside the worry Lucifer had tampered with things no angel should ever meddle with.

* * * *

For the next weeks Michael spent all his spare time with

Lucifer. He knew he neglected his other friends, but the pleasure he found in his new love was all he could think about.

Gabriel brought up the subject of Lucifer first. "Lucifer's preference for your company has been noted," he commented over dinner one evening.

Lucifer had duties to attend to, and Michael already missed his presence at his side. Still, he was happy to have the opportunity to spend time with Gabriel and Raphael.

"Has it?" Michael replied with a shrug.

"The son of the morning has never shown such attention to another angel before," Gabriel said. "Some even say he's entirely untouched."

Michael ducked his head. He now knew Lucifer had indeed been a virgin before Michael. In one way, he still was, for Lucifer had been surprisingly reluctant to let Michael take him anally. That didn't mean Michael had any intention of spilling Lucifer's secret to the other archangels. Michael didn't think it any of their concern if Lucifer had had no former lovers or a hundred angels in his bed at once. All that mattered was that he now shared Michael's bed and he wanted it to stay that way.

"Is he as well formed beneath his robes as they say?" Raphael asked with a grin.

Michael laughed and his face warmed. "I'm not telling you anything, so you'd better turn your attention back to your food."

"I'll take that as a yes," Raphael said.

"He's an angel, just like the rest of us," Gabriel pointed out. "Of course he's handsome in body. We all are. What I want to know is how he feels about Michael."

Gabriel and Raphael focused their stern gazes on Michael, who shifted uncomfortably. Truthfully, he wasn't entirely sure how Lucifer felt about him. They couldn't get enough of each other sexually, yet they hadn't spoken about their feelings. Lucifer wasn't the most talkative of angels at the best of times, and he tended to stick to neutral topics rather than more personal ones.

"Are you sure you know what you're doing?" Gabriel asked kindly.

"I don't know," Michael admitted. "But I can't give him up. I need him so badly."

"Is that your head talking or your cock?" Raphael asked.

"Both," Michael replied with honesty. He had no intention of letting his sexual urges control his life, but he had enough awareness of his own desires to know there was something almost addictive about the pull Lucifer's body had for him. Yet, it wasn't just Lucifer's body he craved. He enjoyed spending time with him and he wanted to know everything about him.

"Why don't you invite him to dine with us?" Raphael asked. "We'd all enjoy getting to know him better."

Michael avoided Raphael's eyes, unwilling to admit that most times he and Lucifer ate together they ended up having extremely messy sex as well. Somehow he doubted that was what Raphael had in mind when he made his suggestion.

"Don't neglect your other friends," Gabriel warned. "Or your duties."

Michael bristled. He had only been late to his shift for watching over the Garden once, and it hadn't been intentional. He hadn't thought those few minutes had been noticed, though it seemed they had.

After Gabriel's quiet reprimand the conversation turned to more pleasant topics, and by the time they had finished their meal Michael was pleased he had taken the time to catch up with his oldest friends.

* * * *

A few days after his meal with the others, Michael decided to raise the subject of Lucifer spending time with his friends again. The feast day meal, a monthly celebration when all angels gathered in the great chamber for music and merriment, seemed to him to be the ideal opportunity.

"The feast day is nearly upon us," he casually commented.

"Is it?" Lucifer's tone was one of complete disinterest. "I don't bother taking note of such events."

"Why don't you come with me this month? I know Gabriel and Raphael would like to get to know you better."

"Why?"

Michael stared at Lucifer for a moment. "They know we've been spending time together and I thought it might be nice if we all attended the feast as a group."

"You've been talking about me with your friends?"

Michael balked at Lucifer's glare. "I've not been telling them intimate details about our sex life, if that's what you mean. But even the most unobservant of angels has noticed we've been in each other's company. Won't you come to the feast with me?"

Lucifer's anger disappeared as swiftly as it had arrived. "I'd rather stay here, with you. We can celebrate the day in private."

Michael shook his head. "I'm assigned to assist with the decorations. You could help me."

Lucifer didn't respond to the question, but Michael gave him the details anyway, hoping Lucifer would join him in his duties, and later at the party.

* * * *

When Lucifer didn't arrive at the great chamber by the time Michael had put the finishing touches to the decorations, he had little hope he would attend at all.

A part of him wanted to leave once his tasks had been completed, to find Lucifer, and have their private celebration. But he had never missed a feast day celebration before, and he didn't want to now. He was with his friends and it had been too long since he had spent any quality time with them. Lucifer would understand. Michael would join him later and they would have a second celebration all of their own.

The party continued throughout the day and long into the night. By the time Michael left his friends and flew to Lucifer's home, far in the east, the stars twinkled above the realm and the full moon hung high in the sky.

He found Lucifer sitting on the roof, which didn't appear to be a comfortable place to rest, but Michael glided down to join him there.

"You didn't come to the feast day celebration," Michael said.

"I never said I would," Lucifer replied. "I thought we were going to have our own celebration here?"

"I told you I had duties to attend to," Michael reminded him.

"Yes, but those wouldn't have taken all day and night."

"I thought you might have come to meet my friends," Michael said. "They'd have enjoyed spending some time with you."

Lucifer stared at the night sky. "They're your friends, not mine."

"They could be yours too, if you'd let them."

Michael could tell his words made no difference to Lucifer. It seemed the angel didn't want any more friends, or any at all, since as far as Michael could tell, he didn't seem to have a single one, save for Michael himself.

They sat on the roof in silence, and while previously their quiet times had been comfortable, this wasn't. The tension was almost unbearable. Michael's fingers twitched and he ached to take Lucifer's hand in his own, yet something held him back.

"I should go home," Michael said. "It's been a long day."

He wanted Lucifer to ask him to stay, but he didn't, and when the silence had gone on too long, Michael spread his wings and flew back to his beach. He tossed and turned all night, his bed far too lonely without Lucifer beside him.

* * * *

The tension following the feast day lasted longer than Michael thought it would. He had imagined Lucifer would be back to his usual self by the next day, waiting for him at what Michael had come to consider *their* pool. Instead, Michael arrived there, promptly at dawn, only to find the pool deserted.

Since Lucifer's duties had caused him to miss the odd morning before, Michael presumed this to be the case again. If they had spoken properly the previous night, Lucifer would no doubt have told him he wouldn't be there today.

When Lucifer failed to appear on the second and third morning, Michael flew to his home to seek him out there.

The place was empty, but since Michael had no pressing matters to attend to elsewhere, he chose to wait for Lucifer to return.

Lucifer finally walked through the archway several hours later. Michael's heart leaped to his throat at the sight of his lover. He was as gorgeous as ever, even with the scowl he currently wore.

"Lucifer, where have you been?" Michael asked. "You've not been at the pool."

"I've had *duties*," Lucifer replied with something akin to a sneer. "You know all about those."

Michael's gut churned with a sensation he recognized as anger. He had never felt such a thing before and he didn't like it. Angels weren't supposed to feel anger. The emotion was strange and unpleasant and he fought against it with every fiber of his being.

Calm, stay calm. By sheer force of will he pushed the anger back into himself, shutting it away.

"Lucifer," Michael whispered as he stepped closer to his lover. "If it's truly your duties that have kept you away from me, then of course I understand, but please be honest with me. Have you been avoiding me?"

As he waited for Lucifer to speak, Michael accepted that he already knew the answer to his question, and the truth hurt.

"Is this it then?" Michael asked. "The end of whatever we had together?"

Lucifer rushed over, swept him into his arms, and kissed him soundly. "No, Michael, no. I won't give you up."

"Then you'll be at the pool tomorrow?" Michael asked.

Lucifer nodded and pressed their lips together again.

Michael let Lucifer control the kiss and sighed when they parted.

Somewhere outside a bell chimed. Michael recognized the noon call for duty and, reluctant as he was to part from Lucifer, he had to leave.

"Stay," Lucifer urged as he held Michael against him.

"I'm expected at the pool of visions," Michael replied. "I'll return later."

Lucifer didn't release him from his embrace. "Others can attend to the pool of visions. We could go to *our* pool and make up for missing the last few mornings."

"I can't let others do my duties for me," Michael chided.

"Of course you can," Lucifer argued. "I want you here, with me. Only *you* can fulfill that duty. There are many who can do your other tasks."

Michael was almost tempted, but it wouldn't have been right. No matter how alluring Lucifer's offer might be, Michael wouldn't shirk his responsibilities to spend time with him.

"I have to go," Michael insisted.

"No, you don't," Lucifer replied, his voice rising with every word.

Michael pulled out of Lucifer's arms and walked to the door. "I'll be back later. I suggest you calm down before then, because I won't neglect my duties for you, no matter how much you complain."

"And what about your duty to me?" Lucifer yelled. "I should be first in your life, always. If you love me, you'd put me first."

Michael halted at the door. He had never spoken words of love to Lucifer, yet it seemed he hadn't needed to. His feelings were obviously plain to see. "You are the first angel in my life."

"Am I?" Lucifer asked. "You spent the feast day celebration with your friends and now you're leaving me again."

"You could have joined me and my friends for the party," Michael reminded him.

"And now?"

"I have duties."

"Which you're putting before me," Lucifer snapped. As Michael watched, Lucifer's wings darkened, for the first time he could recall. They didn't change to black, but Michael could detect a definite hint of gray to them, a sign of his temper Michael had never seen before.

"We all have our tasks in this realm," Michael said. "Me, you, everyone. We all serve the greater power and He will always come first."

The bells chimed again and Michael knew he would have to fly like the wind to arrive at the chamber in time to take over from the current watcher. He didn't have time to continue his discussion with Lucifer. Their argument would have to wait until later. He had more important things to attend to.

* * * *

"You're almost late," Gabriel commented as Michael landed clumsily outside the chamber containing the pool of visions, a wondrous device that could show the watching angel anyone or anything they wished.

Michael smiled. "But not quite," he replied.

"Where have you been?" Gabriel asked. "You haven't been at any meals the last few days. Have you been spending all your time with Lucifer?"

Michael shook his head and walked into the chamber. Metatron nodded a greeting and rose from the stone bench so Michael could take his place.

"Anything to report?" Michael asked.

"All is quiet," Metatron confirmed. "I'll leave you to your vigil and go find something to eat."

Michael's stomach growled and he remembered he hadn't eaten properly all day.

"Did you have dinner?" Gabriel asked once they were alone.

"I forgot," Michael admitted. "It's been a strange day."

"Strange how?"

Michael sat on the bench and concentrated on the pool, focusing intently until the Garden appeared in the waters.

"I'll go find you some food," Gabriel offered. "Then we can talk."

"There's nothing to talk about," Michael said.

"I disagree, but if you insist, I'll do the talking and you can listen."

Michael didn't like the sound of that any better, but time had long since taught him the futility of arguing with his friend.

It didn't take Gabriel more than a few minutes to find food for the two of them and return to Michael's side.

"What's happened?" Gabriel asked. "Or would you like me to guess?"

"It's nothing."

"You've changed, Michael," Gabriel said. "No, don't say anything. I gave you your chance to tell me what's bothering you, but you declined. Since you've become involved with Lucifer, you've not been yourself. You've always been the calmest amongst us, the kindest, and the fairest. Now, you seem conflicted and I think it's the influence of the son of the morning. Maybe you would be better off ending things now, before you get hurt."

"I've wondered the same thing," Michael admitted. "But I think I'm in love with him."

"Think?"

Michael shook his head. "I *know* I am."

"Is it that he doesn't feel as strongly for you?" Gabriel asked.

"No."

"Then you're sure of his affections?"

"He's never spoken words of love, but I believe he does care for me. That's not the problem."

"Then you admit there is one?" Gabriel encouraged him to open up and Michael found that talking about his concerns helped a little.

"Lucifer is upset with me for attending the feast day celebrations."

"I thought you invited him to join us," Gabriel commented. "Raphael and I want to get to know him."

"He declined to attend, but is angry I did, rather than returning to him once I'd completed my duties."

Gabriel sighed. "Raphael and I wouldn't have minded if you'd left to spend time with your lover. We can see how much you care for him."

"That's not the point. You and Raphael mean a lot to me too."

"We'd have understood."

"I know." Michael wondered whether he should mention their argument or not. He had a suspicion he knew what Gabriel would say, but he wanted a fresh opinion on the matter. "He wanted me to stay with him this afternoon."

"You mean after you've ended your vigil here?" Gabriel asked.

"No, he didn't want me to come here at all today."

"You can't neglect your duties for him," Gabriel warned. "Nothing comes before our duties, you know that."

Michael shot Gabriel a quick scowl. "Of course I know that. I'm here, aren't I?"

"In body, yes, but in spirit you seem to be with Lucifer." Gabriel gestured toward the pool of visions. "Since activating the pool, have you been concentrating on what you see in the waters, or on your disagreement with Lucifer?"

Gabriel had hit the nail on the head. Even though he had left Lucifer, Michael was still neglecting his responsibilities. He focused on the waters and the tranquility of the

Garden of the Creator, where mankind made their home. Sometimes he envied the humans their blissful existence. He had known such times once, but the more centuries that passed, the more discontented he seemed to become. Now, torn between his love for Lucifer and his angel duties, he wanted even more to regain what he had lost.

"You know what must come first," Gabriel said as he rose from the bench. "Lucifer cannot place himself above the power of the most high, and it's not fair for him to ask you to do so. You need to stand up to him and let him know you won't be pushed into making a decision that could see you cast out of this realm."

Michael watched Gabriel leave, before concentrating on his duties, firmly pushing Lucifer from his thoughts until he had time to himself to focus on him.

* * * *

Although Michael had intended to return to Lucifer once his vigil at the pool of visions was done, he found himself flying in another direction entirely, and as he made his way through the clouds he let his thoughts drift to his lover.

His feelings for Lucifer clouded his judgment and he didn't want to continue in this way. He could admit to himself, if not to Gabriel, how close he had come to staying with Lucifer this afternoon. The temptation had been fleeting but real. More than anything else, the knowledge he had come so close to willfully neglecting his duties scared him.

Lost in the clouds and his thoughts, Michael didn't notice the sky darkening. It was fully dark when he finally altered his course and headed home.

He landed on the beach, his bare feet sinking into the cool sand. He saw the glow of a light from within his hut and quickened his pace.

Michael wasn't surprised to find Lucifer seated on his bed.

"Where have you been?" Lucifer asked.

"Flying."

"Where to?"

"Just flying aimlessly around, trying to get my thoughts into some sort of order." Michael sat across from Lucifer and met his eyes. "I don't want to fight anymore."

"Me neither," Lucifer said and he held out his arms.

Michael hesitated a moment. "I won't neglect my duties for you."

Lucifer nodded and, although Michael sensed he wasn't entirely happy with his words, he seemed to accept them.

Satisfied they had put their quarrel behind them, Michael crawled into Lucifer's arms and let the angel hold him.

They didn't make love that night, but Michael felt closer to Lucifer than he ever had before. They had reached an understanding and for now that would be enough.

* * * *

When Michael woke Lucifer had gone. The sun had already risen and Michael realized he had missed their morning rendezvous at the pool. He hoped Lucifer understood he hadn't meant to sleep so late.

He gathered his crumpled robes together and flew for the pool as fast as he could. Lucifer's robes were on the bank, though Michael could see no sign of the angel on the cliff side or in the water.

"Lucifer?" Michael called.

A chuckle came from behind him, but when he spun round no one was there.

"Lucifer, where are you?"

A moment later Lucifer appeared in front of him and Michael's jaw dropped in surprise.

"I'm right here," Lucifer teased.

Michael raised his hand to touch Lucifer's cheek. "How did you do that?"

"The same way you could, if you knew how," Lucifer replied. "All angels have the ability, they just don't know it."

"How did you discover this?" Michael asked.

"I asked," Lucifer said, though he refused to specify who he had questioned. Instead he changed the subject by producing a beautiful blue sapphire from behind his back. He raised it in front of Michael's face and squinted at the gem.

"It's a beautiful stone," Michael said. "Is it from the pool?"

Lucifer shook his head. "No, this is from somewhere else. I've been searching for an exact match for your eyes and I think I've finally found it."

Michael smiled fondly and watched as Lucifer encased the gem between his hands and closed his eyes. "What are you doing?"

"Shush," Lucifer hushed him.

Michael kept silent until Lucifer opened his hands again, and when Michael looked down he saw the precious stone had been crafted into a necklace with a fine gold chain, so delicate Michael thought it might snap if he touched it.

"Here," Lucifer said, and he placed the chain around Michael's neck. "My gift, for you. I hope you'll accept this one."

Michael touched the stone where it rested against his chest. The necklace still held the warmth from Lucifer's hands, though he knew it would soon cool. "Thank you."

Lucifer smiled brightly and swept Michael into his arms for a kiss. Michael shrugged out of his robes and let them pool at his feet.

"Are we good now?" Michael asked. "No more arguments?"

Lucifer drew him down onto the grass and they made love at the side of the water. Michael pushed aside the fact Lucifer hadn't answered his questions. Instead he chose to believe they had turned a corner and come to an understanding.

As Lucifer sucked Michael's cock into his mouth, any thoughts of their disagreements vanished from his mind.

When they were together he didn't doubt Lucifer's feelings, even if he never spoke words of love. His actions told Michael all he needed to know.

Chapter Three

Michael and Lucifer came to an understanding, and, although things weren't perfect between them, they managed to avoid any more arguments. Michael tended to his duties and if he neglected his friends a little, neither Gabriel nor Raphael complained. They understood the depth of his feelings for Lucifer and didn't try to come between them.

From Michael's point of view he had good friends, a caring lover, and he intended to keep both.

The only problem he could see appeared to be Lucifer's growing jealousy, and Michael wasn't alone in having noticed.

"There are concerns about Lucifer," Raphael said when Michael took his place at the dinner table. Lucifer had his own duties tonight and Michael was taking the opportunity to spend time with his friends.

"Concerns?" Michael asked.

"His jealousy and pride," Raphael replied.

"Lucifer can be a little jealous of the time I spend away from him, but we understand each other now. He knows I'll always put my duties first."

"But *he* doesn't," Gabriel said. "He's been neglecting his own tasks and his lack of attention has been noted."

"What?" This was the first Michael had heard about this. As far as he was aware, Lucifer was amongst the favored ones and with good reason.

"There are those who say his pride will be his downfall," Raphael said. "He sets himself too high and there are too many who do not see the wrong in this."

Michael watched Raphael and Gabriel exchange a look. "What?"

"There's talk about you," Gabriel admitted.

"Me?" The food in front of him no longer held any appeal, and what he had already eaten sat heavily in his churning stomach.

"Most of the angels who embrace Lucifer's way of thinking are lesser beings. You're an archangel."

"So? I haven't heard any rumors about Lucifer or these other angels."

"Because you've been so wrapped up in your relationship with him," Gabriel replied. "He's gathering followers."

"Followers?" Michael echoed. How had he failed to notice this? From what he had seen, Lucifer hadn't changed from the lone angel he had first watched from the side of the pool.

"They aren't open about it," Raphael explained. "To be so would be too dangerous."

"Lucifer craves worshipers of his own," Gabriel said.

"No, he doesn't," Michael argued. "He barely even talks to anyone besides me."

Raphael shook his head. "They don't need to talk to him to worship him. They simply have to believe in him and his way of thinking."

"His way of thinking isn't any different from the rest of us," Michael pointed out.

"Isn't it?" Gabriel asked. "Has any other angel asked you to neglect your duties for them?"

"That's different," Michael argued.

"No, it's not," Raphael said. "If you were to choose to devote yourself to Lucifer instead of Him..."

"I would never!"

Raphael raised his hand to halt Michael's protests. "You're walking a fine line and we're worried about you."

"There's no need to be."

Gabriel took hold of Michael's hand in a firm grip. "There are those here who feel perhaps Lucifer shouldn't have a place in this realm."

"But he's one of the favored ones," Michael reminded them. "No one would dare cast him out."

"*He* would," Gabriel said. "Be careful, Michael, lest you lose your place here too."

* * * *

Michael worried about Gabriel's and Raphael's words for many of the following days. He casually listened for any of the rumors they had talked about, and was concerned to find that angels *were* talking. He wondered if Lucifer knew what others said about him. Michael could see only one way to find out, and he raised the subject a couple of weeks after his discussion with his friends.

"Lucifer, can I ask you something?"

Michael supposed they weren't in the best place for a serious conversation, but since they spent so much of their time in bed, it was here or at the pool, where there was the additional risk of someone overhearing them.

Lucifer smiled and nodded. "Ask away. What do you wish to know?"

Michael had thought this through a great deal and had chosen his words carefully. "Have you heard the rumors some of the other angels are saying about you?"

"Are they talking about my sexual prowess? If so, you should consider it your duty to dispel any slanderous lies."

"I'm serious," Michael said, ignoring the teasing.

Lucifer sighed. "There are always rumors about the favored ones. What are they saying about me this century?"

"That you have worshipers, and are setting yourself up as the most high, even above Him."

Lucifer laughed loudly and shook his head. "I can't control what other angels think."

"I know, but are you encouraging angels to look to you in the same way we look to Him?"

Lucifer eased out of Michael's arms and turned his back

as he sat on the edge of the bed. "They don't need any encouragement."

"Lucifer, don't you see how dangerous this is?" Michael shivered as a sudden chill ran down his spine.

"Dangerous?" Lucifer peered at him over his shoulder. "Is thinking for yourself any more dangerous than blindly following the flock?"

"Is that what you think of me?" Michael asked. "Do you see me as some kind of mindless sheep?"

"No, of course not. I know you'd stand by me, no matter what, and your feelings for me set you apart from the rest of the pack."

"I won't worship you," Michael said.

"I've never asked you to," Lucifer replied. "Except with your body."

Michael smiled and inched closer to Lucifer's side. He gave him a quick kiss, but he had no intention of letting the subject drop. "And the others?"

"They do not share my bed, only my way of thinking."

Michael took Lucifer's face in his hands. "Think about what you're risking, please. Discourage those who would turn away from Him. Show them where your loyalty lies."

"*You* have my loyalty," Lucifer replied.

"That's not what I meant. I'm content to come second to Him. It's the way it should be."

"What if I want more?" Lucifer asked. "I want to be first in your heart, Michael. Can you give me that?"

Michael sighed and couldn't meet Lucifer's eyes. "You are first amongst all the angels, but I cannot place you before Him. Please don't ask me to."

Lucifer turned his back again and Michael feared he had given him the wrong answer, but he could not lie to Lucifer, any more than he could lie to himself.

* * * *

Michael woke to the sound of bells chiming in the early

hours of the morning. They had never rung at such a time and, for a few moments, he wondered if he had imagined them. When they sounded again he crawled from his bed, rubbing sleep from his eyes. He had no idea what had happened, but he knew if he flew to the main concourse he would probably find out.

Outside the sky was dark with clouds, and thunder rumbled in the distance. Lightning struck over the mountains and rain poured down on him, soaking his wings until they were sodden, making the task of flying difficult. Thunder crashed overhead as the storm worsened. Michael had never seen such a sight and it frightened him more than he wanted to admit. The realm of angels never had anything other than clear skies with occasional fluffy white clouds. What could have happened? He flew swiftly to his destination.

On the concourse, Michael found lots of sleepy angels milling around, but no one with any answers to his questions. He scanned the crowd for the rest of the archangels. He still hadn't seen any of them when he heard Gabriel calling his name.

"Michael? Michael?" He sounded panicked, something Michael had never heard before.

"Over here," he called back, using his wings to rise above the crowd a little and make himself visible to his oldest friend.

"This way," shouted Gabriel, in a slightly less concerned tone. He pointed to an archway Michael couldn't recall seeing when he'd last been here. A new building had been created on the concourse, something that hadn't happened in more than a millennium.

Michael flew to Gabriel's side and landed beside him. "What's happening?"

Gabriel pulled him into his arms, holding him tightly enough to leave bruises.

"Michael, thank goodness," Raphael said as he too wrapped his arms around Michael.

"Um, thank you both, but what in the realm is happening? Why are the bells ringing, why is it stormy, and what's this new archway?"

"Come inside," Gabriel said. "This is a new chamber, specifically for archangels."

"It is?" Michael followed his friends curiously. There had never been any kind of separation of archangels from lesser angels — there had never been any need. Why now did He — for only He could create such a place in this realm — believe such a chamber was required?

Inside the building the floor sloped down to the center of the chamber. Fifteen chairs set in a circle faced inward, one for each of the archangels present. Behind the chairs, curved benches had been set against the walls. At the moment they were empty. Michael searched the faces for Lucifer, but he wasn't there. As one of the highest-ranking angels, even above the regular archangels, Michael supposed he hadn't been summoned with the rest.

"Take a seat, everyone," Gabriel said. "We have much to discuss and precious little time."

Michael looked at the other archangels, most of whom seemed to be as in the dark about why they were there as Michael.

"For those of you who don't know what has happened this night, let me explain," Gabriel said. "The unprecedented has happened. One of the most powerful angels in this realm has fallen from grace."

Michael frowned as he tried to figure out who was missing from their number. Only the favored ones, such as Lucifer, weren't present. When he glanced over at Raphael he would not meet his gaze and for the first time Michael began to worry. *Could Gabriel be talking about Lucifer?*

"Not only has this angel fallen," Gabriel continued, "but many of the lesser angels have followed him — a third of their number, in fact."

A third? Michael could hardly believe his ears. How could so many of their kind have turned away from what they had here?

"Which angel has fallen?" Metatron asked. No one needed to ask which angel he referred to. The lesser angels were a great loss, but the powerful angel they followed was the crux of the problem.

Michael held his breath as he waited for Gabriel to answer the question.

"Lucifer," Gabriel said, meeting Michael's eyes for the first time.

Suddenly every gaze in the room was on him, and Michael shifted uncomfortably in his seat.

"Thankfully, as you can see, Michael has not followed Lucifer down the destructive path he has chosen to take." Gabriel smiled at him and Michael understood why he and Raphael had greeted him so strangely when he had arrived on the concourse. They had obviously feared he might have fallen too.

"What happens now?" Metatron asked. "To Lucifer and the others, I mean?"

Gabriel turned his attention back to Metatron and the room in general. "The realm of angels is now barred to Lucifer and those who have followed him."

"Where are they?" Azrael asked. "If they aren't here, where have they gone? The Garden?"

"They aren't in the Garden," Gabriel confirmed. "At least not right now."

"But?"

"We believe Lucifer has been there and he has corrupted man."

The room erupted with voices raised in horror.

"What?"

"How could this happen?"

"When?"

"Can it be reversed?"

Michael stayed silent. No angel set foot in the Garden without express purpose, and interfering with the choices of man was strictly forbidden. What had Lucifer done?

"Man has eaten the forbidden fruit," Gabriel said. "This action cannot be undone and the decision has been made to send them from the Garden. The Creation is vast and we trust they will soon find shelter and thrive in their new environment. The bigger problem is Lucifer and his followers."

"Where's Lucifer?" Raphael asked. "Has he been traced yet?"

"He has," Gabriel confirmed. "Lucifer has created a new realm and he and his followers are hiding within it."

"A new realm? Where did he acquire that sort of power?"

Michael wondered the same thing. He knew Lucifer to be one of the most powerful archangels alive, and he had temporarily created the lake on the other side of the mountains, but a whole new realm was completely unprecedented. No angel should possess the power of creation and certainly not enough to bring into existence an entire realm.

"He has observed the Creator for countless centuries and it would appear he has learned many things during this time. Lucifer's new realm is vast and growing by the hour."

"I want to talk to him," Michael said and everyone in the room stared at him once again.

"I would advise against that," Gabriel replied. "Lucifer is no longer the angel you knew. He is much changed."

"I need to see him," Michael insisted.

"Perhaps the pool of visions?" Raphael suggested. "I think we all need to see what Lucifer has become, Michael most of all."

Gabriel nodded and they filed out of the room, making their way to the chamber situated a little farther across the concourse. Outside they found many angels still congregating, waiting for answers. The archangels didn't stop to explain as they hurried past.

The pool of visions was guarded, as always, by an angel, who watched over the Garden for the Creator.

"Any change?" Gabriel asked as they approached.

The angel shook his head. "No sign of man at all."

Gabriel nodded. "You may leave now. Your vigil is over."

The angel left without question and the archangels crowded round the pool.

Michael took the central position and touched the water with his finger. He concentrated on Lucifer, whispering his name out loud, and a moment later the pool shimmered to reveal someone Michael didn't recognize.

Around him several angels gasped.

Lucifer sat on an uncomfortable-looking throne in a large room that seemed to be some sort of cave. Not a single gem adorned the walls, and there were no other furnishings at all.

Michael forced himself to study Lucifer. He couldn't stop himself from cringing at the sight of the golden horns protruding from his head. The strawberry-blond hair Michael had been running his fingers through just the day before fell in soft waves over his shoulders. His robes were black and, although his wings weren't visible, Michael had a feeling they too had changed from the soft, white feathers he loved stroking when Lucifer had slept on his stomach.

"Michael?" Gabriel asked. "Are you well?"

Michael nodded. "I have to speak to him. I need to understand what has happened."

"You can't go to him," Gabriel said. "Lucifer's new realm is blocked to angels. We've already tried to go there."

"He'll open it to me," Michael replied.

Gabriel sighed. "Lucifer has named his new realm the Underworld and no angel may set foot inside without pledging allegiance to him and him alone. Those who have done so are as altered as he is." Gabriel touched the water and the image changed, showing strange creatures, the like of which Michael had never seen before.

"What are they?" he asked.

"Former angels, who have chosen to worship Lucifer," Gabriel explained. "This is what they have become. Is that what you want?"

Michael shrank back from the pool. "No, of course not."

"Good," Gabriel said.

"But I still need to talk to him," Michael insisted.

"If you can find a way, without becoming what you see here, I won't stop you."

Michael felt a hand on his shoulder and he turned to Raphael.

"I'm sorry, Michael, truly. I know what he meant to you."

The rest of the archangels stepped back and, at Gabriel's request, they returned to their new chamber. After a few minutes, Michael followed them and they all took their seats once more.

"The fallen angels must be stopped," Gabriel said. "They need to turn back to the light and renounce Lucifer or…"

"Or what?" Metatron asked.

"Or they need to be destroyed," Gabriel finished.

"Destroyed?"

"They cannot be allowed to live," Gabriel said. "They are too powerful and are already creating havoc in the Creation."

Michael didn't need to ask how much trouble they could have caused in such a short amount of time. Everyone knew time moved differently in the realm of angels and a day there might be a century on Earth, or sometimes a day on Earth might be an eternity for the angels.

"Angels aren't killers," Metatron said. "We are peaceful."

Gabriel stood and his wings spread out behind him, pure and white. His robes changed from soft fabric to metallic plates and a matching helm appeared on his head. When he stretched out his arm he held a blade aloft. "From this day, we have a new purpose, the destruction of the demons, by whatever means necessary."

One by one the archangels stood, their garments changing from robes to armor, and they took their places at Gabriel's side.

Michael rose last and, when he did, his own clothes transformed to match the others. The sword in his hand felt strange and heavy. He didn't like it, and from the expressions on the faces of his fellow archangels he suspected he wasn't the only one.

"The war against the demons has begun," Gabriel announced.

The cheer from the rest of the archangels was hesitant and Michael couldn't bring himself to join in at all. What could have happened to Lucifer to bring them to this? He *had* to know.

* * * *

As soon as he left the archangels, Michael flew to Lucifer's home, hoping against everything he had seen that there had been some kind of mistake. The creatures in the pool of visions couldn't be real, and while the man sitting on the throne bore a striking resemblance to Lucifer, maybe it wasn't him at all.

Michael found Lucifer's home deserted. Every room was empty. Even the furniture had gone.

"Lucifer?" he called, though he didn't expect an answer.

It therefore came as something of a surprise when Lucifer, in his new demonic form, appeared before him.

"Michael, I knew you'd come," Lucifer said. "I trusted you would make the right choice."

"Tell me this is a mistake," Michael begged. "They say you're barred from this realm, and that you've turned away from Him."

"Barred?" Lucifer chuckled. "There are no barriers that can keep me from you."

"And have you forsaken the light?"

"This is the new world order," Lucifer replied. "And you have a place in it, ruling at my side."

"I don't want to rule anything. I never did."

"Then I'll rule the world and you'll be my consort."

Michael shook his head. "Are you even listening to yourself? What has happened to you? Why have you turned away from Him?"

"My eyes have finally been opened," Lucifer replied. "Come with me and see for yourself."

"No."

Lucifer held out his hand. "Michael, you know how I feel about you."

"Do I?" Michael asked. "You've never spoken of your feelings. For all I know you consider me with as much contempt as you do the rest of the angels."

"How could you think that?" Lucifer said and Michael could hear the shock in his voice. "You are everything to me. I care for you more than anyone or anything in any world."

"Do you? Then come back to me, undo whatever you've done to the other fallen angels, beg forgiveness, and be restored to the light."

"That's not possible," Lucifer said. "The past cannot be rewritten and each of my demons made their own choice. Only they can choose to return to what they used to be. They are not my slaves. They have the free will to make their own decisions."

Michael had a feeling Lucifer spoke the truth, though it didn't make it any easier to hear.

"I won't join you," Michael said. "I stand with the rest of the archangels."

Lucifer's blue eyes flashed red for a moment and Michael stepped back in horror. "You would strike against me?"

Michael raised his sword and pointed the blade at Lucifer's throat. "I would not want to, but, if I have to, I will."

"Such weapons cannot harm me, any more than they can you," Lucifer said.

Michael stepped closer and let the sword nick the skin of Lucifer's neck, drawing a tiny drop of blood. "This is no ordinary sword. It has the power to bring you down and, while it would pain me to do so, I will if I have to."

Lucifer casually brushed the sword to the side and shook

his head. "You will not harm me, Michael. Not after all we've shared."

"Turn back to the light, Lucifer," Michael begged. "Don't leave me."

"I'm not leaving you," Lucifer replied. "I'm right here. All you have to do is take my hand and we'll be together for the rest of eternity. Together, we would be formidable."

Michael closed his eyes and blinked back the tears he didn't want his lover to see. Lucifer was lost to him and he didn't know how he would go on without him. For one terrifying, fleeting moment, Michael considered taking Lucifer's hand and accepting all he had to offer. He pushed the thought aside before he did something he would regret.

When he opened his eyes he thought Lucifer might have gone, but he found him still there, standing arm's length away.

"Oh, Michael," Lucifer whispered. He raised his hand to Michael's face and cupped his cheek gently. "One day I hope you'll change your mind and join me. There will always be a place for you at my side. You only have to ask."

"It won't happen." Michael raised his hand to the necklace he had not removed since the day Lucifer had placed the jewelry round his throat.

Lucifer touched the stone, which glowed red for a moment before transforming back to its usual blue color.

"What did you do to it?" Michael asked.

"I've turned the sapphire into a key," Lucifer replied. "No angel can set foot in the Underworld, but your necklace is now a key to my personal chambers there. When you're ready to take your rightful place at my side, use the key to come to me and I will welcome you back into my bed, my arms, and my life."

"How does it work?" Michael asked.

Lucifer smiled. "Just say my name while touching the stone."

Michael nodded to acknowledge that he understood. "I won't fall from grace for you."

"Not yet perhaps," Lucifer replied. "But I can wait however long it takes for you to accept your destiny."

"My destiny is to continue my work as an archangel."

"No, Michael. You are mine and one day you will reign at my side. It may not be this year, or even this century, but one day you'll take your true place. It's only a matter of time. Whatever it takes, I *will* convince you to join me."

Michael watched Lucifer vanish from sight, and he knew he would not return to his former home again. They were of different worlds now, and on opposing sides of a war. Michael knew he should cast aside the gemstone, but the necklace was the only gift Lucifer had ever given to him, or at least the only one he could keep. He couldn't bear to part with it, especially knowing it was the last link he had to the angel he had loved more than any other.

He should probably tell Gabriel and the other archangels of his meeting with Lucifer, but he knew he wouldn't. Some things didn't need to be said out loud. He had made his choice and the decision was still too raw for him to talk about.

Maybe one day he would confide in his friends. In the meantime they had a war to fight and Michael had to learn to use the sword he held, because the demons he had seen in the pool of visions had powers they couldn't even begin to imagine.

Chapter Four

Michael stared out over the battlefield and the army of demons congregating on the other side of the plains. From his vantage point, in the air above his own army, he could see the angels were vastly outnumbered.

Lucifer had recruited more demons during the centuries since his fall. His army was composed of thousands of humans, every one eager to sell his or her mortal soul for the promise of power, vengeance, or whatever else Lucifer and his demons offered them.

Gabriel flew up to join him. "This battle will decide things once and for all," he said.

"I know."

"Lucifer has been spotted at the rear of the eastern flank."

Michael's heart leaped at the name of his former lover and he touched the sapphire he still wore round his neck.

"Do you think he'll fight personally?" Gabriel asked.

"If he has to," Michael replied. "We've already seen he is perfectly capable of fighting his own battles."

"What of you?" Gabriel pressed.

"I think I've proved where my loyalties lie by now," Michael replied sharply. "If I intended to join him, I'd have done so long ago."

"You haven't seen him in person since he fell," Gabriel pointed out.

Michael didn't correct him.

"You still wear his gift," Gabriel commented.

Michael dropped his hand and lowered his gaze.

"It's all right to remember your love for him. Just don't let your feelings cloud your judgment now."

"I won't."

Michael gazed at his own army of angels from high above and knew many of them wouldn't see another dawn. One of them might be the angel to kill Lucifer. Michael's heart ached at the fleeting thought.

"You've been a good leader these last centuries," Gabriel said.

Michael acknowledged the compliment with a nod. He still didn't think Gabriel had made the right choice when he had stepped down from his position as unspoken leader of the archangels. Any time Michael asked him about his choice, he simply said he thought the one who knew Lucifer best would be more suited to defeating him. Michael disagreed but had stepped into the role with an ease that sometimes worried him. He didn't want to lead others into battle. He wanted a life of peace, with the man he loved beside him. Unfortunately, the man he loved was across the other side of the battlefield, leading an army of demons whose sole purpose was the destruction of all things good.

"We should report back to the others," Gabriel suggested.

Michael agreed and they flew to the tent situated at the rear of the ranks of angels.

Raphael greeted them with a sharp nod. "Did you see any fallen angels?"

"No," Michael confirmed. "I don't think any more have left our side. Only Lucifer remains."

Gabriel agreed. "Those who fell initially have all been captured or destroyed centuries ago. Those we face now are merely their offspring or converted humans. They won't have the same powers as their predecessors, who we faced in the first war."

Michael studied the battle plans laid out across the table. So many angels had followed Lucifer to the Underworld and not a single one of them had forsworn the leader of the demons.

"They may not have the powers, but they outnumber us five to one," Raphael said. "This fight won't be easy."

"What fight ever is?" Michael asked. "Killing should never come easy, and certainly not to an angel."

Raphael gripped his sword and glared at the table. Michael considered how his friend had changed over the centuries since the creation of the demons. Raphael had become a formidable warrior with little compassion for the enemy. His first instinct was always to kill them rather than to try to bring them back to the light. Michael, meanwhile, always tried to save their souls before striking the killing blow. Although his attempts to save the souls of the demons had been unsuccessful, Michael continued to persevere. He had to believe it possible, or where did that leave him and Lucifer?

Gabriel pointed at the map. "Lucifer has been reported here."

"Lucifer himself?" Raphael asked. "It's been many years since he stepped out of the Underworld."

"Nevertheless, the reports come from several scouts. He's here, readying himself for battle."

"Then the war ends today," Raphael announced. "Lucifer's reign will soon be over."

Michael couldn't meet Raphael's eyes. The thought of his friend killing his former lover made him nauseated.

"Even if Lucifer falls today, there's still an entire army of demons to deal with," Azrael pointed out. "Not only the demons who haven't come to fight, but those who will flee the battle before the end. Not all demons are fighters."

"Azrael is right," Gabriel agreed. "The sexual predators aren't here, nor are most of the demons who prey on greed."

"The fear demons are here in force," Raphael said, "as well as those who thrive on hatred. We need to warn our angels where those numbers are congregating."

Michael nodded and Raphael departed to speak to his angels and pass the word along. The rest of the archangels, except Gabriel, did likewise.

"Michael, how are you doing?" Gabriel asked.

Michael shrugged. "I'm ready to do what I have to. This

is just one more battle, isn't it?"

"A battle where Lucifer would appear to intend to fight," Gabriel reminded him. "Raphael intends to take him on personally."

"He does?" Michael had suspected as much, but hearing Gabriel's confirmation still hurt.

"Yes. How are you with that?"

"I'm dealing with it as best I can." Michael glanced back at the table rather than meet Gabriel's gaze. He couldn't afford to fall apart now. "Can we organize our ranks so Raphael is well away from Lucifer?"

"And who would you put in Raphael's place?" Gabriel asked.

"Myself," Michael replied. "If it comes down to single combat against Lucifer, I should be the angel fighting him."

"I don't think that's wise."

"It probably isn't, but I can't bear to think of either of them killing the other. I continue to hope Lucifer might come back to us."

"You still believe that?" Gabriel sounded sad, as though he thought Michael wasted his time. "After all these centuries, you honestly think Lucifer might suddenly give up his throne in the Underworld and return to the light?"

"I *have* to believe it," Michael replied. "Otherwise, I'm the worst sort of fool for loving a monster all these years."

"No one who knows you could ever call you a fool."

"Raphael might disagree."

"Raphael sees everything as black and white. There is good and evil and nothing in between. But even he would not call you a fool."

"Not to my face."

"Not ever," Gabriel corrected. "He wouldn't follow your leadership if he didn't respect you."

"I don't want him fighting Lucifer," Michael said. "I'd rather take him on myself."

"Can you really do what's necessary when you're standing face to face with him?" Gabriel placed his hand on

Michael's arm. "We don't want to lose you."

"I've been fighting for centuries while Lucifer has been hiding out in the Underworld. I have the advantage in this fight."

"That's not what I meant. If you, an archangel, should fall, the power the demons would draw from you could turn the tide against us."

"I won't fall."

"You don't know that. Lucifer can be most persuasive — just look at the sheer number of demons in his army. Far more humans are giving up their souls to join his cause than are becoming angels. If you should meet, face to face, you don't know how you'll handle the confrontation."

Michael touched his necklace and turned to face Gabriel. "I *have* already seen him since he fell." He was careful not to say Lucifer's name while he touched the sapphire.

"What? When? Why didn't you tell us, tell me?"

"It was right after he fell," Michael said. "I could barely believe what had happened and I went to his house, hoping there might have been some sort of mistake. He came to me there."

"In the realm of angels?" Gabriel grabbed Michael's arm. "Lucifer has access to the realm?"

"He said nothing could keep him away from me. We spoke for a few minutes and he left. I've not seen him since."

"You should have told us he can enter the realm."

"Perhaps, and if he'd come back again I would have said something. Before he left he indicated the realm of angels held nothing for him, save me."

"What else did he say to you?" Gabriel asked.

"He asked me to join him," Michael replied. "I refused, of course."

"Of course." Gabriel hugged him briefly and patted his back. "Were you tempted?"

Michael didn't want to answer, but his oldest and best friend deserved honesty. "Yes."

Gabriel smiled. "Thank you."

"What for?"

"For giving me the truth. If you had said no, I wouldn't have believed you."

The sound of a horn came from outside the tent. The battle was about to begin.

Michael checked his sword and armor and faced Gabriel. "I resisted temptation and have done whatever has been necessary to bring about an end to this war."

Gabriel clasped Michael's arm and squeezed. "God speed, my friend."

"You too."

Michael left the tent and flew above his angels, the ones he had personally recruited and trained from the souls of humans who had ascended to Heaven. Today he would face Lucifer and one way or another this impasse would come to an end.

When the trumpets sounded, the angels charged across the field. Some, like Michael, flew, while others ran on foot. Not every angel felt comfortable going into battle with their wings visible. They were vulnerable to attack and did have a habit of getting in the way at precisely the wrong moment.

The battle cry from the demons rang out across the field, but the angels didn't hesitate in their assault.

"Onward," Michael yelled as he flew ahead, his sword outstretched toward the section of the army of demons he wanted his own angels to attack.

To his left Azrael drew his bow, his weapon of choice, and fired one arrow after another into the demon horde. Thankfully an angel's quiver always had an endless supply of arrows and, when fired by an archangel, they always hit their mark. One demon after another fell, but thousands still stood.

Michael's angels reached the demons and, with their swords raised, they swept through the ranks, slicing and stabbing at any demon in their path. Michael studied the demons, searching for those who seemed to be in charge, finally spotting a large bull-like creature shouting commands from his chariot. Michael flew down at speed, his sword raised, and with one clean swing of the blade he decapitated the demon and flew up out of range.

The loss of one of their leaders didn't seem to bother the demons. Michael suspected, in the heat of the battle, most of them hadn't even noticed.

Michael swerved to avoid a demonic fire arrow aimed in his direction as he chose his next target. A huge snake demon, slithering through the angels, below their line of sight, caught Michael's eye and he realized the creature headed in the direction of the tents. Michael swooped and sliced the snake in half, only to find he faced two smaller demons. When he struck the first, it too split and formed two more demons.

His sword useless against such a creature, Michael flew over to one of the torches at the edge of the camp and returned to the snakes with fire as his weapon. He thrust the torch at the largest remaining snake and set it alight as easily as a bale of straw. The snake writhed in pain, catching against the smaller snakes, which caught fire too. Finally the flames consumed each part of the demon, leaving no trace it had even been there.

His target destroyed, Michael flew back to the battlefield once more.

With the exception of Azrael, who still fired arrows from above the battle, the rest of the archangels were nowhere in sight.

Michael took out two more powerful demons with timely blows from his sword and was searching for another when he spotted a flash of gold high on the opposite hillside. Even though the glint came from some distance away, Michael felt in his gut it was Lucifer watching from the hill and he flew in his direction.

He was still some distance away when he realized his instincts had been correct. Lucifer, his gold horns glinting in the sunlight, rose from his seat on a boulder and drew his sword.

Michael increased his speed and let loose a battle cry as he flew at Lucifer. He could tell the moment Lucifer recognized him. The fallen angel lowered his sword, just a little, hesitation clear in his stance. Michael pressed on and swung his sword at Lucifer as he landed in front of him. Even caught by surprise at the identity of his attacker, Lucifer parried Michael's blow with ease.

"It's been a long time, lover," Lucifer said.

Michael raised his sword again, but he faltered slightly at Lucifer's words and the soft tone he used.

"Don't you have a kiss for me?" Lucifer teased.

Michael didn't trust himself to speak. He needed Lucifer to fight him, not talk to him as if they lay tangled beneath the sheets after making love. He circled Lucifer, keeping his sword raised, stopping only when he no longer had his back to the battlefield. He needed to see if someone approached him from behind.

"My demons won't attack you unless I tell them to," Lucifer said, having clearly guessed Michael's thoughts. "They have their orders."

"You think you have control of any of those creatures?" Michael asked. "Look at them. They're monsters."

"They won't harm *you*."

Michael raised his sword to Lucifer's throat. He saw the tiny scar from the last time he had stood in this position. He cringed at the memory.

Lucifer swept Michael's blade aside with ease. "You can still take your place at my side. It's not too late to join me."

"Never," Michael snarled as he swung his sword at Lucifer, hoping this would be over quickly, one way or another.

Lucifer didn't waste any more time or energy with words. He met Michael's strike with one of his own, and the clang of their swords echoed across the hillside. Michael's arm wavered at the force of the blow, but he maintained his grip on the hilt of the sword and swung round to strike again.

For a demon who had done precious little fighting on

the front lines during the recent years of the wars, Lucifer was astonishingly adept with the blade. He met each of Michael's thrusts with ease and Michael stumbled at the realization this fight wouldn't be as easy as he had first thought.

Michael flew above Lucifer, striking down at the fallen angel as he let his wings carry him out of range. Lucifer's wings, hidden until now, appeared and he left the ground as well. No longer pure white feathers, his wings were dark gray and appeared leathery in texture. Michael could have wept at the visible evidence of what Lucifer had become. Even more than the horns, the wings broke Michael's heart.

Caught up in his sorrow, Michael didn't see Lucifer's next sweep of the sword. The blade caught his shoulder, drawing blood and sending pain shooting down his arm. Thankfully it wasn't his sword arm, even if the wound was still agonizing.

Michael screamed, letting loose one blow after another at Lucifer, his blade moving too fast for a human to see. Lucifer, however, had no such difficulty and now they fought in earnest.

The sky darkened, day turned to night, and the battlefield became quiet. The two armies retired to their respective tents, ready to rest before returning to the field tomorrow.

Michael saw Gabriel hovering in the distance for several minutes before he flew back to their camp to tend to his troops. Michael knew Gabriel and the other archangels would see his own angels cared for too.

Lucifer didn't seem to have any intention of ending their personal battle and, even though Michael yearned for this to be over, he couldn't walk away.

Time meant little as they fought high in the clouds. Their armies were mere specks on the ground and the lights of the torches glowing dots.

Dawn arrived, and, shortly after, Michael heard the sounds of renewed fighting below. Echoes of swords striking metal and arrows screaming through the air joined the clang of Michael's and Lucifer's swords meeting, over and over again.

Michael drove Lucifer back to the ground, only for Lucifer to turn things about and corner him in the rocky crags of the hills. Michael fought his way out of the dead end and drove Lucifer into retreat.

They took to the air again, soaring through the clouds each seeking to gain the upper hand, but neither ever quite managing it.

Another day ended and still they battled. Down below, the two armies once again retired for the night. Michael could see countless dead on the ground, both angels and demons. It was impossible to tell which army had the advantage.

Tonight, Raphael and several other archangels joined Gabriel and they stayed to watch Michael and Lucifer for nearly an hour. When the archangels seemed to understand that the two of them had no intention of stopping, most of them went back to the camp. Gabriel stayed longer, but eventually he too flew to the ground.

The stamina of angels wasn't endless and even archangels needed to recharge eventually. With the coming of the new dawn, Michael felt the strain of his prolonged fight. His arm ached and his wings were tiring. He decided to rest the latter by returning to the ground once more. Lucifer followed him, and in the light of the rising sun he could see the strain their fight had put on Lucifer. One of his wings bled in several places and a fine layer of sweat covered his body. The fallen angel didn't seem quite as steady on his feet as he had been either. Michael didn't know how long they could keep this up, but he knew he wouldn't last another twenty-four hours. He just had to hope he lasted longer than Lucifer.

As the day wore on, Michael began to notice changes to Lucifer. His eyes, which had occasionally flashed red, now remained that color rather than blue. Where previously the only signs of his demonic nature had been the gold horns and altered wings, now the rest of his body changed too. His legs, which Michael had once loved to feel wrapped around his body, became furred and his bare feet transformed into cloven hooves. His chest remained the same in form, but his skin darkened to black. When they locked swords at close quarters Michael saw Lucifer's fingers had become talons with sharp points.

How did I ever love this creature?

Michael continued his thrusts with renewed energy, and finally, he won the upper hand, pushing Lucifer back repeatedly, until the fallen angel was the one cornered in the rocks.

An earthquake shook the ground beneath them and Lucifer's sword slipped from his fingers.

Michael raised his blade, knowing this was the moment he had been waiting for. He could end the war right now with one true blow.

Lucifer grasped blindly for his lost sword and Michael could see the fear in his eyes. He hesitated and Lucifer took advantage of his weakness to retrieve his blade and fend off the delayed blow when Michael finally delivered it.

He had had his chance and he had failed. Michael berated himself as Lucifer went on the attack. His failure could mean the end of all of them. He couldn't kill Lucifer, even after being given the opportunity. The only way this battle could end would be with Lucifer's sword buried in Michael's chest.

Night fell once again and still Michael and Lucifer fought. Only now Michael merely defended himself, not seeking to gain the upper hand.

Gabriel flew to the hillside to check on him again, but this time he didn't stay long. Michael suspected he might be going to fetch reinforcements. It must have been obvious to anyone who saw them that Michael was losing this fight. But Gabriel didn't return and Michael continued the fight for his life. He thought he heard the sounds of screams and fighting in the distance, but couldn't let his concentration lapse to investigate the noise.

Rain had been pouring for much of the afternoon and the ground had become increasingly slippery. In flight, the bad weather didn't make much difference, but on the ground the mud made things much more difficult. Michael stumbled repeatedly as he tried to keep his balance, but the wet grass was treacherous. One particularly hard clash of their swords caused Michael to lose his footing completely and he tumbled down the hill, losing his sword in the process and hitting his head on a rock.

When he had recovered Lucifer stood over him, his sword poised at Michael's chest. Michael sighed and closed his eyes, knowing his battle had arrived at the inevitable conclusion.

He waited for the killing blow, but it didn't come. He dared a glance to see what had happened. Had Gabriel come back after all? No, they were still alone.

Lucifer had withdrawn his sword and leaned against one of the huge rocks surrounding them. *Why hasn't he finished this?*

Michael stared at Lucifer as he changed form, restored once again to the beauty Michael knew so well. His wings remained, as did the horns, but the rest of him converted back to a more human appearance.

Lucifer stalked over to him and Michael tried to find the strength to move, but now he had stopped he couldn't seem to summon any energy. Exhaustion had set in and all he could do was wait for the end. Lucifer stood over him for several long minutes before he tossed aside his sword and fell to the ground beside him.

Michael could hear how short of breath Lucifer was.

He closed his eyes and wondered what they would do now. Would they rest and start again with their energy renewed? Or would it be more sensible for them to return to their armies and let someone else take on the task of killing each other, since neither appeared capable of ending the other's life?

Michael still had his eyes shut when he felt the heaviness

of a body climbing on top of him. His eyes flew open and he saw that Lucifer had straddled him. His hands were over Michael's throat and for a brief, terrifying moment Michael wondered if Lucifer intended to strangle him with his bare hands.

But Lucifer didn't squeeze the life from him. Instead he took Michael's face between his hands and leaned down, pressing their lips together in a kiss that was both strange and familiar.

Michael took a moment to wonder what could possibly be going through Lucifer's mind. Why would he choose to kiss him at such a time? Then he realized Lucifer was *kissing* him and it had been so long since they had last done this. It had been too long, too many lonely centuries where he'd gone home each night to an empty bed.

After a few seconds of hesitation Michael sighed into the kiss and opened his mouth to let Lucifer in.

Michael had missed this so much. He hadn't wanted to admit it, but with Lucifer's lips on his own he couldn't deny the truth. Even now, after all these years, he still wanted Lucifer as badly as he ever had.

Lucifer pulled back a little and gazed into Michael's eyes. Michael nodded in reply to the unspoken question and unclasped his armor. Lucifer sat back to give him room to undress and to remove his own battered robe.

"Come here," Michael said once they were both naked, with nothing between them except Lucifer's gift, the key Michael had never used.

Lucifer pushed Michael's legs apart and kneeled between them. "I can't go slowly," he warned. "It's been too long."

"I know," Michael replied. "Just take me however you want to."

Lucifer nodded and encouraged Michael onto his hands and knees. It wasn't Michael's favorite position, but right now he wanted Lucifer any way he could have him. Lucifer didn't waste time with preparation. He speared Michael with one swift thrust and Michael bit back his scream, desperate to keep quiet in case someone heard them. He knew if his fellow archangels saw him right now they would destroy them both.

"You're tight," Lucifer said. "Has there been anyone else since me?"

Michael shook his head. "No one. Only you, Lucifer."

"Good." Lucifer pulled out nearly all the way before driving in again. Michael pushed back to meet his thrusts relishing the long-forgotten feeling of being so completely filled by his lover.

Michael keened quietly as Lucifer thrust into him again and again. He needed Lucifer so badly. He always had and he suspected he always would.

Lucifer continued to pound into him until Michael's arse burned. He eased his legs apart a little more, spreading himself as wide as he could for Lucifer's pleasure. His cock hung between his thighs, thick and heavy with need.

It had been too many years and they were both so desperate for this, it didn't take long before Lucifer whispered a warning he was close.

Michael felt the heat of Lucifer's release filling his arse and his own balls drew up as he neared his own climax. Lucifer continued to thrust, spilling his seed deep inside him, and Michael couldn't stop his loud scream of pleasure when he too came, his semen spurting onto the ground beneath him.

Lucifer pulled Michael back onto his knees and took hold of Michael's sensitive cock, pumping him repeatedly while Michael cried out in ecstasy.

"That's it, Michael, scream for me," Lucifer whispered in his ear. "Call my name."

"Lucifer," Michael breathed, no more able to disobey the quiet command than he could have stopped the sun from rising.

"Louder," Lucifer demanded. "Scream my name to the heavens."

Michael sobbed and shook his head. If anyone heard him they would come here and see what he had done. If such a thing should happen it would be the end of both of them, and more than anything Michael didn't want this to end. There had to be a way for him to be with Lucifer without losing himself in the process.

"Join me," Lucifer said. "Take your rightful place at my side."

"No."

"It's where you belong."

"No."

"How can you doubt it?" Lucifer asked. "You're naked in my arms, with my cock and my seed filling your arse."

"I can't be what you want me to be." Michael ducked his head, but he made no effort to pull himself away from Lucifer.

"You are everything I want," Lucifer said. "Fiery, passionate, and loyal. I *won't* give you up."

"I won't turn demon for you."

Lucifer kissed Michael's neck, hard enough that Michael knew it would leave a mark. "Then where do we go from here?" he asked. "I can't lose you again."

"You never did," Michael replied. "I've always been yours and we both know it."

"Yet you won't join me."

"I can't."

Lucifer reached to stroke Michael's cock once again. Michael whimpered and shook in Lucifer's arms.

"Let's sleep and we'll talk again in the morning," Lucifer suggested.

Michael cringed as Lucifer withdrew from him. The pain lasted only as long as it took Lucifer to take it away with the touch of his finger.

"You can still do that?" Michael asked.

"I still have all my angel powers. I should have eased my way when I took you, but I confess I wanted to cause you some pain, for leaving me alone all these centuries."

Michael stroked Lucifer's cheek and gave him a tender kiss on the lips. "I understand. If I had been in your position,

I would probably have done the same thing."

Lucifer appeared to doubt his words, and Michael didn't press it. It made no difference since Lucifer had never let Michael take him when they had been together in the realm of angels. He had no idea what sort of lover Michael would be if he were the one on top. Maybe one day they would both find out.

But first they needed to find a way to make this work. Lucifer had no intention of returning to the light and Michael wasn't prepared to become one of his lover's demons. If anyone, angel or demon, should discover what they had done it would be the end of everything.

Lucifer picked up his short robe and placed it on the ground, the fabric extending and spreading to cover a much larger area than it should have. It seemed Lucifer had learned some new tricks as well. Lucifer sat on the robe and held out his hand to Michael, who took it without hesitation.

Michael sank down beside Lucifer and let the fallen angel take him into his arms again. He curled into Lucifer's side, and when he closed his eyes he fell asleep almost immediately, something he hadn't achieved since the last time he had slept with Lucifer.

Chapter Five

Michael woke the next morning to the feel of lips pressing against his chest. When he opened his eyes he saw Lucifer paying homage to his nipples, kissing them and sucking the nubs into his mouth.

"Has the battle started again?" Michael managed to ask.

"The trumpets haven't sounded yet," Lucifer replied. "Now, what should we do today?"

"I need to go back to the army," Michael said, even though he was reluctant to leave their sheltered cocoon in the rocks.

"You've not changed your mind about coming with me?"

"You know I can't."

For a moment Michael thought about leading Lucifer to the cells, deep in the mountains, in the realm of angels.

"The cells won't hold me," Lucifer whispered.

Michael couldn't tell if he had read his mind or merely guessed the direction of his thoughts.

"They might contain lesser angels, but not one as powerful as me."

Michael believed him without question.

"The archangels will kill me when they find out you've failed," Lucifer said. "Can you at least stay with me until they come?"

Michael drew Lucifer closer for a kiss. He could do that. He could be with Lucifer when the end came, even if he could not destroy him personally.

Or maybe there was another way.

The idea formed in Michael's mind even as he savored Lucifer's kiss.

"There may be another option," he whispered after they

parted.

"Hmm?" Lucifer kissed his neck, clearly not listening too closely.

"Who would believe the leader of an army of demons would let an archangel walk away unscathed?"

"Anyone who ever saw us together?" Lucifer suggested.

"But who has?" Michael countered. "You never were particularly sociable. We've been fighting for days now, and no one except us saw how the battle ended. If I go back to the camp they will assume I've defeated you."

"What exactly are you saying?" Lucifer asked. "Even if you did lie to the other archangels — and I can't believe I'm hearing you suggest such a thing — they would soon discover the deception."

"Not if you went into hiding," Michael said as the idea took shape. "You have the power to become invisible. You could use it to stay out of sight. Let everyone believe you've been killed, and no one will be searching for you."

"Why would I want to hide?" Lucifer said. "I'm leader of a great army. What would I have to gain by giving that up?"

Michael kissed Lucifer's ear before whispering into it. "Me."

They formed the plan quickly, and if Michael was surprised at Lucifer's easy capitulation, he refrained from commenting on the same.

Michael left him with a final lingering kiss and flew back to the camp just as the herald was about to sound the start of the battle again. He raised his hand to stop him blowing the horn and hurried to the archangels' tent.

As he soared through the camp he saw the place was in disarray. Tents had been burned to the ground, some still smoldering in the early dawn light. The camp had been attacked during the night, and Michael now understood why Gabriel had not returned with reinforcements.

Inside one of the few remaining tents, he found Gabriel announcing the morning strategy. His friend glanced up at

Michael's entrance and his eyes widened in astonishment. Michael felt a slight twinge of annoyance that Gabriel's expression signified he hadn't believed him capable of winning the fight against Lucifer. Then he remembered he hadn't.

"Michael!" Gabriel rushed round the table and pulled him into his arms. "You must be exhausted."

"I'm good. I slept a little last night."

Gabriel stepped back and guided Michael to a cushioned chair. "Is it over?"

Michael nodded.

Gabriel faced the rest of the archangels. "Spread the word. With Lucifer defeated the tide will turn. We will be victorious and this war will end today."

The archangels dispersed to pass on the news. Gabriel remained with Michael and when they were alone he took hold of his hand.

"How are you?" he asked kindly.

"I'm fine."

"Are you sure?" Gabriel sounded doubtful. "Perhaps you're in shock. Maybe you should go home and leave the rest of us to finish this off."

Michael didn't want to run away, but the days of battling Lucifer had taken their toll. Even though he had slept a little the previous night, the few hours on the hard, damp ground hadn't been enough. Right now he wanted to spend another week curled up in bed, preferably with Lucifer in his arms.

"Go home, Michael," Gabriel said. "That's an order."

Michael gave him a smile. "I thought I was in charge around here?"

"I took over command while you were busy. You can have your position back once you've rested. Now go home."

Once Gabriel had left, Michael breathed a sigh of relief. He hadn't needed to concoct an elaborate set of lies. Maybe later that would be necessary, when his friends asked for details, but right now they were satisfied to make assumptions, ones Michael didn't intend to correct.

The sound of the horn was loud, but the cheers of victorious angels almost drowned it out.

Michael closed his eyes and concentrated on home. A moment later he sat on his beach, watching the waves lap against the golden sands.

He cast his armor aside and lay back on the dunes. Was the war truly going to end today, or was it merely moving on to another stage?

He wondered where Lucifer was right now. Had he kept his side of the bargain or had he revealed his presence after all?

Perhaps the archangels had already discovered Michael's deception and were even now considering how to deal with him.

No, he couldn't let himself think that. Lucifer wouldn't betray him. He was as tired of this war as Michael, he was sure of it.

Closing his eyes, Michael slept, while the battle raged on Earth.

* * * *

Michael woke when Gabriel shook his shoulder.

"It's over," Gabriel said. "The demons have retreated to the Underworld. Without Lucifer leading them they've fallen into disarray. They'll no doubt regroup in time, but it gives us the opportunity to recruit and hopefully be better prepared when the next war starts."

"The next war?" Michael didn't want to think about another war.

Gabriel sat beside him. "It'll come eventually. Only the destruction of every living demon could end it all."

"Or every living angel," Michael pointed out.

Gabriel acknowledged his comment with a nod.

"What were our losses?" Michael asked.

"All the archangels have survived, but we lost a great

many lesser angels. Metatron's losses were the heaviest."

Michael wasn't surprised. Metatron, known as the Scribe, had never been comfortable fighting, and the angels he had recruited over the years were of a similar disposition.

"What of Raphael's angels?" Michael asked. Many of his friend's angels were healers and often torn between fighting the demons and healing their fallen comrades, putting themselves in further danger in the process.

"He's lost many, as expected, but his favorites survived."

Michael was glad for the small mercy. He knew Raphael took it harder than any of them when he lost one of his angels, often considering it a personal failure on his part.

"There's one more thing before I go," Gabriel said. "We couldn't find Lucifer's body."

"You searched?" Michael whispered.

"Of course. He was once one of us. We had hoped to bring him home."

"His home hasn't been here for a long time," Michael said.

"Still, I thought you might have wished to say a proper farewell to him. We can still have a memorial service for him, if you want."

Michael shook his head. He couldn't go through with such a sham, not without confessing what he had done.

Gabriel patted him on the shoulder and stood to leave. "Goodnight, Michael. I'll see you tomorrow in the archangels' chamber for the debriefing."

Michael watched Gabriel walk away before he made his way to his house, a slightly larger abode than it had been all those centuries ago when he had sat here on the beach with Lucifer. The world had moved on a great deal since then. Perhaps it was time he took another look at modern architecture and did some more remodeling. The work would help take his mind off things, or at least he hoped so.

* * * *

The debriefing the following day was relatively swift.

Michael said little. The archangels had made assumptions about what had happened and he'd let them. He kept his responses short and to the point, only lying when he absolutely had to, and keeping it as brief as possible. Even so, the guilt nearly tore him apart.

He had never willingly lied to anyone before, and to do so now was killing something inside him.

As he sat in his chair, listening to the archangels discuss the remaining demons and strategies for how to deal with them in the coming years, Michael's thoughts drifted. Was this how it started? Had he taken the first step toward falling from grace himself? How many lies did it take before he was lost?

When Raphael asked him a question more than once, Michael did his best to concentrate on the meeting, but still his worries lingered.

Would there soon be another fallen angel in the Underworld?

* * * *

For several weeks, Michael resisted the temptation to use his key to the Underworld. It helped that Gabriel kept a close eye on him, rarely leaving him alone for long periods of time, and encouraging him to socialize with the rest of them, even when he would rather have wallowed in his misery and guilt alone.

After a while Gabriel began to give Michael some time to himself. Michael had often been a loner and no one thought it unusual that he wished to enjoy the solitude on occasion.

Michael touched the gem and whispered Lucifer's name. At first nothing happened. Then the world shimmered around him. One moment he was seated on the grass by their pool, the next he sat in the center of a luxurious bed in a lavishly furnished cave.

"Michael?" Lucifer grinned and ran across the room, leaping onto the bed and tackling Michael as he toppled him onto the covers. "You're here, at last. You don't know how many times I've considered risking everything by traveling to the realm of angels to find you."

"Why didn't you?"

Lucifer ducked his head. "I feared you may have changed your mind."

"No, I haven't, as you can see."

Lucifer smiled and kissed him briefly. "Have you any idea how dull it is to be invisible to everyone? Even worse when the only man who knows you're alive is in another realm, and the one realm I can't view from here."

Michael hugged Lucifer and laughed with sheer joy at being in his lover's arms again. "I'm thinking you might have missed me."

Lucifer kissed him again and tore at his clothes. "Whatever gave you that idea? I'm just deathly bored."

Michael grabbed Lucifer's hard cock and gave it a squeeze. "I think it's a little more than boredom," he teased as Lucifer bucked into his hand.

"You could have come sooner," Lucifer chided.

"I've been watched. My friends are concerned for my wellbeing. It's hard to slip away when you're monitored every minute of every day."

"I'll have to teach you how to shield yourself from the eyes of others," Lucifer told him. "It isn't so hard to achieve, and if you're going to visit me here, you should take the time to master the ability."

Michael's first instinct was to refuse the offer, until he remembered Lucifer had been able to make himself invisible even before his fall. The power wasn't demonic, simply an angelic ability Michael had yet to learn. "I'd like that," he said. "And I'm sorry for not coming sooner."

"It matters not," Lucifer said. "You're here now and I'm not going to let you out of my bed until you've been well and truly fucked."

"I can't wait," Michael said. "But I need to know something first."

"Ask quickly. I can't wait much longer."

Michael drew in a breath for courage. "There are many handsome demons among your ranks."

"There are, but that's not a question."

"How many have you had in your bed?" Michael asked.

Lucifer pulled back and stared at him in astonishment. "You think I've been unfaithful to you?"

"It's been centuries," Michael reminded him. "I've watched you for much of that time in the pool of visions. I've seen you laughing and flirting with many men, both humans and demons."

Lucifer sat back. "Yes, I laugh and flirt with my followers and the humans. It means nothing. Have you ever seen me do anything more than flirt?"

"No."

Lucifer nodded. "That's because there has been no other except you. I have ached for you since the moment we parted. You are the only one to ever share my bed, either in the past, the present, or the future. I want no other but you. Do you understand me?"

Michael nodded.

"Say it out loud," Lucifer ordered. "Do you understand what I'm saying to you?"

"Yes," Michael whispered.

"Good," Lucifer said. "I came to your bed a virgin." He took Michael's hand and placed it over his groin. "*Your* hands are the only ones to have touched me this way. I have only ever tasted *your* lips, *your* cock, *your* seed. Yours is the body I crave day and night. I won't give you up, Michael."

"I'm here," Michael said. "I shouldn't be, and I'm risking everything by coming here, but I can't stay away from you either."

Lucifer swept Michael into his arms and rolled him over the covers. Michael groaned as Lucifer rubbed against him, grinding their cocks together.

"Tell me you love me," Lucifer begged. "Please, Michael, let me hear the words I've longed for all these lonely years."

Michael couldn't deny him such a small thing. "I love you, Lucifer, more than anything."

Lucifer kissed him as they rocked against each other. Michael wrapped his legs around Lucifer's waist, holding him in place above him.

"Will anyone hear me if I scream?" Michael asked.

"My chambers are completely soundproof," Lucifer assured him. "Yell as loud as you want, no demon will hear you."

Michael took Lucifer at his word, and when he came a few minutes later, he screamed out Lucifer's name so loudly he thought the entire Underworld must surely have heard him anyway.

Afterwards, he rested his head on Lucifer's chest and closed his eyes, shutting out reality for a few blissful moments.

"How long do you think we can keep this secret?" Lucifer asked.

"For as long as we can," Michael replied. "It's just a matter of time until one of the angels searches for me in the pool of visions and sees me here in your arms."

"The pool cannot show anything here," Lucifer said.

"We've seen the Underworld many times in the pool," Michael said. "We've watched you in your throne room, holding court."

"Yes, but you've not seen this chamber, have you?"

Michael thought about it and realized he hadn't.

"These rooms, my private chambers, are shielded from all angelic methods of spying," Lucifer explained. "So long as we remain within my rooms, we're invisible to the archangels."

"Then this is the only place we can be together?"

"We can be together anywhere, but this is the only place we can be sure of not being caught."

Michael supposed that would have to do. He could see about putting some of his own touches on the chambers, maybe bring Lucifer some of the gems from his former home too. He was still contemplating decorating the cavern when Lucifer raised a problem Michael hadn't yet considered.

"What are you going to tell the archangels if they ask where you've been when they can't see you in their spying pool?"

"I don't know," Michael said. "I hope they trust me enough to not search for me in the pool."

"Do you truly think they won't notice your absences?"

Michael sighed. It was only a matter of time before they questioned him. They had wondered where he was at breakfast when he had been spying on Lucifer. His friends were far too observant at times.

"Let's not worry about such things today," Michael said. "We've been apart too long. Let us enjoy this time together while we can."

Lucifer didn't argue. He ran his fingers through Michael's long hair and held him as he slept.

* * * *

For the next few years Michael slipped away to see Lucifer in the Underworld every chance he could. He cherished the time spent with his lover as they rediscovered the pleasures to be found in each other's body.

Occasionally Lucifer raised the idea of Michael joining him in the Underworld permanently, but he didn't press the issue when Michael refused.

Michael didn't dare meet Lucifer anywhere except his private chambers, and he soon began to think of the rooms as his second home. He spent as much time there as he did in his own beach house.

Secure in the knowledge that if the archangels suspected anything they would have raised their concerns long ago, Michael soon forgot how observant Gabriel in particular could be.

* * * *

"Good morning, Michael," Gabriel said as Michael arrived back in his beach house.

Michael nearly jumped out of his skin at the sound of an unexpected voice in the dark. "Gabriel! What are you doing here so early?"

"Waiting for you."

"What for? Is something wrong?"

Michael lit the lamp on the table. In the illuminated room he could see the worry on Gabriel's face.

"You tell me," Gabriel replied. "Where have you been all night?"

Michael shrugged. "Out."

"Out where?"

"Just out."

"Michael, please don't lie to me. I'm going to ask you one more time. Where were you last night?"

Michael didn't want to lie, yet he could not tell the truth either. Gabriel wouldn't understand. No one would. "Does it matter?"

Gabriel stood and walked over to him. He reached for Michael's necklace and touched the stone. "You still wear Lucifer's gift."

The moment Gabriel spoke Lucifer's name the room shimmered and the two of them found themselves standing in Lucifer's chamber.

"Did you forget something, Michael?" Lucifer asked as he turned round. "Oh fuck."

Michael wasn't sure who appeared more shocked, Gabriel or Lucifer.

Gabriel recovered first, dropping the necklace back against Michael's chest and stepping over to a nearby chair, which he dropped into heavily.

"Gabriel?" Michael whispered. "I can explain."

"Don't." Gabriel raised his hand. He didn't seem angry, just disappointed, which to Michael was even worse. "You lied to us. You lied to *me*. I thought we were friends. I knew you were keeping something from me, but I never imagined your secret to be *this*. How do I get out of here?"

"Just think of home and you'll be there," Michael replied quietly.

Gabriel didn't waste any time with more questions. He disappeared from the room in an instant.

Lucifer hurried across the room and took Michael into his arms. "Stay here and you never have to face the archangels again. Take your place at my side."

Michael shook his head. "I must go back. I have to explain."

"Explain what?" Lucifer asked. "How you lied about my death and have been sharing my bed ever since?"

"I owe it to them to face the consequences of my actions. Do you understand?"

"No," Lucifer said. "I don't."

Michael sighed and stepped back from Lucifer. He couldn't always think clearly when Lucifer took him in his arms. "I'll be back soon."

"Will you?" Lucifer said. "Do you honestly believe the archangels will let you come back to me, now they know where you disappear to?"

Michael didn't know, but he guessed he would soon find out.

Lucifer gave Michael one last kiss before he stepped back and sat on the bed. "I'll be waiting for you, and you know my offer still stands. If I'm about to be resurrected, I want you at my side."

Michael didn't tell Lucifer again that he would never turn demon. They had already discussed the topic countless times. Michael couldn't help but wonder what he would do if he was forced to choose between his home, his brethren, and his love for Lucifer.

* * * *

When Michael arrived in the realm of angels the place was relatively quiet. No one stared at him or whispered as he passed. He guessed word of his deception had not yet spread to the lesser angels. He couldn't see any archangels around. Suspecting they might be in their chamber, he headed in that direction.

Inside the room he found all fourteen archangels engaged in a heated discussion, which stopped as soon as they saw him.

"Michael," Gabriel said. "Take your seat."

He did as he was told and waited in silence.

Gabriel sighed. "I'm sure I don't need to tell you I had no choice other than to tell the rest of the archangels what I saw today."

Michael nodded.

"Is it true?" Raphael asked.

"You doubt my word?" Gabriel snapped.

"No," Raphael replied. "But I need to hear it from Michael's own lips. Does Lucifer live?"

"Yes," Michael stated.

"And you have been meeting with him in secret?"

"Yes."

"To what purpose?" Raphael asked.

Michael frowned at the question and glanced at Gabriel. What had he told them?

Gabriel gestured for him to answer the question.

"Sex," Michael said.

Raphael gaped at him while Gabriel stifled a smile.

"How long?" Raphael questioned.

"Since the last battle," Michael confirmed.

"The battle where you claimed to have killed him," Raphael snarled. "Do you expect us to believe you spared his life simply because you wanted to fuck him again?"

Michael bristled at Raphael's tone. "Actually, he usually fucks me, if you must know."

The archangels fell silent at Michael's words. Eventually Gabriel spoke. "Did you plan this deception before the last battle?"

"No."

Gabriel shook his head. "Michael, talk to us. We can't understand what you've done if you don't try to explain."

"Do you intend to fall?" Raphael asked.

"No." Michael put as much surety into his tone as he could manage.

The archangels sighed collectively.

Gabriel stood and signaled for the end of the meeting. "We'll reconvene this afternoon. I wish to speak to Michael alone."

Michael would rather have got the meeting over with right now, but it was clear he had no say in the matter.

The archangels exited the room, leaving Michael alone with Gabriel. The latter stood and walked to one of the observation benches, waving for Michael to join him.

"Oh, Michael, what have you done?"

"I never meant to lie."

"Do you really love him so much you'd betray all of us?"

"I don't see my actions as a betrayal."

"What do you call it?" Gabriel asked. "Lucifer has fallen from grace and set himself up in direct opposition against Him. The two of you faked his death and you lied to us. By your own admission you've been sneaking around to have sex with him."

"I love him."

"I know you do. That I never doubted. But you must see this cannot continue."

"I can't lose him again," Michael said.

"You may not have a choice," Gabriel replied. "Before you arrived we were discussing the options and decided you must stand trial for your actions."

"Trial?"

"Yes. That's why I need the truth from you. Michael, how close are you to falling?"

Michael bowed his head. He wished he could answer Gabriel's question. He didn't want to fall, but perhaps the choice wasn't his. Maybe it never had been.

Chapter Six

Michael sat in his seat as the rest of the archangels gathered. He hadn't eaten with the others, preferring to sit alone with his thoughts until the trial began.

Gabriel took center stage once again. Michael knew, without being told, Gabriel had resumed his position as leader of the archangels. Michael no longer deserved the honor.

"We all know why we're here," Gabriel said. "Archangel Michael has confessed to deceiving us by lying about his defeat of Lucifer. He has continued in this lie so as to engage in a relationship with the fallen angel and leader of the demons. We need to decide what is to be done about this."

"It must end, immediately," Raguel stated. Michael recalled how Raguel had suffered several personal losses during the war and Michael wasn't surprised at his words now.

Gabriel raised his hand. "First I want Michael to speak. Michael, why did you do this?"

"You know why," Michael replied.

"Yes, I know, but not everyone here does."

"I love him," Michael said. "It's that simple."

"He's a fallen angel, a demon," Raguel shouted. "How can you love such a creature?"

"I loved him from the moment I saw him. The son of the morning, as he was then, was all I ever wanted in a lover and a life mate. I can't turn off my feelings for him any more than I can stop the sun from rising."

"He's a monster."

"He's lost his way," Michael insisted. "He still has a chance to return to us."

"You don't believe that, do you?"

"I have to believe it," Michael replied. "I couldn't love him if I didn't."

"He doesn't deserve your love."

Michael smiled at Raguel. "*Everyone* deserves love. Surely you know that? It's the code we've always lived by."

Raguel glared but declined to comment.

"Michael is right," Gabriel said. "Now we must decide, by vote, whether relationships between angels and demons should be banned."

"I vote to ban them," Raguel said.

"And I vote not to," Michael replied.

"You cannot vote in this matter," Raguel argued. "You have a vested interest in the outcome and your vote is biased."

"We all have bias on whatever we vote for," Michael pointed out.

Gabriel halted their argument. "Michael, in the circumstances, I think Raguel is right. You should not vote in this matter."

The stab of betrayal at his friend's words hit him hard, but he held his tongue.

Raphael spoke next. "I vote *not* to ban relationships."

"I too," Metatron said.

One by one the archangels cast their votes, some agreeing with Raguel, others with Michael. By the time Gabriel's turn to speak came, the outcome was clear. Relationships would not be banned. For Michael it still came as a relief when Gabriel confirmed his vote was not to ban relationships either.

Michael slumped in his seat and closed his eyes as he gave a quick prayer of thanks. When he opened them again Raphael stood before him. "Thank you, my friend."

Raphael smiled. "I don't want to lose you just yet, Michael, and I think if we forced you to choose between us and Lucifer, right now, today, you'd choose him."

Michael threw his arms round Raphael's neck and kissed him on the cheek. Gabriel came to join them and he hugged him too. One by one the archangels who had voted to let him continue seeing Lucifer approached him and he offered them his thanks.

When all who remained were the ones who had chosen to oppose him, Michael stood in the center of the room and spoke to them too.

"I know you don't necessarily believe he can be saved, but Lucifer still has a great capacity to love. He can still come back to the light."

"Then perhaps you can make it your mission to achieve such a great feat," Raguel suggested. "If you truly believe what you say, it shouldn't be a problem. You can bring him back to the fold in time for dinner."

Michael glared at Raguel, annoyed by his flippancy.

"That isn't such a bad idea," Raphael said. "Do you think you can save him, Michael?"

"I believe so, but it would take time."

"Then we're in agreement," Gabriel declared. "Michael, you will continue your relationship with Lucifer, and in the process, bring him back to us."

Michael nodded. "I accept this mission."

"Now, we should bring Lucifer before us," Gabriel said. Several archangels shouted their disapproval, but Gabriel silenced them with a glare. "Go fetch him, Michael."

Michael touched the stone at his neck and whispered Lucifer's name. He found his lover pacing his bedchamber, an expression of worry on his face.

"Michael!" Lucifer ran to him and nearly lifted him off his feet as he hugged him. "I thought I'd never see you again. Are you here to join me for good?"

"No," Michael replied. "I'm here to bring you before the archangels."

Lucifer stepped back. "No."

"They aren't going to destroy you," Michael explained.

"And they aren't going to stop me visiting you either."

"Then what do they want to see me for?"

Michael couldn't blame Lucifer for being suspicious. In his place he would have been the same.

"They want to talk to you," Michael said.

"Are you sure?"

"Yes."

"What if you're wrong? What if it's a trick?"

Michael took Lucifer's face between his hands. "You're forgetting who you're dealing with. They aren't demons, schooled in deception — they're angels, for whom honesty comes naturally."

Lucifer raised an eyebrow.

"Well, most of the time," Michael amended, in light of his own recent lies.

"You're too trusting," Lucifer said. "This could still be a trap."

Michael kissed Lucifer on the lips. "If they want to hurt you, they're going to have to go through me first."

Lucifer sighed and nodded. "I'll hold you to that."

Michael took the two of them back to the realm of angels and directly into the archangels' chamber.

"This is new," Lucifer commented as he gazed around.

"Take a seat, Lucifer," Gabriel said, gesturing to a chair that had been placed in the center of the room while Michael had been in the Underworld.

Lucifer sat and Michael stood beside him rather than sit on his own chair. He wanted to make sure Lucifer knew he was there for him.

"Lucifer, I assume Michael has told you of our decision to allow him to continue his relationship with you?"

"He has."

"We have decided Michael's new primary mission will be to bring you back to the light."

Lucifer laughed loudly. "What? You're serious?"

"Very," Gabriel replied.

"It's not going to happen," Lucifer said. "I'm quite happy

where I am now. I'd much rather Michael joins me."

"I don't doubt it," Gabriel replied, "but nevertheless this is our decision. Now, before you return to the Underworld, we need to clear up a few things. Firstly, how many demons are aware you survived the last battle?"

"None," Lucifer replied.

"Are you sure?"

"Yes. I can stay hidden quite sufficiently."

"What is the state of the Underworld at present?" Raphael asked.

"It's rather drafty and we lost the only decent cook in the final battle," Lucifer replied with a smirk.

Michael nudged him in the shoulder. "Answer the question," he whispered.

Lucifer rolled his eyes. "The most powerful of the demons are still fighting over my throne. The rest are either watching the show or roaming the earth for new recruits."

"Who is the most powerful demon, besides you?" Gabriel asked. "Who is poised to lead your army if you remain hidden?"

"I don't know yet," Lucifer said. "The would-be kings are killed by their rivals as quickly as I can learn their names. My throne is becoming dusty from lack of use."

"Then what you're saying is no one is leading the demons at the present time?"

"Yes, that's right. It's wonderfully chaotic down there."

"And on Earth," Gabriel commented without the enthusiasm Lucifer had shown. "This cannot be allowed to continue."

"I'm sure some enterprising demon will take the throne eventually," Lucifer said.

"The archangels would prefer it to be sooner rather than later."

"The Underworld is *my* realm," Lucifer reminded them. "Who sits on the throne has nothing to do with you."

Michael thought Lucifer had a point, but he held his tongue. He had a feeling his opinion wouldn't count for much right now.

Gabriel glared at Lucifer. "Until the end of the war we knew who we were dealing with and what powers you wielded."

Lucifer smirked. "You think you know *all* the powers I have?"

"Probably not," Gabriel admitted. "Which means you will always have the advantage over us, as well you know. That being the case, what harm is there in us knowing who sits on the throne?"

Lucifer nodded. "Very well, I'll send word as soon as a new king is crowned."

"That's not good enough. We want the leader to take his or her place by the end of the day."

"The end of the century would be a far more realistic timescale."

"Today," Gabriel insisted. "We have been monitoring the Underworld daily since the war, and we have a fair idea of who the likely contenders are for the dubious honor of taking the throne."

"Congratulations," Lucifer said. "If you're so confident, perhaps you'd care to wager on the identity of the new king."

"There is no point in placing bets since we're going to decide who the leader will be before you leave this chamber."

"Oh, we are, are we?" Lucifer replied.

"Yes," Gabriel confirmed. "You will have an equal say in this matter, but the issue *will* be settled today."

Michael leaned over to whisper into Lucifer's ear. "Does it *really* matter who sits on the throne? Don't argue with Gabriel just for the sake of it. Stability in the Underworld surely has advantages for the demons, just as it does for everyone else."

Lucifer sighed. "You're quite right, Michael. Very well, Gabriel, show me those you believe have the potential to take the throne and I'll let you know who could be powerful enough to reign for longer than it takes his rivals to sharpen their swords."

Gabriel gave him a small smile. "Good. You will see the throne is occupied immediately you return to the Underworld. We also want your word, as a fallen angel, that you will keep the most powerful living demon within the Underworld, to prevent that creature from leading the demons into war."

Lucifer laughed. "And how do you suggest I do all this, when no demon knows I live?"

"You will have to reveal yourself to the new king," Gabriel said. "As you're so fond of pointing out to us, you are the last of the fallen angels, and therefore have powers the rest of the demons lack. Imprisoning a single demon, while remaining hidden from the rest, should be a relatively simple task."

"I don't like it, but I see you give me no choice," Lucifer said.

"No, we don't," Gabriel agreed. "Now, let us get this over with. I'm sure you don't wish to be here any longer than necessary."

Michael nudged Lucifer before he made another off-color remark and the archangels began their debate as to who the new king should be. Lucifer answered any questions put to him, and Michael believed his responses to be open and honest. It took several hours, but finally the matter was settled.

Lucifer stretched his arms above his head and yawned. "Is that all?" he asked. "Or am I free to go now?"

"No, there's one final matter we must discuss before you leave," Gabriel replied. "I'm aware you have been in this realm on at least one occasion since your fall."

Michael gasped and Lucifer glanced at him, hurt on his face that Michael had spoken of their meeting to Gabriel without telling him.

Gabriel didn't give either of them time to speak. "Past trespasses will be forgotten, but from this day forward you,

Lucifer, are not to set foot in this realm unless it is because you are being summoned to our presence, or if you seek to come before us to renounce your demon nature and return to the light. This is non-negotiable. If you are seen in this realm without permission, you will be killed."

Lucifer nodded. "You have nothing I want here. As long as Michael can continue to visit me, I don't care."

"Michael can visit you in the Underworld," Gabriel agreed.

"And on Earth," Lucifer added. "I'm tired of our time together being confined to my chambers."

Gabriel shook his head. "You are to remain in the Underworld. We do not wish you to roam the earth."

"Gabriel, please," Michael pleaded. "You've seen the Underworld for yourself. You can't make him stay there."

"His presence on Earth has too great an impact on humans."

"That's not fair," Michael argued. "You never mentioned any of this before. You can't imprison him in that place."

"It's too dangerous to have him walk the earth."

Lucifer raised his hand to Michael's arm and patted it gently. "It's all right, Michael. I'll agree to this demand."

"There's one more thing," Gabriel said. "Michael's key to the Underworld."

Michael touched the gem. "What about it?"

Gabriel held out his hand. "Such a device is too dangerous, especially since it can be activated by others beside you. We can't have angels wandering the Underworld, and I'm sure Lucifer will agree with me."

"Oh yes," Lucifer said. "I do detest having uninvited angels wandering round my chambers."

"Then I suggest you take that necklace and keep it in the Underworld."

"No!" Michael clasped the sapphire.

Lucifer shook his head. "I can remove the magic, so the stone is merely a decorative ornament once more."

"If you do that, I won't be able to visit you," Michael

pointed out. "This is my key to the Underworld, to you."

"You can find another way," Gabriel said. "Lucifer, remove the power."

Lucifer held the stone between his hands and whispered words Michael couldn't hear. When he released the necklace he confirmed it was done.

Gabriel requested that Lucifer go into an antechamber, then touched the necklace, speaking his name out loud. When nothing happened he summoned Lucifer back in.

"Is there anything else?" Lucifer asked. "Or is that enough demands for the moment?"

"We *could* change our minds," Gabriel reminded him.

"I have a request," Michael said.

"What is it?" Gabriel asked.

"I want to take Lucifer to my beach one last time before he leaves. I want to watch the sunset with him."

"Michael, don't push your luck," Lucifer warned. "They could still cast you out of here."

Gabriel sighed. "You don't understand us at all, do you?"

"You mean you'll agree to his request?" Lucifer asked.

Gabriel glanced around the room at the other archangels. Some nodded, others shrugged, Raguel shook his head. "Go watch the sunset, both of you."

Michael smiled and took Lucifer's hand. It wasn't much, just a sunset on the beach, but it was more than he had thought they could ever have again, and he intended to make the most of it.

* * * *

"It's just as I remember it," Lucifer said as they wandered down the beach, hand in hand.

"Is there no way for you to see this realm from the Underworld?" Michael asked.

"No. Whenever you are here, you're lost to me."

Michael squeezed Lucifer's hand and guided him to his favorite spot on the beach, between his house and the sea.

"Do you think the archangels are watching us right now?" Lucifer asked once they had settled down on the sand.

"No, they trust me." Michael wasn't sure why they trusted him after everything he had done since the battle, but they did. "Why do you ask?"

Lucifer used his free hand to stroke Michael's cheek. "Because I remember the first time we sat here."

"Me too."

Lucifer grinned and lowered his hand, brushing his fingers along the seam of Michael's robes. "How about it then?"

Lucifer slipped his hand between the folds of Michael's robes, aiming straight for his cock. Michael gasped and moaned as Lucifer took him in hand, stroking him firmly. He rested his forehead on Lucifer's shoulder and let himself be carried away by the sensations his lover drew from him. No one had ever managed to make him feel even a fraction of the emotion Lucifer did.

When he came, he gave a long moan of desire collapsing into Lucifer's arms, shaking and gasping.

"I've always loved your beach," Lucifer said. "So calm and peaceful. Sometimes I think I could stay here forever."

"You could," Michael replied. "If you return to the light, this could be *our* beach. You'd never have to leave me again."

"Don't spoil this," Lucifer whispered. "I don't wish to argue, not tonight."

Michael nodded and faced the sea. He didn't have to fulfill his mission tonight—in fact, he would have been reluctant to believe Lucifer if he had agreed so easily. He should simply enjoy the evening and the time they had together.

Lucifer held him close and, in comfortable silence, they watched the sun sink below the horizon.

When it was fully dark Michael touched his necklace. "Did you really remove the magic from the stone?"

"Yes, of course. I don't want any more unexpected visitors stumbling into my chambers. Besides, Gabriel would have known if I hadn't."

"Have you had any thoughts about how I can enter the Underworld now the stone doesn't work?"

"You could take your place at my side," Lucifer suggested.

"Besides that," Michael said.

"One day," Lucifer murmured.

Michael shook his head and Lucifer sighed.

"Perhaps something more conventional would suit," Lucifer said. He pointed to the cliffs at the edge of the sea. "Come with me and let us see what we can do."

Michael followed Lucifer along the beach until they stood at the rocky incline.

"Place your left hand on the cliff side," Lucifer said as he did the same with his right.

The rocks were rough and sharp, but Michael was curious to know what Lucifer had in mind.

Lucifer held out his free hand to Michael, who took it without question.

He watched Lucifer close his eyes and mumble something under his breath.

Michael felt the rocks move under his fingers and he tried to pull his hand away.

"Don't!" Lucifer ordered. "Leave it."

Michael didn't question. He held his hand in place even as the rocks continued to shift. A vertical crack appeared halfway between their two hands, stretching from the ground to a point almost half a foot above their heads. The crevice widened as the rocks broke apart, leaving an opening in the cliff.

"There, it's done," Lucifer said.

Michael peered into the gap in the cliff, but the opening was too dark to see anything. Lucifer, however, had clearly thought ahead and, when he stepped into the darkness, a sconce on the wall lit the way. Since Lucifer still held his hand, Michael had no choice other than to follow him into the tunnel and down the stone stairs.

Once he was inside, the rocks behind him moved again

and closed, sealing the path.

Michael gasped and turned back.

"It's all right," Lucifer assured him. "The door will open whenever you need it."

Michael didn't need to ask where they were going. The tunnel already felt like the Underworld.

"Can anyone open the doorway?" Michael asked.

"No, only you or I. No one else even needs to know it's here. In fact, I'd rather they didn't. I don't allow angels to wander around the Underworld." Lucifer glanced back at him. "Present company notwithstanding, of course."

Michael smiled and continued to follow Lucifer down the seemingly endless flight of steps. Finally they arrived in Lucifer's familiar chambers.

The tunnel closed behind them, leaving no trace it had ever been there.

"To open it again, from here or the beach, all you need do is see the tunnel in your mind, and there it will be."

Michael stared at the wall and, sure enough, the tunnel appeared the moment he thought of it.

"Surely you don't want to leave so soon?" Lucifer asked. He stripped off his robes and climbed onto the bed. Michael's arse clenched at the sight of Lucifer's thick erection. No, he wasn't going to leave yet.

Chapter Seven

In the following weeks, Michael and Lucifer settled into a routine. Michael continued with his regular angelic duties in the afternoons, before joining Lucifer in the Underworld for their evening meal. He stayed every night in Lucifer's bed and returned to the realm of angels each morning.

He ate breakfast with Gabriel and Raphael, who always appeared relieved to see him.

Gabriel accepted Michael's relationship with Lucifer and did his best to understand it. Raphael, however, struggled and his relationship with Michael became strained.

Michael didn't realize how far apart they had grown until the morning he joined Gabriel for breakfast and found Raphael wasn't in his usual place.

He tried not to let the absence bother him, but deep down he could tell things had changed between them, and, if he didn't bring Lucifer back to the light, their friendship might be damaged forever.

Michael enjoyed his time with Lucifer, but since they were confined to Lucifer's quarters there was little they could do besides talk, eat their evening meal, and have sex. Lucifer offered to show Michael around the Underworld, keeping the two of them invisible from the masses. Michael refused the offer. The thought of seeing the torture of humans who had strayed from the light made him ill.

Despite the long debate about who should rule the Underworld, the new king hadn't lasted as long as had been anticipated. His death at the hands of a rival who had not even been considered by the archangels and Lucifer came as quite a surprise. The new ruler of the Underworld was crowned and there was talk amongst the demons of renewing the war. The time had come for Lucifer to reveal himself again and Michael was pleased to see him do so without any need for persuasion.

The latest king of the demons raged when he discovered he was Lucifer's prisoner, but he was no match for a fallen angel. Lucifer had powers the rest of the demons lacked, and he had no hesitation in using them. The king took the throne and the glory that came with the position, while Lucifer retained the power.

Talk of war died down, the king making the excuse that they needed to increase their numbers a great deal before taking to the battlefield again. Last time, even though they had outnumbered the angels, they had failed. Next time things would be different, but it would take time to prepare. The demons appeared satisfied and began recruiting in earnest.

Michael and the rest of the archangels were doing the same. Each new soul to arrive in the realm of angels, a place commonly known as Heaven, was considered by the archangels, and, if they were deemed worthy, they earned their wings. Michael carefully chose the souls to take under his command, making sure those who followed him had compassion, open minds, and the capacity to love unconditionally.

The archangels, Michael included, had agreed it shouldn't be common knowledge that Michael and Lucifer were engaged in a relationship. Still, Michael believed in planning ahead, and if word should get out, he wanted to be sure the angels under his command would accept what he had done. There were no guarantees, of course, but Michael took every precaution he could.

Guiding new angels took up much of Michael's time, but he never forgot his primary mission.

* * * *

"You're late," Lucifer complained when Michael stepped into his chambers shortly before midnight.

"It's been a long day," Michael replied, and he grabbed a slice of pie from the spread on the table.

"I know." Lucifer pointed at the wall behind him, revealing a view of the earth, and the castle where Michael had attended to witness the passing of a great lady, who had devoted her time to the welfare of those less fortunate. Her death had been agonizingly slow and Michael had stayed at her side throughout, before guiding her to the realm of angels and her new calling.

"You've been watching me?" Michael asked.

"There's little else I can do here besides wait for you to warm my bed."

Michael could hear the boredom in Lucifer's tone and he knew the fallen angel was beginning to feel the effects of his long confinement in the Underworld.

"This is becoming hard for you, isn't it?" Michael asked.

Lucifer groped him through his robes. "Yes, it certainly is."

Michael chuckled and batted Lucifer's hand away. "You know what I meant."

"Yes, I know." Lucifer stepped back. "I don't want to spend eternity in the Underworld. I wish to walk the earth again. I want to feel the sun on my face and the wind in my hair. Can you not speak to the archangels and ask them to relax their rules?"

"I'll ask, but I don't hold out much hope they'll agree."

"Ask anyway."

Michael nodded then proceeded to distract Lucifer the best way he knew how.

* * * *

It came as no surprise to Michael when his petition to the rest of the archangels failed. They voted unanimously to keep Lucifer confined to the Underworld, a decision Lucifer raged about for weeks.

"They can't keep me here," he shouted. "They have no power over me."

"If you break the bargain, you could lose me," Michael said.

"You'd begrudge me a few hours on Earth?"

"No, of course not, but if you break the rules, what's to stop them forbidding us from seeing each other at all?"

"You would come to me anyway," Lucifer said. "You know you can't stay away."

"Please don't put me to the test," Michael replied. "Let us enjoy what we have."

"You enjoy it," Lucifer snarled. "*You* get the freedom to walk the earth whenever you wish. You can travel to any realm you want, even mine, while I'm stuck here, forgotten about and treated in a manner unbefitting my position."

"Lucifer, please be reasonable. You turned from the light and the archangels can't allow you to wander the earth unchecked."

"Do you still count yourself among their number?" Lucifer asked in a tone of mild curiosity. "Only you refer to *them* in a way that doesn't seem to include you any longer. Have you reconsidered my offer?"

Michael hadn't even realized he hadn't included himself when he'd spoken. "*We* can't allow you to leave here," he amended.

Lucifer continued to grumble until finally Michael had had enough of his complaining for one day.

"I'm going home," he declared. "I'll come back in a day or two, when hopefully you'll be a little more reasonable."

Michael didn't give him a chance to argue. He headed to the wall and opened the tunnel. Then he climbed the steps up to his beach with a heavy heart. He held on to the hope he would be able to bring Lucifer back to the light, but at times like this doubts began to creep in, and he wondered whether he was being drawn into the darkness instead.

* * * *

Michael found himself spending more and more time on Earth, searching for the purest of souls. He tried not to neglect Lucifer too much, but sometimes it couldn't be helped. He expected Lucifer to make more of a fuss whenever he arrived late to his chambers, but he was surprisingly tolerant. Too tolerant, Michael mused, his suspicions rising by the day.

He discovered the reason for Lucifer's calm demeanor quite by chance.

The human whose soul he had gone to Earth to guide had a great number of friends, which wasn't unusual in the least, but one of those acquaintances had a soul almost as pure as the man whose life was drawing to a close. Curious as to who this youth was, Michael traveled back to Earth as soon as he had settled the new soul in the realm of angels. He didn't expect to see Lucifer sitting on a bench in the middle of the town square.

The young soul forgotten, Michael approached Lucifer and waited for him to realize he had been seen. Lucifer's reaction, as soon as he saw Michael, made it clear he hadn't expected to be caught.

"Do you want to explain what you're doing here?" Michael asked.

Lucifer smiled and raised a tankard. "Enjoying a drink of ale. Would you care to join me?"

Michael folded his arms across his chest. "How long have you been coming to Earth?"

"The earth is my domain as much as it is yours," Lucifer replied.

"You promised to remain in the Underworld."

"Who was the young man you were ogling earlier?" Lucifer asked.

"You've been spying on me again?"

Lucifer tossed his tankard aside, spilling the contents onto the grass. "Answer the question, Michael. Who is he?"

Michael picked up the discarded mug and set it on the arm of the bench. "A waste of perfectly good ale, wouldn't you say?"

"Who is he?" Lucifer repeated. "He must be important if he not only distracts you from your duties but draws you back here so soon, when you would usually be eagerly running to my bed by this time. Is he fucking you?"

Michael glared at Lucifer. "I'm not going to dignify that question with an answer. I suggest you go back to the Underworld and calm down."

"Calm down?" Lucifer shouted. "You're letting some pathetic human fuck you, when you could be with me."

Michael's temper rose and he loomed over Lucifer. "You dare to accuse me of infidelity?"

Lucifer leaped up from the bench. "Is he fucking you? Or is it the other way round? Are you fucking him because I won't let you fuck me? Is that it?"

Michael slapped Lucifer in the face, recoiling immediately at the horror of what he had done. He had never struck another in hot blood before. Lucifer appeared equally shocked. He raised his hand to his cheek as he stared slack-jawed at Michael.

He couldn't deal with this right now. All thoughts of the pure soul he had come back to Earth for were forgotten. He had to get out of here. Without a word, Michael fled to his beach in the realm of angels and collapsed onto the sand. He stared at his shaking hand as though he didn't recognize it.

What have I done?

Lucifer had broken the rules and accused Michael of being unfaithful, but that didn't excuse Michael's behavior. His mind was in turmoil as he attempted to come to terms with his actions.

Michael didn't leave the beach all night. He watched the waves roll in beneath the starry sky and, when the sun rose behind him, he felt slightly less conflicted and knew what he had to do.

* * * *

Michael found Gabriel working away in his garden, tending his exotic array of plants.

"Gabriel, can I talk to you?"

Gabriel looked up and his smile of greeting disappeared instantly. "What's wrong, Michael?"

Michael followed Gabriel into the gazebo and took a seat opposite him. "I need your advice."

"Of course. You know I'll try to help you any way I can. What's happened?"

"It's Lucifer," Michael replied. "We had an argument last night."

"What about?"

Michael flushed. "It doesn't matter what we fought about, what bothers me is how I acted. I struck him."

Gabriel whistled softly. "You lost your temper?"

Michael nodded. "I didn't mean to."

"Lucifer tries the patience of many of us," Gabriel said. "Are you any closer to bringing him back to the light?"

Michael sighed. "Sometimes I wonder if I'm closer to following him into the darkness."

Gabriel leaned forward and encouraged Michael to meet his eyes. "I'm glad you've told me this."

"What am I going to do?" Michael asked. "I don't want to fall, but I feel as if I'm already slipping. I'm no nearer to saving Lucifer now than I was when I agreed to the mission. I don't know what to do."

"You could end your relationship with Lucifer," Gabriel suggested. "If you feel the danger in being with him is too great, then step away."

Michael shook his head immediately. "I can't walk away from him. I still love him."

"Then perhaps you need to go to the Underworld and make your peace with him," Gabriel said. "If he's there, that is."

Michael gaped at Gabriel.

"Lucifer has been leaving the Underworld for some time now. The rest of the archangels are aware of this and have been waiting to see if you would tell us."

"I didn't find out until last night," Michael said. "I know I should have said something just now, but..."

"But it wasn't the most pressing concern," Gabriel finished. "It's all right. I trust you would have told us soon."

"I'm not so sure," Michael admitted. "I've kept Lucifer's secrets before. This is just another one, isn't it? Another lie I'm telling to protect him, and one more step into the darkness."

"Lucifer deceived us all," Gabriel reminded him. "No one ever suspected he could fall so far or take so many with him. You know He still loves him, so why shouldn't you? Caring for him isn't the same as worshiping him."

Michael nodded. "Why haven't the archangels raised the matter of Lucifer going to Earth?"

"Because he hasn't been doing any recruiting while he's been there," Gabriel explained. "It took only a few days to figure out what he was doing."

"Which is?"

"He goes where you've been," Gabriel said. "I think perhaps he does so to try to be closer to you when you're apart."

"And you've known this for how long?"

"Several months. One of Azrael's charges spotted him on Earth and assumed an angel had fallen. His horns marked him as a demon, but she could sense his angelic powers too."

"Does the charge know she saw Lucifer?"

"No. We let her continue to believe a lesser angel had left us, and since then the archangels have taken on the task of monitoring Lucifer and keeping track of his movements."

"Then he is still believed dead?"

"Yes, and we intend to keep it that way. His reappearance now could be devastating. His followers might even claim it to be resurrection."

Michael didn't think Lucifer wanted it known he still lived, but he had been wrong about so many things, he couldn't say for sure.

"Go make your peace," Gabriel said. "Then perhaps some time apart from Lucifer might help."

"I can't leave him."

"I'm not suggesting you do, not permanently anyway. But sometimes stepping back from a situation can give you some perspective."

Gabriel was correct, but Michael didn't know how Lucifer would take the news of any separation, no matter the duration.

* * * *

"I'm sorry," Lucifer said the moment Michael entered his chamber. "I should never have doubted you. I know you'd never take a mortal into your bed."

"There's no one—mortal, angel, or demon—in my bed apart from you."

"I know." Lucifer replied. "Am I forgiven?"

Michael stepped closer. "Am I?" he asked. "I'm sorry I slapped you. I don't know what I was thinking."

"You had every right to be angry after what I said," Lucifer assured him. He rubbed his cheek. "Just don't make a habit of it."

"I'll try not to," Michael promised.

He wandered over to one of the chairs, avoiding the bed, because if he ended up there tonight, his resolve would crumble.

Lucifer went to the bed and stretched out. "What are you doing all the way over there? Take off those robes and come here."

Michael remained in his seat. "I don't think we should have sex tonight."

Lucifer laughed momentarily before he realized Michael wasn't joking. "Don't be ridiculous. Come to bed."

Michael shook his head. "I think it would be best if we spent some time apart."

"We already spend too much time separated," Lucifer argued. "Your duties take you away from me all the time."

"I'm not going to argue with you about this," Michael said. "I'm telling you what I've decided. I'm going to go back to the realm of angels shortly and I'm not sure when I'm going to be back here."

"I'll expect you here tomorrow evening," Lucifer stated.

"Are you listening to what I'm saying?"

"Yes, but we both know you'll be here tomorrow, as eager for my cock as ever."

"No, I won't," Michael insisted. He stood and reopened the tunnel. "I don't expect to see you again until I return here. And, just so you know, the archangels are aware you've been going to Earth."

"You betrayed me?"

"I didn't have to tell them, because they already knew, apparently long before I did."

"Why haven't they tried to stop me?"

"You'd have to ask them."

"I'm asking you."

Michael walked into the tunnel. "Goodnight, Lucifer."

* * * *

Each morning and every night Michael sat on his beach, staring at the cliff. The temptation to open the entrance to the Underworld grew every day. He missed Lucifer constantly.

Every day his resolve weakened a little more and he didn't know how much longer he could stay away.

Two months had passed when Michael felt the presence of a familiar body wrapping around him in the middle of the night.

"Lucifer?" Michael murmured sleepily.

"Shush," Lucifer replied. "Don't say anything. Just let me

hold you."

He should send him away. They were in the realm of angels, where Lucifer was strictly forbidden to be. If the archangels discovered him here, he would be killed.

Michael took Lucifer's hand and pulled his arm around him. He could feel the hardness of Lucifer's erection against his arse and he pushed back toward it. He closed his eyes and went back to sleep, secure in Lucifer's embrace.

When he next woke, it was to the sensation of a warm mouth wrapped around his cock, sucking him gently.

"Oh, Lucifer," Michael moaned. "I've missed you. Don't stop. Oh, that's it, right there. Suck harder, Lucifer, harder. Yes!"

Michael came in Lucifer's mouth with a cry of pleasure after just a few minutes. It had been far too long.

When Lucifer's lips met his own Michael could taste himself and he moaned in delight. He spread his legs apart and Lucifer slid into position.

"Tell me you've missed me," Lucifer said.

"I have, I have."

"Tell me you still want me."

"I want you, Lucifer, so badly."

"How badly, Michael?"

Michael took hold of Lucifer's cock and guided him between his legs. "Fuck me, Lucifer."

Lucifer didn't hesitate. With one swift thrust he claimed Michael's body for his own once more. Michael gave up any control he had to Lucifer and didn't regret it in the slightest.

Michael lay there while Lucifer pounded into him. He cried out encouragement as their bodies moved in a fast and punishing rhythm.

"Two months," Lucifer growled. "That's how long it's been since I've seen you. I never thought you'd stay away so long. If I'd known, I wouldn't have agreed to the separation."

"You didn't agree," Michael reminded him between gasps of breath.

"You're quite right," Lucifer replied, right before he thrust into Michael with enough force to lift him from the bed. "I didn't agree then and I don't now."

Michael howled with pleasure and his cock rose once more.

Lucifer slowed his pace to a less punishing rhythm. "That's it, Michael."

Michael moaned and sighed when Lucifer stopped fucking him and began making love to him instead. He grasped for Lucifer, needing to touch him. He knew, even without Lucifer saying the words, he had been forgiven for deserting him these last months.

Lucifer came first, spilling his seed inside Michael, who, with a few strokes of his hand on his cock, reached his climax for a second time, even though he didn't have anything left to spill.

Michael guided Lucifer down to lie across his chest, careful not to let him leave his body. He wanted to feel his lover inside him as long as possible. He didn't want to let him go.

From the way he snuggled closer, Michael suspected Lucifer felt the same way. "Two months," Lucifer whispered. "I never thought you would stay away from me so long."

"We've been apart for longer than that," Michael reminded him. "During the war, remember?"

"That was when I thought I'd never have you in my life again," Lucifer said. "There are few angels who would willingly take one such as I into their bed."

"They don't know you as I do," Michael replied. "They see only what you've become."

"And what do you see?"

Michael smiled. "I see the angel I fell in love with and what he might be again, if he could only find his way back to the light."

"You still think you can save me?"

"Yes, but you shouldn't have broken the rules by coming

here."

Lucifer smirked. "Rules are made to be broken. You should try it more often."

"I don't think the archangels would agree with you."

Lucifer sighed sadly. "I knew the consequences of coming to you, but I couldn't stay away another day. I will accept my punishment."

"You'll only be punished if you get caught," Michael whispered, barely able to believe he spoke the words, even as they left his lips.

"You're one of the archangels," Lucifer pointed out. "It's your duty to turn me in for punishment."

"You know I won't."

Lucifer's smile widened. "I know. Just as *you* know you should."

Michael accepted the truth in Lucifer's words and took another step toward the darkness. He knew there would be no going back. Lucifer had come here to test him and Michael had failed again.

The knock on the door wasn't entirely unexpected, though it came sooner than Michael would have hoped.

"Come in," he called and a moment later Gabriel entered the room.

"You could at least have made me wait until you'd got out of bed and dressed," Gabriel complained. "Your presence is required in our chamber. Both of you."

Gabriel left the room, though Michael could see him outside through the window, waiting to escort them. Was this it? Had he finally crossed the line that would lose him his wings? Michael wouldn't blame the archangels if they decided to cast him out of the realm. Lucifer would be delighted, but Michael's stomach churned at the thought.

Once they were decently robed, and Lucifer had made sure his demonic features were suitably hidden, Michael and Lucifer followed Gabriel to the archangels' chamber. No one gave them a second glance. They were simply three angels going about their business.

Inside the chamber the rest of the archangels waited.

"Had a pleasant night, did we?" Raguel asked.

"Why yes," Lucifer replied easily. "You might like to try it sometime."

"Excuse me?"

"Sex," Lucifer said. "You might find you enjoy it."

"Take a seat, Lucifer," Gabriel interrupted, pointing to the center of the room. "You too, Michael."

Lucifer sat, winked at Michael, and patted his lap.

Michael stifled a smile and took his usual place in the circle of archangels.

Gabriel called the room to attention. "Lucifer, you are here in this realm in direct contravention of the agreement between yourself and the archangels."

Lucifer didn't say anything.

"Well?" Gabriel asked.

"What do you want me to say?" Lucifer replied. "I know I'm here. I was horny."

Michael nearly choked on his tongue.

"Lucifer," Gabriel said, "Michael asked for time away from you. You had no right to deny him this."

"He didn't seem upset to see me last night," Lucifer said. "I believe his exact words were 'suck harder' and 'fuck me'. Hardly the words of someone who didn't want me here."

Michael's face burned as the rest of the archangels focused their attention on him. Lucifer's tongue would be the death of him, one way or another.

"We'll come to Michael's part in this shortly," Gabriel said. "We are aware he is not entirely without blame in this matter."

Lucifer rose and moved to stand between Michael and the other archangels. "Michael didn't ask me to join him last night. I came to him uninvited."

"That's not the point." Gabriel gestured to Lucifer to retake his seat. "Michael should have brought you to us immediately after he became aware of your presence. He didn't, and we don't believe he had any intention of doing so."

Michael ducked his head, knowing the accusation had hit the mark.

"I believe he was a little distracted by my cock up his arse," Lucifer said.

"Lucifer!" Michael hissed. "You're not helping."

Lucifer ignored him, although he did walk back to his seat.

"Returning to your presence here," Gabriel said, "you are aware of the punishment, Lucifer?"

"I am."

"We swore if you entered this realm without permission we would have no alternative other than to destroy you."

"Please feel free to try," Lucifer replied.

"Did you imagine it to be an idle threat?" Gabriel asked.

Lucifer shrugged. "If you're going to kill me, do get on with it."

Raguel rose from his seat, drawing his sword and pointing it at Lucifer. "Gabriel, may I have the honor?"

Gabriel raised his hand and Raguel sat back down, though he kept his sword in his hand. Then he turned to Lucifer again. "Lucifer, can you give me one good reason why I shouldn't let Raguel use his sword to exact justice?"

Lucifer smirked at Raguel. "Because he doesn't know one end of a sword from the other?"

Raguel charged across the room, his sword raised.

Michael didn't hesitate. He leaped from his seat and dove between Raguel and Lucifer. "No!"

Raguel barely stopped in time. "You would give your life for this monster?"

"He's not a monster," Michael said. "And yes, I would."

"Why?"

Michael reached out blindly behind him and when Lucifer held his hand he took strength from him. "Because I love him."

Raguel raised his sword again, this time pointing it at Michael. "He doesn't deserve your love. He doesn't

114

understand such emotions and he never will."

"This isn't about what Lucifer feels for me," Michael said. "It's about what I feel for him. I love him and I would sacrifice myself to protect him. I won't let you kill him, not like this."

"Sit down, Raguel," Gabriel ordered. "You too, Michael."

Raguel reluctantly walked back to his seat, but when Michael tried to do likewise Lucifer kept hold of his hand and tugged him onto his lap. Michael sighed and shifted so he was more comfortable. He should take his proper place, but with Raguel still brandishing his sword, perhaps it might be better to stay close to Lucifer. He told himself that was the only reason, though when he felt the swelling of Lucifer's cock beneath his arse he certainly wasn't complaining.

"Michael?" Gabriel asked.

Lucifer wrapped his arms round Michael's waist. "He's fine right here."

Michael nodded. "Let's just get on with the meeting."

Gabriel didn't seem impressed with the new seating arrangements but clearly wanted to get on with the proceedings. "Lucifer, I'll ask you again, why should we not exact justice on you?"

Michael didn't give Lucifer a chance to reply this time. "This isn't justice, Gabriel, and you know it."

"He's broken the rules."

"I know he has, but he doesn't deserve to die for visiting me."

Gabriel tapped his fingers on the arm of his chair. "What punishment would you decree *is* deserved?"

"What?"

"You say he doesn't deserve to die," Gabriel said. "So, what would be your punishment?"

Michael shrugged. "Confining him to the Underworld?"

"That's where he was supposed to be in the first place."

Lucifer cleared his throat. "I would relinquish some of my powers."

Gabriel leaned forward. "Continue."

"I have many powers. If you are truly willing to spare my life, I would give some of them up, permanently."

"Which powers?" Gabriel asked.

"His invisibility power?" Raguel suggested. "To stop him wandering through realms undetected."

"No," Michael argued. "Without that power he would also be seen in the Underworld, and the demons would know he lives."

"Michael's correct," Raphael agreed. "Lucifer must retain that power. I would suggest his power to convert humans to demons is the one to be relinquished."

Lucifer gasped and Michael squeezed his hands before he said something foolish.

Raphael rose to continue. "We already know Lucifer hasn't just broken the rule about entering this realm. He has been on Earth as well. I would recommend the relaxation of the rule about going to Earth, if Lucifer agrees to give up his power of conversion, and if he agrees only to go to Earth when accompanied by an archangel."

Michael checked with Lucifer, who nodded imperceptibly.

"There are many demons recruiting these days," Lucifer told him. "I'm not one of them. The only one I wish to bring into the Underworld is you, and for that to happen, you must fall of your own volition. No power of mine can bring it about."

"He agrees," Michael said.

Gabriel stood and walked toward them. Lightning flashed through the room as the bargain was sealed. "Then it's done."

"And Lucifer is allowed to be on Earth now?" Michael clarified.

"Yes, but only when an archangel is with him, and he is not to set foot in the realm of angels," Gabriel replied.

"Thank you," Michael whispered. He couldn't wait to see the changing world with Lucifer at his side.

"Don't thank me yet," Gabriel warned. "We haven't

talked about your own actions."

Michael cringed.

Gabriel nodded. "You have deceived your fellow archangels on more than one occasion. This latest deception cannot go unpunished."

"I know."

"I'm sorry, Michael, but we have no choice except to strip you of your wings."

Michael thought he might be sick.

"No!" Lucifer shouted. "You can't do this to him. He's an archangel and that's all he's ever known. Out of all of you, he is the only one with the capacity to love unconditionally. If you take away his wings it'll destroy him."

If Lucifer hadn't been holding him so closely, Michael felt sure he would have tumbled to the floor. A few moments ago he had relished the thought of spending time on Earth with Lucifer. Now his dream had shattered. The archangel escorting him on Earth would be someone else.

"You have no say in this matter," Gabriel said.

"You can't punish Michael for my actions," Lucifer said.

"We aren't. We're punishing him for his own lies and omissions."

Michael slowly eased his way out of Lucifer's embrace. "I'm sorry, Lucifer, but Gabriel is right. We both know I had no intention of turning you in this morning. I must face the consequences of my actions."

Lucifer tried to pull him back into his arms, but Michael stepped out of his reach. He faced Gabriel, then knelt on the floor, his head bowed.

"No!" Lucifer screamed again, throwing himself from his chair and gathering Michael into his arms. "Take all my powers, confine me to the deepest pit in the Underworld, anything you want, but don't do this to him."

"It's all right," Michael said. "This is justice."

"No, it's not," Lucifer argued. "Gabriel, please. Whatever you want from me, it's yours."

Gabriel smiled. "It's clear Lucifer cares for you a great

deal, Michael. He might try to pass his feelings off as merely sexual, but I think maybe you were right after all. He does care for you."

"Of course I do," Lucifer yelled. "Do you think I'd be here in this realm if I didn't?"

Gabriel took Michael's hand and pulled him to his feet. "Go take Lucifer back to the Underworld."

"I don't understand," Michael said. "What about my wings?"

Gabriel chuckled. "Your wings are right where they should be. Did you really believe we'd strip them from you?"

"Yes," Michael whispered.

"Then perhaps you don't know us as well as you think you do," Gabriel replied.

"I don't understand."

"They were testing me," Lucifer explained.

"Correct," said Gabriel. "I needed to know whether Michael's faith in you is justified. Your defense of him tells me it is. For as long as you have the capacity to love, there's hope you can be saved."

"Then you had no intention of taking my wings?" Michael asked.

"No, of course not."

"Then what *is* my punishment?"

Gabriel smiled. "I'm thinking of getting a gardener, on a short-term contract for, say, a hundred years."

"You're going to make me weed your garden?" Michael had never enjoyed gardening and Gabriel knew it.

"And prune my roses, clean my pond, and everything else my little corner of paradise needs." Gabriel nodded thoughtfully. "I'll be overseeing your work personally. You can use your time working in my garden to update me with full reports regarding your mission."

Michael smiled and nodded. "I can live with that."

"Goodbye, Lucifer," Gabriel said. "I hope to see you back amongst us soon."

Michael wanted the same, but he didn't share Gabriel's optimism. Lucifer's journey back to the light would be a long one, for no other angel had fallen quite so far as he had. Michael vowed he would be with him every step of the way.

Chapter Eight

While Michael didn't exactly enjoy gardening, he did find it pleasant to spend more time with Gabriel and he was truly sorry he had been neglecting his oldest friend so much. Raphael sometimes joined the two of them as well, and Michael felt they might be making some progress in restoring their friendship to what it had once been.

He just wished he was making progress with his mission to save Lucifer.

Now Lucifer was free to visit Earth with him, their relationship wasn't as tense as it had been, but they had fallen into an easy routine and had reached something of an impasse.

"I don't seem to be getting anywhere with him," Michael admitted as he continued his task of weeding the flowerbed under Gabriel's kitchen window. "I don't think he wants to come back to us."

"Of course he doesn't," Raphael said. "I still say we should have taken him up on his offer of anything to save your wings and told him to give up all his demonic powers and return here."

"No one can be forced into the light," Gabriel said. "He has to come here of his own free will, without coercion, bribery, or trickery."

Raphael snorted. "All the things he is so familiar with."

"He's not that bad," Michael said.

"He's a master manipulator," Raphael replied. "He has you wrapped around his little finger."

"We're equals in our relationship."

"Do you honestly believe that?" Gabriel asked.

"Don't you?" Michael countered.

Raphael answered the question instead. "Lucifer is pulling all your strings and you don't even know it. He has all the power between the two of you, and I'm not talking about angel or demon powers, I mean the other kind. He's the one in charge and, as long as that remains the case, you'll never save him."

"You think he manipulates me?"

"When he snaps his fingers, you go running to his side. You've lied for him over and over again. We're worried about you."

"I've not kept anything from you since Lucifer was last here," Michael insisted as he tried to keep hold of his temper.

"We're just worried about you," Gabriel assured him. "We see signs in you that were, in hindsight at least, seen in Lucifer before he fell."

Michael shivered. "You do?"

"The isolation from the rest of us, as well as the lying."

"That's why you wanted me to do your gardening, isn't it? To keep me from distancing myself."

"Yes. We don't want you to fall, and we're worried Lucifer's influence over you is too great."

"I've never been the most sociable of angels," Michael reminded them. "Socially inept, I believe you called me once."

"Making light of serious concerns is another trait Lucifer has," Raphael commented.

Gabriel nodded his agreement. "You say you and Lucifer are equals in your relationship, but I disagree. He's in charge of you, and, as long as it remains that way, you're in danger of falling. You need to stand up to him and stop being manipulated, or Raphael's correct, and you'll never be able to bring him back to the light."

Michael didn't think he was being manipulated by Lucifer, so he asked his friends to tell him when they thought he was being, so he could see for himself.

* * * *

A few days later, Raphael raised the subject again. "Michael, where are you going?"

"The Underworld," Michael replied.

"I thought you were going to go there after your shift on the new souls' gate?"

"I was, but I was late visiting Lucifer yesterday. I'm going to have lunch with him, come here for my shift, before heading back down for dinner."

"Was that your suggestion or Lucifer's?" Raphael asked.

"I don't remember."

"Honesty," Raphael reminded him.

Michael frowned and closed his eyes, running through the conversation with Lucifer in his mind. "Lucifer raised the idea of lunch first," he admitted. "But I agreed to it."

"And if you hadn't agreed?"

Michael considered the question carefully before accepting the truth. Lucifer would have pouted and nagged him until he had changed his mind. It was easier to go along with his plan right from the start.

"This is an example of Lucifer manipulating you," Raphael said, "just in case you haven't figured it out."

Michael sat on a nearby bench. "If I don't meet him for lunch he may come searching for me."

"He's not allowed in this realm."

"He'll be worried."

Raphael waved his hand in the direction of Michael's beach. "Go to lunch, but next time something like this arises, you need to stand up to him. You can't always be at his beck and call."

* * * *

It didn't take long for Michael to learn to recognize when Lucifer was cajoling him into doing what he wanted. If he hadn't been so besotted with him he would probably have noticed long before Raphael had pointed it out to him.

"You don't have to go back yet," Lucifer whispered into Michael's ear.

"Gabriel's expecting me to help watch over his new recruits while they're on Earth for the first time."

"Isn't that *his* job?"

"Yes, but he can only be in one place at a time and with so many new angels under his tutelage he's struggling a little."

"You have your own duties to attend to," Lucifer pointed out. "You shouldn't have to make up for his deficiencies too."

Michael ignored the dig at Gabriel and grabbed his discarded robes from the foot of the bed. "I'll see you this evening."

He could feel the heat of Lucifer's body against his back and he steeled himself for what he knew would be coming next.

"Come back to bed," Lucifer purred. "You've been working too hard recently. You need to relax, and I know *exactly* how to help with that."

Michael eased himself out of Lucifer's arms and made to leave. He donned his robes and tied them securely. He hoped the expression on his face made it clear to Lucifer that he wasn't going to talk him around this time.

When he met Lucifer's gaze he saw his lover scowling, his lower lip sticking out in a familiar pout.

"You're actually going to leave me?" Lucifer asked.

"I told you, I'll see you for dinner later this evening."

Lucifer turned his back on him. "If you're sure you can spare the time," he muttered.

Michael rolled his eyes, leaned over, and kissed the crown of Lucifer's head. "Stop sulking. I'll see you later."

Lucifer ignored him, but Michael felt far better about himself as he left the Underworld. He would take back control of his life, whether Lucifer wanted him to or not.

* * * *

Michael arrived in the Underworld hungry and tired. Helping Gabriel had been an interesting experience — their methods of training recruits differed greatly — but combined with his own duties, it made for a long day. He hoped Lucifer had stopped sulking and was in a better frame of mind than when Michael had left him this morning.

It came as something of a surprise to find Lucifer's chambers empty and no sign of dinner on the table. He wondered if Lucifer planned to take him out somewhere on Earth, but if that was the case, where had he disappeared to?

"Lucifer?" he called.

He was met with silence.

Michael wandered through Lucifer's chambers, wondering how long he should wait for him. His stomach growled, but he resisted the temptation to leave immediately. Lucifer had his own duties to attend to — perhaps he had been held up with the demon king.

He hoped Lucifer hadn't gone to Earth without him. He had no doubt none of the other archangels had taken him there. Besides Michael, only Gabriel had escorted Lucifer on Earth, and he had done so just once. Gabriel had told Michael he wanted to speak to Lucifer privately, so Michael had brought Lucifer from the Underworld and left him in Gabriel's charge for a couple of hours. Neither his best friend nor his lover had told him what they had discussed.

Since Gabriel, nor any of the other archangels, had asked Michael to bring Lucifer to Earth, if he had gone there, he had done so without permission and in contravention of the agreement. Michael hoped he was simply somewhere else in his own realm of caverns.

In all the times Michael had been to the Underworld he had never ventured anywhere besides Lucifer's chambers. Now, with nothing to do other than pace, he found himself curious as to what lay beyond the walls. After an hour the temptation became too much and he opened the doorway into the main part of the Underworld. With Lucifer's help, he had long since mastered the art of invisibility, so, after making sure he could not be seen by any wandering demons, Michael went in search of his lover.

The rest of the Underworld was dark, dreary, and far too crowded. If the archangels had been on a recruiting drive, the demons had been doing likewise, and they appeared far more successful in their efforts. Michael had thought the angels had a fair idea of the current number of demons, but he had been wandering the Underworld just a few minutes before he realized how wrong they were. They should have been keeping a closer eye on the Underworld, and he would see this rectified when he returned to the realm of angels.

Dozens of winding tunnels branched off the main route, but Michael didn't venture down any of them. Many of the demons seemed to be heading in the same direction, and Michael followed them. He soon found himself in a large cavern he recognized from the pool of visions as the throne room.

The demon king, a scaled creature with two heads, roared with laughter as four lesser demons fought in the center of the room. The fighters had drawn quite a crowd, including his absent lover.

Lucifer sat on the steps to the side of the throne, equally enthralled with the entertainment, and oblivious to Michael's presence.

Michael watched him for a moment or two before walking over to the steps leading to the throne. He knew Lucifer would be able to see him when he drew close enough. No matter how hard he tried, Michael had never been able to hide himself from his lover for more than a few moments.

"Lost track of time?" he asked, keeping his voice low, so none except Lucifer could hear him.

Lucifer glared at him with such animosity Michael stepped back in surprise. "I thought we had an agreement about angels wandering around the Underworld?"

"Angels?" the demon king asked. "What angels?"

Lucifer smiled at the king. "Nothing for you to concern

yourself with. Just an intruder."

The demon king took him at his word and carried on watching the fight.

"Is that what I am now?" Michael asked. "An intruder?"

"You have no business being in this part of the Underworld. Perhaps you should go have dinner with Gabriel?"

Michael sat on the step beside Lucifer and made himself comfortable. Two could play at this game. "So, who is your money on to win this fight?"

"What?" Lucifer blinked at him with an adorably confused expression. Michael considered this a vast improvement on his earlier display of temper.

Michael gestured to the fight. "I think the black-horned demon will win this one. He seems to have some rather sneaky moves."

"They're demons. They all have sneaky moves," Lucifer replied. "You need to go back to my chambers. If the horde down there should discover your presence here, I might not be able to protect you."

Michael glanced at the demon king. Even though Michael remained invisible, and he was pretty sure no one except Lucifer could see and hear him, the demon king was aware of his lover's presence and could no doubt hear Lucifer's half of the conversation. His lover made no effort to lower his voice at all.

"Your demon king is listening to your words most intently. Perhaps you should send your thoughts to me instead of speaking."

"Let him listen," Lucifer muttered. "He might learn a few things. Why are you here, Michael?"

"We had dinner plans, remember?"

Lucifer snorted. "I had plans for you this morning, but you weren't so anxious to spend time with me then."

The demon king squinted in Michael's direction and he could tell he was trying desperately to see who Lucifer spoke with.

"I had duties," Michael said. "Now, are you going to

come to dinner, or do we need another separation?"

Lucifer laughed. "You'll be back in my bed before the end of the week."

"*I'm* not the one who sneaked into the realm of angels, and my bed, not so long ago."

Lucifer grumbled under his breath and, although Michael didn't catch what he said, it appeared from his chuckle the demon king did.

"Perhaps we could take this discussion somewhere a little more private," Michael suggested.

Lucifer ignored him and nudged the demon king. "Would you care to wager on the outcome of the fight?" he asked.

"Which fight?" the demon king whispered, presumably so he didn't appear to be talking to himself. "The one on the floor or the one between you and — what was his name? — Michael?"

Lucifer glared at the demon king, who cringed and backed up as far in his throne as he could. "You forget your place."

The demon king nodded fervently.

Satisfied, Lucifer focused his attention on Michael. "As I've told you before, angels have no business wandering the Underworld. Either you go back to my chambers and wait for me there, or the next battle put on for the entertainment of my demons will be the archangel Michael, taking on all comers."

The demon king gaped momentarily at Lucifer. However, this time the creature held his tongue.

Michael knew Lucifer had the power to make Michael visible to the demons. His powers were amplified in the Underworld, while Michael's were weakened. That didn't mean Michael thought he would carry out his threat, and even if he did, Michael was perfectly capable of defending himself.

"You weren't listening to me at all this morning, were you?" Michael asked. "I'm not going to allow you to continue to manipulate me."

"*I'm* ruler of this realm," Lucifer reminded him. "You do

what *I* say and go where *I* tell you. You have two choices. I suggest you think fast because the current fight is almost over and my demons will be anxious for a new battle to enjoy."

Michael stood and shook his head. "I take the third option."

As he walked away he saw from the corner of his eye the black-horned demon raise his arms in victory as the defeated demons writhed in pain at his feet.

Michael walked back to Lucifer's chambers at a relatively slow pace, giving his lover plenty of time to catch up to him if he wanted to. By the time he reached the tunnel, Michael could tell Lucifer had no intention of chasing after him. He glanced at the bed, and for a moment his resolve wavered and he considered waiting for Lucifer to join him.

"No," he told himself firmly. "You are *not* going to be manipulated."

He repeated the words like a mantra as he ascended the stone stairs back to his beach.

* * * *

The next day Michael debated whether to go to the Underworld at all, but in the end he did. Despite threatening Lucifer with another separation, he didn't want one. He just hoped Lucifer didn't force him into a position where he had no other option.

Lucifer waited for him in bed, naked and aroused. Unfortunately for Michael, he wasn't alone in his chambers. A young man reclined in a chair, drinking wine, and stroking his exposed cock.

Anger flared as Michael stared at the man.

"Human or demon?" he asked.

"Can't you tell?" the stranger asked and when he met Michael's gaze his eyes were blood red. A demon then.

"Get out," Michael ordered.

"These are *my* rooms," Lucifer stated. "*I* say who stays

and who goes."

Michael glared at him before stalking over to the demon. "Don't make me ask you again."

The demon laughed. "I don't take orders from angels."

"Lucifer," Michael said, "tell this creature to leave."

Instead of doing as Michael said, Lucifer patted the covers beside him and the demon hurried to join him on the bed. "Gregor has offered to keep me company when your duties take you away from me. I thought you might enjoy meeting him before he begins his new role in the Underworld."

Hearing Lucifer hadn't yet fucked the demon helped quell some of Michael's anger. Lucifer was calling his bluff, manipulating him yet again.

"Remove Gregor's memories of you and send him away," Michael said. "The last thing you need is for some lower-level demon to brag to the rest of your followers about your continued survival."

"Maybe I want everyone to know I'm still around," Lucifer suggested. "I might earn a little respect back. Humans don't even fear my name anymore."

Michael had heard enough. He might not be at full strength in the Underworld, but he wasn't powerless. He produced his sword and pointed the blade at the demon's throat. "Or I can silence him myself, permanently," he suggested.

Lucifer didn't bother to come to Gregor's defense. "You wouldn't dare."

Michael poked the demon with his blade, just hard enough to draw blood. Gregor squeaked and scooted away. "Get out."

This time the demon obeyed him and he scurried from the room. Lucifer waved his hand after him and, when Michael asked, confirmed he had wiped his memory.

Michael kept his sword unsheathed as he faced Lucifer. "If I ever find another man in your bed again, it's over."

Lucifer stretched lazily. "You know you'll always come back to me."

Michael raised his blade to Lucifer's throat. "I'm not

talking about our relationship," he clarified. "I'll finish what I started on the battlefield. This is your last chance, Lucifer."

"If you kill me, you'll have failed your mission. How will the rest of the archangels take that?"

Michael laughed, though there wasn't much humor in it. "Most of them would be delighted to hear I've come to my senses."

When he thought he might have made his point, Michael lowered his sword and stared at Lucifer for several long minutes.

"I'm going home now."

"You're not coming to bed?" Lucifer asked.

Michael gave him an annoyed scowl. "Strangely, I'm not in the mood right now."

Lucifer gave Michael's groin a deliberately provocative look. "Are you sure about that?"

Loose-fitting robes might hide most things, but sometimes even they weren't enough. Michael had no doubt Lucifer could see how turned-on he was.

Lucifer slid from the bed and took Michael's sword out of his hand. "You shouldn't wave that around. Someone might get hurt."

Michael gasped as Lucifer set aside his blade with one hand and grabbed his aching cock with the other.

"Oh yes," Lucifer whispered. "Let's go to bed and I'll take care of this problem for you."

Michael grasped Lucifer's wrist. "Not tonight."

"Are you sure I can't tempt you?" Lucifer purred into his ear and Michael shivered. "Come on, Michael, stop being so awkward."

Michael pushed Lucifer away and he tumbled onto the bed. With lightning-fast moves, Michael pushed Lucifer onto his back and climbed on top of him. "I don't want to be fucked tonight. Though I might be persuaded to fuck *you*."

Lucifer stared at him in silence. Never once had he let Michael top him, and Michael doubted he would start now.

"I didn't think so," Michael said.

"Wait!" Lucifer grabbed Michael's arm before he could pull away and leave. Then, in a movement completely unexpected, Lucifer eased his legs apart and offered him a small nod.

Michael took a minute to process what Lucifer was saying to him. After so many centuries of refusing to let Michael fuck him, he had been sure of the answer before he made the suggestion. Yet Lucifer had called his bluff.

With a shaking hand, Michael reached between Lucifer's legs and stroked a finger round his hole. He expected Lucifer to stop him, to change his mind when push came to shove. He tested him with the tip of his finger, pushing the tiniest fraction into his opening, and Lucifer moaned with blatant desire.

All thoughts of going home vanished as Michael scrambled across the bed, searching for Lucifer's stash of oil on his bedside table. He found the half-empty vial and moved back to his previous position.

Lucifer had never appeared more beautiful to Michael, or more tempting.

"Get on your hands and knees," he ordered and Lucifer hurried to obey him.

Michael dribbled oil over Lucifer's hole and his own fingers. He rubbed his slippery digits along Lucifer's crack and eased his index finger inside him.

Lucifer groaned at the intrusion, relaxing without any urging from Michael. Thrilled at his response, Michael pulled his finger almost completely out, then thrust it in again.

"More," Lucifer begged and Michael complied by inserting a second finger along with the first.

"Tell me if it's too much," Michael said.

"Not enough," Lucifer replied. "Fuck me, Michael, fuck me now."

Michael wasn't sure Lucifer was fully prepared for his cock, but with the power to remove pain with a single touch, he decided to give Lucifer what he wanted. He removed his fingers and after coating his erection with the rest of the oil, he spread Lucifer's buttocks and pushed his way in.

Lucifer howled, and for a moment Michael wondered if he had misjudged the situation. Then Lucifer moved against him, eager for more.

Michael put a hand on Lucifer's back and held him still. "Not this time."

"I need you." Lucifer whimpered. "Please, Michael."

"Listen to me," Michael said. "I need to be the one in control right now. Do you understand?"

Lucifer nodded.

"When I'm topping you, *I'm* the one in charge."

"Yes," Lucifer agreed. "Anything you want, just fuck me already."

Michael kept his thrusts deliberately slow and steady.

"Harder," Lucifer begged.

Michael leaned over him so his mouth was as close to Lucifer's ear as he could manage. "I'll go harder when *I'm* ready," he whispered. Then he nipped him on the shoulder, quick and hard.

"Yes," Lucifer cried.

He wanted to make this last, because he had no idea when Lucifer would let him top him again. Unfortunately, finally being allowed to take charge and top his lover meant he was as eager as Lucifer. He managed to keep his pace slow for the first couple of thrusts, before his passion took over.

"Who's in charge?" asked Michael, his voice short and breathless.

"You, you are," Lucifer replied.

"Say it again."

"You're in charge. Fuck, Michael, right there, yes!"

Michael did as Lucifer begged, fucking him with abandon. He gripped Lucifer's hips, hard enough to leave bruises, if his lover had been mortal. He wanted to say more, but he was too far gone to form words. Lucifer cried out in pleasure, clenching around Michael's cock as he climaxed.

"Lucifer!" Michael screamed when he came, buried inside his lover for the first time.

Michael collapsed on top of Lucifer, where he lay panting for breath. When he thought he could form words again, he gave it his best shot.

"Lucifer?"

"Hmm?" his lover murmured. To Michael's ears he sounded well and truly fucked.

"I want you to promise me something," Michael said.

"Promise what?"

"That you won't take another lover for as long as we're together."

Lucifer rolled over and stared at Michael. "Did you *really* think I would have fucked that pathetic excuse for a demon?"

Michael shrugged. "I don't know. When we're here, like this, I'd say no, but…"

"But what?" Lucifer prompted.

Michael turned on his side to meet Lucifer's eyes. "I never thought of myself as the jealous type, but if my reaction to Gregor is anything to go by, I guess I must be."

"I like you jealous," Lucifer teased. "Especially when the result is sex *this* good."

"I don't want to wonder whether you've taken another lover while I've been away. I hate the idea of anyone else touching you. I know you don't feel as much for me as I do for you, but —"

"What?" Lucifer interrupted as he brushed Michael's hair back from his face. Michael lowered his gaze. "Surely you know by now how much I love you?"

"Do you?" Michael asked quietly. "You've never said the words."

"I'm a fallen angel, or to give me my true title, which I know you don't like to use, even though we both know it's true, a demon. We aren't supposed to love."

"You never said the words before you fell either," Michael pointed out.

"I must have."

"No, you didn't. Believe me, I'd know if you had."

Lucifer remained quiet for a long time before he finally spoke again. "I'm sorry."

Michael smiled and kissed Lucifer on the lips, sliding his tongue into Lucifer's mouth, tasting him and drawing him nearer. Lucifer *loved* him. He didn't doubt it, especially now he had spoken the words out loud. Which meant Michael could save him, maybe not today, or even this century, but one day.

When they parted, Lucifer's smile matched Michael's.

"I love you, Michael," Lucifer whispered. "I have ever since the first day I caught you spying on me. I should have told you, and I'm sorry I didn't. I want no other in my bed."

Michael believed him and he curled up in Lucifer's waiting arms, content at last.

"Besides," Lucifer added, "now I know what I've been missing all these centuries, I intend to make up for lost time."

Michael smiled. He had a feeling he would enjoy taking charge in their relationship, just as much as Lucifer seemed to enjoy giving up control.

* * * *

Back in the realm of angels, Michael found Gabriel relaxing in his garden.

"You look like the cat that got the cream," Gabriel commented as Michael sat next to him. "I take it things are going better between you and Lucifer?"

Michael nodded. "We've come to an understanding."

"Is he closer to returning to the light?"

"I think maybe he is," Michael replied.

"And he's going to stop manipulating you?" Gabriel asked.

Michael snorted. Lucifer had tried to persuade him to stick around this morning, neglecting his duties once more, with the promise of letting Michael top him again. This time Michael had recognized the ploy for what it was, and with one stern glare at Lucifer, his lover had backtracked. The calculation had vanished from Lucifer's eyes and had been replaced by pure lust. They had reached an understanding, and Michael found himself content with their relationship for the first time in centuries.

"He'll try," Michael told Gabriel, "but he won't succeed in his manipulations, not now I recognize what he's doing. I honestly believe he doesn't even realize he does it."

"Oh, he knows *exactly* what he's doing," Gabriel argued. "He's a demon. Manipulation is what he does."

"It's because of what he is that I think he doesn't realize. It's so ingrained in him now, he can't help himself."

"If he's ever to come back to us, he'll have to learn to stop."

"I know, and I'm going to help him."

"How, if he doesn't know he's doing it?"

Michael smirked. The temptation to tell Gabriel he intended to fuck the habit out of him was awfully tempting, but he knew the archangel didn't want to hear about their sex life.

"On second thoughts, I'd probably rather not know," Gabriel said.

Michael was still chuckling when he arrived home, after leaving Gabriel to find Michael more jobs to do in his garden the following day.

For the first time Michael believed Lucifer saw him as his equal. He had earned his respect as well as his love. Now all he had to do was bring him back to the light.

Chapter Nine

Michael and Lucifer settled into a routine of sorts, spending their nights together and most of their days tending to their duties in their separate realms. They also spent time on Earth, watching the world changing around them.

Michael felt as if he were making progress, albeit slowly. It therefore came as something of a surprise when he heard the reason for the latest summons calling him to the archangels' chamber.

Raguel took center stage as soon as Michael, the last to arrive, had taken his seat.

"I'm here to request we vote again on whether to ban relationships between angels and demons."

Michael frowned. As far as he knew, Lucifer had been toeing the line and keeping to the rules set out for him. Had he misjudged him so badly? What had happened that Michael wasn't aware of?

Raguel pointed at Michael and glared. "Michael has set a dangerous precedent and now we see the repercussions."

"Precedent?" Michael asked. He glanced round at his fellow archangels and from the expressions on their faces several of them appeared to be as confused as he.

Metatron cleared his throat. "One of my angels has been found to be in a relationship with a demon for the last ten years."

"A relationship she concealed and lied about," Raguel shouted. "Like someone else I could mention."

"I thought you already did mention him," Gabriel pointed out.

Raguel faltered momentarily at Gabriel's comment. "We can't have angels getting involved with demons. They're too easily corrupted. I demand we vote again on this issue."

Metatron rose from his seat and faced the rest of the room. "No angel outside of this chamber is aware of Michael's continued relationship with Lucifer. Allisandra does not know of any rules relating to such relationships."

"All the more reason for relationships to be banned," Raguel argued. "She shouldn't have been consorting with a demon at all."

"He had targeted one of her charges," Metatron explained. "During the assignment they came to know each other and she recognized his attraction to her. She used this to her advantage and distracted him from her charge."

"That sounds more demonic than angelic," Raguel said. "Manipulation and using her body to get her own way is hardly behavior befitting an angel."

"Maybe at first," Metatron agreed. "However, once her charge had completed the task Allisandra had been assisting him with, the relationship with the demon became more conventional."

"Conventional?" Raguel roared. "It's an abomination."

Michael cleared his throat and Raguel had the grace to appear apologetic for his outburst.

"I'd like to hear from Allisandra," Gabriel said. "Does everyone agree?"

"Yes," Michael replied, along with most of the other archangels.

Metatron left the chamber and returned a few minutes later with the angel in question. Slight and blonde, Allisandra wore an expression of horror at being brought before the archangels.

"Take a seat, my dear," Gabriel said, and the angel stumbled to the center of the room. "I have a question or two for you, if you don't mind?"

Allisandra nodded, though from the shaking of her hands, Michael suspected her fear hadn't diminished.

"Why didn't you tell Metatron about your relationship with the demon?" Gabriel asked.

"His name is Janos," Allisandra said, unexpected steel in her tone.

"Apologies," Gabriel replied. "I was not aware of his name. Now, why didn't you tell Metatron?"

Allisandra shrugged. "He's a demon. I knew if I told anyone I'd never be allowed to see him again."

"Quite right," Raguel snapped, earning him a glare from Gabriel.

Gabriel turned back to Allisandra with a kind smile. "Has Metatron ever raised the subject of relationships with demons with you?"

"No."

"And what is your belief as to whether demons can be saved?" Gabriel asked. "Brought back to the light, to join us here?"

Allisandra hesitated. "I don't know."

Gabriel smiled. "*He* says anyone can be saved, demons included."

Allisandra nodded in acknowledgment of his words.

"Very well," Gabriel said. "Let's vote."

Michael raised his hand. "I have a question first, if you don't mind?"

"Of course," Gabriel replied.

Michael turned to Allisandra. "Do you love Janos?"

"Yes, I do."

Michael smiled and deferred back to Gabriel.

Gabriel took charge and cast his vote, once again agreeing not to ban relationships between angels and demons. Raguel, voting second, cancelled out Gabriel's vote with his own. One by one they went round the circle. When it came to Michael's turn he found himself cut off by Azrael, who voted immediately after Raphael, seated on Michael's other side.

"I haven't voted yet," Michael interrupted.

"You can't vote on this matter," Raguel argued. "It would

be entirely inappropriate. You have too much bias on this subject."

"Everyone has their own opinion on everything we vote for," Michael pointed out. "I have a right to vote on this, the same as I have on any other issue."

Michael could tell Allisandra was confused as to what was happening. To an uninformed angel there could be no reason at all why an archangel should not be allowed to cast a vote on any issue. He took only a moment to decide to be completely open about the situation. If necessary, he, or Metatron, could remove any memory of what he said once she left the chamber.

"My relationship with Lucifer is not the issue here," Michael stated. "This is about all angels and all demons and I have a right to a say in the matter."

"Your relationship with that creature is what started all this," Raguel snapped.

"Since it isn't common knowledge Lucifer even lives, I fail to see how I can be held accountable for the acts of other angels and demons," Michael argued.

"Michael is right," Gabriel interrupted. "Allisandra's actions were entirely independent and Michael cannot be held responsible for those."

"Well, of course *you'd* agree with him," Raguel muttered. "You're his best friend."

"I *was,*" Gabriel amended. "However, I think you'll find Lucifer has that honor these days."

Michael smiled and shook his head. "Sorry, Gabriel, you're not getting rid of me so easily."

Raguel groaned. "Regardless of who Michael considers to be his best friend, I think we're all in agreement his relationship with Lucifer clouds his judgment on the current matter."

"Or maybe it gives me a new perspective?" Michael suggested. "I say again, I have a right to vote on this matter. I waived my vote last time because, as you recall, only my own relationship with Lucifer was at stake. Now it isn't."

"Perhaps we should vote on whether Michael can vote?" Azrael offered in a teasing tone.

"That won't be necessary," Gabriel replied. "As an archangel, he has a right and I don't intend to try to take that from him. Michael, how do you vote?"

Michael already knew his vote wouldn't make a difference. There were only two angels left to vote after him, Azrael and Metatron, and even if they both voted to ban relationships, which privately Michael considered to be highly unlikely, their votes would still not be enough to pass the motion.

He also knew he hadn't been given enough time to truly consider the matter. Right now the fate of Allisandra and her demon took second place to his thoughts about how the vote could have separated him from Lucifer, if the angels who had already voted had all agreed with Raguel.

"Michael?" Gabriel prompted.

"We all know how *he'll* vote," Raguel said. "Not that it'll make any difference now. Can we get on with this?"

Michael shot Raguel a smirk worth of Lucifer himself. "I abstain," he announced.

"What?" Raguel spluttered. "You can't abstain."

"Yes, he can," Gabriel said. "Many archangels, including you, have abstained from voting on various issues over the centuries."

"But after all that nonsense about having the right to vote!" Raguel sounded incensed and his face turned almost purple with rage.

Michael's own temper rose and he stood. "If I relinquished my right to vote on this issue today, we all know that would be setting a precedent and I would never be allowed to have my say on this again. In the event this matter is brought to the chambers again, I want to ensure I can exercise my rights, just as the rest of you do."

"Then why don't you vote now?" Raguel asked. "If you want to exercise your rights so badly, here's your chance."

"I don't feel I can make an unbiased decision on this

matter today," Michael explained. "While it's clear some of you had advance warning of what this meeting was called for, I did not. To cast my vote with fairness I would need time to consider the repercussions. I therefore abstain today."

Azrael interrupted Raguel before he could respond. "I vote against banning relationships."

"I too vote against," Metatron hurried to add.

Gabriel stood and clasped his hands together. "Then the matter is decided, and this meeting of the archangels is concluded."

Michael gestured to Metatron and took him aside to quickly request Allisandra's memory of his relationship with Lucifer be removed. It would be too dangerous for everyone if Lucifer's continued survival were to be known.

He was about to leave the chamber when Gabriel called him over.

"What is it?" he asked.

"Did you go out of your way to annoy Raguel?" Gabriel asked. "I thought he might draw his sword on you, he was so angry."

"I can handle him."

Gabriel sighed and ran his hand through his hair. "You could have voted. It's not like your vote would have made a difference to the outcome."

Michael shook his head and smiled sadly. "It makes a difference to me. I'm the one who has to live with my choice. Can I make a request?"

"Of course, what is it?"

"Next time this matter comes up for voting—and we both know it will, because Raguel is never going to let this go—can I have a little advance warning as to why it's being raised, who is involved, and some time to process things and consider the matter?"

Gabriel didn't respond for several long minutes. "Why do you want to know who is involved?"

"Because I would wish to speak to them privately before

the vote. If an angel — any angel — were to be told they could no longer be with their lover, they would have to choose."

"Choose what?"

"Whether to give up their love or their wings," Michael replied. "No angel can come to such a decision on a moment's notice."

"You would give up your wings for Lucifer?" Gabriel asked.

"I don't know," Michael admitted. "And that's why I'm asking for some time, just a few days will do, the next time Raguel demands a vote."

Gabriel nodded. "Agreed."

Michael left the chamber with Gabriel and found Raphael waiting outside. He had obviously been listening to their conversation.

"You would never give up your wings," he said. "You've never known anything other than this existence."

Michael walked with his two oldest friends toward the arch where the newly deceased were constantly arriving in the realm. He had duties there today, which would take his mind off the recent meeting. He didn't agree with Raphael's comment, but he didn't disagree either. Truthfully, he had no idea at all what he would do if he had to make the choice to give up such a massive part of his life. Either option would involve tearing out a piece of his heart.

All he could do was hope the day never came when he was forced to choose.

Chapter Ten

It had been nearly two months since Michael had last escorted Lucifer on Earth. He supposed he couldn't blame Lucifer for wanting to torture him a little, given the circumstances. He just wished his lover had chosen another form of punishment besides shopping.

"What do you think?" Lucifer asked as he smoothed his hands over the seat of the black leather trousers he was trying on. To Michael's untrained eye, they appeared exactly the same as the last pair, and all the others before.

"You look good," Michael dutifully replied. He wondered whether he should comment on Lucifer's shorter hair but decided against it. The shoulder-length waves were a drastic change from his former, longer style and Michael wasn't entirely sure he liked it.

"You didn't even look properly," Lucifer complained.

Michael tried, probably unsuccessfully, to stifle his sigh of impatience. "You *always* look good. Are you getting that pair?"

Lucifer studied himself in the mirror, twisting this way and that.

"Why don't you just do what the rest of us do, and use your powers to alter your clothes to whatever you want?" Michael asked.

Lucifer laughed. "Where's the fun in that?"

"Where's the fun in shopping?" Michael mumbled under his breath.

Lucifer heard him anyway and he bent down to whisper in his ear, "Just imagine how you'll enjoy tearing them off me later."

"Peeling them off is more likely," Michael said. "Are you sure they're the right size?"

"Oh yes," Lucifer replied. "I think I'll take them all."

Michael stared at the pile of clothes Lucifer had previously tried on and discarded. It was a good job angels had unlimited funds no matter the country or era.

Finally, they exited the clothing store and were back out in the sunshine. Michael breathed in the fresh air with relief. Why Lucifer wanted to be cooped up inside shops after being confined to the Underworld was a mystery to him.

They strolled down the street, hand in hand, enjoying the unseasonably warm weather.

A couple of youths sneered at them as they passed, and Michael caught the word 'queer' from one of them. Humans had become most intolerant over the centuries.

Lucifer clearly heard the slur too and glared at the young men. "I'll be seeing you later," he told them with a cold smile, his eyes flashing red.

Michael nudged Lucifer and they continued on their way. "You shouldn't scare the humans so."

"I didn't scare them at all. That particular gang has beaten several gay men over the years and is on the fast track to my realm. I have every intention of reminding them of our encounter today when they arrive."

"You aren't supposed to show yourself to your demons," Michael reminded him.

Lucifer laughed. "They won't be demons. They aren't worthy of the name. I often show myself to humans who have pissed me off during their lives. It brightens up my days immensely."

Michael rolled his eyes. As an angel he shouldn't condone Lucifer's behavior, yet he couldn't bring himself to begrudge him the small pleasure either.

"How's your new king settling in?" Michael asked in an effort to change the subject.

"As well as can be expected," Lucifer replied. "He's pissed

off at the whole mess."

"Any attempts on his life yet?"

"Not yet, but it's only a matter of time. Tristan simply isn't demon king material. Without a killer instinct, I'm sorry, but he won't last a year."

Michael suspected as much. With all the demon kings who had come and gone over the years, Tristan was the latest, and the first one Michael had a vested interest in. Tristan was a sex demon, a rather reluctant incubus who, through a strange twist of fate, had found himself the even more reluctant king of the Underworld. What made him particularly notable from Michael's point of view was the fact Tristan had two lovers, one of whom was an angel recruited by Raphael. The trio had been in a relationship while Tristan had been human, but events seemed to be conspiring to tear the three men apart.

"Lucifer..." Michael hesitated. They had been apart for too long and he had no wish to ruin the pleasant mood.

"What is it?"

Michael shook his head. "Nothing."

"It must have been something. What's bothering you?"

Michael wasn't sure how his words would be received, but he had to try. "Tristan had two lovers before his imprisonment in the Underworld, Alastor, one of your demons, of course, and also Machidiel, one of Raphael's angels."

"Yes, I know."

"Machidiel misses him."

Lucifer raised an immaculately shaped eyebrow. "Then he knows what he has to do."

"He won't give up his wings and he won't fall."

"Then he doesn't love Tristan as much as he claims, does he?"

Michael glared at Lucifer. Was that a jibe at him? He had thought they were past those sorts of comments.

Lucifer hurried to reassure him, but Michael remained unconvinced.

"I'm sorry," Lucifer said. "I didn't mean *you*. Tristan misses the angel too."

"His name's Machidiel, though he prefers Mac."

Lucifer huffed. "I know what his name is. Tristan has already mentioned him…frequently. I simply don't wish to take the trouble to remember it. As I said, this king won't last long at all."

"Still, it might be useful to remember the name of Tristan's lover."

"Why?"

Michael squeezed Lucifer's hand.

Lucifer, who often surprised Michael with his astuteness, guessed what he was about to say. "Absolutely not! I won't permit some random angel to go wandering round the Underworld."

"Even when doing so would help your king settle into his new home?"

"Tristan is going to have to get used to his new quarters, and unless Mac intends to turn demon, they won't be sharing them."

Michael drew Lucifer off the main street and into one of the city's many alleyways. He pushed Lucifer against the wall with one hand and groped him through his trousers with the other. "Are you sure I can't convince you?"

Lucifer groaned and tilted his head back, banging his skull on the bricks. "Oh, Michael, I've missed this."

"Have you missed *me*?" Michael asked. From the corner of his eye he could see humans passing by the end of the alley. No one glanced in their direction, but that might change if Lucifer moaned any louder.

"You know I have," Lucifer replied. He dropped his shopping bags, unfastened his belt, and undid his fly.

Michael didn't need any form of direction. He slid his hand into Lucifer's trousers and took his hard flesh in hand. "Are you sure I can't convince you to give Tristan a little one-on-one time with Mac?"

"Fuck, Michael, shut up and suck me."

"So demanding," Michael teased as he dropped to his knees.

Another glance at the alley entrance revealed no one. They had time for this, especially since Lucifer wouldn't last long at all.

Although he usually preferred to take his time, Michael didn't dare, not considering their current location. Instead he took Lucifer into his mouth, sucking in as much of the flesh as he could manage and massaging the underside with his tongue.

Lucifer gave a strangled gasp and grabbed Michael's hair. He bucked into Michael's mouth with hard thrusts that hit the back of his throat.

Michael closed his eyes and concentrated on giving Lucifer as much pleasure as he could. The better his mood, the more chance there would be of changing his mind about Mac. Michael had learned a thing or two about manipulation during his years as Lucifer's lover, and he intended to put them to good use right now.

Lucifer screamed as he came and Michael tasted the bitter tang of his cum on his tongue, filling his mouth, and he swallowed it eagerly.

When he had finished, Michael tucked Lucifer's dick back into his trousers and sat back on his heels. "Are you sure I can't convince you?" he asked again.

"Convince me of what?" Lucifer replied with a rather dazed expression.

Michael stood and took Lucifer's face in his hands. "Just for an hour. No one has to know."

Lucifer ground his teeth. "No. Now drop it, Michael. You should know, after all these years, you're no match for me when it comes to these games. Stick to what you do best—keeping me happy."

Michael bristled at Lucifer's words. Was that all Lucifer wanted him for? Someone to warm his bed and suck his cock on demand?

No, he couldn't believe that. Lucifer was just annoyed

with Michael pestering him and he'd lashed out.

From the stubborn set of his jaw, Michael had a feeling manipulating Lucifer wouldn't be as easy as he first thought. He decided to drop the subject for now.

* * * *

Something had to be done. Michael's attempts to talk Lucifer into letting Mac into the Underworld had fallen on deaf ears time and again. Now Tristan's demon lover was lost to the imprisoned king as well.

It was time for Michael to put his foot down.

Whether Lucifer liked it or not, Michael intended to escort Mac into the Underworld to see Tristan, while relationships between angels and demons were still permitted by the archangels.

The latest vote — at the behest of Raguel, once again — had been the closest yet. Michael had abstained again, but he feared the time would come when he could no longer do so. The day would arrive when he had to make a choice, and he dreaded it.

Thinking of the vote reminded Michael that his relationship with Raphael may never again be as it once was. When one of his oldest friends had changed his mind and voted for the ban Michael had felt the betrayal like a punch to the gut.

Michael grabbed a bottle of wine and a couple of glasses and guided Mac out through the back door of his house and onto the beach. The building had changed a great deal over the centuries, while the peaceful beach remained the same as ever.

They sat on the sand and Michael poured them each a glass of wine. Michael took a sip and noted that the alcohol was stronger than he had thought when he had purchased the bottle on his last trip to Earth. Perhaps it would help loosen his tongue. Save for when he reported to Gabriel, he hadn't spoken of Lucifer directly in such a long time.

He didn't like to remind the rest of the archangels of his continual failure to bring his lover back into the light.

At least Mac already knew Lucifer was alive. Michael wouldn't have to convince him of the truth of that.

They talked of Tristan, and specifically of his need to feed from an angel to satisfy the incubus which resided within him.

"Could Lucifer be persuaded to let Tristan feed from him?" Mac asked.

Those words were the opening Michael needed. "I doubt it. Lucifer tends to do as he pleases and for all his faults — and believe me, he has many — infidelity is not one of them."

"What do you mean?"

Michael smiled. "He's a terrible flirt, but he would never be unfaithful to me."

Mac nearly dropped his glass at Michael's words. "What?"

"Lucifer and I are lovers," Michael explained. "We were together before he fell and despite what he has become, I cannot give him up."

Mac sat in stunned silence as Michael proceeded to tell him all he needed to know about his relationship with Lucifer. The wine had certainly done its job in loosening his tongue, and Michael suspected he might have ventured into the realm of too much information, but Mac didn't stop him. He listened intently until Michael had finished.

Michael answered his questions, and when there was nothing more to be said, he rose and silently cursed his inability to hold his alcohol. Maybe if Lucifer was really angry at what he was about to do, Michael could simply plead drunkenness.

"Now, how about we go set your Tristan to rights?" Michael said.

"What do you mean? You have a way to help him?"

"Lucifer is my lover, in every sense of the word. He is also as much a prisoner in the Underworld as Tristan." Michael didn't explain about Lucifer being permitted on Earth, provided an archangel accompanied him. Lucifer still considered himself a prisoner at such times, and he made no secret of the fact he hated the position he was in.

"You have a way to get to the Underworld?"

Michael held out a hand to Mac. "Come. Let us go where *most* angels fear to tread."

Michael led Mac along the beach until they arrived at the cliff where Michael opened the cave with his mind.

"Be careful of the steps," Michael warned. "They're very worn."

"Had a lot of use, have they?" Mac teased.

Michael glanced over his shoulder and winked. "Oh yes."

Unlike his beach house, the stairs to the Underworld hadn't changed at all. The cold, hard stones were lit by the same ancient sconces they had always been. There was no modern lighting here.

Finally they reached the end of the stairs and Lucifer's quarters. Although the room was little more than a cave, there had been some changes here. The luxurious bed had been a recent purchase and Michael had spent many hours with Lucifer, breaking it in.

"Michael, is that you?" Lucifer's voice came from the bathroom. Michael suspected he was still trying to sort out the plumbing. For some reason, modern facilities didn't seem to want to work properly in the Underworld, no matter how much time Lucifer spent swearing at the equipment. The shower ran hot for only a few seconds before the user was doused in icy water. It was, in Lucifer's words, 'bloody ridiculous'. How could the hottest place in any realm refuse to deliver basic hot water?

"No, it's your other lover," Michael called back. He nudged Mac and smiled. He was still feeling ever so slightly tipsy.

Lucifer laughed loudly. "I'll be there in a minute. I want you naked and ready for me."

Michael's face heated. Maybe he should have warned Lucifer he intended to bring Mac into the Underworld. No, he reasoned, if he had mentioned his plan to him, he'd have refused, just as he had before. *Wait a minute!* If he wanted Michael naked he was probably stripping off himself right about now.

"I've brought company," Michael shouted quickly. He didn't want Lucifer strolling into the room with everything on display. "You'd better be decent when you come in here."

Lucifer appeared a moment later, thankfully dressed. "Michael, you know the rules."

"You once told me rules are made to be broken."

"Nevertheless, I can't have angels wandering around the Underworld as though out for a morning stroll."

"Tristan needs him. You know he does." Michael stepped forward and ran his hand up Lucifer's arm. "I know you remember what it's like to be separated from the other half of your soul, because I remember it myself."

"Does Machidiel wish to turn demon?" Lucifer asked.

"No," Mac replied immediately, his voice firm.

"Then you have no business here in the Underworld."

"Lucifer," Michael murmured into his lover's ear. "No one would ever know if you were to allow them some time together."

"You're going to be difficult about this, aren't you?" Michael hid his smile as he heard the wavering in Lucifer's tone.

"Yes."

Lucifer sighed. "How difficult?"

Michael had found just one way to truly manipulate Lucifer, and that was to withhold sex from him. He just hoped Lucifer didn't figure out Michael was bluffing. "I'll be too busy consoling Mac after the loss of both of his lovers to spend much time down here for a while."

"You enjoy being with me too much to stay away for more than a few days."

"Mac will be devastated for weeks, if not months." Michael shook his head sadly. He couldn't meet Lucifer's eyes. His lover would know he was lying.

"Months?" Lucifer glared at Mac.

"Maybe even years," Michael suggested. "Alastor has been reborn. He could live to be a hundred before he's able to return to Heaven and help pick up the pieces."

"You know as well as I do, you could not stay away from me for so long."

"I did once before," Michael reminded him. "It was many centuries from the time you turned demon to the last night of the battle."

"Damn it, Michael." Lucifer pulled him into his arms and turned to Mac. "You've got one hour."

"I thought you had more stamina than that," Michael teased, even as he wondered if he might be pushing his luck.

Lucifer mock-glared at him. "Fine. I'll summon him back here later."

Without a word, Lucifer sent Mac from the room.

"You've sent him to Tristan's chambers?" Michael asked, just to be sure.

"Don't you trust me?"

Michael nodded. "Yes, of course I do. Now, I believe you mentioned something about getting naked."

Lucifer's cock rose to poke him in the stomach at Michael's words. "Get undressed and on all fours on the bed, *now*."

Michael hurried to comply. He could tell Lucifer needed to take charge this time. While they had been equal in the bedchamber for centuries now, there were times when Lucifer needed to exert his authority. Especially when Michael had successfully manipulated him.

Lucifer followed him onto the bed and immediately dove between Michael's buttocks, licking at his hole and nipping the exposed flesh. Michael keened as Lucifer rimmed him thoroughly.

"Ready?" Lucifer asked.

They hadn't used lube, but Michael didn't care. He needed Lucifer in him and he had to have him now. "Fuck me," he begged.

Lucifer entered him with one swift thrust and Michael howled as his arse stretched and burned.

Michael held still as he forced himself to relax. Gradually the pain subsided and the pleasure began. "Move, Lucifer, please, I need you."

Lucifer pounded into him relentlessly and Michael loved every second of it.

"Bringing angels into *my* domain," Lucifer growled. "Do you think I can't tell when you're manipulating me?"

"Hoped," Michael gasped.

Lucifer increased his pace and Michael's cock brushed against the covers beneath him. Pre-cum dripped onto the silk sheets and he could tell he would come without his dick being touched.

"Manipulative archangel," Lucifer shouted. "You need to take your place at my side here. I can't live without you much longer."

"You have me."

"I want forever. Angels aren't supposed to manipulate, but you do it so well."

Michael shut his ears to Lucifer's pleas. Instead he concentrated on the feel of Lucifer buried in his arse, his lover's balls slapping against his buttocks, the hands gripping his hips, holding him in place.

"Fall for me," Lucifer cried. "Michael, you've made me wait so long. Join me forever."

Michael screamed as he came. He would have collapsed onto the bed, except Lucifer held him in place as he continued to fuck him.

"Yes!" Lucifer yelled and Michael felt the heat of his lover's release in his arse.

They fell onto the sheets in a sweaty, sticky mess.

Lucifer wrapped around him and sucked on his ear. "Soon, Michael," he whispered.

Michael shivered a little. He didn't want to admit Lucifer made a valid point. He *had* used rather underhand methods to get Mac into the Underworld. His actions weren't entirely worthy of an archangel, even if they had achieved the desired result.

* * * *

Michael played with Lucifer's hair as his lover slept. He should leave soon, but the feeling of contentment made him reluctant to depart.

Lucifer stirred and blinked sleepily at Michael, a smile slowly spreading across his face. "You have to admit, there are *some* advantages to having a sex demon on the throne of the Underworld."

"But does the rampant sex drive outweigh the increase in crimes of a sexual nature?" Michael asked.

Lucifer ran a finger down the length of Michael's cock, which rose instantly at the touch. "Even you couldn't get it up again this quickly without our current king."

Michael chuckled. "You've been sleeping for nearly an hour. I've been half hard for most of the time, and my arousal has nothing to do with your current king."

Lucifer sat up. "An hour?"

"Yes. I should be leaving soon."

Lucifer scowled but didn't try to talk him into staying. Michael smiled to himself when he thought on how much progress he had made with his lover over the years. A few centuries ago, Lucifer would have tried his best to talk him into staying in his bed.

Michael kissed Lucifer deeply, thrusting his tongue into his mouth and moaning in pleasure. A few more minutes of this and he wouldn't need Lucifer to talk him into sticking around, he'd be throwing him down on the bed and fucking him into oblivion. As much as he didn't want to admit it, the increased sex drive was due to Tristan being on the throne. In the months since Michael had first brought Mac to the Underworld, the young king's powers had grown at an alarming rate. The repercussions of letting Tristan feed

154

from an angel couldn't be ignored for much longer.

* * * *

Michael arrived back in the realm of angels to find Gabriel on his beach.

"Have you been waiting long?" Michael asked.

"Not very, but I wanted to speak to you before you began your shift."

Michael checked the time and cringed. They only had a few minutes.

"You've been spending a lot more time with Lucifer recently," Gabriel commented in a deceptively casual tone.

Michael bristled defensively. "I've not been neglecting my duties."

"I never said you were, but I'm worried about you."

"There's no need to be. I'm perfectly well."

Gabriel took his arm and swung him gently round to face him. "Are you?"

Michael nodded, but he knew the response was automatic. "I'm not sure."

"What's bothering you?" Gabriel asked.

Michael didn't know how to put his concerns into words. It sounded so silly when he thought about the problem. Too much sex with his lover seemed a ridiculous dilemma to have.

"Ah," Gabriel said.

Michael scowled. "I wish you wouldn't poke into my mind without warning."

"I know you don't like me to, but sometimes you're so hard to read and you never were one for confiding in others."

Michael couldn't deny that Gabriel spoke the truth. "What do you think? Am I being ridiculous?"

"No. The effects of the present king of the Underworld are felt on Earth and it stands to reason the impact would be even more powerful in the Underworld itself. It's simply a matter of time before we feel the ripples here too."

"You think so?"

"It's a certainty."

"We can't go on this way," Michael said. "When I'm in the Underworld I can barely keep my hands off him."

"That's always been a problem for you," Gabriel teased, nudging him in the arm.

"Not as bad as this," Michael admitted.

Gabriel sighed. "I've called a meeting of the archangels' council for midnight tonight."

"You have?" Michael could tell from the harshness of Gabriel's tone the reason for the meeting was serious.

"I think we need to consider separating Machidiel and Tristan."

Michael had been thinking the same thing.

"Tristan's powers grow as long as he feeds on Mac," Gabriel continued. "You should think about things before the meeting."

"I don't need to," Michael replied. "I hate to say it, but I should never have taken Mac to the Underworld. If I had known what would happen throughout the world by letting Tristan feed from him, I'd…"

Gabriel patted his shoulder. "You had no way of knowing. None of us did. This situation is completely unprecedented. You did what you thought was for the best, reuniting the two of them when they needed each other."

"I know, but it doesn't make it any easier to accept I made the wrong choice."

They had arrived at the training grounds, where Michael's latest recruits waited for him to show them the best way of handling their new wings.

"I'll see you later," Gabriel said, leaving Michael to greet the new angels before the council meeting.

* * * *

Michael could see the fury in Mac's eyes, even from across

the room. He wished he had had the opportunity to speak to him before the council meeting and the unanimous vote to separate the angel from his demon lover, permanently.

A part of him wished he could avoid the confrontation he knew would follow the meeting, but Michael had never lacked courage and he saw no point in putting off the inevitable.

He let Mac rage at him and kept a tight rein on his own temper as he calmly explained the reasoning behind the decision.

Throughout it all, he wondered how he would have reacted if the archangels had voted to separate him from Lucifer. His fury would have been legendary, and who knew, it still might be one day, if the worst ever happened.

In the here and now, however, what was done was done, and all they could do was watch and wait to see what happened when Tristan could no longer feed from his angel lover.

* * * *

Lucifer groaned, and not in a good way.

"What is it?" Michael asked. He had just opened a bottle of wine, but from the scowl on Lucifer's face, he wondered if he should have bothered.

"Machidiel is talking to Irdu and Ardat about me."

Michael cringed. He had guided Mac into the Underworld for the last time, to say a final goodbye to Tristan now his reign had ended, the only way it could, with his death. Irdu and Ardat, the incubi and succubi leaders, had been with their king at the end, but what had happened in the few minutes since Lucifer had sent the angel to Tristan's chambers?

"Damn it," Lucifer snarled. "He's told them I'm alive."

Sometimes Michael thought it might be better if Lucifer couldn't hear everything his demons said about him. He knew Lucifer shut out the voices most of the time, but occasionally, such as now, the conversation was too important to ignore.

"What are you going to do about it?" Michael asked.

Lucifer raised his hand to halt Michael's words and Michael let him listen to the discussion happening elsewhere in the Underworld.

"I have to go to step in," Lucifer said. "Your angel is determined to track down Tristan."

"Didn't you just send Mac to him?" Michael questioned.

"To his body," Lucifer confirmed.

Michael rolled his eyes. "He needs to speak to him properly. You know I meant to send him to his soul."

"I'll be back shortly," Lucifer said.

Michael waited impatiently for Lucifer to return. He filled his glass and took a drink of the wine while he worried what was happening.

A few minutes later Lucifer returned, with guests. Mac, he recognized, as well as the newly deceased Tristan's soul. Thankfully, in the Underworld, the souls of the deceased remained corporeal, the better to inflict punishment on those who deserved it. For Tristan it meant he could cling to Mac after so long apart. The other two stunning demons were strangers to him. He guessed they were Irdu and Ardat, the male and female leaders of all sex demons. They were truly beautiful.

Irdu was dark-skinned with jet-black hair spilling over his shoulders and down toward his arse. He wore a silken kilt and little else. Ardat, his female counterpart, was his opposite in every way. Her pale hair was white-blonde, and her skin creamy and flawless. She wore even less than Irdu, her beaded gown covering little and leaving her breasts completely exposed.

Michael had never been attracted to women, always preferring the male form, yet he felt himself drawn to the succubus, just as much as her lover.

"Are we having a party?" Michael asked. His arousal had surged the moment Lucifer and the others had appeared, and Michael wasn't entirely sure it was Lucifer causing his body to react in such a way.

"*Lucifer, a moment of your time please,*" he asked telepathically, even though he disliked communicating in such a way.

His lover understood his meaning and everyone in the room froze apart from the two of them.

"Why am I rock hard all of a sudden?" Michael asked.

"You're in the presence of two of the most talented sex demons ever to walk the earth," Lucifer pointed out.

"Can you make them stop whatever it is they're doing?"

"No. You'll have to put up with an aching cock for a while. You'll get used to it. I find their company quite pleasant, actually."

Michael snorted. "Why does that not surprise me? What are they doing here?"

Lucifer wouldn't meet his eyes all of a sudden and Michael's heart began to race for an entirely different reason.

"Lucifer, what have you done?"

"How much do you want Tristan's soul released from the Underworld?" Lucifer asked.

Michael frowned. "What do you mean?"

Lucifer stalked across the room and pulled him into a crushing embrace. Lucifer kissed him hard, and Michael felt his lover's stiff member press against his own erection. "I love you, Michael, and I'm doing this for you and your young angel here."

"Doing what?"

Lucifer pressed his forehead to Michael's and sighed. "I can't release Tristan's soul just because you and Machidiel want me to."

Michael didn't understand, but he didn't have time to question his lover further. Michael dropped back into his seat as Lucifer stepped back to his previous position and the room came to life once more.

"Irdu and Ardat have challenged me for the release of

Tristan's soul," Lucifer explained.

"Challenged how?" Michael asked, though he had a feeling he already knew the answer to his question.

"If they can make me come, I release Tristan's soul," Lucifer explained. "If they cannot, it proves Tristan was willingly unfaithful to his lovers whilst in the Underworld, and his soul remains here, forever."

"You're going to have sex with them?" Michael asked telepathically.

"If you tell me you don't want me to, I'll…"

"No," Michael replied. *"If this is the price for Tristan's soul, so be it."*

"I won't last long," Lucifer admitted. *"They are most talented."*

Michael smiled to himself as he realized what Lucifer was telling him. He could not simply release Tristan's soul, but he had accepted a challenge he couldn't win.

"Oh, this should be interesting," Michael said out loud.

"You aren't going to stay and watch, are you?" Lucifer asked.

"Of course I am," Michael replied easily. "I intend to make sure there isn't any cheating happening."

"I would never betray you." Lucifer climbed onto the bed.

Michael knew he spoke the truth. This wasn't a betrayal. His lover, selfish in so many ways, was helping him the only way he could.

Irdu and Ardat joined Lucifer, while Mac and Tristan took a seat beside Michael.

Michael tried to concentrate on his conversation with Mac, but the sight of his lover and the two demons was more distracting than he would ever have imagined.

He had thought he'd be jealous of seeing Lucifer with another man, yet right now Michael didn't feel anything other than painfully aroused. He had no doubt it was because of the presence of the two sex demons currently crawling over his lover.

Ardat took Lucifer's thick cock between her lips while

Irdu fed Lucifer his own rod, encouraging the fallen angel to suck him.

"*Michael, fuck, Michael!*" Lucifer's words whispered across his mind and Michael let the connection between them open completely.

"*You look ravishing,*" Michael said. "*It's taking every bit of my willpower to stay in my seat right now.*"

"*If you join us, I'm done.*"

"*I won't be coming over there. I'd rather not give Mac and Tristan any more of a show than they're already enjoying.*"

"*Are you enjoying it?*" Lucifer asked.

Michael watched as Lucifer tried to hold back his orgasm by gripping the base of his cock. Irdu laughed and pulled Lucifer's hand away. He whispered something in Lucifer's ear, but Michael could make out what he said.

Lucifer had been right. He wouldn't last long.

Michael rubbed himself through his robes.

"You find the sight arousing?" Mac whispered.

"Oh yes," Michael replied, his eyes never leaving his lover. He had never thought himself a voyeur, but right now he couldn't think of anything that could give him more pleasure than watching the two sex demons drive Lucifer to the brink of an orgasm. He would be coming in his robes in a matter of minutes. The longer Irdu and Ardat pleasured Lucifer, the more aroused Michael became. He knew their powers caused him to feel this way, but he didn't care. He just wanted to enjoy being in the moment.

"I think perhaps I might try to persuade Lucifer to invite them to our bed on occasion." The words had left Michael's mouth before he had even thought them through. Was he seriously considering taking two more demons into his bed?

He had never wanted anyone else since the day he had first seen Lucifer. But the thought of taking Irdu's cock into his mouth, as Lucifer had done just moments ago, made his mouth water.

Then there was Ardat. Her plump lips would look perfect

wrapped around his member.

Mac had taken two lovers into his bed at once, but Michael had always been jealous of the mere idea of sharing Lucifer with anyone.

Was the power of the two demons eclipsing his jealous nature?

Image after image raced through his mind. Lucifer fucking Irdu, while Irdu claimed Ardat. Michael would give a great deal to see that, and even more to watch Irdu pounding into Lucifer while his lover sucked Michael's cock.

Again, Michael tried to concentrate on his conversation with Mac, but he was only half there. The rest of him was on the bed with Lucifer, who was too far gone to communicate telepathically. He was close to coming, which meant Tristan would soon be free to leave.

Mac would have to take him to the realm of angels, because Michael had no intention of leaving Lucifer tonight.

Lucifer came in Ardat's mouth and failed the challenge beautifully. Michael stood, uncaring that everyone in the room could see his erection practically poking through his robes. He walked to the succubus and kissed her deeply, the familiar taste of Lucifer's cum pleasant in his mouth, yet a little strange.

"Thank you," he said after he had parted their lips.

"What are you thanking her for?" Lucifer growled from where he lay prone on the bed.

Michael smiled to himself. Yes, he should be thanking Lucifer as well, and later, when they were alone, he would. Until then, he would ensure Lucifer's reputation remained intact. To everyone else in the room, he had failed the challenge despite his best efforts. Only Michael knew he had never stood a chance.

Chapter Eleven

When Michael and Lucifer were alone, Michael's head felt clearer than it had been in the presence of Irdu and Ardat. They were truly talented demons. Michael couldn't recall ever being so turned on without being touched. Still, something bothered him and he didn't know how to raise the subject with his lover.

"What is it?" Lucifer asked, clearly having noticed Michael's wandering thoughts.

"I don't know," Michael admitted. "I can't believe what we did today."

"What *I* did, you mean?"

"Not just that," Michael replied. "I was practically pleasuring myself as I watched the three of you on the bed. Even though Mac and Tristan sat right beside me, I couldn't keep my hand off my cock."

Lucifer laughed. "Is that all that's bothering you?"

"Isn't that enough?"

Lucifer kissed him briefly. "Did you know every time Irdu or Ardat walk the earth there's a baby boom in the towns or cities they go to? Just having them near makes everyone want to fuck the nearest warm body."

Michael could believe it quite easily. "I desired them, even Ardat. I've never had such feelings for a woman before."

"She's a demon, not a woman," Lucifer reminded him. "It doesn't change what your sexual preference is, her powers ensure you want her, just as Irdu's make you crave him."

"Is it the same for you?"

"Yes, though perhaps not to the same extent as for humans, angels, and lesser demons. If their powers didn't work on me, I could have won the challenge, because they would have given up long before I came."

"Thank you for deliberately throwing the challenge to allow Tristan to leave the Underworld."

"You're welcome, though I will deny it with my last breath if you tell anyone else. Still, even if I hadn't let them win, if they had persisted, they would have made me come eventually, purely because of what they are."

They lay quietly for several minutes until Lucifer spoke again.

"Did you mean what you said about inviting them back into our bed?" he asked.

Michael frowned. *Did I?* "I don't know. I meant it at the time, but I think part of the reason I said it was the desire I felt at the time. Now things are clearer, I'm not sure. What do you think?"

"They would be honored, but I don't want to share you."

Michael chuckled. "I didn't think I would like it, but watching you with them was almost intoxicating."

Lucifer leaned onto his side and stroked Michael's bare chest, still slick with sweat from their lovemaking. "If watching them pleasure me brings you joy, then I will let them into our bed, but they are not to touch you, understand?"

Michael's heart raced at the possessive lust in Lucifer's eyes. He nodded slowly.

"You are *mine,* and mine alone," Lucifer continued. "No man, woman, angel, or demon will touch you while I draw breath. My cock is the only one your lips are allowed to touch. I'm the only one allowed to fuck you or kiss you. You'll taste no man's seed except mine, unless you're licking another's from *my* body. You spread your legs only for me, Michael."

Lucifer dipped his hand between Michael's thighs and Michael instinctively opened to allow him access to his arse, still aching from earlier. Michael moaned as Lucifer rubbed him intimately.

"This is mine," Lucifer growled. "*You* are mine, body and soul, make no mistake about it. Do you still want me to allow the demons into our bed?"

Michael gasped and nodded. "Yes."

Lucifer stilled in obvious surprise. "Even knowing they will touch me and not you?"

"Yes."

"But you want them to bring you pleasure too." It wasn't a question and Lucifer already knew the answer, since everyone who saw Ardat and Irdu wanted them sexually.

"Not if it brings you pain," Michael replied quietly.

They were in agreement and Lucifer climbed out of bed and gathered their robes from the floor. "Put that on and I'll summon them."

"Why do I need to dress?" Lucifer's eyes flashed and Michael understood immediately. "You don't want them ogling me."

"No, not while we're negotiating terms."

Michael didn't bother to argue. He pulled on the garment and tied the cord. It covered him, but at the same time did nothing to hide the fact his cock was hard. When Lucifer summoned the incubus and succubus a moment later, the tent in his robes became even more obvious as his erection grew to almost painful proportions. Michael barely managed to stop himself from stroking off.

The demons bowed before Lucifer, but their eyes were trained on Michael, still on the bed and no doubt appearing completely debauched.

Lucifer, still naked, took a seat beside the bed. "You heard Michael's invitation to you," he said.

"We did," they replied in unison.

"My lover enjoyed watching you with me, and wishes to do so again. I have agreed to allow this because I delight in giving him pleasure."

Irdu raised an eyebrow and smirked. "Is that the only reason?"

Ardat gave a light tinkling laugh. "He liked what we did

to him and wants more of the same."

"I do," Lucifer admitted. "But if Michael didn't want you in our bed, make no mistake, you would not be here right now."

Irdu smiled at Michael. "Then we give our thanks to the archangel and look forward to showing him our gratitude in other ways."

Lucifer growled quietly. "He accepts your thanks, but that is all."

Irdu and Ardat wore twin expressions of confusion.

Lucifer rose and towered over the two kneeling demons. "While you are in our bed, you will not touch him."

"And out of the bed?" Ardat asked mischievously. "I quite like the idea of him fucking me on the couch."

Lucifer glowered at her and even from across the room Michael saw her flinch. "He is *mine*. You will not touch him."

Ardat didn't seem to know when to curb her tongue. "Can he touch us?"

"No," Lucifer snapped. "Do you agree to these terms?"

Irdu nudged Ardat before she could say anything else. "So, to clarify, what you're saying is, you are inviting us to your bed for your pleasure, but not for Michael's."

"Michael will derive pleasure from watching the three of us together."

"Not exactly a fair deal for him, is it?" Ardat commented. "Why force him to masturbate when there are three others in the room who would be happy to help him come?"

Lucifer grabbed the demon by the throat and yanked her to her feet. Had she been human, he might well have choked her with such a move, but demons were made of sterner stuff. "You will not touch him, understand?"

Michael scrambled off the bed and touched Lucifer's arm. "She understands. Now release her before Irdu loses his temper."

Lucifer turned his attention to the other demon and saw what Michael had already spotted. The incubus was dangerously close to attacking him, even if such a move would result in nothing except two needless deaths.

With a snarl of anger Lucifer pushed Ardat away.

Michael stepped between his lover and the demons. "As you can see, Lucifer is a little possessive of me."

Ardat rubbed her throat, the marks from Lucifer's grip already fading. "A little?" she muttered.

Michael shrugged and smiled. "Very well, let's say insanely possessive. Now, if you wish to share our bed, you will have to agree to the rules Lucifer sets down for you. If you don't, I can't guarantee I'll be able to stop him if he loses control, especially since I'm likely to be lost in my own pleasure at the time."

Irdu nodded. "Sex with us can make a person lose control, so what if *you* touch *us*?"

Michael glanced at Lucifer. "He makes a good point."

Lucifer paced back and forth for several minutes before finally coming to a halt beside the bed. "Very well, a compromise." He pointed at the two demons. "You don't suck him, fuck him, or kiss him. You have enough control over your own urges to manage that."

"It's not exactly a compromise," Ardat argued.

"I haven't finished," Lucifer snapped. "Michael, as you point out, could lose himself in the pleasure, and if that happens he may touch you without consequence for as long as it takes me to persuade him to focus his attention on me."

Ardat opened her mouth, but Michael shook his head quickly, warning her to hold her peace.

"Do you agree to these terms?" Lucifer asked.

Irdu and Ardat communicated silently for several minutes. Finally the two demons bowed low before Lucifer once again. "We agree."

Michael returned to the bed and climbed onto the mattress.

"Eager?" Lucifer asked.

Michael's lips twitched as he tried to suppress his smile.

"May we see the archangel?" Irdu asked. "His body, that is?"

Lucifer scowled but nodded.

Michael undid the cord and slipped the robe from his shoulders. The fabric pooled around his waist, securing his modesty for a little longer.

Lucifer crooked his finger and Michael rose to his knees, his movement causing the robe to fall the rest of the way, revealing his erection to the hungry gazes of the two demons — and Lucifer, of course.

Ardat approached the bed first. "I had heard archangels are the most beautifully formed of all beings, and now I see the tales are true."

Lucifer joined Michael on the bed and knelt beside him. He ran his hand down Michael's chest, over his abdomen, and let his fingers skim the hard cock that twitched at the slightest touch.

"Irdu, join us," Michael said.

The demon slipped onto the bed and crawled as close as he could without risking touching Michael.

"What's your pleasure?" Lucifer murmured into Michael's ear.

"I…" Michael saw Irdu lick his lips and he craved the feeling of the demon's mouth wrapped around his cock, but he didn't dare ask for that. He tore his eyes away from Irdu and met Lucifer's gaze. "Suck me, while Irdu fucks you."

"*No one has ever fucked me except you,*" Lucifer told him telepathically.

Michael could tell he didn't want the demons to know of his lack of lovers despite his longevity.

Michael stroked Lucifer's cheek as he kissed him deeply. "*If you don't want this, just say so. We can send them away.*"

"*It's rather hard to say no to you when your tongue's in my mouth.*"

Michael sat back and chuckled. "Sorry."

Lucifer inched back to put a little space between them. He waved his hand to freeze the two demons out of the conversation. "I don't know if I can let another man fuck me. You know how long it was before I let you."

"I know."

"Are you disappointed in me?" Lucifer asked.

"Disappointed?" Michael shook his head, surprised at Lucifer's question and what it revealed about his lover's fears. "Of course not. But I think we should talk about your boundaries. What are you comfortable with?"

Lucifer's gaze flickered to the demons. "I liked them sucking me, and I enjoyed sucking Irdu. I think I'd be okay with them rimming me too."

"What about you fucking them?" Michael asked.

The expression of desire on Lucifer's face answered his question. Lucifer wanted the two demons, and despite being the one to instigate this, Michael recognized the twinge in his gut as jealousy. He squashed it down and concentrated on how he had felt watching Lucifer coming. He never appeared more beautiful than when he was in the throes of an orgasm.

"I have an idea," Lucifer said. "How about we suck each other while our new friends rim us? Then I'll fuck Irdu, while he takes Ardat."

"And what am I doing while that's happening?" Michael teased. "Or had you forgotten about me?"

"You get to fuck me."

Michael frowned. "I'm not really sure about the logistics of that one."

Lucifer cocked his head to one side. "It might be something we have to work up to."

Michael shook his head and smiled fondly at his lover. "Let's see what our companions have to say. After all, they are here for their own pleasure as well as ours."

Lucifer unfroze the two demons who either didn't notice or didn't comment on the time lapse. He gave them the details of what they had decided upon.

Thankfully neither of the demons commented on the change of plan.

Michael let Lucifer guide him into position and after

several moments of jostling limbs the four of them were finally ready. Michael took Lucifer's cock between his lips and sucked the head lightly, while at the same time Lucifer licked at Michael's own throbbing erection. They had done this many times before. The position was familiar and almost comforting.

Then came the unfamiliar sensation of another set of hands on his body, slowly parting his buttocks, carefully so as not to knock him from Lucifer's mouth. He felt warm breath ghosting over his hole and a tongue, too long for that of a human, delving into his arse, licking him more intimately than Lucifer ever had, stroking his prostate with perfect accuracy.

On the other side of Lucifer, Ardat gave Michael's lover the same attention.

Michael closed his eyes and concentrated on the varying sensations, his senses close to overloading. He sucked Lucifer with increasing desperation, taking as much of his length into his mouth as he could manage.

He sensed a slight drain on his angelic powers and could tell Irdu was feeding from his energy. He couldn't kill him, but Michael knew he would have to be careful not to leave himself too vulnerable. It was safe for the moment, though.

With a moan of pleasure, Michael stroked Lucifer's heavy balls, fondling them gently. Lucifer mimicked him and Michael sucked him harder in response.

The four of them became increasingly noisy while they slowly continued to pleasure each other.

Michael tasted Lucifer's seed as he began to spill into Michael's waiting mouth. He sucked harder and Lucifer released Michael's cock to scream out his release.

Ardat and Irdu drew back when Lucifer came, and Michael nearly cried out at the loss of the demon's tongue massaging his prostate.

Lucifer took a while to come to his senses, by which time Michael's own climax had retreated somewhat.

"Fuck his mouth," Irdu whispered into Michael's ear.

"What are you and Ardat going to do?" Michael asked.

"Enjoy the show," they replied together.

"Come here," Lucifer ordered, though his voice remained groggy.

Michael crawled up his lover's body and straddled his chest. The two demons moved position so they knelt at Lucifer's head. They kissed deeply before turning back to Michael.

"You taste good," Ardat commented.

Lucifer gripped Michael's arse and tugged him closer. He opened his mouth wide and Michael didn't need any further encouragement. He pushed his way slowly into Lucifer's mouth and, when he was sure his lover wasn't going to choke, he began to slowly thrust.

In front of him, Ardat took hold of Irdu's cock and stroked it in time to Michael's movements.

Lucifer encouraged him to quicken his pace and Ardat did the same.

Irdu came first, spilling across Ardat's fist. The succubus raised her hand and licked his cum from her fingers, her eyes on Michael the entire time.

"Want a taste?" she asked.

"You'll taste no other man's seed unless you're licking it from my body," Lucifer reminded him.

Michael shook his head, too breathless to form words.

Ardat held out her hand. "Are you sure? I think you might like it."

Michael suspected he would, but he wasn't so far gone he had forgotten Lucifer's terms. He slowed his thrusts a little and gathered his breath. "How long until he comes again?"

"A few minutes," Ardat said. "Maybe less, with the power boost rimming you gave him."

"Make him come over Lucifer," Michael ordered.

Ardat grinned. "Is this another rule?" she asked.

Michael nodded.

"I think I want some rules of my own," Ardat said as she and Irdu crawled back down the bed. "I want to taste the cum of an archangel."

"You can't suck me," Michael reminded her.

"I know, but there's no rule stopping me from tasting you after you've come in Lucifer's mouth, is there?"

Michael's heart constricted. She was talking about kissing Lucifer—*his* lover—and Michael didn't like the idea at all. Now he understood exactly where Lucifer was coming from. "No."

Ardat smiled. "You two are really quite perfect for each other, aren't you? Both so sweetly jealous. It's almost as if you don't *trust* each other."

"I could change my mind about having you in here at all," Michael said. "If I say I want you gone, you'll never share Lucifer's bed again."

"You think he can resist us?" Irdu asked. "*No one* can do that forever."

"He can," Michael replied. "I trust him."

"Then why won't you let me kiss him?" Ardat questioned.

Michael didn't answer her, and, after he came in Lucifer's mouth a few minutes later, he climbed off his lover to the opposite side of the bed where the two demons sat. Too far gone to form words, he nodded at Ardat, giving her silent permission to kiss his lover.

She leaned in, licking her lips, then lapped at Lucifer's, tasting Michael's seed. Michael cringed, unable to watch without his jealousy rising.

Suddenly Lucifer pushed her off and wiped his hand across his mouth. "No."

"Lucifer?" Michael asked.

"You don't enjoy watching her kiss me, so it doesn't happen again," Lucifer explained. "My kisses are yours alone, agreed?"

Michael threw his arms around Lucifer's neck and kissed him, tasting himself as well as his lover. "Agreed," he said. "No one gets to kiss you except me."

Lucifer pushed him down onto the bed and thrust against him. "Leave us," he told the two demons, who seemed to sense the shift in mood and vanished instantly.

"You've sent them away for good?" Michael asked. Something akin to disappointment hit him sharply.

"No, just for now," Lucifer replied. "When you want them to join us again, let me know."

"What if you want them here?" Michael asked.

Lucifer rubbed against him, and Michael spread his legs wider so Lucifer could claim him fully. "I won't," Lucifer said as he speared Michael with one smooth thrust, nailing his prostate as efficiently as Irdu had managed with his tongue.

Michael relaxed and let Lucifer fuck him with abandon. He shouted and screamed his pleasure, and afterwards he whispered words of love into Lucifer's ear, even though he could tell his lover slept, exhausted at last.

* * * *

It took a while before they found a good balance between the four of them. Lucifer refused to back down on any of his rules, and, after Michael's own jealous reaction to seeing Ardat kissing his lover, Michael didn't blame him.

They invited the two demons to join them once every couple of months, for a single night of carnal pleasure.

Michael had no illusions about what was in it for the two sex demons. Each time they came to Lucifer's bed they fed from Lucifer and from Michael himself. They took just enough power to ensure their survival during the battle for the throne of the Underworld, and Michael tried not to begrudge them. He wasn't happy to discover Lucifer's survival was now common knowledge in the Underworld, but there was little he could do about it.

In the seclusion of Lucifer's chambers, what they did together privately seemed perfectly natural. However, when he went home, to the realm of angels, Michael began to harbor doubts. He needed to confide in someone, and as always Gabriel was his first choice.

Michael had now worked in Gabriel's garden for many years, far longer than their initial arrangement, and some days he even enjoyed it. Today, when it was just the two of them there, laboring side by side, it was easy to open up and talk.

"Can I ask you something, in confidence?" Michael asked.

"Of course, what is it?"

"You won't speak of this to anyone?" Michael pressed. "Not even Raphael?"

Gabriel stopped digging and frowned at him. "Are you still at odds? I thought things had improved between you, now the business between Machidiel and his lovers has been resolved."

"It is, which is why I don't want to risk rocking the boat again, at least not yet. Things are a little too raw between us, if you know what I mean?"

"I won't speak to him about whatever you tell me," Gabriel promised. "Though I'm sure I don't need to remind you secrets do have a tendency to come out sooner or later."

Michael understood that very well indeed. "It's about Lucifer."

"It usually is," Gabriel commented dryly. "What's he done this time?"

"Nothing!" Michael shook his head and hurried to reassure Gabriel that Lucifer had been behaving himself. "I guess I should have said it's about my relationship with Lucifer."

"What about it?" Gabriel asked.

Michael focused on tugging a particularly stubborn weed from the flowerbed. "We've been having sex with other demons," he finally blurted out.

"You've been cheating on each other?" Gabriel's tone conveyed his disbelief.

"No, never!" Michael met Gabriel's horrified gaze. "I meant we've been inviting other demons into our bed, the incubi and succubi leaders, in fact."

"Irdu and Ardat?"

"Yes."

Gabriel whistled. "And how are you enjoying sharing your body with a woman after all these years with only men?"

Although Gabriel rarely spoke of his own sex life, Michael knew enough to be well aware of the fact Gabriel was what the modern world referred to as an equal opportunities lover.

"It's different," Michael admitted, "but we've not, er, you know, gone all the way."

Gabriel snorted. "You've just admitted to me you're sharing your bed with three demons at once — and I know you don't see Lucifer as such, but he is — yet you can't say the word 'sex'."

Michael scowled at Gabriel and tossed down his gardening fork. "Fine, I've not had sexual intercourse with her, okay?"

"Then what have you been doing?" Gabriel raised his hand. "On second thoughts, I'm not sure I want to hear. What exactly *is* the problem? Apart from the obvious, which I doubt has even occurred to you."

"What do you mean by that?" Michael asked. He sounded defensive even to his own ears.

Gabriel sighed and rose from the ground. He held out his hand to help Michael to his feet. "This has obviously been happening for a while, yet you're only now telling me. That means you've been lying to me again, even if it was by omission."

"I know, and I'm sorry."

"Don't worry about it. Now, what's the problem you want my advice about?"

Michael walked through the gardens, not seeing the beauty in the fresh blooms, nor smelling the scents of the flowers. "I'm worried I'm no longer enough for Lucifer."

"Why do you think that? Does he have sex with these demons when you're not there?"

"No, he'd never do that to me."

"Has he told you you're not enough, or indicated he no

longer wants you?"

"No."

"Then he's shown a preference to your other lovers, over you?"

Michael frowned as he considered Lucifer's behavior in the bedchamber. "I don't think so."

"Then why do you think you're not enough for him?" Gabriel asked. "Has he ever given you cause to believe that?"

"No, I guess not."

Gabriel sat on a metal bench with a rose motif, and Michael sat beside him. "Lucifer loves you. You were the only angel he ever took notice of before he fell, and you've been the one constant presence in his life from that day until this. Throughout all these centuries, you have been enough for him. Have faith, my friend."

Michael nodded. "I guess maybe I needed to hear the words out loud. When I'm with them, I don't question what we're doing, but I wonder how much of that is because of what they are."

"Probably most of it," Gabriel replied. "What do you feel for Irdu and Ardat?"

"Lust, desire."

"Love?"

"No."

"And you still love Lucifer?"

"Of course, that goes without saying. I can't even imagine life without him."

Gabriel wrapped his arm round Michael's shoulder and hugged him close to his side. "Keep loving him as much as you do right now, and one day you'll bring him home."

"Do you *really* believe that?" Michael whispered.

"Don't you?"

"I used to, but now I wonder if love is enough."

"Don't let your doubts lead you from your path. Everyone can be saved, even your newest lovers."

Gabriel always seemed to know the right thing to say.

Michael wondered whether anything ever bothered him and if he ever doubted himself. He smiled as he recalled something Machidiel had once said to him, a comment about how Michael always seemed calm. Things weren't always as they appeared. For all Michael knew, Gabriel battled inner conflicts too. The thought didn't sit well with Michael. Why wouldn't Gabriel confide in him if that were the case?

"What's with the frown?" Gabriel asked.

"Why don't you ever confide in me?" Michael replied without thinking.

Gabriel laughed. "Where did that come from? You know everything about me."

"I don't even know if you're seeing anyone at the moment," Michael said. "You haven't mentioned anyone in years."

"That's because I've not been involved with anyone in years."

"Aren't you lonely?"

"Sometimes, but I can find company when I need to."

"Who?"

"No one you know," Gabriel said. "Why do you want to know about me all of a sudden?"

"Because I'm trying not to be so self-absorbed. If you ever wanted to talk to me about your troubles, I want you to know I'm here for you."

"I know, but I promise, I don't have any troubles to talk about."

"Are you sure?"

Gabriel hesitated just a little too long.

"What is it?"

Gabriel stared at the clouds. "I worry I'm not a good leader for the archangels."

"You're doing a better job than I ever did."

"You underestimate your own abilities. Who do the lesser angels come to for guidance?"

"Whoever happens to be available?"

"No, they go to you," Gabriel said. "You're more approachable than the rest of us."

"Being easy to talk to doesn't make me a good leader."

"The angels would follow you anywhere, and you know it. I think you should resume your previous position as our official leader."

Michael hung his head. "I don't know."

"I've called a meeting for us to vote on it."

"You've what? Are you sure you want to give up the post?"

"Positive. Now, come on, let's start pruning the roses round the gazebo."

Michael followed Gabriel and soon they were back at work, and if Gabriel seemed to be gathering together a large bouquet of roses, Michael wouldn't comment on it. He hoped whoever they were for appreciated the gift, as well as the archangel who had grown them.

* * * *

Michael fidgeted in his chair as the archangels took their seats for Gabriel's meeting. He felt as nervous now as he had any time he had been caught in his lies about Lucifer. He had been a poor leader, and he couldn't understand why Gabriel thought he should take on the role again.

Behind him, the public gallery remained empty. This meeting was only between the archangels, for things would be discussed that weren't common knowledge, specifically Michael's relationship with Lucifer.

Gabriel took his seat last and called the rest of the archangels to order. "I've decided to relinquish my role as leader of the archangels," he said without preamble.

A whisper of dissent rippled through the room. Everyone seemed as surprised as Michael had been.

"Most of the lesser angels, and all mortals on Earth, believe Michael to be our leader still, and I think he should step back into the role he handled so well and for so many years."

"Absolutely not," Raguel said. "Unless he intends to give up consorting with Lucifer."

Gabriel glared at Raguel. "We're not here to discuss Michael's relationship."

"Maybe we should be," Raguel argued.

"I'm not giving up Lucifer," Michael stated clearly.

Raguel rolled his eyes. "What a surprise."

"I think Michael should take up the position again," Raphael interrupted.

Michael could barely contain his surprise.

Raphael shrugged. "As Gabriel said, most still believe you to be our leader anyway. I've certainly never bothered correcting anyone who has mistakenly referred to you as such."

"That's not a good enough reason," Raguel argued. "It simply means we should have been more vocal in announcing Gabriel as his successor."

"The reason we kept it quiet is because we wanted to avoid the questions of the lesser angels as to why," Gabriel pointed out. "Besides, I only ever took the post temporarily. I never intended to usurp Michael's place for this long. It's time for him to take it back."

Michael saw several archangels nod at Gabriel's words.

"But look what happened when I was in charge before," Michael said. "I didn't exactly set the best example, did I?"

Gabriel laughed. "You led us through the years we were at war and brought us victory and peace over the demons."

"Peace brought by deception and lies," Michael reminded him.

"Without you, Lucifer might still be leading an army of demons to this day," Raphael said quietly. "Only his feelings for you allowed him to walk away. I may not agree with all the choices you've made, but Gabriel is right. *You* were the one who ended the war."

"The war was centuries ago. I've done nothing worthy of a leader since, and plenty that isn't."

Gabriel smiled. "You're right, the war was centuries ago, as was the last occasion you tried to willfully deceive us. It's time for you to take your rightful place again. Are we all ready to vote?"

The archangels nodded and one by one they cast their votes. Raguel, unsurprisingly, voted no, but everyone else said yes. Gabriel turned to Michael last of all. "What do you say, Michael? Are you ready to take charge of us again?"

Michael laughed and shook his head. "I don't know that I ever had much control over you. Just answer me one question, truthfully."

"You dare to impugn Gabriel's honesty?" Raguel snapped.

Gabriel sighed but ignored his fellow archangel. "Ask and I'll try to be as honest as I can."

"Why do you really want this?" Michael asked. "And why now?"

"Because of what we talked about earlier."

"What do you mean?" Michael couldn't think of anything they had spoken about that could have led to this.

"You confided in me today — don't look at me like that, I'm not going to repeat what you told me — but because you took so long to tell me, it made me realize there are still barriers between us, and I think my taking your place is one of them. You are torn between your love for Lucifer and your friends here. The longer this continues, the stronger your ties to Lucifer and his world become, and the weaker your links to us. By resuming your role as our leader, however nominal the position is, your bonds with us are strengthened, and you're reminded of who you truly are and where you belong."

Michael ducked his head, his eyes watery at Gabriel's words.

He didn't see Gabriel leave his seat, didn't even know he had moved, until he felt his strong arms wrap around him.

"I don't want to lose you," Gabriel whispered into his ear. "You're my best friend and I love you. Be the archangel you were born to be, our leader."

Michael nodded. "Very well."

Gabriel stepped back and smiled. "Thank you. Now all is as it should be, or it will be when you bring Lucifer home."

Michael grinned back. "Does this mean I no longer have to work in your garden?"

Gabriel laughed. "I don't know about that, I kind of like having you around there."

Michael didn't admit it, but he enjoyed spending time in Gabriel's garden too. Besides, he wanted those bonds between himself and the other archangels to remain strong, and this would help.

"My place could do with redecorating," Raphael teased.

"Don't push your luck," Michael replied with laugh.

"What are you going to do for your first act as our official leader?" Gabriel asked.

"Call this meeting to a close and go for lunch?" Michael suggested, earning a round of applause from the room. Even Raguel managed to crack a smile. Perhaps there was hope for Michael yet.

Chapter Twelve

Michael soon settled back into his role as leader and he took great pains to maintain his relationships with the rest of the archangels, including Raguel.

He had finally told Raphael he was sharing his bed with Irdu and Ardat, and, while the look of utter horror on his face had almost been amusing, the renewed rift the knowledge had created between them wasn't funny at all. Of course, Michael should probably have told Raphael privately, as he had Gabriel, rather than blurting it out as he had. It had taken nearly ten years, but they had finally come to an understanding, where Michael kept the details of his sex life to himself, and Raphael lived in blissful ignorance of the same.

The incubus and succubus always expressed delight at being invited into Lucifer's chambers and they definitely kept things interesting.

Michael should have known it was only a matter of time before they went too far. Each time Irdu and Ardat joined them for a night of pleasure, his control came a little closer to slipping.

After thirty years, even Lucifer seemed to be affected by the all-encompassing lust of having two sex demons in their bed.

Lucifer pulled Ardat into a passionate kiss. Michael watched Lucifer and Ardat together and didn't feel the jealousy he had previously experienced. Desire coursed through him and he grabbed Irdu's hair and pulled him round to face him. Their kiss was hard and brutal, more teeth than lips as they battled for dominance with their tongues.

Then another mouth was on his and he tasted the familiar lips of his lover. The kiss softened and Michael moaned as Lucifer lowered him to the bed.

He felt two sets of lips on his balls and he canted his hips upward. The demons weren't supposed to suck him, and technically they weren't, but they were tiptoeing close to the line. If Lucifer saw them he would be furious. Michael should tell them to stop, but what they did to him felt so good.

Lucifer withdrew from the kiss and Michael whimpered.

The demons at his groin pulled back as well, but Michael could tell Lucifer had seen what they had been doing. He waited for the explosion, but it never came.

Michael caught the triumphant glance Irdu and Ardat exchanged, but it was seemingly lost on Lucifer, who stared at Michael as though he couldn't tear his eyes away from him for more than a second.

"Are you sure?" Michael asked, not entirely certain he could believe what he was seeing.

Lucifer tugged Michael into a sitting position and sat behind him, one leg on either side of Michael's thighs.

"Which one do you want to ride your cock?" Lucifer whispered into Michael's ear.

"Either, both," Michael breathed.

"Time to make a choice," Lucifer murmured.

"If I choose Ardat, can Irdu fuck me afterwards?" Michael asked. For a moment he wondered if he had gone too far with his suggestion, then Lucifer's erection nudged his rear and he knew his lover was equally turned on by the idea.

"Ride him, Ardat," Lucifer ordered.

The succubus gracefully crawled over the bed and lowered herself onto Michael's cock.

"Oh fuck." Michael gasped, savoring the sensation of burying himself in a woman for the first time in his life. It felt different from being inside Lucifer, but just as good. Her body opened to him easily, and he slid into her warmth.

Ardat rode him expertly, seeking her own pleasure. "You'll never know another woman like this," she said. "Only I can make *any* man want me. Even an archangel, who has known only men, cannot resist what I offer him."

Michael watched Irdu slide up behind Ardat and grope her breasts, toying with her nipples, and displaying them for Michael and Lucifer's enjoyment.

Ardat threw back her head, drawing power from Michael with each breath she took. Her hair cascaded down her back and she cried out as she climaxed.

Michael followed her a moment later, spilling his seed inside her willing body.

Irdu drew Ardat away and laid her down on the bed. "Suck them," he said, gesturing to her breasts. "I want to watch you do that before I take you."

Michael glanced at Lucifer who nodded, and the two of them dove eagerly onto Ardat's breasts, sucking at the peaks. Michael marveled at the way the buds hardened and peaked at even the slightest touch. They were far more sensitive than his own nubs or even Lucifer's.

Lucifer seemed equally enamored with Ardat's other breast and Michael wondered why they had not done this before.

Michael watched Irdu bend over Ardat's groin, part her thighs and bury his face between her legs.

Ardat gasped and clung to Michael and Lucifer by their hair.

Lucifer continued to pay homage to the succubus, but Michael craved something else. He could see Irdu's thick cock hanging between his legs and Michael's arse ached to feel it inside him.

When Ardat came for the second time, Irdu finally sat back and stared at Michael.

"Fuck me," Michael said.

He didn't wait for a response. He rolled onto his hands and knees, knowing Irdu would do as he asked. The demon had made no secret of the fact he wanted this.

Lucifer, leaving Ardat lost to her climax, knelt in front of Michael and held out his cock, stroking the length with slow, deliberate movements. Pre-cum already dripped from the tip and Michael leaned in to lap it up before the semen hit the covers.

Behind him, Irdu prepared him quickly. Michael pushed back against the rod at his arse.

"Fuck!" Michael swore when Irdu entered him.

"You're so beautiful, Michael," Lucifer said. "Irdu, fuck him hard."

Michael nodded. "Yes, oh yes."

Irdu took them at their word and began to pound Michael with a ferocity that sent him stumbling into Lucifer. "Scream for me, Michael," Irdu demanded.

Michael shouted, yelled, and screamed, his entire body thrumming with desire. Irdu fed from him, just as Ardat had, and some part of him could tell they took more power tonight than they ever had before. They couldn't drain him or kill him, so Michael let them.

Lucifer remained in front of him, his cock hovering near Michael's mouth. When a particularly powerful thrust moved him forward, Michael took the opportunity of swallowing Lucifer's dick, taking it deep into his throat.

"Michael, fuck!" Lucifer cried.

Michael gulped around his length and Lucifer gurgled in response.

Irdu didn't falter or break his stride at all. He continued to fuck Michael as hard as he could, his cock hitting Michael's sweet spot again and again.

Lucifer came down his throat and Michael reluctantly let his sensitive flesh go.

Michael howled as Irdu drove into him again and again. His own shaft ached to be touched, Michael didn't care who by.

Then Lucifer took Michael's face in his hands and kissed him. When Lucifer tried to pull away, Michael raised one of his hands and took hold of the back of Lucifer's head, keeping him in place.

Behind him, Irdu didn't seem to be showing any sign of slowing his pace. Michael's arse had never taken such a pounding. Sex with Lucifer had been rough on occasion, but nothing compared to this. Irdu's stamina was legendary for a reason, no one, angel or demon, could keep up with him.

"How are you doing?" Lucifer asked against Michael's lips.

Michael groaned. "My cock...touch...please..."

Lucifer didn't need telling twice. He eased Michael onto his knees and Irdu slowed just enough to ensure he didn't pull out. Lucifer took Michael's erection in his hand and Michael screamed in pleasure, coming instantly at the touch. Then everything went black.

* * * *

When Michael came round he found himself cradled in Lucifer's arms and the two sex demons had departed. For the first time in what seemed like years his head felt clear of lust. He shifted slightly and felt Lucifer's stiff erection beneath him. His own spent cock twitched. Maybe not entirely clear of lust, then.

"Welcome back," Lucifer said with a smile. "How are you doing?"

"What happened?"

"You passed out when you came. According to Irdu it's a common occurrence when he fucks mortals. He left here rather smug about his prowess."

Michael let Lucifer help him sit up. He winced at the pain in his sore arse.

"Sore?" Lucifer asked.

"What do you think?" Michael muttered. "I feel well and truly fucked."

"You were," Lucifer reminded him. "Here, let me help."

Michael nodded and spread his legs so Lucifer could reach between them. A few soft touches from his lover, combined with his whispered words, and the pain receded as though it had never been there. "Thank you."

Lucifer smiled but declined to comment.

Michael curled up at Lucifer's side and rested his head on his shoulder. "Did you send the others away?"

"No, they left of their own accord. They had got what they wanted."

"What do you mean?"

"To fuck and be fucked by an archangel," Lucifer explained. "There are few demons who can claim to have experienced such a thing. Just three, in fact, and they were all here in this bed last night."

Michael frowned. "Why do I feel as if I've been used?"

"Because you were," Lucifer replied. "Demons are self-serving at the core and Irdu and Ardat are no exception. The power they syphoned from you last night will give them a boost for the next millennium. They won't be back here again any time soon."

Michael had thought there might be a chance he could save the two sex demons and bring them back to the light. Finding out they had simply wanted to feed from him, before casting him aside, didn't sit right with him.

"Don't be so disheartened," Lucifer said. "You enjoyed last night, didn't you?"

Michael nodded. "Yes, I did. What about you?"

Lucifer remained quiet for several minutes, and Michael wondered if he intended to answer the question.

"Yes, I enjoyed it, more than I thought I would. Watching Irdu fuck you aroused me in ways I never imagined. And before, when Ardat rode you, I couldn't tear my eyes away."

"No jealousy?" Michael asked, just to be sure.

"No, but…"

"But what?"

Lucifer chewed on his lip. "Last night was fucking, pure and simple. I'm not jealous of that, because it's different from what there is between us."

Michael understood what Lucifer said because he felt

exactly the same. When he and Lucifer came together, particularly when they were alone, they made love. Michael had always understood the difference, and he smiled at the thought that Lucifer did too, even if his lover couldn't quite put it into words.

They slept a while in each other's arms, and when they woke they made love together, slowly, steadily, and gently. After the night before it was exactly what they needed.

When Michael returned home, leaving Lucifer with a last lingering kiss at the entrance to the tunnel, he had no regrets at all.

* * * *

Michael talked to Gabriel and Raphael about the sex demons' departure from Lucifer's bed. Neither of his friends appeared surprised at his revelation.

"They're demons," Raphael pointed out. "They played the two of you like a pair of fine instruments and you let them."

"Raphael, please," Gabriel chided.

"He's right," Michael interrupted. "They've been using their powers on us the whole time, ensuring our desire for them remained ever present, even when they weren't with us. They have the most addictive personalities I've ever come across. They wanted to feed from me and I let them."

"Are they going to try and take the throne of the Underworld?" Gabriel asked. "We can't have another sex demon on the throne."

Michael shook his head. "I think they just want to ensure their own survival. They've been lying low since the present king took the throne, and I believe they'll continue to do so."

"If you hear anything to the contrary, you must tell us," Gabriel warned.

"I will."

"What about Lucifer?" Raphael asked. "Is he any closer

to being saved?"

Michael didn't know the answer to that question. He didn't feel as if he was losing Lucifer to the Underworld, but nor did he believe he was making any progress in bringing him back to the light.

"You'll get there," Gabriel assured him kindly. "Have faith."

Michael nodded, but he couldn't help seeing the expression of skepticism on Raphael's face. He suspected his own might be similar.

* * * *

Michael didn't expect to see Irdu and Ardat again and didn't mourn their loss. Lucifer was enough for him. It therefore came as a surprise to find Ardat standing in front of him as he walked down a busy street on Earth some six months later.

Ardat, who had never been even remotely modest, wore a long hooded cloak that covered her from head to toe. If the clothes hadn't looked so out of place in the modern world, Michael might not have noticed her at all.

"Michael," Ardat said. "I must talk to you privately."

Michael gestured toward a nearby alley, but the demon shook her head.

"It has to be somewhere no demon can see."

"There's no such place," Michael replied.

"You lie."

Michael sighed. "The only place I know is the realm of angels, and if you set foot there, you'll be killed."

"No, I won't," Ardat replied.

Michael raised an eyebrow in question, but Ardat stood her ground.

"Take me to your realm, in chains if you have to. I throw myself on the mercy of the archangels."

"Do you realize what you're saying?" Michael asked.

"Yes." Ardat held out her hands, her wrists together.

Michael shook his head but did as she asked, binding her wrists together and also her ankles. Then he took her to the realm of angels, despite his reservations.

As soon as he arrived, Michael summoned the archangels to their chamber.

"I wished to speak to you alone," Ardat complained.

"If you hope to leave this realm alive, you'll speak in front of all the archangels," Michael told her. "Should you be discovered alone with me in this realm your life would be forfeit immediately."

Ardat took the seat in the center of the room as the rest of the archangels filed into the room, expressions of confusion on all their faces.

Michael took his own seat, facing Ardat. "For those who don't know her, this is Ardat, leader of the succubi. She wishes to speak to us."

"I wish to speak to *you*, alone," Ardat corrected.

"Since you refused to tell me what you want on Earth, you have two choices. You speak to me here, or not at all."

Ardat glared at him and Michael realized this was the first time he had been in her presence when she wasn't using her powers on him. While he could still appreciate her beauty, he felt no sexual desire for her at all.

"I wish to be hidden from the demons," Ardat said.

"You wish to come to the light?" Michael asked.

Ardat snorted and sneered. "Hardly. This isn't something I want to do—it's more of a necessity in my rather unique circumstances."

"And what circumstances are those?"

Ardat stood and reached up awkwardly with her bound wrists to unfasten the tie of her cloak. The fabric dropped to the floor, revealing her usual attire beneath. The beaded gown left her breasts entirely exposed and did little to hide her modesty. They also revealed a secret the cloak had previously hidden.

"I'm carrying your child," the demon declared.

Michael opened and closed his mouth several times while

the archangels reacted in shock. Michael had only told Gabriel and Raphael about his relationship with Ardat. It was obvious from the gasps and exclamations they had kept his confidence in this matter.

"Lying demon," Metatron shouted and the rest of the archangels echoed his words.

"Quiet!" Michael roared, bringing the room to order once more.

The archangels settled down immediately.

"Why do you believe the child is mine?" Michael asked.

Before Ardat could reply, Metatron interrupted again. "Are you saying this creature *could* be carrying your baby?"

Michael turned to Metatron, two seats away. "Yes, that's *exactly* what I'm saying."

"I can't see why anyone is surprised by this," Raguel said. "Michael's will has always been weak, and this is just another example of why he should never have resumed his position as our leader."

Michael stared coldly at Raguel until he lapsed into silence. Turning back to Ardat, he gestured for her to speak.

"I have carried many children over the centuries," Ardat said. "Some have been Irdu's, some the spawn of other demons, others have been part mortal. After so many I know the signs to show what manner of being I carry in my womb. This time what I carry is different—I feel your aura inside me, just as surely as I felt your cock within me the night we came together."

Gabriel approached Ardat and held out his hand toward her slightly rounded belly. "May I?"

The demon gave her consent and Gabriel touched her for several moments. When he stepped away he approached Michael.

"She speaks the truth," Gabriel said, quietly so no one else in the room would hear him. "You know what this means?"

Michael nodded. A child born of a demon and an angel wasn't entirely unheard of. There had been several born during the last few centuries. What made this different was that Michael wasn't any lesser angel, he was an archangel, and Ardat was the leader of all female sex demons. The child would be in danger from the moment he or she was born.

"The Underworld won't be safe for the child," Michael said. "The aura will mark him or her as part angel, and a target."

"I'm surprised they haven't already realized what Ardat carries," Gabriel commented.

"She and Irdu have been feeding on me for years," Michael replied. "The angelic power boosts they have enjoyed will have helped to mask the child, but once it's born that will no longer be the case."

Michael faced Ardat once more. "Does Irdu know?"

"He's aware of the pregnancy, but that's all."

"Where is he now?"

Ardat shrugged. "I've no idea. He has not been in my bed for a couple of months. He's probably with one of his other lovers. He tends to crave men when I'm with child. He'll come back to me in time."

"What do you want from Michael?" Gabriel asked.

"I wish to be hidden from all demons until the birth, and afterwards I want Michael to take the child and keep it safe."

"A child cannot live in this realm," Gabriel said. "In the realm of angels no one ever ages, including children."

"I don't care where you send the child, as long as it is away from demonic dangers."

"Don't you wish to raise the child yourself?" Raphael asked. "If you were to come to the light, we could hide you both on Earth."

Michael nodded. "Raphael is correct. While we cannot hide a demon on Earth, as a mortal we could shield you."

"Demon is what I am," Ardat replied. "I have no wish to come to the light."

"Why not? You clearly care for the child you carry, and putting another before yourself is one of the first steps to being saved. Some might say it is the most important one."

Ardat visibly recoiled. "Carrying the child of an angel, having so much goodness inside me, is making me weak."

Michael turned to Gabriel. "Any suggestions?"

"Can't I stay here?" Ardat asked. "Just until the birth?"

"You'll not age while you're here," Michael told her. "If you were to remain in this realm, the child would never be born."

"Then you can't help me?" Ardat rose from her seat.

Michael halted her with a raise of his hand. "You cannot stay here, and we cannot shield a demon on Earth, but there is someone who can hide you."

"Are you talking about God?" Ardat spat out the final word as though it left a foul taste in her mouth.

"He cannot help you unless you come back to the light," Michael replied. "I'm talking about Lucifer."

"Absolutely not." Ardat looked as if she might bolt, but the chains preventing her from making a run for the doors also stopped her from exiting the realm with her powers.

"As you know, Lucifer is most adept at hiding. He's also powerful enough to protect you from the demons in the Underworld."

"Lucifer has grown weak over the centuries," Ardat replied. "He is not the demon he once was."

Michael smiled. "No, he isn't, but he *is* a fallen angel, the only one of his kind, and his powers eclipse ours. He is the only one who can hide you."

"And what do you think he'll say when he discovers I'm carrying your child?" Ardat asked. "I doubt he'll be pleased."

Michael shrugged. "Lucifer, if you'll recall, was present at the conception. Since he doesn't require a lesson on the birds and the bees, I doubt he'll be as shocked as you seem to think."

"Perhaps we should summon him here?" Raphael suggested. "I must admit I'm curious to see his reaction."

Michael would rather have spoken to Lucifer privately, but

with the rest of the archangels nodding he acknowledged it would be best to deal with the situation entirely openly.

Lucifer appeared in the room instantly after Michael called him. He glared at the archangels in front of him, though his expression softened when his eyes landed on Michael. "Whatever it is, I didn't do it."

Gabriel chuckled. "I think we're all in agreement that, in this case, Michael is the one who *did it*."

Michael glared at his best friend.

"Did what?" Lucifer asked.

Michael sighed and pointed behind Lucifer.

Lucifer made a choking noise as he took in the sight of the pregnant demon in the center of the room. When he turned back to Michael he gave him a smirk. "Congratulations, or is it commiserations?"

"I think we'll stick with the former," Michael replied. "Ardat is concerned for the safety of our child."

Lucifer snorted. "I suspect her own skin is her primary concern."

"Nevertheless, she has come to us for protection."

"And what does that have to do with me?" Lucifer asked.

"The archangels cannot hide one demon from the others. It isn't within our power. It *is* within yours."

"You want me to hide her from the entire Underworld?"

"Yes."

Lucifer shook his head. "Ardat is one of the most popular demons alive. Her disappearance will be noticed. In fact, I'd already heard rumors she hadn't been seen at the usual functions. Now I see why."

"Can you hide her or not?" Raphael asked. "If you can't, say so now."

"My chambers are shielded from any demonic spying. She could stay in them for the duration of the pregnancy."

"I would be honored to share your bed again," Ardat offered.

"I never said anything about that," Lucifer snapped. "I have no intention of staying there with you. I'm sure I can find a cavern to hole up in for a few months."

Michael didn't like the sound of that at all. "Perhaps Lucifer could stay here with me until after the birth?"

"No!" Raguel shouted. "Demons have no place in this realm."

Michael glared at the archangel and Gabriel placed a calming hand on his arm before facing Raguel. "If Lucifer gives up his home to Ardat, he'll need somewhere to stay. I think he should stay with Michael."

"He doesn't have to leave his home," Raguel said. "Who will keep an eye on this demon and assist her with the birth if Lucifer is lounging around on Michael's beach?"

"Do I look like a damn midwife?" Lucifer snarled.

"I don't need any man's help with giving birth," Ardat added. "I've managed perfectly well in the past with my attendants."

"Where are they now?" Michael asked. "Do you trust them?"

"I only summon them when the time comes, and no, I don't trust them. Perhaps you might provide a couple of angels to attend me?"

Gabriel nodded. "I'm sure that can be arranged. So, everything is agreed? Ardat will move into Lucifer's shielded chambers in the Underworld, Lucifer will stay here with Michael, and we'll provide a couple of angels to assist with the birth."

"I don't agree with Lucifer staying here," Raguel reminded him.

"Yes, we know," Gabriel replied. "Does anyone else have any objections?"

The room remained silent.

"Then it's settled," Gabriel said.

"There's just one more thing we need to sort out," Michael said. "Who's going to raise the child?"

Lucifer shook his head. "Don't look at me. I don't do dirty nappies and midnight feeds. As soon as it's born, I want it out of my chambers."

Michael chuckled. "I'm sure no one would expect you to raise the child, even if it were safe for him or her to remain in the Underworld, which it isn't."

"I have an idea," Raphael said quietly from his seat. "If you could come with me Michael, we need to pay someone a visit."

Lucifer promised to escort Ardat to his chambers and return to Michael's home. Michael agreed to meet him at his beach later and followed Raphael.

"Where are we going?" Michael asked.

"Earth. You might want to change into modern clothing."

Michael did as Raphael suggested with merely a thought. "Can you be a little more specific about where?"

"Italy."

Michael sighed. "Are you being deliberately evasive?"

Raphael laughed. "Sorry, but I thought you might enjoy the surprise."

"You don't think I've had enough surprises for one day?"

Raphael led him down the path toward a busy square. People milled about the place and a group of children played a game of tag. At first Michael didn't see him, but then Tristan turned his head and the spark of recognition lit.

"Machidiel and his partners are living here?" Michael asked.

"For about a year now—Alastor's work keeps them traveling around a lot." Raphael glanced at his wristwatch. "Machidiel and Alastor should be here soon."

"Have they had any more demon trouble?"

"No, not since we stepped in to send a certain nuisance packing ten years ago. They've been living good lives, though they aren't as complete as they might like. Adoption is hard enough for two gay men—when there are three in the relationship, it creates an additional obstacle."

Michael suddenly understood why they were here and what Raphael was suggesting.

"Two former demons and a former angel," Raphael

commented. "What better protection for such a unique child? And there is the added bonus of them being acquainted with you already, so they won't mind you visiting. You could be a part of your child's life, instead of simply watching events unfold from the sidelines."

"They would do that for me?" Michael asked.

Raphael smiled. "Why don't we go ask them?"

Michael saw that Alastor and Machidiel had arrived on the square, where they greeted Tristan with hugs and smiles. They seemed very happy together.

"Good afternoon," Raphael greeted the three mortal men. "How are you enjoying Italy?"

"Raphael!" Machidiel gaped at the archangel. "And Michael, what are you doing here?"

"We're here to see you, of course," Raphael replied.

"Is there something wrong?" Machidiel asked.

"No," Michael assured him quickly. "But Raphael believes we might be able to help each other."

"Let's go somewhere we can talk quietly," Raphael said.

"Our villa isn't far," Machidiel said, pointing the way.

The five men drew plenty of stares as they walked down the street. Michael was pleased to see that neither Machidiel nor his lovers took any notice of the appreciative glances sent in their direction. Three in a relationship had to be tough, but they seemed to have things under control.

Once they arrived at the villa, Tristan poured them each a glass of wine and they sat in the garden, enjoying the evening sun.

"So, what's this all about?" Machidiel asked.

Raphael smirked at Michael. "Do you want to tell them, or shall I?"

Michael rolled his eyes. "Go ahead, I can tell you're just dying to blurt it out anyway."

Raphael grinned and turned to the others. "Michael's knocked up a demon."

Michael nearly choked on his wine. Machidiel and his partners appeared as if they had swallowed their tongues.

"Um," Machidiel stammered. "I thought you were with, er, Lucifer."

"I am, but you'll recall Ardat?"

"The leader of the succubi?"

"Yes, that's her."

"Then the demonic duo are still sharing a bed with you and Lucifer?" Machidiel asked, though Raphael's revelation made the answer to the question obvious.

Alastor and Tristan remained quiet, probably because most of this was news to them. They had no memories of their lives as demons, although Machidiel had no doubt provided them with the essentials, which wouldn't include details of Michael's tangled mess of a love life.

"Ardat and her incubus counterpart, Irdu, shared our bed until earlier this year. It would appear that during our last night together, I managed to impregnate her. She carries a child that is part demon and part angel, a combination that makes him or her a target. Ardat is in hiding until after the birth, but she cannot raise my child in the Underworld. And, as you know, no one ages in the realm of angels. The only option, therefore, is for the child to be raised on Earth, by someone who knows of the existence of angels and demons, and the realms the rest of the human race live in ignorance of."

"Are you asking what I think you are?" Machidiel asked.

"I'm asking if you, Alastor, and Tristan would consider raising my son or daughter." Even as he spoke the words he felt his stomach sink. Could he give up his child so easily?

"And let Michael stop by to visit, of course," Raphael added. "Because I think it's a foregone conclusion he'll lose his heart to this baby the moment he takes him or her in his arms."

Machidiel took Michael's hand and squeezed it. "My partners and I will need to discuss this, but I thank you for the honor, whatever we decide."

"Thank *you* for even considering doing this," Michael replied. "I promise I'll provide whatever you need, official papers, funds, whatever you require."

"I have a question," Tristan said.

"Of course, what is it?"

"When you say this child is half demon, what sort of demonic powers are we talking about?"

It was a fair question, and Michael wasn't sure he had all the answers. This was unprecedented. "I'm not sure the child will have any demonic powers, but if he or she does, they will no doubt be of a similar nature to those of Ardat—in other words, they'll be of a sexual nature and will manifest when the child reaches maturity."

Michael hoped the demonic aspect of his child didn't put the three men off the idea. If they refused, Michael hoped Raphael had another plan up his sleeve, because Michael had nothing.

Machidiel invited the two archangels to stay to dinner, and the five men shared a pleasant meal together. Afterward, Michael and Raphael left the trio to talk things over. They didn't have to make a decision right away, there was a little time before the baby arrived. It would also give Michael time to think about whether he could go through with this at all.

Chapter Thirteen

When Michael returned to his home, he found Lucifer sitting on his beach, staring out over the waves, just as Michael enjoyed doing. Gabriel watched the fallen angel from the kitchen, no doubt keeping an eye on him. It would not be a good idea to let Lucifer wander the realm alone. Who knew what mischief he could get into?

"Where have you been?" Gabriel asked. "I think Lucifer is getting impatient."

"Raphael and I were visiting Machidiel and his partners."

"Ah, I see."

"Do you?"

Gabriel nodded. "I can't think of anyone better to raise your child."

"They haven't agreed yet, and neither have I."

Gabriel patted him on the shoulder. "They will, but why wouldn't you?"

"I never thought I'd be a father. This is probably the only chance I'll get. Do I really want to give that up?"

"You cannot live as an angel on Earth," Gabriel said.

"I know." If he wanted to take on the role of a father and give his child a normal life, he would have to do so as a mortal.

"Could you really give up your wings, not to mention Lucifer?" Gabriel asked.

"Yes, I could. If the child were a mortal it wouldn't even be a question. My concern is that without my powers I can't protect him or her if I need to. My child will be a target and as a mortal I'd be powerless."

"You know what Lucifer would say?"

"Lucifer is selfish. He would say whatever suits him."

"Perhaps you should go talk to him. Maybe he'll surprise us."

Michael nodded, said goodbye to his best friend, and went to join Lucifer on the beach.

"Are you settled in?" Michael asked.

Lucifer smiled at him and kissed him on the lips. "I am now. Where have you been?"

Michael explained, again, where Raphael had taken him and the reason why. Lucifer, predictably, thought it a marvelous idea. With someone else raising Michael's child, it meant Michael could devote more of his time to keeping Lucifer happy. Michael had no doubt Lucifer's response was selfish in origin, though he wished it were not so.

"It's an option," Michael agreed. "I'm not sure whether they'll agree, though, and even if they do, I'm not sure I'm ready to give my child to someone else to raise."

"You wouldn't have time to raise a child on Earth as well as attend to your archangel duties."

"No, but I wasn't thinking of trying that. Besides, angels are forbidden from residing permanently on Earth without giving up our wings. After a year I would have to become mortal."

"Of course you must," Lucifer agreed. "It's one of the many rules He has decreed with which I disagree."

Michael had no wish to argue about the laws the angels lived by. "The earth is the kingdom of man. If an angel wishes to live amongst mankind, he or she must live as they do, without powers. I accept that and will make my choice accordingly."

"You'd give up your wings?"

"Maybe."

Lucifer shook his head. "You're an archangel. It's all you've ever known, all you've ever been."

"I know."

"You don't even know if you could survive as a human."

"I guess I'd find out."

"What would happen to us if you gave up your wings?" Lucifer asked. "You couldn't visit the Underworld, and I couldn't go to Earth unless one of the other archangels escorted me, and we both know how unlikely that would be. We'd never see each other."

"I know, but that's not what's important."

Lucifer glared at him. "I thought *I* was important to you."

"You are, of course you are."

"But I'm never first in your life, am I?" Lucifer muttered. "How many more hundreds of years are you going to put everyone else before me?"

Michael sighed and buried his face in his knees. "How many hundreds of years is it going to take before you believe I love you?"

"I know you love me, but that's not what I'm asking. I'm tired of being the last one you consider whenever you need to make an important decision in your life."

"That's not true and you know it," Michael snapped. "I am *always* putting you first, because you make such a fuss when I don't."

"You're seriously considering giving up your wings to raise this child, aren't you?"

"Yes, I am."

"What's stopping you?" Lucifer huffed under his breath. "Obviously your feelings for me don't factor into your decision."

Michael had heard enough. "Is that what you think? *Really*, Lucifer? I should be considering how my choice will affect my recruits. I need to think about whether Gabriel will take on the role of leader of the archangels again. I need to be sure I can protect a child without my wings and powers. But the only thing I can think about right now is how you'd survive if I did this!"

Lucifer cringed away from him as Michael lost his temper for the first time in centuries.

"The entire world does *not* revolve around you," Michael raged. "I'm going to be a father and, whether you like it or not, my child *is* going to come before you. The sooner you accept it, the better."

Michael didn't wait for Lucifer to reply. He stormed back to the house and crawled into bed. He lay awake for hours, but Lucifer didn't join him. Finally, shortly before dawn, Michael went to the window overlooking the beach. Lucifer hadn't moved from his place on the sand. Michael yearned to join him, but he didn't want to fight again. Instead he dressed and went for a walk.

He didn't know how he wound up in Gabriel's gazebo, but he was still there when the archangel rose and found him there the next morning.

"Aren't you supposed to be monitoring Lucifer?" Gabriel asked.

"We had a fight."

"Already?" Gabriel shook his head. "You've not even been living together for a day. How are you already fighting?"

"He doesn't like the idea of me giving up my wings to raise the baby myself."

"Lucifer is nothing if not predictable."

"I know. I should have waited before bringing it up, let him get used to the idea of me being a father."

"Should haves are a waste of time," Gabriel said. "He knows what you're considering and he has to deal with it."

"I should go back and talk to him," Michael replied. "Not to mention, as you rightly pointed out, I'm supposed to be keeping an eye on him."

"I suspect Lucifer has too much on his mind right now to be considering recruiting angels to his cause."

"I hope so."

Gabriel walked Michael back through the garden. His presence was reassuring as always, but ultimately Michael had to make his own choices and follow his heart. He wished he had any idea as to what he should do.

Michael arrived home to find Lucifer asleep in his bed. Exhausted after his own sleepless night, Michael slipped in beside him and wrapped his arms around his lover. He closed his eyes and slept at last. Maybe things would look better when he wasn't so tired.

* * * *

They slept until early afternoon, and although Michael could have stayed in bed for another hour or two, he had to head to the training grounds. Lucifer came with him, causing quite a stir amongst the lesser angels, none of whom had seen him before. He radiated power and was clearly one of the reclusive favored ones. Michael didn't introduce him to his recruits and no one spoke to Lucifer, who watched silently from the sidelines. The archangels had decided it was for the best not to draw attention to Lucifer if they could avoid it.

"What are you going to do about them?" Lucifer asked after Michael had finished work for the day. "Your recruits, I mean."

"The other archangels will take care of them for me."

"Can they teach them everything you can?"

"No, just as I couldn't teach an angel everything Gabriel, or Raphael, or any archangel could."

Michael wanted to take Lucifer's hand as they walked along the main concourse, but he didn't dare. They drew enough stares from the angels they passed already. Michael had no intention of feeding the rumors by revealing the true nature of his involvement with Lucifer. Even if most didn't recognize the fallen angel, there were some who were old enough to remember him, at least if they looked closely enough. The fewer angels who knew they were lovers, the safer it would be for everyone concerned.

"Let's check on Ardat," Michael suggested when they arrived back at the beach.

They visited the demon for a short while, just long enough to ensure she was settled and safe. She made it clear she didn't want them to disturb her and they soon left her and headed back to the realm of angels.

"Dinner on Earth?" Michael asked.

Lucifer agreed and Michael took him to Earth, finding a pleasant, quiet restaurant. They ordered their meals and ate in comfortable silence.

Only when they had begun dessert did Lucifer raise the subject Michael had hoped to avoid for at least the duration of the evening.

"What will you do if you give up your wings?" Lucifer asked.

"Raise my child, of course."

"I know that. I meant for a job, to earn money. Where are you planning on living?"

"I don't know. I've not thought about it yet."

"You'll be living as a human—don't you think it's something you should be thinking about? You've never lived without your powers."

"Neither have you," Michael pointed out.

"No, and I don't intend to. But look at it this way. We're sitting here in a restaurant you didn't have to book a table at, because you used your powers to get us in here. When we've finished you'll be able to pay because your wallet will have the exact right amount of money in it, no matter what we ordered. When you go to your cupboards at home, they always have what you need in them. Other than the occasional treat you buy here on Earth, you never have to shop and you don't have to hold down a job to make money. You've never had to pay bills. You have no idea what it's like out there."

"And you do?" Michael countered. "You don't exactly have a nine-to-five job yourself."

"I'm a demon. I know humans and human needs, because I preyed on those needs for years."

"Most of the human race manages to survive without angelic or demonic assistance. I'm sure I'd be able to get by."

Lucifer looked as if he wanted to say something else, but for some reason he held his tongue. Michael tried prompting him, yet Lucifer remained stubbornly silent.

Michael pretended to let the subject drop as they sipped their coffee. In reality he did something he had never done before. He used his powers to delve into Lucifer's mind to see what he was thinking.

"He doesn't even realize he'll be a bigger target than his child. Every demon alive will want the honor of slaying the archangel Michael. I won't be able to protect him. I'll be trapped in the Underworld while he's vulnerable on Earth. They'll both be dead within a year, and I'll be powerless to prevent it. I'm going to lose him. I'm going to lose him. How can I be expected to watch him die?"

Michael closed his eyes and disconnected from Lucifer's mind. Spoken out loud, Michael would have brushed aside Lucifer's words as his usual selfish attitude, thinking only of how it would affect him. That his lover had kept them to himself made Michael consider them closer.

Could Lucifer be correct? Would Michael be targeted by demons if he gave up his wings?

Who was he kidding? Of course he would. Michael had been the one to lead the angels during the great war. He was instantly recognizable to every demon alive. As soon as word got out he had given up his wings the demons would search every corner of the earth until they found him. He would be powerless to stop them killing him and the child.

A child could be hidden, especially if only a select few knew of its existence. Michael was another matter entirely. He couldn't expect the other archangels to neglect their duties to protect him, even though they wouldn't hesitate to do so if he were to ask.

Michael didn't speak of what he had heard of Lucifer's thoughts and his lover never brought the subject up. They returned home and Michael took Lucifer to bed, making love to him until the early hours of the morning.

For the next few days they settled into a routine and Michael mulled over the decision of what he should do. He didn't want to give up his child, but he had to do what was best for the baby. Leaving Lucifer under the watchful eye of Raphael, Michael headed to Gabriel's garden, seeking his best friend's advice once more.

"Do you think I'd be in danger from demons if I chose to live as a mortal?" Michael asked, getting right to the point.

"Yes, I do." Gabriel sounded sure of himself. "You've been a thorn in the side of every demon who has crossed your path since the day Lucifer fell from grace. They'll be queueing up for the pleasure of killing you if they discover you've made yourself vulnerable by living as a human. You know, as well as I do, every angel can hide their angelic aura from demons, but only while we retain our powers. If an angel gives up his or her wings, they lose the power to hide their aura, and it shines out like a beacon for demons everywhere. As an archangel, your aura will be the brightest on Earth. And, while most former angels are ignored by demons, that won't be the case with you. Your face is instantly recognizable to everyone in the Underworld and that will be your downfall."

"My child will have the same aura," Michael pointed out. "He or she will be equally vulnerable."

"If the child is raised by Machidiel and his partners, any demon will assume they have used a surrogate and the aura is inherited from Machidiel. No one is likely to suspect the child might be yours."

"They might if I visit them as frequently as I would wish."

"Then you'll have to be careful," Gabriel said. "I know you'll always put the welfare of your child first, even if it means stepping back and letting others take on the role you would like to have for your own."

"I feel as if I'm being selfish by not taking on the duties that are mine."

Gabriel shook his head. "If you were a regular human, with a child on the way, you know as well as I do you'd never shirk from your responsibilities. These are unusual circumstances, and you're not just some random mortal. You're an archangel, and like it or not, you have many enemies. You need to do what's best to protect your child from those forces."

"I know. I just wish the decision wasn't quite so hard. I'm ready to give up my wings and face up to my responsibilities."

"If you feel that's the best course of action, I'll stand by your decision."

"I don't know if it is," Michael admitted.

"Well, you have a while yet before you need to make your choice, perhaps things will seem clearer once the baby is born."

Michael nodded. He hoped that would be the case, because right now he felt torn in different directions and he had no idea what to do for the best.

* * * *

Michael paced on his beach, waiting for news from the Underworld. Ardat had refused to allow his presence in the chamber when she went into labor, and no amount of arguing would change her mind. Instead, he was forced to wait for the news from the two lesser angels who had gone into the Underworld to assist with the birth.

Finally, one of the angels appeared in the entrance. "It's a girl," she called as she waved Michael over.

Michael ran to the tunnel, Lucifer close at his heels.

He was halfway down the steps when he realized Lucifer was no longer behind him. He wanted to see his child, but he had a duty to ensure Lucifer wasn't left unattended in the realm of angels. Sighing with frustration, he did an about face and hurried back up the stairs. He met Lucifer at the entrance.

"What are you doing?" Michael asked.

"Just taking a last look at the sea," Lucifer replied. "Ardat will be going back to her former residence, and I'll be expected to return to the Underworld. No more playing house with you, I'm afraid."

"I'm sure she'll need a day or two to recover," Michael pointed out.

"She's a demon," Lucifer reminded him. "She's no doubt already recovered and eager to be on her way."

Michael didn't believe him, but when they arrived in Lucifer's chambers he discovered he wasn't far from the truth.

Ardat was out of bed, dressed in her usual attire and brushing out her long hair. If it weren't for the newborn baby sleeping in the arms of the angel, Michael would never have believed the demon had just given birth.

"Ah, good, there you are," Ardat said. "You have a daughter. Lucifer, thank you for the use of your chambers. I'll be leaving in just a few minutes, if you'd be so kind as to fetch my belongings from your bathroom."

Lucifer gaped at the succubus, not because of her eagerness to depart, which he had predicted a few moments before, but rather, Michael suspected, because she spoke to him as if he were an errand boy.

"Don't you want to know about our plans for raising the child?" Michael asked.

"Not especially," Ardat replied as she began applying her makeup.

"But she's your child," Michael reminded her.

"Yes, I know. I've just spent fourteen hours in labor, giving birth to her. I've done my part, now it's your turn."

Ardat rose, gathered together her belongings, and took the items from one of the other angels, who had gone to get them from the bathroom for her. "I'll leave you to it."

"Wait!" Michael grabbed her arm. "What about your daughter? You haven't even told us her name."

"You can name her," Ardat said. "I'm just relieved to be feeling my old self again. No more angelic influence over me, thank Lucifer."

"Don't thank me for it," Lucifer muttered.

Ardat shrugged and strolled toward the door. "Farewell, lovers."

"She just walked out on her own child," Michael said. "Doesn't she care at all?"

"She's a demon," Lucifer replied. "Now, have you decided what you're going to do with the little bundle of joy?"

Michael took the baby from the angel and gazed into the most perfect face he had ever seen. He smiled and the world seemed to fall away, until it was just him and his daughter.

"You need to think of a name," Lucifer said. "If you're going to raise her yourself."

Michael sighed. "I wish I could, I really do, but we both know I can't."

"What?"

Michael didn't blame Lucifer for being surprised. They had avoided the discussion about what would happen now for weeks. Raphael had stopped by a month before and confirmed Machidiel and his partners would be willing to raise the child. Which meant Michael had a choice, and it had proved to be the most difficult of his life.

"If I give up my wings to raise her, I'll be powerless to protect her from all the demons who want my head on a pike. We both know they would come for me as soon as word got out, and this sort of secret can't be kept for long."

"Then you're going to leave her in the care of Machidiel and the others?"

"She'll be safe there, and I'll be keeping a close eye on her."

"And you're happy with this decision?"

"No, not entirely, but I'd never forgive myself if she were to be harmed because I was unable to protect her."

"Are you going to name her?" Lucifer asked.

"I'll let Machidiel and his partners choose her name. After all, they'll be her parents. I'll just be the doting uncle."

Lucifer leaned in close and brushed his hand over the baby's head. "Do you think they'd object to a second uncle stopping by now and then?"

"I'm sure they wouldn't," Michael replied with a smile. "Let's take her to her new home."

* * * *

"Are you sure about this?" Machidiel asked as he took the baby from Michael's arms and placed her in the crib Lucifer had just conjured from thin air. Lucifer had decorated and furnished the nursery in a matter of seconds, and Michael had provided all the documentation the family would ever need to ensure the child was secure in her new home.

Michael nodded, his eyes watery. He couldn't speak, not yet.

"She needs a name," Lucifer said.

"We've already decided on them," Machidiel replied with a smile. "You know, just in case."

"Michelle Lucy," Tristan said. "We thought her names should reflect her parentage, without being too obvious."

"I'm not one of her parents," Lucifer pointed out.

"Not biologically," Tristan agreed, "but, as Michael's partner, you'll be playing just as big a role in her life as he will."

Michael nodded and rubbed his eyes. He wasn't going to cry, not in front of everyone. "Take care of her, okay?"

"She'll want for nothing," Machidiel assured him.

Alastor and Tristan were already cooing over Michelle, and Michael could tell she was going to be spoiled by her three fathers.

Lucifer took hold of his hand. *"Are you okay?"*

Michael shook his head.

"Home?"

Michael nodded. He couldn't hold it together much longer.

"We'll stop by later in the week to see how she's doing," Lucifer said.

"You don't want to stay a while?" Alastor asked.

"Not tonight," Lucifer replied. "I'm going to take Michael home."

Michael felt three sets of eyes focus on him and he made a concentrated effort not to break down. "I'll see you soon," he said.

A moment later he collapsed in Lucifer's arms and let his lover carry him to bed. He wept for a long time, but Lucifer held him throughout, murmuring soothing words into his ear and promising him things would work out in the end.

Michael cried himself to sleep, hoping he had made the right decision but accepting he would never know for sure. No one could foretell the future, not even an archangel, and it was impossible to predict what might have happened had he made a different choice.

* * * *

Michael pulled himself together before he went to visit his daughter. The decision had been made and he had to trust he had made the right choice. Michelle would be loved by three caring men and watched over by an archangel and the most powerful demon of all.

The first visit was the hardest, but as the weeks and months passed it became easier.

Sometimes Lucifer joined him for the visits, and other times Gabriel and Raphael chose to accompany him. Mostly, Michael went alone.

Every time Michael visited he made sure to keep a close eye out for any demons in the vicinity, searching with both his eyes and his powers. It was only because he was so vigilant that he noticed Ardat's presence at all.

Doubling back on his tracks he snuck up on Ardat before she was even aware of his presence.

"Going somewhere?" he asked the demon casually.

She tried to use her powers to depart, but Michael had already put her on lockdown. She wasn't going anywhere until he allowed her to. His daughter lived just a few hundred yards away and her safety was his top priority.

"You can't keep me here forever," Ardat snarled.

"I don't intend to," Michael replied. "Just long enough for you to answer my questions. What are you doing here?"

"Taking a walk through the city. Searching for someone to spend the night with. Are you volunteering?"

"No, and I don't believe you. What are you really doing here?"

Ardat tilted her chin stubbornly before she apparently realized Michael had no intention of letting her go without hearing the truth. "I wanted to see her, okay?"

"Why?"

"Because she's my daughter. What more reason do I need?"

Michael snorted. "You weren't so maternal the day she was born. You couldn't get away from her fast enough. Why are you here now?"

"Curiosity."

"Is that all?"

"Isn't it enough?"

"Is anyone with you?" Michael asked. "Does anyone know you're here? Were you followed?"

Ardat laughed. "Aren't we being just a little paranoid?"

Michael grabbed the demon by the throat. "Answer the questions, or I swear you won't live to see tomorrow."

"I'm alone," Ardat wheezed and Michael eased up on the pressure. "I just wanted to see her. I wasn't even going to talk to them, but they walk her through the park in the pushchair at this time."

"You've been spying on them?"

"Yes."

"How did you find her?"

"I'm her mother."

"That's not an answer."

"I can find all of my children," Ardat explained. "We share a bond that can never be broken."

Michael studied the demon for several long minutes. He could detect no signs she was lying to him, and gave every appearance of being here merely to see the daughter she had walked away from the day she had been born.

"If you're followed, you place her in danger."

"I'm not a fool," Ardat snapped. "I've survived all these centuries by using the wits most demons don't believe I possess. Her angelic aura is strong, and she is becoming more angel than demon."

"She's being raised by a former angel," Michael pointed out.

"That would explain it." Ardat hesitated. "Is she happy?"

"She's still a baby, but she seems to be."

"Good. Can I go now?"

Michael nodded and released Ardat from the locks he had placed on her. She vanished immediately. He hoped she wasn't looking to cause trouble, but he had to warn Machidiel and the others she was lurking around, just in case. He would also be monitoring the area even more closely himself.

* * * *

Once he had discovered Ardat was in the area, Michael found her watching Michelle and her parents more and more frequently. She was always alone and never came too close to the villa. Michael sometimes observed her from the pool of visions as well, and when he did, he felt more reassured as to her intentions. If she planned on doing anything untoward, she could easily try to do so when he wasn't a physical presence on Earth, standing in her way.

"Maybe she's rediscovered her maternal instincts?" Gabriel suggested.

"Perhaps, but I don't like this uncertainty."

"Unfortunately, we can't stop her from spying. She's right about the bond that ties her to her children. Wherever her daughter is, Ardat will find her."

"I guess we'll just have to keep a close watch on her."

"We already are." Gabriel patted Michael on the shoulder. "Try not to worry so much. Your daughter is healthy, well loved, and you get to see her frequently."

"I know. I just don't trust Ardat not to have another

agenda."

"She's a demon. She probably has a dozen different plots going at any given time. All we can do is prepare for whatever she and the rest of her kind throw at us."

Michael nodded. Gabriel was right. He had to stop worrying and trust they had all done enough to keep his daughter safe.

Still, the longer Ardat watched over her child, the more Michael wondered if she regretted her decision to walk out of her life. If she truly had no agenda, her actions now showed a great deal of fondness, maybe even love, for her daughter. Any demon who could love another and put their safety and happiness before their own could be saved. Had he given up on Ardat too soon?

* * * *

"Ardat was watching Michelle again today," Michael commented to Lucifer, curious to hear his lover's thoughts on the behavior of the demon.

"If you're asking me to stop her, I can't, not without imprisoning her in the Underworld, and while her presence might be concerning, it doesn't warrant confinement."

"I'm not asking you to do that. I thought perhaps her affection for Michelle might be a sign of her stepping toward the light. Maybe I should have tried harder to save her."

Lucifer roared with laughter until tears ran from his eyes and he wheezed so badly, if he were human, passersby might have thought he required medical attention.

"It wasn't that funny," Michael huffed. "I really do think her behavior is because she cares."

"Ardat cares about no one except herself," Lucifer replied. "She would throw Irdu to the lions to save her own skin, and they've been lovers for centuries."

"Then why do *you* think she's watching her?"

"Curiosity, and to keep tabs on her, ready for when she comes into her powers."

"Her angelic powers are already beginning to develop," Michael said.

"They are?"

Michael nodded. At three years old, his daughter already had the power to heal herself, though she wasn't old enough to realize the importance of what she did.

"It's probably her demonic powers that interest Ardat," Lucifer commented. "And those won't appear for at least a decade."

"If that's all Ardat is hovering around for, maybe she'll get bored before then and leave her be."

"Ardat is a demon and she's an expert at playing the waiting game. When Michelle's powers appear, she'll be ready."

Michael didn't like the sound of that, but there was nothing he could do. Lucifer might be convinced to confine Ardat to the Underworld, but Michael didn't want them to go to such an extreme unless Michelle's safety deemed it absolutely necessary. Perhaps it would be best to bide their time and wait until Ardat revealed her true purpose.

Later that night Michael thought back on Lucifer's words. He had a feeling Ardat wasn't the only demon playing the waiting game. Lucifer was too. Despite Michael's insistence he wouldn't fall from grace, he knew Lucifer still hoped he would. Yes, demons were good at waiting, and Lucifer was the expert.

Chapter Fourteen

Michelle grew up with three doting fathers, as well as her devoted Uncle Michael and Uncle Luc. They had decided that introducing Lucifer by his full name might not be the best of ideas. It might raise a few awkward questions.

Michael spent a lot of time on Earth, visiting his daughter every day he could manage. Lucifer came with him once or twice a month, and even Gabriel and Raphael had stopped by to see the youngster on special occasions. Michael adored his little girl, and if his heart ached when she spoke her first word of "Dada" to Tristan, he tried not to let it show.

The years passed and Michelle's angelic powers grew with her. She healed fast, a little too quickly for a human, but hadn't suffered any serious injuries that would make it obvious. She was a natural healer, something that delighted Machidiel, who worked at the local hospital. He confided his hopes she would one day follow in his footsteps. She also had the ability to calm people with her touch, though she probably had no idea she was even doing it.

Her demon heritage couldn't be denied forever, though, and at fifteen years old the young beauty had a trail of young boys, and more than a few girls, following her around like a gaggle of geese.

Michael knew his daughter's other powers would manifest soon and the talk he had been dreading could no longer be put off. They had to tell her the truth about her parents.

Sitting in Machidiel's lounge, Michael fidgeted nervously, and even Lucifer seemed more on edge than usual.

"Maybe we should wait a little longer," Michael

suggested. "Doesn't she have exams soon? We shouldn't distract her from those."

"Her exams aren't for a while yet," Tristan said. "And is there ever going to be a perfect time for this discussion?"

"She already knows she's adopted," Alastor pointed out. "We've always been honest with her about that, not that you can really hide the fact when you're being raised by three men and not a woman in sight. Besides, sooner or later she'll notice the two of you don't age."

"I'm surprised she hasn't already," Tristan admitted.

"It's the otherworldly stuff I'm worried about," Michael said. "Not to mention telling her I'm her father."

Lucifer chuckled. "If she gets angry about that, just tell her who I am and that should be enough to take the heat off you."

"Not helping," Michael muttered.

Lucifer pulled Michael into his side and put his arm around his shoulders. "Stop worrying so much. Michelle adores you even more than the men who raised her, because you let her get away with far more than they do, and spoil her rotten."

"Here she comes," Alastor said with a nod to the window.

Sure enough Michelle headed toward the front door, and she didn't seem to be in the best of moods. The door slammed behind her, rattling the glass.

"In here, now," Machidiel called.

Michelle appeared in the lounge entrance, a sulky expression on her face.

"What did we say about slamming doors?" Machidiel asked.

"I'm not to take my temper out on inanimate objects," Michelle recited, as though she had repeated the words several times before.

"Then don't," Machidiel said. "If we have a problem we discuss it and deal, okay?"

Michelle nodded.

"So, what's happened?" Tristan asked.

"Paulo was being a jerk again," Michelle said.

"Who's Paulo?" Lucifer asked.

Michelle looked in their direction and her face lit up. "Uncle Luc, Uncle Michael! I didn't know you were visiting today." Michelle tossed her bag onto the floor and ran across the room, launching herself into Lucifer's lap, kissing him on the cheek, then turning to Michael and doing the same. "I've not seen you in ages."

"You saw us just last week," Michael pointed out with a chuckle.

"Exactly, that's like a lifetime ago."

"So, who's Paulo?" Lucifer repeated.

"Just a boy at school," Michelle replied. "He's not even worth talking about. He's an idiot."

"Then why let him upset you?" Michael asked.

Michelle's reply was a typical teenage response. "He just does."

"What has he done now?" Alastor asked.

"He said you were all going to go to Hell," Michelle muttered. "His uncle's a priest and he's been giving sermons about the evils of being gay."

Lucifer snorted. "I'd love to know who started all these rumors about homosexuals going to Hell."

"Paulo said it's the word of God," Michelle said.

"It's not," Michael told her firmly. "No one is going to Hell because of who they love. You can take my word for it."

Michelle didn't seem convinced. "Since you haven't died, you can't know for sure."

"No, I've not died, but you can trust me on this one."

"Michelle," Machidiel said as he walked across the room then crouched in front of the sofa. "I'm not going to Hell, and neither is anyone else in this room." His gaze flickered to Lucifer, who tried to smother his smile but wasn't quite quick enough.

"What's so funny?" Michelle asked. She glared over her shoulder at Lucifer. "Are you laughing at me?"

"Of course not, darling," Lucifer assured her. "It's just your dad knows I have a reservation in Hell, though not for sleeping with your Uncle Michael."

"Why do you think you're going to Hell?" Michelle asked. "Have you got some dark and murky secrets in your past?"

"Oh yes, but they're secret," Lucifer teased. "Now, we're not here to chat about my misdemeanors, so what are you going to do about this Paulo?"

"I already did something." Michelle displayed her knuckles and Michael saw they were bruised and the middle one had split.

"Have you been fighting?" Machidiel asked.

"No, I just punched him a few times until he shut up."

"Yes, that would be fighting," Machidiel said. "You're grounded for the rest of the week."

"Dad!"

"No arguments."

Michelle turned to Alastor and Tristan. "Papa? Daddy? Maria's having a party on Friday."

Tristan and Alastor shook their heads. "You know the punishment for fighting."

"It's not fair," Michelle whined. "Everyone else is going to be there."

"*Everyone else* hasn't been fighting with Paulo," Machidiel pointed out. "Now, your Uncle Michael has come to talk to you about something important, so why don't you two take a walk in the garden?"

"Maybe this isn't the best time," Michael said. "Michelle obviously has a lot on her mind today."

"Stop scrambling for excuses," Lucifer scolded.

Michelle seemed to forget about her fight as she looked at Michael with curiosity. "I'll come for a walk with you. It's not as if I can go anywhere else now."

Machidiel stepped back so they could stand and Michael led his daughter out into the garden. Lucifer said his goodbyes and promised to visit again the following week. Michael knew, as soon as he left the room, Lucifer would go to the Underworld, since Michael technically no longer escorted him.

"What did you want to talk to me about?" Michelle asked as they wandered through flowerbeds nearly as well kept as Gabriel's.

"It's about your parents," Michael replied, unsure where to start now the time had finally arrived. Perhaps he should have prepared a speech.

"What about them?" The tone of her voice didn't convey any great interest.

"Have you ever wondered about who they are?"

"Oh, you mean my birth parents?"

"Yes."

Michelle shrugged. "I've not really thought about them. I've got my dads and you and Uncle Luc. What do I need any more parents for?"

"Then you're not even the slightest bit curious about them?"

"Maybe a little bit, but I don't want to upset my dads by trying to find them or anything."

Michael guided his daughter to the stone wall round the fountain. "Let's sit down."

Michelle dipped her hand into the water and flicked a few drops. "Do you know who my birth parents are?"

"Yes."

Michelle gazed at her reflection in the water. She didn't face Michael when she spoke. "Do you know why they didn't want me?"

The words hit him like a punch to the gut and Michael struggled to maintain his composure. "I don't know about your mother, but your father wanted you very much."

"Not that much," Michelle replied. "If he did, he'd have kept me, wouldn't he? There are plenty of single dads out there these days. Even if my mother wasn't interested, he could have tried."

"It's not quite so simple," Michael said. "There were complications you don't know about."

"Such as?"

Michael hesitated. How did he begin to explain? "Your parents... They aren't exactly normal."

"What's normal these days?" Michelle asked. "I'm being raised by three men who have sex with each other, and to me, that's normal."

"So, you've, er, had *the talk*?" Michael asked. "Um, the birds and the bees one, that is."

Michelle snorted. "Three times. It was *so* embarrassing the first time. By the third time I could have given the speech myself, and probably done a better job than Papa did."

"Do I want to know why you had the talk three times?"

"I think they all thought the others wouldn't go through with it."

Michael chuckled.

"Um, that's not what you want to talk to me about, is it? I *really* don't need to hear it again."

"No, like I said, I need to speak with you about your parents."

"Do they want to see me?" Michelle asked. "Do my dads know?"

"Your dads know everything I'm telling you today."

"You've not told me much of anything yet."

"Cheeky." Michael smiled indulgently. "This is hard, you know. I think I'd rather be giving you that other talk right now."

"Why is it hard?" Michelle asked.

Michael took his daughter's hands in his own and drew a deep breath. "I think perhaps it might be easier to show you."

Readying himself for her reaction, Michael transported them both to his beach, changing into his robes and revealing his white wings to her for the first time.

Michelle gasped. "Oh my stars. Where are we? Holy crap! You have *wings!*"

"This is where I live," Michael said, gesturing to the luxurious beach house at the edge of the dunes. "We call it the realm of angels, though you'd probably know it better as Heaven."

"I though Heaven was all clouds and stuff."

Michael smiled. "The main concourse is more as you would imagine Heaven to be. That's where the newly deceased arrive, and we like to ensure their transition to this realm is as smooth as possible. But everyone's idea of Heaven is different, which means this realm has just as many locations as you would find on Earth. For me, this beach is the most perfect place I can imagine. Others may prefer the mountains or the forest. One man's Heaven may be another's personal hell, and all should feel safe and secure in this realm."

Michelle reached out toward his right wing but stopped short of touching the feathers.

"Go ahead," Michael told her. "They're real."

"You're an angel? Holy crap, you're a fucking angel."

"Your language is appalling," Michael told her. "I think I might be having a word with your dads about that when we get back."

"I'm sorry, but you're an *angel.*"

Michael smiled. "Yes, I am."

"Is Uncle Luc an angel too?"

"He used to be, and I keep hoping one day he will be again."

"How does that work?" Michelle asked. "I thought once you were an angel it was forever."

"It usually is, but sometimes things don't work out quite as we would want them to."

Michelle took a few steps in the direction of the house. "Does Uncle Luc live here with you?"

"No."

Michelle frowned. "I always thought you two lived together. You act as if you've been a couple for a long time. I guess now I know why you never invited me to visit you."

"Your Uncle Luc and I have been in a relationship for centuries, and even though we can't live together, we are very much committed to each other." Michael hesitated a moment, but he had brought Michelle here to tell her the truth, and that meant the whole truth. "Your Uncle Luc is better known by other names. Usually I call him Lucifer."

"The devil?" Michelle whispered. "Uncle Luc is the devil?"

Michael smiled. "Yes."

"How long have you known?"

"Forever. I fell in love with him when he was an angel. He used to live in those distant mountains you can see on the horizon. He fell from grace a long time ago, and I've made it my life's work to bring him back to the light."

"Wow. When you said you'd been together centuries, you really meant it, didn't you?"

Michael let the two of them into the house. "But we're not here to talk about me and Lucifer, we're here to talk about you."

"I thought you were going to tell me about my parents?"

Michael smiled and drew in a deep breath.

"You're my father, aren't you?" Michelle blurted out. "*That's* why you've brought me here, isn't it?"

A part of Michael was relieved she had figured out the truth without him having to say the words, but her shock didn't tell him anything about what she thought of the revelation. "Yes," he said, because it was the only word he could manage to force from his lips.

He couldn't face her, couldn't bear to see whatever was in her eyes. Would she be disappointed or angry?

"Uncle Michael, are you okay?" She placed her hand on his arm and Michael felt his inner turmoil recede as though it had never been there. Her powers were strong. To bring calmness to an archangel was something most angels could never achieve.

Michael finally faced his daughter. "Shouldn't I be asking you that question?"

"I'm fine," she replied with a smile. "Though I'm not sure *why* I'm taking this so well. I feel like I should be shocked and angry at being lied to, but I'm not."

Michael knew the reason for her calmness was her angelic nature, but he wanted to give her time to digest what he had told her before he dropped the next bombshell.

"I guess I'll be the only girl in school with *four* fathers," Michelle continued. "What do I call you? I've already got a Dad, a Papa, and a Daddy."

"You can still call me Uncle Michael. Your dads are the ones who raised you."

A knocking sound came from the front door. Michael was tempted to ignore it, but few angels disturbed him at home, and it could be something important.

"I'd better see who that is," Michael said. "Wait here, okay?"

"I can't exactly go home," Michelle pointed out.

Michael nodded as he went to answer the door.

"Gabriel, what brings you here?" he asked.

"I need your help with one of my charges," Gabriel explained. "But I see you're busy. Hello, Michelle."

Michelle waved from the sofa. "Hi, Uncle Gabe, er Gabriel? As in the angel Gabriel?"

"Yes," Gabriel replied. "We thought perhaps having uncles by the names of Gabriel, Raphael, and Michael might be a bit obvious."

"You mean Uncle Rafe is an angel too?"

Gabriel laughed. "You're too smart for your own good, you know that? I'll stop by tomorrow, Michael."

"No," Michelle interrupted. "Father can go with you. I'll just stay here and relax. Do you have a telly?"

Michael laughed and his heart warmed at hearing his daughter refer to him as Father. "No, there's no television here, but I'm sure I can find something to keep you occupied for a little while." With a snap of his fingers he produced Michelle's homework and passed the books to her.

"Father!"

"That's just cruel," Gabriel said. "You bring her to our paradise and make her do school work. Come on, munchkin, we'll give you the tour."

"Great!" Michelle tossed aside her school books and ran to the door. "What do I get to see first?"

"Now you've done it," Michael said. "She'll want to come here all the time now."

Michelle laughed as she waited for them on the path. "Oh look, *they* have wings too."

"All angels have them," Gabriel said. "We just don't generally show them on Earth."

"Can I see yours? Do they just burst out of your clothes?"

Gabriel turned round and let his wings appear, thankfully without tearing his garments.

Michelle clapped in delight. "Are they heavy?"

"No. They're light as a feather, or a lot of feathers would probably be more accurate." He spread his wings wide and hovered a few inches off the floor.

"Show off," Michael coughed into his hand.

Gabriel laughed and they set off after Michelle, who rushed ahead of them to see everything in sight.

"I take it your news went well?" Gabriel whispered as they followed Michelle toward Gabriel's home, occasionally calling out the direction for her to take.

"So far, but she doesn't know everything yet."

"Obviously she knows you're her father, and an archangel, but what doesn't she know? Just so I don't accidentally say the wrong thing."

"She knows who her Uncle Luc is, but that's about it. She doesn't know about her mother, or her own powers."

"I'm sorry I interrupted. I didn't realize you intended to bring her here."

"It was a spur of the moment thing."

"Clearly she's taken the news about her biological father well."

"Yes, she has, much to my relief."

"You sound surprised. You forget, she's half angel herself, and whether she knows it or not, her nature will always be one of acceptance."

"She's only half angel," Michael reminded him. "She's half demon too."

"Let's hope that news goes down as well as the rest."

Michael pushed the uneasy thought from his mind and changed the subject. "What is it you need my help with?"

"One of my angels has become involved with a demon, a pain demon to be precise."

"Ah." Michael nodded. It had become quite common over the centuries for the archangels to let Michael know when one of their charges became a little too friendly with an inhabitant of the Underworld. Michael took them under his wing, so to speak, and also ensured that Lucifer was aware of the relationship. He also made sure to give the angels advance warning of any petition — usually brought to the table by Raguel — to ban such relations.

Gabriel's charge was working in the garden when they arrived, and Gabriel soon put all idle hands to work, while he supervised.

Michelle, Gabriel was amused to discover, was as ambivalent about gardening as Michael.

By unspoken agreement, Gabriel set Michelle to work in one part of the garden, weeding the petunias, while Michael and Adam, Gabriel's charge, talked quietly as they trimmed the hedge on the other side of the house.

Once Michael had made it clear his door was always open if Adam needed advice, he went back to Michelle, thankfully before she uprooted Gabriel's prized peonies by mistake.

"I guess we have to go home soon," Michelle said. "My dads will be wondering where I've disappeared to."

"They won't even know you've been gone," Michael told her. "Time moves differently here. I'll return you home in plenty of time to get your homework done before dinner."

"Or I could stay here and you can tell me about my mum?" Michelle suggested with a sneaky grin.

"What do you want to know about her?"

"Her name would be a start."

"Her name's Ardat."

"Did you love her?"

Michael had hoped for a few more easy questions before getting to the tough ones. "My heart belongs to your Uncle Luc," he reminded her.

"I know, but you must have had *some* feelings for my mum, or you wouldn't have had sex with her. Does Uncle Luc know you cheated on him?"

"I never cheated on Lucifer," Michael quickly assured her.

"Did you have a fight or separate or something?"

"No. It wasn't like that." Michael hesitated. How did you go about explaining to your fifteen-year-old daughter that you and your lover had invited other people — demons — into your bed? Then he remembered Michelle was being raised by three men in a relationship together. She was also smart enough to figure it out on her own, if given enough time. "Your Uncle Luc and I invited your mother to be with us."

"Oh." Michelle blushed and ducked her head.

"There's something else you need to know about your mother. She's not human either. She's a demon, and an extraordinarily powerful one."

"My parents are an archangel and a demon. Wow."

"You're taking this awfully well."

Michelle frowned at him. "There's more, isn't there?"

"Yes, and I think you might know where this conversation is going."

Michelle studied the knuckles on her hand. The bruises had vanished and the cut appeared days old, rather than hours. "Sometimes I see other kids with cuts and bruises that last for days or even weeks. My bruises disappear in just a few hours."

"We thought you might have noticed that."

"I asked Papa about it once, but he just told me not to worry about it. Later that night I heard him talking to Dad about it, but I couldn't hear all of what they were saying.

It's not normal to heal this quickly, which I guess means *I'm* not normal, am I?"

"It depends on your definition of normal," Michael replied. "Because of who your parents are, this is normal for you."

Michelle scowled at him. "But I'm not human, am I?"

"No, you're half angel and half demon. The accelerated healing comes from my side of the family, as do some of your other abilities, including being able to calm people down with a touch. You'll also find it easy to see auras of those who are, or have been, angels. You can probably already see them, though you won't have known what they were."

"Sometimes, when I see Dad out of the corner of my eye, I think he's glowing."

"That's his aura. Your dad used to be an angel, but he gave up his wings to live a mortal life because he loved Alastor and Tristan so much. Sometimes an angel might hide their aura, especially when they're on Earth, but those who give up their wings, like your dad, can't. Now you're maturing, your powers are growing, which is why we felt it was time to tell you who you are."

Michelle nodded and stood to pace the room for several minutes. Michael gave her all the time she needed, and finally she returned to her seat beside him. "I'm glad you told me. A few people have said things before about how I seem to heal quickly. I just didn't know why."

"Well, now you do. You don't just have angelic powers, though—you're also half demon, which means you'll be getting some gifts from your mother too."

Michelle frowned. "Like what?"

"Your mother, Ardat, is the leader of the succubi."

"The suck you what?"

"Succubi. Specifically, she's a demon who feeds from sex. It's highly unlikely you'll need to do that, but some of her powers will manifest in you over the next few years."

"What sort of powers?" For the first time Michelle

appeared scared, and Michael couldn't blame her. Finding out she was part angel was one thing—discovering she was part demon was another matter entirely.

"We're not sure, but we think you'll be giving off an aura that will make those who come into contact with you desire you. In fact, we believe you already are. Your dads tell me you have a lot of boys and girls following you around these days, and while part of that is probably because you're a bright, pretty young woman, some of it could be because of your demonic talents."

"Can I control these powers?" Michelle sounded panicked.

Michael took hold of her hands and used his own ability to calm to help her. "In time, you should be able to, yes, but I'm afraid I can only help you with the angelic ones."

"Can Uncle Luc help with the demonic ones?"

"We'll ask him, but he's not a succubus, or the male equivalent, which is an incubus, so he may be as ignorant about them as I am."

Michelle sighed. "And to think, a few hours ago my biggest worry was whether my dads were going to go to Hell."

"At least now you'll believe me when I say they're coming here," Michael teased. "Your dad had a home here, and it's ready for the three of them when they reach the end of their mortal lives."

"I can't wait to tell Paulo he's wrong."

Michael shook his head. "I wouldn't recommend that."

"But he's…" Michelle sighed. "He'll just think I'm crazy, won't he?"

"I'm afraid so, but at least you'll know he's wrong, and when the time comes, you'll be able to visit your dads here."

"I'll be able to come and go from here whenever I want?" Michelle brightened considerably and Michael didn't need to read her mind to figure out where her thoughts had gone.

"Yes, you'll be able to come here, when you're older and you've learned how to travel from one realm to another, but it'll take many years to accomplish that."

"Years?"

"Yes. So, you won't be able to sneak here while you're grounded." Michael smiled. "At least not all the time."

"Maybe I'll just ask Uncle Luc to let me hang out with him," Michelle suggested with a smirk. "Having the devil for an uncle has to have some advantages. He should support me when I get in trouble."

Michael laughed. "Good luck with that. Let me know how it goes."

Michelle stuck out her lower lip in a fake pout, but she threw her arms around Michael's neck and hugged him hard. "I'm glad you're my father."

Michael hugged her back. "And I'm glad you're my daughter."

They had one more stop to make before they returned to Earth. Michael took his daughter to the chamber containing the pool of visions. At the very least, Michelle should be able to see what her mother looked like. As she gazed into the pool Michael realized in a few more years she would be able to see her mother simply by viewing her own reflection. She already shared her mother's pale skin, her white-blonde hair, and tall, slim figure. Michelle would be a great beauty and a heartbreaker. Michael hoped her own remained intact, though he suspected life would have a few more surprises in store for a girl born to an angel and a demon.

Chapter Fifteen

The relief that his daughter had taken the news of her parentage so well was enormous. Michael had been dreading her reaction for years, but her angelic nature had shone through. Perhaps it helped that Michael had been such a large part of her life, even though he hadn't raised her. Whatever the reason, the revelation didn't seem to have much of an effect on Michelle's day to day life. She went to school, did her chores and homework, and socialized with her friends, at least when she wasn't grounded.

Michael and Machidiel helped her to come to terms with her growing powers, ensuring she knew what needed to be hidden from the rest of the human race.

The demon powers were a little harder to deal with. Lucifer, whose powers weren't of a sexual nature, despite the almost supernatural allure Michael felt from him, couldn't help much.

Ardat, who had been watching Michelle for so long, was now conspicuously absent. Michael even tried asking Lucifer to track her down in the Underworld. As worrisome as it had been when she'd been lurking around on street corners, not knowing what she was up to had to be ten times worse.

"She's been partying hard," Lucifer reported. "Rumor has it she and Irdu are traveling and recruiting personally in Scandinavia. Don't worry about her. I'm sure she's lost interest in Michelle."

Michael couldn't shake off his worry. "Why, though? Michelle is just coming into her powers, this is when I'd *expect* her mother to be watching."

"The powers your daughter inherited from you are far stronger than her demonic powers."

"Because I'm helping her hone her angelic powers."

"Well, you keep doing that, and if Ardat resurfaces, we'll deal with it. In the meantime, how about you come back to bed? It's been far too long since we had sex."

Michael smiled at Lucifer, who had been patiently waiting for him to finish pacing. He supposed he had been neglecting his lover a little. Between his duties as an angel, an increasing number of angels forming relationships with demons, and spending time with Michelle, it didn't leave Michael much time for Lucifer. A twinge of guilt hit him in the chest and he climbed onto the bed, and into Lucifer's welcoming embrace.

* * * *

A few more years passed, and still Ardat didn't show herself. Michelle left school and went to university. To Machidiel's delight she had decided to go into the medical profession, though she appeared to be leaning toward research. Her days were filled with studying and Michael took a step back, leaving her to live her life, and returning to his primary mission.

Michael wished his saving of Lucifer was going as smoothly as his relationship with his daughter. He didn't believe he was any nearer bringing Lucifer back to the light now than he had been a thousand years ago. He didn't doubt that Lucifer was capable of love, but it wasn't enough to save him. His love wasn't selfless and never had been.

Michael could sense Lucifer's growing impatience with Michael's continued refusal to join him in the Underworld. The quarrels Michael had thought were behind them returned and Lucifer's barbed comments about Michael's priorities became more frequent and more pointed.

As always, when he felt as though he had reached a dead end, Michael turned to Gabriel, hoping for some words of wisdom.

"I don't know if I'm ever going to save him," Michael confided. "He never seems to change."

"I think he has," Gabriel replied. "He clearly loves your daughter, and you."

"But love's not enough, is it?" Michael didn't need Gabriel to answer the question. If all it took was love, Lucifer would have been living back in the realm of angels a long time ago.

"He'll come back to us one day," Gabriel said as he took Michael's hand. "Don't give up on him."

"I'm not. I can't."

Gabriel tightened his grip. "I know you, Michael. I know how your mind works, and I can tell you're losing hope."

Michael sighed and released himself from Gabriel's hand. Gabriel knew him far too well. "I just don't feel I'm getting anywhere with him. If I could just see some sign I'm getting through to him."

"There are signs, if you know where to look."

"Like what?"

"Like the way his eyes follow you around the room. How he can't be near you without touching you."

Michael snorted and shook his head. "That's just desire. It doesn't mean anything other than he wants to get me into bed."

"What are you thinking, Michael? What are you *really* thinking right now?"

"I don't know. Maybe I'm just tired."

Gabriel remained quiet for a minute or two, and Michael could tell he was poking into his thoughts. Normally he would have minded, but he doubted Gabriel would be able to make sense of his muddled mind anyway.

"A separation?" Gabriel asked. "You're considering a separation?"

Michael frowned. He didn't want to leave Lucifer, not even for a little while. Time apart hadn't helped last time, and he didn't think it would now either. He hadn't even realized that the idea had been there until Gabriel had said the words.

"Have you talked to Machidiel about this?" Gabriel suggested.

"No, why, do you think he could help?"

"Perhaps. He is, after all, the only angel to ever bring a demon back to the light."

"Two, if you count Tristan," Michael replied.

"I think we can agree those circumstances were a little different. I'm talking about Alastor. He was a demon for centuries, and yet look at him now."

"Unfortunately, it's not likely I'm going to be in mortal danger at just the right time for Lucifer to sacrifice himself to save me," Michael pointed out. "As an archangel I'm a little hard to kill."

"The way you fought on the battlefield, I'd say impossible," Gabriel agreed.

"It's a moot point anyway. Lucifer might love me, but not to the detriment of his own life."

"I disagree."

Michael didn't see the point of arguing. His life hadn't been in jeopardy for centuries, and, as things stood at the moment, it wasn't likely to be any time soon.

Unless...

"Michael?" Gabriel grabbed his arm. "What is it?"

Michael shook his head, banishing the thought that had popped into his mind so suddenly. "Nothing, I'm just in a rut. Next week Lucifer will no doubt do something to surprise me, and my faith will be restored."

"I hope so. I hate to see you so defeated."

"I'll be fine," Michael assured him.

They worked a while longer, and when Michael went home he felt a little better. Yet he couldn't help glancing at the archway of reincarnation as he passed. Other angels had chosen that path, but never an archangel.

No. He turned away from the archway and pushed the thought aside. To be reborn wouldn't help him. How could he hope to save Lucifer if he had no memory of what they had shared all these years?

Chapter Sixteen

A crash of thunder woke Michael from his sleep, and for a moment he felt disoriented. There was no thunder in the realm of angels. It never rained and no storm clouds marred the skies.

Yet thundering it was.

Michael leaped out of bed and pulled on his robes. He raced to the archangels' chamber and summoned those who were currently on Earth, the rest already woken by the thunder and pounding rain.

"What's happening?" Metatron asked.

"I think we all know what's happened." Raguel had to shout to make himself heard over the storm. "It's exactly what I've been saying for centuries—no good will come from angels getting involved with demons."

"You don't know that's what has happened," Gabriel replied.

"Look at the sky," Raguel snapped. "When was the last time you saw a storm in this realm?"

Michael shivered. The last time had been so long ago he had almost forgotten it had happened. It had been the morning after Lucifer had fallen, taking a third of the angels with him.

"I'm going to speak to Lucifer," Michael said. "He'll be able to confirm if an angel has fallen."

"Summon him here to answer us all," Raguel demanded, before Michael had even made it to the door. "I don't trust you to report back accurately."

Michael bristled at the accusation, but he did as Raguel requested, summoning Lucifer into the chamber to speak to the entire council.

"Good morning," Lucifer said as he took the chair in the middle of the room. "Interesting weather we're having, wouldn't you say?"

Michael tried to read Lucifer's mind, but he was out of practice and Lucifer seemed to be blocking him. He guessed they would have to extract the information the old-fashioned way. "Lucifer, what do you know about what's happening?"

"Well, thunder is created when—"

"Lucifer, we don't have time for this," Michael snapped. "Has an angel fallen?"

"Yes, several, in fact."

Michael felt sick to his stomach. "How many?"

"I'm not sure, somewhere between two and three dozen."

Raguel cleared his throat. "And how many of those angels were sleeping with demons?"

"I wouldn't know," Lucifer replied lazily. "I have a policy whereby I mind my own damn business when it comes to who my demons are fucking."

"Lucifer…" Michael made the warning in his voice clear.

"I *don't know*," Lucifer insisted. "I have better things to do with my time than poke my nose where it isn't wanted."

"Find out," Michael demanded. "I want you to report back here within the hour with the exact number of fallen angels, as well as how many were in relationships with demons."

"Things are a little busy in the Underworld right now," Lucifer replied as he made a show of studying his nails. "There's something of a party atmosphere down there."

"I don't care," Michael snapped. "You have one hour."

Lucifer glared from his seat, right before he transformed into his demon form. The last time Michael had seen him this way had been on the battlefield. It hadn't scared him then, but it terrified him now.

"You don't tell me what to do," Lucifer snarled. "I'm not one of your precious recruits. I'm Lucifer himself and I don't take orders, I give them."

Michael rose and pulled his sword from the scabbard he normally kept hidden. He pointed the blade directly at Lucifer. "One hour."

Lucifer vanished, and Michael began the long wait for him to report back.

An hour passed, then two. The storm lessened, though the rain continued to pour down. The sky darkened again, this time as night fell, and still Lucifer did not appear.

Finally, Michael could give him no more time. Raguel had been calling for the meeting to be reconvened most of the day, and while most of the others were content to give Lucifer a little more time, no one, not even Michael, could agree to wait indefinitely for the contrary fallen angel to return.

Michael and Gabriel talked quietly at the side of the room. Raphael joined them, his expression grim.

They had all been making inquiries throughout the day and their best guess was that thirty angels had fallen, most fairly new angels, all recruited in the last few decades. None were as powerful as those who had fallen with Lucifer. It didn't make any difference to the seriousness of events.

Michael had called a meeting of all the angels currently known to be in relationships with demons, and while most had attended at his home early that afternoon, there were two absentees. A second summons to those missing had gone unanswered.

Now the archangels had to deal with the repercussions of whatever had happened to draw so many angels to the darkness.

"I think you should go to the Underworld and see what's keeping him," Gabriel suggested. "The fallen angels might be staging some sort of coup."

"Even combined, they don't have the power to take on Lucifer," Michael replied. "As an angel he had more powers than any of the archangels. None of the lesser angels who've turned demon could overthrow him."

"What do you think is keeping him?" Raphael asked.

"I don't know."

"I agree with Gabriel, you should at least try to speak to him, and bring him back here if you can, before we reconvene."

Michael nodded. "Give me one hour. If I'm not back by then, start without me."

Gabriel agreed and Michael announced his intentions to the rest of the archangels. Raguel and his supporters protested, before eventually agreeing to give Michael time to visit the Underworld.

When he arrived in Lucifer's chambers, Michael found them empty. He didn't enjoy venturing into the rest of the Underworld, but he had done so before and the situation certainly called for it tonight.

As he had during his previous visit to the main Underworld, Michael made his way to the throne room. He wasn't surprised to find Lucifer there, along with a huge crowd of demons and the fallen angels. Lucifer, visible to everyone, lounged on the throne he had once relinquished yet had now apparently reclaimed.

Michael kept himself invisible from everyone, including Lucifer, as he made his way through the throng.

Unfortunately for Michael, while he could hide himself from most of the inhabitants of the Underworld, Lucifer had always been more powerful than a single archangel. The closer he got to Lucifer, the weaker his shield became, and by the time he reached his lover, Lucifer's eyes were firmly fixed on him.

"Are we going to have another discussion about angels wandering my domain?" asked Lucifer, his words slow and slurred.

"Have you been drinking?" Michael asked, though the empty tankard beside him probably answered his question.

"Of course," Lucifer replied with a grin. "This is a celebration. Join us, have a drink, loosen up a little."

Michael rolled his eyes. He could count on his fingers

the number of times he had ever seen Lucifer intoxicated. Alcohol rarely affected his lover. Power, however, went straight to his head. The boost the fallen angels had given him had reduced him to this state.

"We've been waiting for you to return with your report," Michael said. "Or had you forgotten?"

"I think *you're* the one who has a memory problem. If you want to know how many fallen angels are here, take a look, they're right here in this room, you can count them yourself. *They* don't have a problem joining me here, unlike *you*."

"Lucifer, I'm not here to fight with you."

"Who's fighting?" Lucifer filled his tankard with a wave of his hand and took a long swallow. "Just because I'm not running to do your bidding as I have before. I'd forgotten what it's like to have followers with angelic powers."

Michael cringed at having his suspicions confirmed. "This isn't you talking."

Lucifer roared with laughter. "Of course it's me. I haven't felt this good in a millennium. I can't wait for the day you finally join me. The power boost I'll enjoy from the fall of an archangel will be unparalleled."

Michael could see he wouldn't get anywhere until Lucifer had sobered up, which could take months, since his intoxication came from power, rather than good old-fashioned alcohol. He surveyed the room. He soon caught sight of one of the angels who had recently fallen from grace. Unlike many of the demons, she had maintained most of her human appearance, though with her horns, claws, and pointed teeth she would stand out in the crowd in the realm of angels. Michael could feel her lure and felt certain that she had become a sexual predator. How had this happened?

He saw Ardat laughing and joking, and was astonished when she gave him a small wave from across the room. She was more powerful than he had realized, if she could see him despite his shield.

"Go home, Michael," Lucifer said. "Or, better yet, go wait in my bed until I'm ready to come fuck you. That's all you've ever been good for."

"Lucifer, listen to yourself." Michael couldn't give up so quickly.

"No," Lucifer roared. "You listen. I am not some lesser angel to take orders from *you*. I'm the great Lucifer, ruler of the Underworld, the most powerful demon to ever walk the earth."

"I know who you are."

"You know, but you don't understand. You have no place here unless you wish to join me."

"I won't do that."

Lucifer sneered. "No, of course you won't. Well, things are going to change from now on."

"What do you mean?" Michael asked.

Lucifer pulled open his robes and exposed his erection. "Suck me."

A hush fell over the room and Michael realized that the rest of the demons could see him. Lucifer had revealed Michael's presence to the room, just as he had once threatened to. Michael tried to put up his shields again, but Lucifer's power prevented him.

"Well?" Lucifer said. "What are you waiting for? You either take your place beside me, or you get on your knees and suck my cock."

"No."

"Why not?" Lucifer asked with a smirk at the crowd. "It's not like you don't enjoy it. Oh yes, my demons, listen up. I think it's about time you all knew the truth about the archangel Michael. He refuses to become one of us, but he's been spreading his legs for me for centuries. In private he has no such hesitation about kneeling at my feet and taking my cock between those pouting lips."

Lucifer pointed to the space between his legs and a cushion appeared between his feet. "There, I've made it more comfortable for you. Now kneel."

Michael drew his sword and pointed it at Lucifer's chest. "Cover your body and sober up."

"Isn't false modesty a sin?" Lucifer replied with a smirk. "I have no problem with every demon in this room seeing me this way."

"You might not care, but I do."

"Ah, is that jealousy I hear?" Lucifer cupped a hand round his ear and the demons behind Michael howled with laughter. "If you don't suck me, right now, I'll give you something to be jealous about."

Michael stepped forward without lowering his sword. The moment the tip of the blade touched Lucifer's skin the weapon vanished from Michael's hand. For the first time Michael sensed he might be in real danger.

"My powers in the Underworld are without equal," Lucifer said. He pointed to the cushion once more. "You know what you have to do. Or do I summon another to take your place?"

"You wouldn't dare."

Lucifer snapped his fingers and Gregor, the demon he had threatened to take into his bed so many years ago, appeared beside the throne. "You remember Gregor, don't you, Michael?"

Gregor, whose memory had been wiped, seemed a little confused.

"I remember him," Michael confirmed.

"Good." Lucifer smiled at the demon and gestured to the cushion. "Gregor, would you like the honor of sucking my cock?"

Gregor licked his lips as he hurried to kneel between Lucifer's legs.

"No!" Michael shouted, and he pulled the demon back before he took the hard rod into his mouth.

Lucifer smiled. "One of you is going to suck me, Michael. It's him or you, so make your choice."

"This creature will never touch you again," Michael said. He used his powers to send the demon flying across the room, uncaring as to where he landed.

"Kneel," Lucifer demanded.

Michael closed his eyes and with shaking limbs he sank onto the cushion.

"That's right," Lucifer said.

Michael's heart pounded. He could feel the eyes of every demon in the room boring into his back.

"Now suck me," Lucifer ordered.

Michael gazed up at Lucifer, searching his eyes for the love he thought the fallen angel felt for him.

"What are you waiting for?" one of the demons in the crowd called. "If you don't want to taste him, I'll be happy to take your place."

"You heard him," Lucifer said.

Michael nodded and, with a heavy heart, he sucked the tip of Lucifer's cock between his lips. The crowd behind him cheered and laughed.

Lucifer tugged hard on Michael's hair, holding his head in place as he began to fuck his mouth.

Michael closed his watery eyes as humiliation swept through him. What was he doing? How could he let Lucifer use him this way?

Lucifer screamed in pleasure as he filled Michael's mouth with his seed, and Michael drank it down, for the first time in his life finding no pleasure in the act.

Finally, Lucifer was spent and Michael pulled away.

"Stay there," Lucifer said. "I like seeing you kneel at my feet."

Michael couldn't have stood, even if he'd tried. He hung his head, unwilling to meet his lover's eyes.

"Undress," Lucifer ordered. "I want to see you."

Michael didn't move.

"You aren't shy, are you?" Lucifer asked. "You've just sucked my cock for the entertainment of several hundred demons. This is hardly the time for modesty. Now, undress."

Behind him, Michael could hear the demons growing restless again. He untied his robes, keeping his back to the room.

"Stand up and face my people," Lucifer said.

"Lucifer, please."

Lucifer grabbed Michael's arm and pulled him to his feet. He yanked the robe from his body and turned him to face the room. Michael closed his eyes rather than see the demons.

"Look at them," Lucifer whispered into his ear.

Even though he didn't want to, Michael felt a compulsion to open his eyes. He could tell Lucifer was using his powers on him, but was helpless to resist.

"See, my demons," Lucifer called to the room. "Here stands before you the legendary archangel Michael, who laid claim to my defeat in the great war. Look upon him and see him for what he truly is."

"He's a liar!" a female demon shouted, to the cheers of the rest.

"Lucifer's whore," a second creature yelled.

Michael couldn't take any more and he tried to use his powers to leave, but Lucifer blocked him, trapping him in the Underworld.

"You leave when *I* say," Lucifer whispered in his ear.

Lucifer let the demons heckle Michael for a while longer, before he raised his hand for quiet.

"My loyal demons, that's enough. What you say of the archangel is true, but there is one more thing he is, and that's mine. One day the archangel Michael *will* rule the Underworld at my side."

"I will never rule beside you," Michael said.

"You will rule *with* me or kneel *before* me. I don't care which."

"Never."

Lucifer smirked at him. "But Michael, you already have."

"I won't worship you."

Lucifer laughed. "You will do *anything* I tell you to, and we both know it. What other angel would do what you have done tonight? Would Gabriel stand here naked before my demons? Would Raphael suck my cock for such an audience? Oh no, Michael. Only you would enjoy doing such things."

"'Enjoy'?" Michael nearly choked on the word.

Lucifer stroked Michael's cock, showing the whole room his arousal. "Oh yes, I think you enjoyed it immensely."

Michael's body betrayed him with every touch of Lucifer's hand. He moaned softly as Lucifer pleasured him.

"Come for me and I'll let you leave," Lucifer said. "I'm sure the rest of the archangels are wondering where you are."

Finally seeing an end to his torment, Michael closed his eyes and let Lucifer stroke him to completion. He would have fallen to the ground, but Lucifer held him upright.

"You said I could go now," Michael reminded him.

"You may," Lucifer agreed. He picked up Michael's robe and wrapped it round his shoulders. "I'll expect you back here tomorrow, at the same time. I do believe my demons would like to see you ride my cock while I'm on my throne. I think you'll enjoy that just as much as they will."

"It won't happen," Michael said as he covered himself up.

"So you say now, but come tomorrow, when the choice is that or watching another take your place, I know you'll change your mind."

Michael didn't even bother to reply. No longer trapped in the Underworld, he returned to the realm of angels, desperately trying to hold things together before he faced the rest of the archangels.

* * * *

Back in the archangels' chamber, Michael took his seat and called the meeting to order. "Lucifer won't be joining us."

Gabriel stared at him questioningly, but Michael avoided his gaze.

"What a surprise," Raguel muttered.

Michael glared at the angel briefly before returning to the matter at hand. "Our estimation of the number of fallen angels would appear to be accurate. If they were all in the main throne room, there are twenty-nine, all lesser angels, who are now a variety of demons."

"They need to be killed," Raguel said. "And don't even dare to suggest they can be brought back to the light. You've had how many centuries to bring Lucifer back?"

"Lucifer has no intention of returning to the light," Michael stated bleakly. He hated to admit it out loud, but he could deny the truth no longer.

"I think we should vote, again, to ban relationships between angels and demons," Raguel declared.

"Tomorrow," Gabriel said.

"No, now!" Raguel insisted. "Before more angels are lost to us."

Michael nodded. "I would request permission to summon those we are aware are in such relationships, so they may see the outcome of the vote."

"That's highly unorthodox."

"But not unprecedented," Michael reminded them. "They can watch from the gallery without participating. If necessary, we can remove their memories of anything they don't need to know."

Raguel snorted. "You mean we'll wipe the memories of your relationship with Lucifer?"

"If necessary."

"I don't believe wiping anyone's memories of your tawdry relationship is required," Raguel argued. "Everyone in this room knows you've been fucking Lucifer for centuries. I think it's about time the general angel population knows too."

"I see no reason why they should," Gabriel interrupted.

"The reason they didn't know before was because Lucifer was believed to be dead," Raguel pointed out. "His survival is now common knowledge amongst demons and I'm quite sure most of the angels are equally aware. Some of them have probably figured it out for themselves by now anyway, at least those who have bothered to put a little thought into the matter."

"If the general population becomes aware of Michael's relationship with Lucifer, it could damage his reputation among those who share your opinion that angels should not engage in relationships with demons."

"Michael's reputation is undeserved."

"It also isn't the important issue here," Metatron said. "Let's vote and get this over with, so we can concentrate on how to deal with the newest fallen angels."

Michael couldn't help silently agreeing with Raguel. His reputation wasn't deserved, and, after his behavior tonight, tawdry was a perfectly accurate word to describe his relationship with Lucifer. He debated whether he should say anything about what had happened, but he could not bring himself to relive the humiliation so soon. He wondered how long it would be before word of his actions reached the ears of the angels. He didn't worry about his reputation so much as his friendships. What would Gabriel think if he knew what Michael had done?

"Summon them, Michael," Gabriel said, distracting Michael from his thoughts.

Michael called forth the angels who were in relationships with demons, and after explaining why they were there, they took their seats.

Raguel voted first, giving his strong opinion on the need to enforce the ban once and for all.

One by one they cast their votes, and Michael wasn't surprised to see that several of the archangels had changed their votes to join Raguel.

Gabriel voted to keep the status quo, as did Raphael, though Michael could tell he had reservations, and he suspected that only their friendship had tipped the scale.

Finally, the day—the moment—Michael had dreaded for years arrived. Seven votes for banning relationships and seven to allow them to continue had been cast. Fifteen archangels, one vote left, and it fell to Michael to break the tie.

For as long as he had been allowed to vote on the issue, Michael had abstained. But his vote had never made a difference to the outcome. Today it would. His choice right now could change the lives of not just him, but of all those angels sitting in the gallery, as well as those who might meet and fall for demons in the future. Their fate was in his hands and he had no idea what to say for the best.

"Well, it seems we're voting to allow relationships to continue," Raguel complained, the disappointment clear in his tone.

"Wait," said Michael, his voice quiet. "I've not voted yet."

"Well, we all know which way *you're* going to vote, don't we?" Raguel replied. "Let's just get this over with and move on to the next order of business."

"You think you know me so well?" Michael asked. "I have never once voted on this subject, but today I'm going to." He faced the gallery. "For those who are not aware, the reason I have always summoned you, to give you warning of these petitions, is because I too am in a relationship with a demon, and have been for many years. As you may already know, Lucifer, who I'm famed for killing in battle, lives. Not only that, he has shared my bed for centuries. If this ban should be imposed, I will be forced to make the same choice as each of you. My lover or my wings. By giving up our wings, we are able to avoid falling from grace, for to do so could bring about another war. Angels have fallen this day, and if this ban had been imposed upon us a hundred years ago, or even fifty years ago, it might have been avoided. I'm sorry, but had I known this day would come, perhaps I wouldn't have fought so hard to ensure we be allowed to love whomever we wish, even if that someone is a demon."

Michael turned to Raguel briefly and nodded. "I vote for the ban."

Raguel nearly fell from his chair in shock, which under any other circumstances might have brought a smile to

Michael's lips.

"Michael, are you sure you want to do this?" Gabriel asked. "Your mission to save Lucifer…"

"Was a lost cause from the moment I accepted it," Michael replied. "My vote is cast. The ban is now effective and no angel present is to leave this room without confirming their choice. Their wings or their lovers."

"What's your choice?" Gabriel asked.

Michael didn't know, but he hoped he would have the answer by the time the rest had made their decisions. "I need some time to decide," he said. "But I give my word, I'll make my choice before this meeting is concluded."

Gabriel nodded and faced the angels in the gallery. "Do any of you have any questions?"

One of the angels, a young man with dark skin and hair, rose to his feet. "What will happen to us if we give up our wings?"

Michael stood to answer the question for everyone in the gallery. "If you give up your wings, you have two choices, whether you wish to keep your lover or start over in a new life. If you're reborn, you will continue without your memories from the moment you walk through the archway of reincarnation, and at the end of your new life you'll be treated the same as you are at the end of every life you live. You may be reborn to another life or given the opportunity to become an angel again. It will be entirely dependent on how you lived your life. The other option, if you wish to continue your relationship, will involve you being relocated to Earth. You'll be given a new identity, a home, and enough funds to ensure you are comfortable until you are settled into your new life."

"What if we give up our wings and our lover no longer wants us?" another angel asked. "What if they were only interested because they wanted us to fall?"

Michael sighed and his thoughts turned to Lucifer.

'You will rule with me or kneel before me.'

He forced himself to focus. "That's a chance you must

take. Only you can decide whether or not you trust your lover."

The angels began to whisper among themselves. There was lots of shaking of heads and worried expressions. They needed a little time to make their choices, just as Michael did.

'You will do anything I tell you to, and we both know it.'

Deciding to give them what time he could, Michael turned back to the archangels. "While they're discussing their options, how about we focus on the issue of the fallen angels?"

"They need to be killed," Raguel said. "If they walk the earth, their presence will have a similar effect to that of Lucifer. Humans will be drawn to them, and demon recruitment will be boosted. The sooner they die, the better."

"Violence shouldn't be the first choice," Gabriel replied. "It should be a last resort, and only when all other avenues have been exhausted."

"Are you forgetting what happened the last time angels fell?" Raguel asked. "It was a long and bloody war."

"Not all the angels who fell were killed," Azrael pointed out.

"None came back to the light," Raguel reminded them. "Those who weren't killed remain imprisoned to this day. They have no more wish to be saved than Lucifer does."

"Has anyone spoken to them recently?" Metatron asked. "Besides their guards, that is."

Michael frowned. He hadn't been to the cells since he had helped escort the last of the captured fallen angels there. That had been long before the final battle of the war.

Around the circle, each of the other archangels shook their heads. Michael felt a pang of shame at how they had neglected to try to bring the previous former angels back to the light. They should have been working on healing them from the start, and if they had, maybe by now some or all of those would have been saved.

"Perhaps some of them might wish to come back to the

light by now," Gabriel suggested.

Michael wanted to agree with Gabriel, but he couldn't. They had tasted the same power Lucifer enjoyed. He didn't doubt they wanted out of their confinement, but they didn't crave the return of their wings, only the freedom and power they had as demons.

"You disagree?" Gabriel asked.

"Yes. If they are as like-minded as Lucifer, they won't want their wings back, only power."

Gabriel stared at him thoughtfully. "I think a short adjournment might be in order."

"Why?" Raguel questioned. "Now Michael is finally talking some sense after all these years, we might actually make some progress."

"I wish to speak to Michael privately," Gabriel replied, and without waiting for a response he stalked across the room, took Michael by the arm, and escorted him into one of the antechambers.

From the corner of his eye, Michael saw Raphael move toward them, but a glare from Gabriel halted him in his tracks.

As soon as the door closed behind them, Gabriel rounded on Michael. "What's going on? What happened in the Underworld?"

Michael shrugged. He didn't want to talk about it. "I realized something I should have figured out a long time ago."

"And what's that?"

"Lucifer doesn't *want* to be saved. He wants to corrupt me. He's been biding his time, waiting for me to fall. He's told me what I wanted to hear and I was foolish enough to believe him. I made a mistake when I accepted the mission to bring him back to the light."

"But you were making progress with him. Look how he is with your daughter. Or even how he is with you. He loves you."

"Does he?" Michael asked. "I'm not so sure anymore."

"What's changed? What did he say to you when you went to the Underworld?"

Michael sat on one of the stone seats and dropped his head into his hands. "It doesn't matter what he said. I saw him for what he truly is tonight and I didn't like it."

Gabriel took a seat beside him. "Talk to me, Michael, so we can try to figure out where to go from here?"

"Lucifer was drunk on power. That's why he didn't report back to us. He was celebrating with the rest of the demons and reveling in the boost to his powers the fallen angels have given him."

"Perhaps you should speak to him when he's more himself again."

Michael snorted. "He's a demon. Tonight I finally accepted that."

"You aren't going to tell me what happened in the Underworld, are you?"

"I can't," Michael admitted. "I…"

Gabriel patted his arm. "It's okay. You don't have to say anything until you're ready."

Michael took Gabriel's hand and squeezed. "Thank you."

"Do you truly believe Lucifer can't be saved?"

Michael nodded. "No one can be forced into the light."

"The cells here won't be able to hold him."

"I know." Michael sat back and stared at the ceiling. "Capturing Lucifer was never an option."

"No."

"I can't kill him."

"I'd never ask you to."

"What do you think I should do?" Michael asked.

"I don't know. Why did you vote for the ban, Michael?"

"Because it was the right thing to do," Michael replied. "We can't risk another war if more angels should fall."

"No, we can't, but are you sure you didn't vote for the ban because of whatever Lucifer said to you in the Underworld?"

"Perhaps that's part of the reason. I always thought one

day I'd be able to bring him back. Now I know I was wrong."

"You've given up on him."

It wasn't a question, but Michael nodded miserably. He felt Gabriel probing into his mind, trying to make sense of his thoughts. Michael pushed him out, desperate to stop him seeing what he had done. The presence retreated and Michael let Gabriel take him in his arms.

"Just hold on a little longer. This meeting will soon be over. Then we'll talk about what you're going to do."

Michael nodded and they embraced another minute or two, before he followed Gabriel back into the main chamber.

"Well?" Raguel asked.

"Well what?" Gabriel replied as he took his seat. "I said I wanted to speak to Michael privately."

"And what did he have to say?"

"Nothing I wish to share with the rest of the room," Gabriel snapped. "I wanted privacy for a reason. Now, where were we?"

Metatron gestured to the angels in the gallery. "We were waiting for you to return to hear the decisions of the angels."

Michael noted that the angels had stopped talking and appeared to have come to their decisions. He wished his own choice had been made, but things were not quite as simple for him. If he should live a mortal life on Earth, he would be a target for demons, just as he would have been had he chosen to raise his daughter personally.

One by one, the angels stepped forward and voiced their decisions. When the final one had spoken he noted there was almost an even number of angels giving up their demon lovers and those surrendering their wings. Of those choosing a life on Earth, none wished to be reborn.

"And what about you, Michael?" Raguel asked. "Have you decided yet?"

"I have," Michael said.

Gabriel stared at him with wide eyes.

"And?" Raguel pressed.

"We all know I wouldn't survive more than a few months

on Earth if I gave up my wings. I would be targeted by every demon in the Underworld from the moment I'm spotted. Without my powers, I'd be a walking target."

"Then you intend to give up Lucifer?" Raguel asked. "I don't believe you'll be able to stay away from him. You'll deceive us, yet again, as you crawl back into his bed the moment he snaps his fingers."

"That's uncalled for," Gabriel said.

"No," Michael interrupted. "Raguel has a point, and I accept his criticism. I also agree with him. I don't think I have the willpower to stay away from Lucifer, which is why I intend to be reborn."

Chapter Seventeen

Michael stood on his beach, facing the cliff wall where the tunnel was concealed. He raised his hand to the stone and focused on the crack Lucifer and he had created all those years ago. Inch by inch, Michael sealed the entrance. Only he and Lucifer had ever been able to open the passage to the Underworld—now Michael had locked it at his end. He wondered how long it would be before Lucifer even noticed what he had done.

"Are you sure you don't want to talk to him before you do this?" Gabriel asked.

"The others didn't have the opportunity to speak to their lovers," Michael reminded him.

"They haven't been in their relationships since time immemorial."

"I don't need to speak to him," Michael said. "He'll try to talk me out of it, and I'm afraid I'll let him."

"What do you think he'd want you to choose?" Gabriel asked. "I know he won't want you to put yourself in danger."

"Won't he?" Michael gave him a smile. "If I were to simply give up my wings and powers, leaving myself vulnerable to demons, and choose him, he would see it as a victory. By cutting my ties with the angels, he would believe I'm taking a step closer to him, and what he ultimately wants."

"You at his side."

"Yes. Though he might be angry at the loss of power my falling would have given him."

"Is that why you're doing this?" Gabriel asked. "Are you afraid you might fall?"

Michael whispered his answer. "Yes."

"You think this is your only choice, don't you?"

"It *is*. I can't live on Earth in this form, and I can't trust myself to stay away from him if I keep my wings. If I should fall, the consequences would be disastrous. Being reborn solves everything."

Gabriel shook his head. "Or you're running away from your problems. Giving up your memories and everything you've ever known is such a drastic step to take. I'm not sure you've thought this through."

"Maybe I *am* running away, but right now I don't see any other option."

"Don't do this, Michael. You can change your mind. Keep your wings, but end things with Lucifer. Maybe he'll respect your decision."

Michael laughed, the first real one since the recent fall of angels. "Your opinion of Lucifer is far higher than mine. Even with the tunnel closed, he'll find a way. He'll stalk me on Earth whenever I'm there, and he'll wear me down until I give in. Knowing me, it probably won't take him too long either."

"He knows he's not allowed on Earth unless he's accompanied by an archangel."

"Do you really believe he's going to stick to the rules?" Michael asked.

"You think he'll leave the Underworld?"

"We might refer to him as a prisoner there, but it's only because he agrees to it. If he wants to leave, he can do so any time he likes. We've all known that for centuries."

"Have you considered what he might do when he finds out what you've done?" Gabriel asked. "He'll be furious."

"What can he do?" Michael replied. "I'll be living a new life, with no memory of him or what we shared. I'll be one man among billions."

"We can try to shield you from him," Gabriel suggested. "Between us, I'm pretty sure the archangels can at least keep him from viewing you from the Underworld while you're growing up."

"Thank you," Michael said.

"Of course, it will be harder to hide you, the older you become," Gabriel pointed out. "And if he searched hard enough, he might find you anyway. You know whenever an angel is reborn they still retain their aura. If he has the entire Underworld hunting for you—and I think we both know that's a distinct possibility—it's only a matter of time before he tracks you down. He may not know it's you at first, but as you mature, he will. While you won't be identical in appearance, there'll be enough similarities to make you recognizable."

"I doubt he'll waste that much time and resources. By the time I'm old enough to be interesting to him, he'll have moved on."

"You don't believe that any more than I do."

Michael couldn't meet Gabriel's knowing gaze.

'One of you is going to suck me, Michael. It's him or you, so make your choice.'

"He'll find someone else," Michael whispered, even though the thought almost killed him.

"I'm not going to talk you out of this, am I?" Gabriel said.

Michael shook his head and began the walk to the archway of reincarnation. "No."

Gabriel matched him pace for pace as Michael strolled along the concourse. Raphael joined them partway.

"He's really going to go through with this?" Raphael asked Gabriel.

"Unless he bolts at the last moment, yes."

"I'm not going to bolt," Michael said.

"Lucifer is going to be furious," Raphael said.

"I've already pointed that out to him."

"And he's still going to go through with this madness?"

Michael glared at Raphael over his shoulder. His friend raised his hands in surrender. He wasn't going to argue with him.

"You do know he'll track you down as soon as he realizes

what you've done?" Raphael commented. "He can't stay away from you, any more than you can remain apart from him."

"Even if he does find me, without my memories he'll soon lose interest. I'll be just another mortal."

"I think you underestimate his feelings for you."

Michael turned to face Raphael and shook his head. "The one thing I have *never* done is underestimate him."

A crowd had gathered by the time Michael arrived at the archway of reincarnation. The rest of the archangels waited for him, along with a large number of lesser angels. All those who had been present in the chamber had gathered, including those who would shortly be going to Earth as mortals. Everyone wanted to see the unprecedented event of an archangel giving up everything to be reborn.

One person Michael hadn't expected, but was delighted to see, was his daughter. He took a few moments to speak with her out of earshot of the others, and she told him she understood what he was doing and why. Each time he saw her, he found himself surprised and pleased by her continuing good nature. She had grown into a fine young woman, and would one day be a great angel herself. Losing his memories of her would be his deepest regret. Unfortunately, it had to be done, and after they had spoken and said their goodbyes, Michael let her walk him back to the archway.

Raguel stepped between Michael and the archway. "I know we haven't always seen eye to eye, but I think you're making the right choice."

Michael nodded. "I hope you're right."

"Gabriel has told us of his plan to shield you from demonic monitoring, and I just want you to know I'll do my part to help."

"Thank you."

Raguel patted him on the shoulder before stepping aside so Michael could move forward a couple of steps.

Gabriel's hand on his arm stopped him from stepping

into the archway. "Don't you at least want to see him one last time before you do this?"

"No." Michael shook his head. "I won't let him talk me out of this."

"I don't mean in person, but you could always check in on him in the pool of visions."

"To what purpose? Torturing myself with my failure? No, it's better this way."

Gabriel sighed and pulled Michael into his arms. Michael hugged him back, then Raphael, and other archangels and angels. He suspected his fellow angels might miss him even more than Lucifer would.

Finally, everyone had wished him well, all words of advice had been offered, and Michael could put off his journey no longer.

Gabriel, who had barely left his side since they had left the archangels' chamber, stayed close to him. So close, in fact, that Michael had to remind him to step back or he might find himself being reborn too.

There was one last thing he had to do before he stepped through the archway. Michael removed his necklace, the gift from Lucifer he had worn for so long, and placed it in Gabriel's hand. "Keep this safe for me."

Gabriel nodded. "Live a good life," he said, and he pulled Michael back into his arms again, this time kissing him deeply on the lips.

Michael's shock at Gabriel's kiss lasted only as long as the kiss itself. As soon as he stepped back, he was through the archway and his new life had begun.

Chapter Eighteen

Michael stirred his coffee, his attention focused on the tech article on his tablet he had been engrossed in for the last fifteen minutes. He didn't notice the man sitting opposite him until he heard a pointed cough.

"You certainly took some tracking down," the stranger said.

Michael frowned. "Do I know you?"

"Very amusing, Michael." The strange man gave him a dazzling smile, revealing straight white teeth.

"How do you know my name?"

The smile slipped from the man's face and was replaced by a frown.

Michael shifted uncomfortably under the sudden scrutiny. "I need to get back to work," he said as he grabbed his coffee and tablet and made a hasty exit from the café.

He had no idea who the strange man had been, but for the rest of the day his mind kept drifting back to him, and to the piercing blue eyes that seemed to see right through him.

When he left the office, late as usual, he thought he saw the blond man watching him from across the street, but on taking a closer look, no one was there.

Still, the feeling of being watched didn't leave him, not even after he'd arrived home. He put it down to nerves and tried to pull himself together.

* * * *

The next day Michael saw the stranger again. The man approached him in the same café, once again taking the seat opposite him.

"So, how long do you intend to keep this up?" he asked.

"I think you've mistaken me for someone else," Michael said.

"You might be going by Michael Smith these days—not the most original of names—but I know it's you. Do you realize it's taken me twenty years to track you down?"

Michael didn't know how this man had found out his name or what to say, except to point out the obvious. "I'm twenty years old, which should tell you, you have the wrong person."

"I don't think so. I'd know you anywhere. My *soul* will always find you."

Michael shivered at the intensity of the man's words, his first instinct to run from the café again.

"You've been playing at being human for twenty years now," the man continued. "It's time for you to come home, to me."

Michael had heard enough. "I don't know who you are, or what the hell you're talking about, but I suggest you fuck off and annoy someone else."

The man reeled back. "Michael, it's me, Lucifer."

"Lucifer?" Michael laughed loudly. "Damn, your parents must have been *cruel* to land you with *that* name."

Lucifer—if that was even his real name—gazed at him in confusion and...hurt? Then his expression changed to one of shock. "What have you done?" Lucifer whispered.

"I don't know what you're talking about," Michael replied.

"You don't remember me." Lucifer shook his head and blinked rapidly, as though he was trying to stop tears from falling, but why would that be the case?

"I've never met you before yesterday," Michael said. "I'm sorry, but I honestly believe you've got me confused with someone else."

"No," Lucifer said quietly. "I'd know you anywhere. I just never imagined you would do *this*."

"Do what?"

Lucifer stood and stumbled back from the table. "I have to go."

Michael didn't try to make him stay. Handsome as the man was, he seemed rather creepy too. He didn't know whether to hope he saw Lucifer again or to pray he didn't.

* * * *

Lucifer returned to the café a few weeks later. This time he seemed to accept that Michael didn't know him and didn't try to insist they had met before.

"I think we should go on a date this weekend," Lucifer suggested.

"Excuse me?" Michael gaped at Lucifer. He had sat at the table ten minutes ago, they had exchanged small talk, somewhat reluctantly on Michael's part, and now he wanted a date?

"Dinner perhaps," Lucifer commented as though Michael hadn't spoken.

"I already have plans this weekend," Michael lied.

"I don't believe you."

Michael scowled. "Why not?"

"Because you've met me now, and I know I'm irresistible."

"Arrogant much?" Michael asked as he checked his watch. He didn't particularly want to go back to the office yet, but Lucifer's tone was so superior, he just wanted to escape his presence.

"You don't need to be back at work for another thirty-four minutes," Lucifer said.

Michael didn't ask how Lucifer knew. "I think I need to start changing round my schedule."

"Why?"

"So stalkers like you can't gather information about my whereabouts at any time of the day."

"I'm not a stalker. I'm the man you're going to spend eternity with."

"Eternity?" Michael snorted. "One lifetime isn't enough for you?"

"I intend to live a *very* long life," Lucifer replied. "And I see you at my side."

With every word Lucifer said, Michael became more ill at ease. When Lucifer talked about forever, Michael could almost believe he meant it literally.

"I see me leaving," Michael said. He stood and grabbed his jacket from the back of his chair. "Please don't come near me again."

Lucifer didn't try to stop him and Michael quickly hurried from the café. He glanced back just once and saw two handsome strangers standing over Lucifer. They seemed angry for some reason, but Michael had no intention of sticking around to find out why.

* * * *

From that day forward Michael's life seemed to take a turn for the worse. Lots of turns for the worse, in fact.

Even though he had never been particularly accident-prone, Michael found himself making numerous visits to the Accident and Emergency department, with injuries ranging from a broken wrist after having someone fall off a ladder on top of him, to a bad case of food poisoning following a date that hadn't been going particularly well to begin with.

He'd even managed to wind up in a car accident resulting in a two-day hospital visit, where he could have sworn he heard a man talking to him while he struggled to regain consciousness. The staff at the hospital insisted that he hadn't received any visitors, but he knew what he had heard.

His love life didn't fare much better. For some reason he seemed to attract the worst men out there. If a man was a layabout, a liar, or a plain old cheat, Michael found him. By the time he approached thirty years of age, he was convinced he would never find the so-called love of his life.

Changing jobs and moving town didn't help either. His mother told him he couldn't run away from his problems, but he told himself a fresh start couldn't hurt. All it seemed to do, though, was introduce him to a new hospital and another social network of men who just weren't right for him.

Bad luck followed Michael wherever he went, resulting in him dodging traffic on the busy high street, while he chased after his over-priced concert ticket, which had flown out of his hand, despite the fact there wasn't a trace of a breeze.

If Michael didn't know better, he'd swear his ticket had a mind and will of its own.

A car horn blared as the driver swerved to miss him. "Wanker!" the motorist yelled.

Michael ignored him.

Ahead of him, the slip of paper was plucked out of the air by a handsome man about Michael's own age. He hoped the man was honest enough to hand it back.

Panting and breathless, Michael finally caught up to his wayward ticket.

"Yours?" The man held the ticket aloft.

Michael nodded.

"You're out of shape," the man teased. "Too much fish and chips, I'd say."

Michael frowned, wondering how this stranger knew his favorite meal. Then again, he was in England, where fish and chips had been a well-loved dinner for over a century. It must have been a lucky guess.

"Can I have my ticket back?" Michael asked once he had found his voice again.

"Sure."

Michael took the paper and tucked it safely into his jacket. "Thanks. I spent a small fortune on that."

"I know." The man took an identical piece of paper from his own pocket. "I just got mine this morning too."

Fate. The word popped into Michael's head, even though

he didn't believe in such things.

"Front row of the balcony."

"Mine too," Michael said.

"I guess I'll see you there then."

The man turned away.

"Wait! What's your name?"

"Gabe," he replied.

"I'm Michael."

"Nice to meet you, Michael," Gabe said. "Take care of that ticket now."

As Michael watched Gabe walk away he considered maybe things were looking up.

At the concert, Michael found himself seated right beside Gabe. They enjoyed the show and afterward they went for a drink together. By the end of the night Michael and Gabe were talking like old friends and had already made plans to meet up the following week too.

Handsome and charming, Gabe quickly became a constant presence in his life. Michael enjoyed spending time with him. They could laugh and joke together as easily as they could debate and talk about the more serious issues of the day. He just wished there was a spark of attraction for him.

Although Gabe was bisexual, and presently without a partner of either gender, he never made a move on Michael. Michael had asked him once why not, and Gabe had told him he saw Michael as the brother he had never had. Michael felt as though he had known Gabe forever.

"Forever is a long time," Gabe replied when Michael told him that.

Michael shrugged. "Don't you ever feel like maybe we've known each other before?"

"Maybe we have, in another life," Gabe suggested.

"Do you believe in that sort of stuff?"

"Yes, don't you?"

"I never really thought about it."

Gabe smiled. "Maybe you should. If you believe death is the end of everything, you'll be rather disappointed when you find out it isn't."

"You sound pretty sure there's an afterlife."

"I am."

Michael wasn't so certain, but he respected Gabe's beliefs.

The restaurant they ate at this evening wasn't particularly crowded, and that was probably why Michael felt the undeniable sensation of someone focusing on him. Trying not to be obvious about it, Michael glanced round the room and, sure enough, there was a vaguely familiar man eating alone and staring right at him.

"What is it?" Gabe asked.

"Nothing." Michael turned his attention back to his friend.

"I just asked you the same question three times. Whatever's distracting you isn't nothing."

Michael shrugged. "Just a guy over there. I thought he was looking at me."

"He is."

"You saw him?" Michael couldn't hide his surprise. "Why didn't you say anything?"

"Forget about him. He's trouble."

"You know him?"

"Yes." Gabe's tone made it clear he didn't want to discuss the man, but Michael's curiosity was piqued.

"Well, who is he? And why do you think he's bad news?"

Gabe sighed. "His name's Lucifer, and believe me when I say he's perfectly named."

"Lucifer?" Something sparked in Michael's memory. A man, in a café, with the same name. He shivered and glanced back at the man across the room. It *was* the same person. Then he remembered the last time he had seen him, when two other men had stood over Lucifer as Michael had scurried away. Gabe had been one of those men.

"I saw you," Michael said. "Talking to him in a café—it must have been ten years ago now—you and some other man."

"I didn't realize you saw us," Gabe said.

Michael wondered if this was some sort of game the three

of them were playing with him, but he swiftly dismissed the idea. Gabe didn't play games.

"Forget about him," Gabe repeated.

Michael nodded, yet his eyes kept drifting back to Lucifer. He couldn't seem to help himself. Even though he now recalled his previous encounters with Lucifer, he felt drawn to him. He tried to push the feeling aside. The man had practically been stalking him, he certainly didn't need any encouragement.

Was it a coincidence he was here, all these miles away from the café where they had once met? Michael hoped it was, because the alternative appeared to be that Lucifer had spent the last ten years tracking him down to the other side of the country.

* * * *

Now he had reappeared in his life, Michael couldn't help seeing Lucifer on a regular basis. The strange man never approached him yet still seemed to be a constant presence. Michael would see him on the bus, in the supermarket, or walking down the street. The odd thing was he never once saw him when he was alone. Gabe was with Michael every single time Lucifer appeared. He mentioned it to his friend once, but Gabe merely shrugged and muttered, "Coincidence."

Michael continued to search for Mr. Right, whoever he might be, but when he was being completely honest with himself, he admitted he wasn't looking too hard. He also accepted that if Lucifer ever did speak to him again, he'd be willing to give him a second chance.

He didn't know why he found the man intriguing. It certainly wasn't Lucifer's manners. Each time they had spoken Lucifer had been arrogant and rude, neither quality being ones Michael found attractive. Yet, Michael couldn't seem to stop thinking about him, or watching out for him around town.

Michael wanted to see him again and maybe find out why he found the man so fascinating.

* * * *

Michael and Gabe sat in the park, eating chips and watching a group of kids kicking a football around on the lawn. Lucifer sat beside Michael, on the opposite side to Gabe. He nicked a chip from Michael's tray, grinning widely as he popped it into his mouth.

"Did you want something?" Gabe asked. "Besides our chips, I mean."

"Just enjoying a summer afternoon," Lucifer replied. "Don't you have somewhere you need to be?"

"Not right now."

"Are you sure?" Lucifer pressed. "Only you're cramping my style."

Gabe rolled his eyes. "You know the rules, Lucifer. I'm not going anywhere."

"Rules?" Michael asked. "What are you talking about?"

Gabe cursed under his breath.

"Keep out of my head," Lucifer said, which made about as much sense as Gabe's comment about rules.

Gabe swore again, and Michael gave him a questioning glance. Gabe shook his head briefly and mouthed, "Later."

Lucifer used Michael's distraction as an opportunity to steal another chip and Michael slapped his hand. "Gabe here has appointed himself your personal bodyguard, or didn't he tell you that? He seems to believe you can't think for yourself."

"I'm sure that's not true," Michael replied.

"Oh, but it is," Lucifer whispered into his ear. "He knows he can't keep us apart forever, but he will insist on acting as a cock blocker for as long as he can. I'm sure *you* don't want that, do you, Michael?"

Michael gulped, nearly choking on his food.

Lucifer didn't give him much of a chance to respond. "I

can do things to your body you've only ever dreamed of. All you have to do is give me a chance to show you."

"Um." Michael glanced at Gabe, who gave no sign of having heard Lucifer's whisper.

"That eunuch has nothing to offer you," Lucifer continued. "I can offer you the world."

"Eunuch?" Gabe snarled, revealing he had heard every word, no matter how quietly Lucifer had been murmuring in Michael's ear.

Lucifer smirked at Gabe. "When did you last get laid?"

"Mind your own business. Besides, what's it been for you, about thirty years, right?"

Michael wouldn't have put Lucifer at older than twenty-five, and certainly no older than himself. In fact, now he thought about it, he realized Lucifer looked just the same as he had when he'd seen him ten years ago. Or maybe his memory played tricks on him.

While he was contemplating Lucifer's age, he and Gabe continued to argue.

"So, how long ago was it?" Lucifer asked. "Tenth century? Or maybe as far back as the eighth?"

Michael finished his chips as the two men squabbled across him like a pair of children. When Lucifer rose to his feet to yell at Gabe, Michael stood as well. He shook his head, tossed his empty tray into the rubbish bin, and walked away, leaving the pair of them to fight it out. He idly wondered if there could be some unresolved sexual tension between the two men but quickly shoved the thought aside. The idea made him unexpectedly jealous, though he didn't want to look too closely at who he was jealous of.

* * * *

Michael dreamt about Lucifer that night, and it was the most erotic dream he had ever experienced.

"It's been so long, Michael," Lucifer whispered into his ear. "I need you so badly."

Lucifer's weight on top of him should have scared him, but Michael reminded himself this was just a dream.

"Tell me you want me," Lucifer demanded.

"I want you," Michael replied. "I don't know why, but I want you so much I don't think I can go another day without you."

"You won't have to," Lucifer told him.

With gentle touches, Lucifer stroked Michael's chest and abdomen, his fingers skimming the waistband of the boxers Michael slept in. Michael's erection strained against the fabric and he moaned in pleasure.

"That's it," Lucifer whispered. "Moan for me, Michael. Let me hear you."

Michael groaned, a wave of desire washing over him at Lucifer's touch. Lucifer responded to his sounds of delight by gripping Michael's cock through the boxers and squeezing. Michael bucked his hips and gave a choked cry. It had been so long since his last boyfriend, and even longer since he had felt so strongly about someone.

Lucifer moved his hand lower, slipping his fingers between Michael's thighs. "Open up for me."

Michael obeyed Lucifer's command immediately, spreading his legs so Lucifer could settle between them.

"Am I dreaming?" Michael asked as Lucifer rubbed their groins together.

"Yes," Lucifer replied. "This is all in your head."

"Are you going to fuck me?"

"Not tonight," Lucifer said.

Knowing this wasn't a one-night stand made Michael happy. His arse ached in anticipation of feeling Lucifer inside him, but he could wait.

"Tonight is just the beginning," Lucifer told him.

Michael nodded and wrapped his legs around Lucifer's thighs, trapping him close. He bucked his hips, feeling Lucifer's hardness against his own.

"That's it," Lucifer gasped.

Michael moaned again and slipped his hands down

Lucifer's back, cupping his bare arse. When had Lucifer undressed? He frowned in confusion before he remembered this was a dream. He tried to imagine his own clothing away, but it seemed his dream world didn't work quite as well as he would have liked. He didn't let it bother him. He had never felt like this before.

Closing his eyes, Michael gave his body to Lucifer without reservation, letting him use him as he wanted. All Michael could do was hold on tight for the ride and he did. Slick with sweat, they moved in a timeless rhythm of perfect synchronization, something Michael had never achieved with other men, yet that seemed to come naturally with Lucifer. Of course, since this was a dream, it stood to reason they would be perfectly matched. There shouldn't be any awkwardness during a sex dream.

"I'm close," Michael shouted and, no sooner had the words left his lips, he felt Lucifer stiffen in his arms. He opened his eyes to the sight of Lucifer on the brink of his climax. Michael cried out as they came, together, with perfect timing.

* * * *

When Michael woke the next morning, he felt as though something momentous had happened, and he smiled at his ceiling.

Beside him, the bed was empty, but the sheets were rumpled, as though someone had been sleeping next to him.

"Lucifer?" he called.

No reply came.

"Just a dream," Michael muttered. He sat up and swung his feet down to the floor, grimacing when he realized he'd had a wet dream, coming in his boxers, something he hadn't done in years.

He stumbled to the bathroom, determined to put the dream from his mind.

By the time he had eaten a quick breakfast and was on his way to work, he felt more like himself again.

Gabe met him partway to the office and they walked the rest of the way together.

"You seem rather perky this morning," Gabe commented. "Something you want to share with me?"

"Just a pleasant dream last night," Michael replied with a smile. "A *very* pleasant dream, if you know what I mean?"

Gabe leaned close with a grin. "Are you telling me you had a sex dream last night?"

"Yeah, and it was *hot*."

"How hot?"

"Hot enough that I came in my boxers like a damn teenager," Michael replied. "And he didn't even fuck me."

"He?"

"Um." Michael frowned when he recalled the last time he had actually seen Lucifer, yesterday in the park. He and Gabe had been arguing. Perhaps it wouldn't be such a great idea to tell his friend he'd had a sex dream about someone he clearly had issues with. "Just a faceless guy. It was kind of dark."

Gabe gave him a doubtful look but didn't question him further about his dream man's identity.

Michael pushed the little white lie from his mind and by the time he arrived at work he had almost forgotten about it entirely.

He didn't forget about Lucifer. In fact, he spent most of the day thinking about him and daydreaming about when he might see him again. He wondered what the enigmatic man did for a living. He didn't seem like a regular office worker and Michael had never seen him in a suit. He never appeared to be in a hurry and Michael had seen him at various times of day. If Michael's schedule was set in stone, Lucifer's was the exact opposite.

The more Michael pondered Lucifer, the less he realized he knew about him. He didn't even know his surname.

Michael smiled to himself. On the other hand, he did

know just how talented Lucifer was in the bedroom, even if it was just in his dreams.

* * * *

Lucifer came to him in his dreams the next night too, this time playing homage to Michael's cock and balls, while not touching any other part of his body, no matter how much Michael begged him. He licked and sucked Michael for what seemed like hours, gripping the base of his shaft with just the right amount of pressure to prevent him from coming too soon.

Michael keened as he tried to thrust into Lucifer's mouth, but Lucifer held him down, preventing him from setting the pace.

This time when he came, it was with Lucifer's lips wrapped tight around his cock.

The next morning Michael expected to wake to another pair of boxers sticky with the evidence of his orgasm, but to his surprise he didn't. The boxers were on the floor — where he had a vague recollection of Lucifer tossing them in his dream — and there was no trace of Michael having come in his dream at all. Unless…

Michael pushed the thought aside. Lucifer hadn't been in his bed last night. It was impossible. Yet Michael checked both the doors to his house anyway, finding each securely locked and bolted.

* * * *

On the third night Michael checked all the doors and windows, locking everything with keys, bolts, and chains. No way was anyone getting into his home tonight.

He went to bed uncharacteristically early, even as he called himself a fool for acting like a kid waiting for Santa Claus to visit on Christmas Eve.

He fell asleep a little before midnight, his disappointment at the empty bed keeping him awake.

"Anyone would think you didn't want me here," Lucifer whispered into his ear.

Michael glanced at the bedside clock and saw it was just after two in the morning. "How did you get in here?"

"*You* let me in," Lucifer replied.

"No I didn't, the doors and windows are locked."

"I know they are, but that's not what I meant. You want me in your bed, and so here I am."

"Am I dreaming?"

"Of course you are," Lucifer said. "But sometimes our dreams are so much better than reality. Wouldn't you agree?"

Michael nodded and launched himself at Lucifer, tearing at his clothes as he searched for the bare skin his fingers ached to touch.

On the previous two nights Lucifer had taken control of their encounters, but tonight Michael needed something else. He pushed Lucifer onto his back and straddled his thighs. He stared at the man beneath him, his torn shirt revealing his beautifully sculpted chest. Lucifer still wore his jeans, and Michael could see the outline of his cock trapped within them. He touched the hardness, stroking lightly and watching the erection grow under his fingers.

Lucifer fumbled with the belt of his jeans, but Michael slapped his hands out of the way.

"Please," Lucifer begged.

Michael laughed now the tables had been turned, but he undid the belt and popped open the already straining buttons. Lucifer didn't wear any undergarments, so as soon as the fly was undone, his cock sprang free. Michael licked his lips, his mouth watering at the sight of the pearly drop of pre-cum at the tip. He wanted to taste Lucifer more than he had ever wanted anything else in his life.

Lucifer gazed at him. "Are you going to fuck me?"

Michael shook his head. "Not tonight."

Lucifer groaned and closed his eyes. "Next time, because I can't wait much longer to feel you inside me. It's been too long."

"How long?" Michael asked.

"It feels like centuries," Lucifer replied.

Michael smiled at the evasive answer. Lucifer certainly had a way with words.

Scooting back down the bed, Michael leaned in and licked at Lucifer's cock, tasting him for the first time. He was tempted to take him into his mouth, as Lucifer had done to him the previous night, but the wicked imp on his shoulder wanted to make Lucifer suffer a little before he came.

Michael kept his touches light and teasing as he worked his way back up Lucifer's body. He sucked on his nipples, then his neck, knowing he would leave a mark on the perfect skin.

He rubbed his arse against Lucifer's cock, teasing both Lucifer and himself with what they both wanted.

Lucifer moaned and Michael captured his lips in a passionate kiss, delving his tongue into Lucifer's mouth, swallowing his moans. When Lucifer's tongue touched his own, Michael's erection swelled. They kissed fiercely, each trying to dominate the other, but Michael had no intention of letting Lucifer take charge tonight. He bit Lucifer's lip, grabbed at his hair, and clawed at his back. Lucifer gave as good as he got, and Michael reveled in the roughness.

"Fuck!" Michael screamed when Lucifer flipped him onto his back. They rolled around on the bed, one on top, then the other, neither prepared to give an inch as they each sought to dominate and control.

Lucifer pulled him into a sitting position and crashed their mouths together once more. Michael surrendered to the kiss before turning it around again, forcing Lucifer to bend to his will.

Michael ground his erection against Lucifer's flat stomach then pushed his arse back to rub against Lucifer's stiff length. He found the perfect angle and rhythm without breaking his connection to Lucifer.

Lucifer's nails, which Michael privately thought needed

to be trimmed, scraped at his spine and dug into his arse. Michael didn't know how long he would last, but he suspected another minute would be optimistic.

"Call my name," Lucifer demanded. "I want to hear my name on your lips when you come."

"Lucifer!" Michael screamed, unable to do anything other than obey Lucifer's command.

"You are *mine*," Lucifer whispered as Michael came back down to Earth. "Nothing can keep us apart. Do you hear me, Michael?"

Michael nodded sleepily. "Nothing," he murmured.

"Remember that," Lucifer said. "It doesn't matter where you go or how many years have passed, I will *always* find you again."

Michael shivered, but the words didn't scare him as he thought they should.

"Your place is at my side," Lucifer continued.

"Your side," Michael mumbled. He rolled into Lucifer's arms and rested his head on his chest, sleepily content and only half listening to Lucifer's words.

"Are you ready to join me now?" Lucifer asked quietly. "Have I waited long enough?"

Michael burrowed closer into Lucifer's embrace and closed his eyes, letting sleep take him. His last thought before he drifted off was how could he be dreaming about going to sleep if he already was?

* * * *

The next morning Michael wasn't surprised to find his bed empty once more. The rumpled sheets were equally expected. Only when he caught sight of his reflection in the bathroom mirror did he start to question his sanity.

His swollen lips looked as though they had been thoroughly kissed. He touched a love bite on his neck and could see another on his hip. He remembered Lucifer clawing at his back, and when he twisted round he could see the clear scratch marks running nearly the length of his spine.

"Fuck!"

Michael ran from the bathroom, going first to the front door, then the back, finding both securely locked, just as they had been the night before. Every window remained locked and bolted. No one could have entered the building without his knowledge.

He grabbed his mobile and called Gabe.

"What is it?" Gabe asked. "Are you running late for work?"

"No, I..." Michael didn't know what to say. He'd had another dirty dream and he'd apparently scratched himself up in the process. Except he couldn't reach the marks easily, so how could he be responsible for them? And he hadn't been kissing himself.

"I'll be right over," Gabe said.

Michael nodded, even though Gabe couldn't see him, and sat on the bed to wait.

It wasn't until Gabe arrived, and Michael opened the door, that he remembered he was naked.

Gabe gave him a sweeping glance and a smirk. "You really are out of it this morning, aren't you? Go put some clothes on before your neighbors call the cops."

Michael hurried to dress, only recalling the scratches Lucifer had given him when Gabe gave a low whistle.

"What happened to your back?" Gabe asked. "Or, should I say, who?"

Michael grabbed a robe from the hook on his bedroom door and covered himself. "I think I had some rough sex last night," he said when he joined Gabe in the living room.

"You *think*? Don't you remember?"

"Yes, I remember everything, but—and this is going to sound weird—I went to bed alone last night."

"You're right, it does sound weird."

"I locked the doors and windows and I *know* there was no one in the house except me. Yet, he came to me again.

278

He just appeared in my bed in the middle of the night. I thought I was dreaming, like the last couple of nights, but then…" Michael gestured to the love bite on his neck and pointed at his back.

"And your mouth looks as if it's spent the night round a man's cock," Gabe added.

Michael touched his tender lips. "No, but we spent a lot of the night kissing, and we weren't exactly gentle."

"I can tell. Did you see who it was this time?"

Michael ducked his head.

"Or, should I ask, are you going to tell me the truth this time?" Gabe amended.

"I've been dreaming about Lucifer," Michael admitted. "I don't know why, but I have. It's not as if I even like him much. If I see him when I'm awake he acts like a stalker or an arrogant jerk."

"That's because he *is* an arrogant jerk."

"Then why am I having sex dreams about him?" Michael asked.

"I think that's something only you can answer," Gabe said.

Michael sighed. "I guess it means I'm attracted to him, right?"

"I think that's a given," Gabe replied with a chuckle. "Even I can see he's a gorgeous specimen of man."

"What's the history between you two, anyway?" Michael had been curious about their past since discovering that Gabe and Lucifer knew each other. "He's not one of your exes, is he?"

"Heavens no!" Gabe appeared torn between appalled and amused at the suggestion.

"Then how *do* you know him?"

"It's a long story."

"Another time?"

Gabe shrugged. "Maybe."

Michael didn't press him. He had soon discovered that Gabe wasn't exactly forthcoming about his life, and Michael didn't wish to pry.

"Perhaps I should give him a chance," Michael said. "Go on a date and see where things lead."

Gabe laughed. "You've had sex with him for the last three nights. I think you're past the first-date stage."

"Dreams don't count," Michael pointed out.

Gabe eased aside Michael's collar and gently touched the bruise on his neck. "Are you sure you were dreaming?"

Michael wasn't, and that scared him more than anything else.

* * * *

Now he was keeping an eye open for him, Michael didn't see Lucifer at all. Nor did he have any more dreams about him. At first he wasn't sure whether to be relieved or disappointed, but as the days became weeks and still Lucifer didn't appear, he accepted it was the latter.

Gabe was also mysteriously absent, but he often traveled for his work, and Michael assumed his career kept him busy this time too.

Lucifer finally reappeared two months later, sitting on Michael's doorstep when he arrived home from work. Gabe, who was also back in town, had walked home with Michael but quickly made his excuses and disappeared round the corner, leaving Michael alone with Lucifer.

"Missed me?" Lucifer asked.

Michael sat beside him on the step. He wanted some answers to his questions, but he didn't know what to ask first.

"No?" Lucifer prodded. "Maybe I should just make my visits nightly. You seemed to welcome me then."

Michael twisted round so he sat sideways, facing Lucifer. "So, you *were* in my bed."

"Of course."

"I thought I was dreaming."

Lucifer chuckled. "Maybe your whole life is a dream?"

"Maybe I need to fit better locks on my doors."

"No lock can keep me out, and we both know it."

Somehow Michael *did* know. Lucifer was scarily determined, and for some reason Michael couldn't fathom, he wanted Michael.

Lucifer shifted position so he faced Michael. He sighed and stared at the corner Gabe had disappeared around. "I've been advised I'm not exactly playing fair with you."

"What do you mean? And advised by who?"

"By Gabe and the rest of his little crew of do-gooders."

"Has he threatened you?" Michael didn't think it sounded like Gabe, but there was a lot he didn't know about his friend, just as he was sure there was plenty Gabe didn't know about him.

"Not recently, and I can handle him anyway."

"What do you mean about playing fair?"

"Gabe thinks luring you to my side with sex is playing dirty. He knows I'm irresistible."

"Did anyone ever tell you you're arrogant?" Michael asked.

"I believe *you* did," Lucifer reminded him.

Michael laughed. "I guess I did, didn't I? So, what are you going to do if you're going to play fair?"

"I'm going to make you an offer," Lucifer said. "One you can't resist."

"Hmm?"

Lucifer gave him a mock frown. "Can you at least try to sound a little curious?"

Michael gave him a wide-eyed stare. "Oh my goodness, what offer? Tell me, tell me, please!"

Lucifer rolled his eyes. "You're the only one who could ever get away with mocking me in such a manner."

Michael grinned. "Okay, I'll be serious. Tell me your offer?"

Lucifer smiled and took his hand. "How would you like to never have another visit to Accident and Emergency?"

"How do you know about those?"

"I know *everything* about you," Lucifer replied.

"And that's your offer, no more trips to the hospital?"

"That's part of it. How about the promotion you've been working toward for the last eight months? The one you didn't get last week."

Michael frowned. He hadn't even told Gabe about the job.

"I can fix up this house for you, furnish the place however you want, no expense spared."

"Is that all?" Michael asked.

"All?" Lucifer echoed. "I'm offering you perfect health, a great promotion, and the home of your dreams."

"In exchange for what?"

"That's the best part," Lucifer whispered. "To get all of that, all you have to do is accept me and agree to be by my side forever."

"You keep using that word."

"What word?"

"Forever."

"It's the right word to use."

"Is it? Nothing lasts forever, least of all relationships."

"Ours will."

"What makes you so sure?"

Lucifer smiled. "You've just had some bad experiences. You seem to attract the wrong type of man."

"Do you include yourself in that number?" Michael waited for Lucifer to say *no* or *of course not,* but he didn't. "Well, how would you go about getting me the promotion?"

"Ask me no questions and I'll tell you no lies."

Michael scowled. "Are you being deliberately evasive?"

"I'm offering you your dreams."

"What do *you* know about my dreams?" Michael asked.

Lucifer ran his index finger down Michael's cheek. "I know more than you think. Do you accept my offer?"

"I don't know."

"Does it tempt you even a little?" Lucifer asked. "Or is there something else you desire instead? I can give you anything you want, all you have to do is ask."

"How about true love and happiness?" Michael replied.

"*I'm* your true love."

"But can you make me happy?" Michael questioned quietly.

Lucifer leered at him. "I can make you *very* happy indeed."

"Be serious," Michael said. "I'm not talking about sex. Do you *really* think you can make me happy for the rest of my life?"

Lucifer frowned, as though he didn't quite understand the question.

Michael stood and smiled at Lucifer. "Let me know when you figure out the answer. Maybe then I'll consider your offer."

* * * *

Michael expected Lucifer to return within a couple of days, with reassurances about how he could indeed make him happy. He was quite disappointed when he didn't show. He was tempted to ask Gabe if he had seen him, but he couldn't manage to work up the courage. He wasn't sure he wanted to know the answer.

He spent a ridiculous amount of time wondering where Lucifer was, even going so far as to try to track him down on the Internet. Unfortunately, with a name like Lucifer and no surname to go on, Michael struggled to find anything that wasn't about the original fallen angel, which didn't help him at all.

Sometimes he thought he sensed someone watching him, but he never saw who it might be. He put it down to an overactive imagination, especially when the feelings lingered while he was alone in his house.

Lucifer might have found a way to enter his home and join him in his bed, but he had been very much present at the time. Unless he had the power to become invisible, Lucifer certainly wasn't hanging around now.

"I'm going to be leaving town," Gabe told him a couple of

months after Lucifer had made Michael his offer.

"Yeah? How long for this time?"

Gabe took a deep breath. "Permanently, I think."

Michael opened and closed his mouth. "Oh. You don't intend to come back at all?"

"No. My new job is on the other side of the world."

"Well, that's, er, great." Michael tried to sound enthusiastic but failed miserably. "We'll keep in touch though, yeah?"

"I'll call you as soon as I'm settled. Maybe you can fly out and visit?"

"I'd like that." Michael wasn't lying, but he couldn't afford the life of a jet-setter. He felt as if he were on the verge of losing his best friend.

At first he heard from Gabe every week, before the calls became monthly, then every few months, until they tapered off to holiday calls. It was hard to maintain a friendship over such a long distance, and, although Michael tried, he found himself talking to Gabe's answering machine more than he did Gabe.

He missed him, but life moved on. He worked and eventually earned the promotion he wanted. He dated, though he never found someone he wanted to move in with or marry.

Michael enjoyed life, though sometimes, particularly at night, when the creaking of the house was the only sound he heard apart from his own breathing, he wondered what would have happened if he had accepted Lucifer's offer. Would Lucifer be with him now, sharing his bed and home, *forever*?

He guessed he would never know.

Chapter Nineteen

Michael lived a long life, something that constantly surprised him, considering how accident-prone he had been from the age of twenty onward.

He suspected the end must be near when he began hallucinating. Gabe, his old friend, whom he hadn't laid eyes on in sixty years, stood at his bedside, looking just as he had the last time he had seen him.

"Hello, Michael," Gabe greeted him with a smile. "I'm here to take you home."

"I think the doctor might have something to say about discharging myself," Michael replied, every word an effort to speak.

"Not that home," Gabe said as he took his hand.

Michael felt strength he hadn't experienced in years flooding his body. He rose with ease, no longer feeling the ache in his back and joints. He wanted to look behind him, and yet at the same time he didn't. Curiosity won out and he glanced over his shoulder. He saw himself, eerily still, and knew his life had ended.

"I guess you were right," Michael said.

"About what?" Gabe asked.

"There is more after death."

"Of course there is."

Michael frowned. "When did you die?"

Gabe shrugged. "I haven't died."

"Then how…?"

Michael gasped as wings appeared on Gabe's back, spreading out behind him, pure white and beautiful.

"I'm here to take you home," Gabe said again.

This time Michael didn't try to argue with him. He let Gabe guide him to whatever came next.

Heaven was just as the stories described, beautiful and bathed in eternal sunlight. Angels walked around, as well as others like Michael, the newly deceased, staring at everything with wonder. Everyone appeared young and beautiful, and when Michael studied his own hands he saw that they too showed no signs of his advanced years.

"I have a confession to make," Gabe said.

Michael raised an eyebrow and waited.

"I was never human," Gabe admitted. "This is what I've always been."

"An angel?"

"An archangel, actually," another angel said. "Welcome home, Michael."

Michael smiled at the second angel. "It's nice to meet you...er?"

"Raphael," the angel replied. "And you've already met Gabriel, of course."

Gabriel shrugged. "I thought Gabe sounded more modern."

Michael laughed. "The archangel Gabriel. No wonder you were so convinced there's life after death."

"Well, I *did* have some inside information," Gabriel admitted. "Now, about my confession."

"It's not that you're an angel?"

"No. There's something else."

Michael waited while Gabriel glanced shiftily at Raphael. "What is it?"

"I stole something from you," Gabriel finally said.

"What?" Michael frowned in confusion. "Everything I ever had is back on Earth. I don't think it matters anymore."

"Oh, it does," Gabriel replied. "I stole your memories, Michael."

"What?" Raphael beat Michael to it with the question. "Oh, Gabriel, you didn't?"

"I don't understand," Michael said. "What are you talking

about? I remember everything. I don't have any gaps or lost time or anything."

Gabriel took his hands in both of his. "Michael, it's extremely rare for an archangel to go to Earth to bring a soul here. We only do so on special occasions, and for very special people."

Michael didn't think that described him, but he sensed more to come.

"Michael, you were—are—an archangel, just like us."

Gabriel appeared nervous as he waited for Michael to react to his statement.

"You can't just blurt it out like that," Raphael scolded. "Michael, come on, let's go somewhere quieter. Gabriel has some explaining to do."

They ended up sitting on a beach that Gabriel and Raphael told Michael was his. He liked it and felt maybe this *could* be his home.

"You decided to give up your wings and be reborn," Gabriel explained. "When a person steps through the archway they lose all memories of their life before that moment. I stole your memories from you, right before you took the final step."

"Why?"

"Because I thought you were making a hasty decision, and this way I could return them to you when you came home."

"You mean now?" Michael said.

"Yes."

"Why did I give up my wings?" Michael asked.

"You thought it for the best," Gabriel said. "Here, let me give you your memories back. Then you'll have the answers to many of your questions."

Michael waited as Gabriel leaned in toward him and kissed him for several long minutes. The kiss wasn't sexual, and there was no desire there, it was something else, though Michael couldn't say what exactly.

When Michael pulled away his memories had been

restored to him, just as Gabriel had promised. There was so much inside his head, he felt overwhelmed and didn't know quite what to think about first.

"Michael?" Gabriel said. "Are you okay?"

"You've seen my memories," Michael replied, unable to meet Gabriel's eyes.

"Yes." Michael could hear no judgment in the quietly spoken word.

"You saw what happened in the Underworld, the last time I went there."

Gabriel took Michael's hand and squeezed his fingers. "Lucifer was drunk on power. He wasn't himself."

"Don't make excuses for him," Michael said. Knowing that Gabriel had seen him kneeling at Lucifer's feet, sucking his cock in front of a room full of demons, embarrassed him even more than the event itself had. "And don't excuse *my* behavior either."

"I'm not," Gabriel replied. "I saw everything that happened, through your own eyes."

"Then you saw how easily he manipulated and used me. All he has to do is hint someone will take my place in his bed and I agree to anything he asks. How long do you think it would have been before I fell from grace?"

"I don't believe you would have," Gabriel replied. "You chose to be reborn rather than risk falling. Your will is stronger than you think."

"I was running away and we both know it. Not that it did any good. He still found me."

"Lucifer is most persistent," Gabriel said.

"We hid you as long as we could," Raphael explained. "Unfortunately, as suspected, the older you grew, the more of a beacon your angelic aura became, until it shone so brightly we could no longer hide you."

Gabriel nodded and picked up the story. "We hoped we wouldn't have to interfere directly, especially when you made it clear you weren't interested after he first approached you. You saw Raphael and me warning him off too—we hoped our threats would be enough to keep him away. Unfortunately, as you know, he decided against leaving you alone, and when we spotted him watching you again, it was decided I would go to Earth to protect you, as your guardian angel. We made a deal with Lucifer that he could only go to Earth to see you when I was in your presence."

"Please tell me you weren't in my bedroom the nights he came to me there," Michael begged, his face heating with renewed mortification.

"No, of course not," Gabriel assured him. "Lucifer never did stick to the rules. After you told me about your dreams we realized what he was doing."

"Do you know why he didn't come back to me again?" Michael asked.

Gabriel and Raphael exchanged a glance.

"What is it?" Michael questioned. "What aren't you telling me?"

Gabriel spoke first. "After you told me he had been visiting you, in what you thought were dreams, we brought him before us. It was agreed that, as you were human, we couldn't stop him from making you a legitimate offer, just as he would any other human. I admit we encouraged him to do so, since it seemed fairer than the way he was using sex to lure you to him. What we don't know is why he stepped back. He told us you refused his offer, but we don't understand why that would have kept him away. When he usually recruited and an offer was rejected, he'd just make a new one, until he got what he wanted. Not that he's actively recruited humans in centuries, not since relinquishing the ability."

"How did he get the power back anyway?" Michael asked.

"Well, I didn't give it him back," Raphael muttered. "I voted against it."

Michael turned to Gabriel. "What happened?"

"When Lucifer discovered what you had done he was

furious. He declared all previous agreements between himself and the archangels null and void. He demanded his power to convert humans back."

"And you just gave it to him?"

"No, of course not. As Raphael said, we took a vote."

"I can't believe that vote passed," Michael said.

"Lucifer made it clear he would do a lot more damage if we *didn't* give him the ability back," Gabriel explained. "With the power boost he received from the second fall of angels, we have no doubt he could have carried out his threat."

"Has he recruited many new demons since the vote?"

Gabriel shook his head. "Not a single one, at least that we're aware of. As far as we can tell, the only one he has tried to recruit is you."

"And he didn't exactly try too hard to win me over," Michael muttered. "I don't understand why he gave up so easily."

"You'll need to speak to Lucifer directly about why he didn't make you a new offer," Raphael said. "Only he can answer all your questions."

"And it'll have to wait, I'm afraid," Gabriel added. "The rest of the archangels wish to speak to you first."

Michael nodded and followed after his friends. He wondered what Lucifer would have to say when they finally came face to face again.

* * * *

The archangels' chamber was just as Michael remembered. Even his seat was there, though he wondered whether it was actually his, or if he had lost his place amongst them forever.

"Welcome back," Metatron said as Michael hovered in the archway between Gabriel and Raphael. "I'm Metatron."

"He knows who you are," Gabriel interrupted. "Unbeknownst to Michael I held his memories in safekeeping for him. They have now been restored to their rightful owner."

Metatron gaped at Gabriel while the other archangels began to whisper. It seemed Gabriel had told no one what he had done.

Metatron recovered his composure and waved them into the room. "In that case, we won't keep you long. I'm sure there are others you'll want to speak to soon."

Michael nodded. He hoped his parents, the humans who had raised him, were here, as well as his daughter.

"Michael, please take a seat," Raguel asked, pointing to the chair in the center of the room.

Michael cast a quick glance at his former place but didn't approach his old seat. When everyone had sat down he was relieved to see that his old chair remained empty. At least he hadn't been replaced entirely.

"You'll no doubt wish to know whether you have earned your wings back," Raguel said. "I'll tell you quite plainly, the answer is no."

The words were a punch to the gut.

"You lived a good life," Raguel continued, "and you resisted temptation, but so do many humans. To earn a set of wings, you must do more."

"Not all of us agree with this," Gabriel interrupted. "Many humans earn their wings over time, without the extraordinary acts of courage and self-sacrifice you seem to think are necessary."

"We each recruit in our own way," Raphael added. "Not everyone follows the same criteria. Some of us aren't quite so selective as to who we believe will make a good angel."

"Nevertheless, the majority have spoken," Raguel stated. "Michael has lived only one life, during which he performed no great acts of bravery or selflessness. He was almost lured to the darkness by Lucifer himself. And, perhaps most importantly, we have to take into consideration that Michael was not an ordinary angel. If his wings were to be restored he would be a powerful archangel again, with far more powers at his disposal than a newly winged human."

"As you point out, Michael is an archangel. He gave up his wings for a reason, and he deserves to have them restored to him now that he's returned to us."

Raguel smiled. "Michael *was* an archangel, and the reason he gave up his wings is still as relevant today as it was the day he chose to be reborn. Even if we were minded to agree on whether he deserves them, he must still make the choice between his demon lover and his wings."

"I think he should speak to Lucifer before he makes his decision," Gabriel said.

Michael recalled why he hadn't discussed the matter with Lucifer prior to being reborn, but perhaps Gabriel had been right. The hurt on Lucifer's face when he had found out Michael truly didn't know him could have been avoided.

"Very well," Raguel replied. "If he wishes to speak to Lucifer, so be it."

"I'd like to talk to him," Michael agreed. "But I'd rather not speak to him today, if that's all right."

"Of course," Gabriel assured him with a smile. "Your home is still your home. Why don't you go there and think things through."

Michael nodded and rose to leave. He felt as though he had come full circle, and perhaps he had. Gabriel had been right, as always. Michael should have spoken to Lucifer before being reborn. After all their years together, he had deserved that much.

* * * *

Michael made one stop before he went home. With Gabriel's assistance, since he could not work it himself without his powers, he made use of the pool of visions.

He looked in on his parents and other family members from his life on Earth, seeing that they had all been reborn to new lives.

He also checked in on his daughter. At first he thought she

too had been reborn, but on closer inspection he realized this wasn't the case.

"We noticed she stopped ageing not long after you were reborn," Gabriel explained. "We're not sure yet if she has stopped completely, or whether she is merely ageing at a much slower rate to humans."

"How is she dealing with that?" Michael asked.

"She's been doing fine. We've been assisting her in faking her own death and forming new identities."

"Thank you."

"She's family," Gabriel said. "Ardat seems to be monitoring her too. She's made contact with Michelle several times over the last few decades."

"To what purpose?"

"She tells Michelle she just wishes to get to know her. If she has any other agenda, we don't know what it is. Michelle is cautious and her angelic powers far outweigh her demonic heritage. She is strong and wise. Don't worry about her too much. We're taking care of her."

Michael nodded as he continued to search for his friends and family through the pool. Once he had assured himself that everyone was well and happy, he said goodbye to Gabriel and walked home.

Chapter Twenty

The next morning Michael still had no idea what he would say to Lucifer, though he suspected he might not have the opportunity to say much at all if Lucifer was still angry about what he had done.

Michael sat on the beach, staring at the cliff face. He supposed he couldn't put it off any longer.

He was halfway to the concealed tunnel when he remembered he no longer had his powers and couldn't open the passage. Cursing himself for being an idiot, he retraced his steps and went to track down Gabriel. He found him working in his garden, just as he had always done. The familiar sight was a welcome one.

"Can you help me open the door to the Underworld?" Michael asked. "I think it's time for me to go see what Lucifer has to say for himself, but without my powers I can't get down there. Can I syphon a little from you, just enough to open the tunnel?"

"He's not in the Underworld," Gabriel said. "He's in one of our cells."

Michael frowned, knowing something wasn't quite right about that. "But our cells could never hold him. He's far too powerful."

"He came here voluntarily," Gabriel explained. "He hasn't tried to escape, though we're all a little puzzled as to why."

Michael was equally confused but simply added the mystery to the long list of questions he already had for his lover.

Gabriel offered to fly Michael to the cells, which were

located deep in the mountains, and Michael accepted. While the journey on foot would have given him the chance to get his thoughts together, he suspected every sensible notion would fly from his head as soon as he saw Lucifer.

They arrived at the cells and Gabriel announced his intention to visit some of the other fallen angels. He explained that he had been speaking with many of them in recent decades, hoping to bring some back to the light. They made arrangements to meet in a few hours, and Michael took the final steps to Lucifer's cell.

The first thing to surprise him was the open door, though since Lucifer could break out whenever he chose, doors seemed rather pointless objects anyway.

Lucifer sat in a cushioned chair, a book in his hand and a cat on his lap. Michael gaped when he recognized the animal as the childhood pet he had grown up with. How in the world had Lucifer tracked the animal down? He had passed away long before Lucifer had located Michael.

"Where did you find him?" Michael blurted.

Lucifer didn't look up from his book as he replied, "He found me. I think he knew one day you'd walk through my door again. He had more hope of your return than I did."

Michael crouched beside the chair and stroked the cat's fur. "Hello, Tom Cat. Have you missed me?"

Lucifer snorted. "The moggy gets a greeting, but I don't?"

"Hello, Lucifer." Michael sighed. "I guess we have a lot to talk about, don't we?"

"You could say that," Lucifer replied, finally meeting Michael's eyes. "I see you have your memories back—Gabriel, I assume—so how about you start explaining?"

Michael took the seat next to Lucifer's. "I'm not sure where to begin," he said. "I assume you know the petition to ban relationships between angels and demons was passed?"

"Yes, Gabriel told me."

"My vote was the one to decide the issue," Michael said.

"It was?"

"Yes."

"Gabriel failed to mention that."

"Aren't you going to ask me why I voted for the ban?"

Lucifer put his book down on the small table. "I assume it's because you were angry with me over my behavior in the Underworld."

"No."

"Don't lie to me," Lucifer said. "I know you were furious."

"Of course I was angry. You humiliated me for the entertainment of your demons. But that's not why I voted for the ban." Michael stood and began to pace.

"It was nearly a week before I even *knew* about the ban," Lucifer said. "When you didn't come back I accepted you were probably angry with me. When I discovered you'd sealed the passageway I wondered if perhaps I *had* gone too far. Gabriel summoned me before the archangels and informed me of the ban, telling me you didn't wish to see me. I presumed you had made the choice to keep your wings. It would have been nice to be consulted, since, last time I checked, there were two of us in this relationship."

"I'm sorry. I should have told you what I intended to do."

Lucifer nudged Tom Cat to the floor and rose to his feet. Michael cringed at the fury in his eyes. "Sorry? You left me without a backward glance, and you're *sorry*?"

"Don't you dare play the victim!" Michael shouted back. "You treated me like a whore in front of your demons. You used your powers on me. You kept me from leaving the Underworld. You manipulated me, just as you've always done, from the moment we met."

"You didn't even give me the chance to make amends."

"You made it very clear what you wanted from me," Michael raged as he rose to stand toe to toe with Lucifer.

"I wanted you to join me."

"You wanted me for sex," Michael yelled, scaring Tom Cat, who jumped up onto a nearby shelf. "Well, you can get that from any of your demons. There were plenty of them there that day who made it clear they'd be happy to take my place. If all you want is a cocksucker, you don't need me."

"Is that what you think?"

"That's what you *said*."

"I promised you I'd never take another into my bed for as long as we're together."

"Then why did you summon Gregor?" Michael asked. "You made me choose between humiliating myself or watching another man pleasure you."

"I knew you'd stop him before his lips ever touched my cock."

"And that's what scared me," Michael replied. "When it comes to you, I'd do anything to avoid losing you to someone else."

"Not anything," Lucifer said.

"Yes, *anything*," Michael argued. "I came too close to falling that day. I didn't want to, but if you'd asked me to fall from grace or watch you fuck another man, I'd have turned demon for you. *That's* why I voted for the ban, Lucifer. Because when an angel loves a demon to such an extent, it's too dangerous to be allowed to continue."

Lucifer's anger dissipated as quickly as it had appeared. He sat back down and Michael returned to his seat too. "You were that close to falling?"

"I won't—can't—turn demon," Michael said. "You know that, you've *always* known that."

Lucifer nodded. "Yes, I know. Even when I had no idea where you were, or what you had done, I knew falling had never been an option. I had demons searching the earth for you for years, until word finally reached me that your aura had been spotted. I raced there, eager to see you again, only to find a human who treated me as if I were a stranger."

"You *were* a stranger to me," Michael pointed out.

"I know," Lucifer said. "That's when I realized how much I had lost, entirely through my own selfish actions. I'm so sorry, Michael. The last time I saw you—in the Underworld, that is—I was drunk on the power boost from the fallen angels. I shouldn't have treated you the way I did. My behavior was inexcusable. I love you, and I beg your forgiveness."

"We've both made mistakes," Michael said. "I knew it was the power boost making you act that way. I should have waited for you to sober up before I made any hasty decisions. I should have at least spoken to you before I fled for Earth. I think it's about time we started communicating properly, don't you?"

Lucifer stuck out his hand. "Agreed."

They shook on it and Michael reluctantly released Lucifer's hand. "So, how long have you been living here in this cell, instead of in the Underworld?"

"Since you refused my offer."

"Why would you choose imprisonment over freedom?"

"Two reasons," Lucifer replied. "Firstly, I wanted to distance myself from the Underworld and the power that makes me say and do things I shouldn't. It's easier to resist temptation when you're removed from it."

"And the second reason?"

"I wanted you to be able to visit me, as you are now. Without your powers you can't open the passageway."

"I could have borrowed some power from one of the other archangels."

"You can do that?" Lucifer asked.

"Yes."

"I never knew that."

"We've learned a few tricks since you were one of our number. Only the archangels can loan powers in such a way, and it has to be agreed, never stolen, but Gabriel wouldn't hesitate to help me."

Lucifer smiled. "I rather like Gabriel, you know? I came to know him quite well while he was escorting me on Earth. I can see why you're friends."

"Hmm. That wasn't the impression I got whenever I saw the two of you together. You were always sniping at each other."

"Angels and demons," Lucifer replied. "It's something of

a habit."

Michael chuckled and shook his head. "Any excuse. You two could have been friends, if you'd given each other a chance."

"Maybe one day we will be," Lucifer said. "So, now you know why I chose to be incarcerated here, what else would you like to know?"

Michael frowned. "I already know Gabriel and Raphael warned you off after you first found me, not that you took any notice of them."

"Your bodyguards told me to stay away, or else. At first I wondered if I should respect your wishes, but when I found out you'd been targeted by some of my more mischievous minions, I defied the archangels to keep an eye on things."

"I was targeted?"

"Gabriel didn't tell you?"

Michael shook his head.

"Didn't you ever wonder why you had so many *accidents* after you first met me? Or why you seemed to attract the wrong type of men?"

"Coincidence?"

"Demonic influence," Lucifer corrected. "I did my best to protect you, and Gabriel helped as well. Between the two of us, we managed to stop the worst of the attacks, without you ever knowing about them. I suppose, I should confess, I didn't exactly do a lot to stop the parade of losers you began to attract, thanks to a group of lower-class sex demons who had put the whammy on you."

Michael had made many enemies over the years, and he supposed he shouldn't be surprised the demons delighted in causing him trouble while he was most vulnerable. "I guess now I know why my love life was so abysmal."

Lucifer smirked. "It wasn't all bad. I recall there were a few enjoyable nights."

Michael glared at Lucifer until his smirk disappeared. "Three nights out of a lifetime of loneliness?"

"You weren't *that* lonely," Lucifer reminded him. "You

had plenty of sex, just not with me."

From the sulky expression on Lucifer's face, Michael suspected he should probably let the subject drop, but there was one more thing he wanted to know. "There could have been more if you'd pursued me a little harder. Why did you disappear on me?"

"You refused my offer," Lucifer reminded him.

"I know, but that wouldn't usually stop you. Why didn't you come back with a better one?"

Lucifer looked away and wouldn't meet his eyes.

Michael left his chair and knelt at Lucifer's feet. "Tell me, Lucifer, why did you give up on me?"

"Because I finally accepted I couldn't give you what you wanted," Lucifer whispered. "I couldn't make you happy."

"That's not true," Michael argued, but Lucifer raised his hand.

"Before I fell from grace, I put pressure on you to place me before all others. Since I fell, all I've done is use you for my own pleasure while trying to convince you to join me in my damnation. I never once thought about what you wanted. With or without your wings, you'll always be an archangel. It's part of who you are, and I had no right to ask you to give that up. Then, after you left me to be reborn, I tried to lure you into my world again. Even knowing you'd gone to such extremes to escape me, I tried to drag you back, at the time when you were most vulnerable. I never made you happy, because I never thought of your feelings, only my own."

Michael took Lucifer's hand and squeezed his fingers. "You love me. *That* makes me happy."

"But it's not enough, is it?"

"I don't know," Michael admitted. "I gave up my wings and ran away rather than face our problems head-on. I was terrified of falling from grace."

"I should never have asked you to."

Michael released Lucifer's hand and turned round so he rested his head against Lucifer's leg, letting his lover stroke his hair. "What are we going to do?"

"I don't know."

They sat quietly and Michael watched Tom Cat play with a bowl of water on the sideboard. The kitty's antics were a pleasant distraction. "He seems to like that bowl," Michael commented.

"He's trying to figure out why he can't see anyone in there," Lucifer said.

"What do you mean?"

"The water is from the pool of visions. Gabriel brought it to me, so I could watch you on Earth. Tom Cat liked to view you too."

"Spied on by my lover and my cat." Michael chuckled. "An unusual pair of voyeurs."

"I didn't watch you have sex," Lucifer told him. "I found it too painful to see you with other men."

"I'm sorry."

Lucifer continued to stroke his hair and Michael closed his eyes, content for the moment to forget everything except what happened in the here and now.

"I can't speak for the cat, of course," Lucifer added. "He could be a secret perv."

Michael laughed and tilted his head to see Lucifer's teasing smile. "Idiot."

"I prefer the term fool."

"Fool then. What else have you been doing in here for the last sixty years?"

"Ask the question you really want to know," Lucifer said.

Michael sighed. Lucifer had always known him too well. "Did you replace me?"

"No." Lucifer tilted Michael's chin. "I swear to you, there has been no other since the day you left me. You have always been the only one for me."

Michael believed him. He should never have doubted his faithfulness. "What have you been doing to pass the time?"

"Thinking."

"About what?"

"Anything and everything. What I want out of life, and what really matters. I even…"

"What?" Michael prompted when it seemed Lucifer had lost his train of thought.

"I talked to Him."

"You did?" Michael was surprised. Lucifer hadn't talked to Him since before his fall from grace, and, from what he could recall, hadn't spoken to Him particularly frequently in the months preceding his fall.

"I asked him to watch over you," Lucifer said. "Not that I needed to ask. He would never turn his back on one of his angels, not even one who has fallen so far as I have."

Michael took Lucifer's hand again and kissed the knuckles. Hearing from Lucifer's own lips that he had prayed for him gave him hope such as he had never felt before. His heart swelled with love for the man beside him.

"Lucifer, will you take me to bed, please?" Michael asked. He wasn't an angel at the moment and they weren't breaking any rules. Michael didn't think he could stop himself, even if they were.

Without a word, Lucifer drew Michael to his feet and led him into the adjoining room. Furniture in the room was sparse, but it did have a large bed, with cream sheets and covers, and that was all they needed.

Michael's fingers trembled as he undid his robes. After so many years in modern clothes, he was relieved to be back in his familiar attire again, yet he still fumbled a little. Lucifer gently pushed his hands aside and undressed him. Michael wanted to do the same for Lucifer, but he was too nervous to even untie the cord of his belt.

When Lucifer had finally undressed them both, he took Michael's hand and guided him onto the bed.

"Just so we're clear, you're not dreaming," Lucifer told him with a wink.

"I know," Michael replied. "I think a part of me always knew you were real, even if I didn't know what you were or how you got into my room in the dead of night."

"No lock can keep me from you," Lucifer said. "Only our own stubborn natures can keep us apart. I'm working on mine, though."

"Me too."

Lucifer smiled and dipped his head to kiss Michael's neck, softly and light as a feather. Michael sighed and closed his eyes, letting Lucifer rediscover his body, relearning all his most sensitive spots.

All it took were a few touches of lips on his skin, firm hands skimming his hips, and Michael was more aroused than he could remember being in years. No one had ever managed to give him as much pleasure as Lucifer did. Each stroke from the tip of a finger sent waves of desire through Michael's body. He felt as though he had been sleeping for a hundred years and only now did he wake from his slumber.

Michael moaned softly as Lucifer worked his way up and down his chest and neck. He felt the press of lips against his ear, jaw, and cheeks. He opened his mouth a little, and Lucifer accepted his silent invitation, kissing him gently. Michael sucked on Lucifer's lower lip, nipping at it when Lucifer tried to pull away.

"Patience," Lucifer whispered.

"It's been too long for me to be patient," Michael complained. "I need you so badly. Lucifer, please."

Lucifer chuckled into his ear, then began trailing kisses back down his chest. He sucked Michael's nipples into his mouth, worshiping first one then the other, until Michael thought he might come from that alone.

Then, before Michael could embarrass himself with his lack of control, Lucifer moved lower again, dipping his tongue into Michael's navel and licking along the line leading to his groin.

Just when Michael thought Lucifer would take him into his mouth, he changed direction, sucking on the skin at his hip, marking him once again.

Half-hard since the moment Michael had walked into

Lucifer's cell, his erection now reached almost painful proportions, and still Lucifer didn't touch him. He felt the dampness of his pre-cum dripping onto his abdomen, and a moment later Lucifer lapped him clean with sweeping strokes of his tongue.

Michael couldn't believe he had given this up for so long. No one knew how to touch him as Lucifer did. What mortal could know just what he needed? Lucifer had learned every inch of his body thousands of years ago, and he remembered every tiny detail.

When Lucifer finally touched his aching cock, Michael moaned, long and low, with pleasure. He planted his feet on the bed, spreading his thighs and opening himself to Lucifer's expert attention.

Michael craved Lucifer's mouth on his shaft, his lips circling him, his tongue stroking his sensitive flesh while he swallowed him deep in his throat.

"Lucifer, please," Michael begged, hoping his lover knew what he craved, because he had lost the ability to form coherent sentences the moment Lucifer's fingers had grasped his dick.

He knew, of course he knew. Lucifer sucked his cock head and teased the tip with his tongue. Michael bucked and moaned, shouting for more. Only Lucifer could give him what he needed.

Michael wanted everything Lucifer could give him and he wanted it now, before he lost his mind to the endless need. He spread his legs wider and Lucifer dipped his head, sucking one of Michael's balls into his mouth. When he had done with the first, he gave the other the same exquisite treatment. His long hair brushed against Michael's erection, causing renewed sparks of desire to shoot through his body.

"Lucifer, Lucifer, Lucifer," Michael moaned, his lover's name the only word he could recall as he spiraled out of control.

A finger at his opening sent him soaring to new heights of pleasure and Michael pushed down against the digit. He expected Lucifer to breach him with his fingers, but once again he surprised him, exploring his anus with his tongue. Lucifer didn't seem in any great hurry to move things on to the next level, something Michael found himself grateful for, because he didn't know when they would have the opportunity to be together again.

Lucifer sat back and pulled Michael into a sitting position so they were eye to eye. "I love you, Michael," he said. "More than anything."

Michael didn't doubt that he meant the words, even if they were spoken in the heat of passion.

"I won't lose you again," Lucifer continued. "I'll do whatever it takes to stay with you. Do you understand what I'm saying?"

Michael nodded, even though he wasn't entirely sure he did. His head was cloudy with lust and he ached to be taken. He needed Lucifer inside him more than he needed to draw breath. He grasped blindly for Lucifer's erection, finding the thick length with his shaking hand.

Lucifer groaned when Michael held him, squeezing gently.

"Need you," Michael said against Lucifer's lips. "If you love me, please don't make me wait any longer. I need you in me, now."

Lucifer pushed Michael onto the bed and eased his legs back. Michael held them in place as Lucifer scrambled into position, lining up his cock with Michael's anus.

"Do it," Michael said. "Now!"

With one smooth thrust Lucifer entered him, filling Michael as no other man ever had or ever could. Only Lucifer could make him feel so completely claimed.

The pain of Lucifer's entry burned for a few seconds, until Lucifer took away his sting with a stroke of his fingers. Michael had definitely missed that with his lovers on Earth, but he at least had the presence of mind not to mention the fact right now. Reminding Lucifer of his life without him on Earth would be a definite mood killer.

Lucifer moved, easing in and out of him with shallow thrusts. "That's it," Michael urged. "Right there, Lucifer, right there."

Michael shouted encouragement until he lost the power of speech. Then all he could do was moan and scream and hope Lucifer understood what he wanted. And Lucifer did. He took Michael's legs and placed them over his own shoulders, all without breaking his rhythm.

They moved together until their bodies became slick with sweat. Michael's cock bobbed between them, and he knew without a doubt he would come without being touched again. He closed his eyes and held on to the last bit of his control, knowing he wouldn't last much longer.

Lucifer shouted out his name, pleading and begging Michael for anything and everything. Lucifer filled him, covered him, and claimed him completely. Michael accepted that he couldn't walk away from Lucifer this time. He wouldn't survive another separation. This one had been too much to bear. He couldn't go through it again, searching his entire life for something that was missing, without even knowing what he sought.

"Michael!" Lucifer screamed as he stiffened and filled Michael with the heat of his release. That was something else Michael realized he had missed, and he savored the sensation of his lover coming inside him, with nothing between them at all. On Earth he had never had unprotected sex, never having found someone he loved and trusted enough to take such a step. He clenched around Lucifer's softening cock, moaning loudly, on the brink of his own climax. Then Lucifer moved inside him again and Michael cried out, coming harder than he ever had before.

When he recovered from his orgasm, Michael realized Lucifer was licking him clean. Michael touched Lucifer's face and, when he had his attention, he beckoned him closer, seeking his lips and the kisses he so desperately craved.

They lay on the bed, kissing languidly, the outside worlds forgotten about. The realm of angels, the Underworld,

Earth, nothing mattered except this room and their own private paradise.

Unfortunately, paradise couldn't last forever, even if Michael would have hoped otherwise. Gabriel would be here soon, searching for him and asking him what his decision would be. Michael wished there was an easy answer to his dilemma.

"Having regrets?" Lucifer asked. He brushed a stray lock of hair from Michael's face, worry evident in his expression.

"No, never."

"Then why the long face?"

Michael forced a smile to his lips.

"It won't work," Lucifer told him. "You're still worried about something, so how about we try that old-fashioned thing called honesty and talk about what's bothering you?"

Michael sighed. "I just don't know what I'm going to do and I need to make a choice soon."

"What are your options?" Lucifer asked.

"Rebirth or you," Michael replied. "I didn't want to make a choice between my wings and you before, so I chose rebirth instead. I'm not going to run away again."

"Gabriel said you decided not to give up your wings because you'd have been a target for every demon in the Underworld who wanted a piece of you."

Michael hesitated before he replied. "Yes."

"You don't sound too sure about that."

"I know I'd have been a target, but I also know you'd have done everything in your power to protect me from my enemies."

"I can't watch you every minute of every day. If I could, you'd never had suffered all those accidents."

"Don't try to make excuses for me," Michael said. "I should have placed my trust in my love for you. Instead I didn't give you the chance to prove yourself worthy of that love. I ran away in a manner unworthy of an archangel."

Lucifer kissed him softly. "Don't be so hard on yourself. I had done little to earn your love and a great deal to drive you away. I never deserved you."

Michael opened his mouth to argue, but Lucifer cut him off with a finger to his lips.

"I didn't, and we both know it. Now we have a second chance to put things right and I think we should consider all our options. What are the choices, as you see them?"

"Well, my wings aren't an option according to Raguel. I didn't do anything worthy enough in my life to warrant being restored to my archangel status. That leaves two choices — rebirth again, or life on Earth with my memories and you as my lover."

Lucifer nodded. "I can see why you've discounted the third option, that being turning demon, but I don't think you've considered the fourth one."

"What are you talking about? These are my options and I think we both know what I'm going to decide. I don't want to be reborn again. I want to remember you from this day forwards."

"I want you to remember me too. But if I were to visit you on Earth, it would only be with one of your archangel friends escorting me. I'm sure you don't want an audience, and now I'm sober, neither do I."

Michael frowned at the reminder of what Lucifer had put him through that dreadful night.

"I'm so sorry," Lucifer told him again. "I'm ashamed of what I did to you. I want to destroy every demon who was present."

"I'd rather just forget about it," Michael replied. "Besides, I'm sure the archangels would give us a little privacy."

"Personally, I'd rather not test your theory."

"I don't see we have any other choice, unless you want to tell me what you think our fourth option is?"

Lucifer smiled and leaned over to whisper in his ear. "What do you think would be a worthy enough act to earn back your wings?"

"I don't know," Michael admitted. "I recruited based on the hearts of humans, not on their acts. But each archangel chooses their angels in a different way, and the majority voted I don't deserve my wings yet."

Lucifer nipped his earlobe then sucked it into his mouth. It was quite distracting. What had they been talking about again?

"Do you think," Lucifer whispered, "saving a fallen angel might convince even the strictest archangel that you're worthy of your wings?"

"Hmm," Michael murmured. Lucifer sucked on Michael's neck and his arousal spiked again.

"What do you think?" Lucifer asked.

Michael blinked at Lucifer, his mind fuzzy. "About what?"

Lucifer rolled his eyes and drew back. Michael whined at the loss of contact.

"I want to go home," Lucifer said.

"These cells can't hold you," Michael pointed out, his head a little clearer now Lucifer had put some distance between them.

"I'm not talking about the Underworld." Lucifer stood and Michael watched him morph into his full demon form. Lucifer held out a clawed hand. "I told you, back on Earth, I would give you anything you wanted, that all you had to do was ask. You don't need to tell me what you want. I already know your deepest desire is the return of your wings. I'll do *anything* to make you happy, Michael."

Suddenly Michael understood what Lucifer meant and his heart raced. He took Lucifer's hand and squeezed his fingers briefly. He blinked back tears of joy, barely able to believe what he saw. Lucifer's horns disappeared, his claws retracted, and his leathery wings transformed back into the soft feathers of an angel. Slowly, every sign of the demon vanished, until the most beautiful angel Michael had ever laid eyes on stood before him.

For the first time in countless centuries, Michael gazed upon the son of the morning in all his angelic glory. The sight left him speechless, just as it had all those years ago, when he'd spied on Lucifer in the pool of jewels.

Almost as if he knew where Michael's thoughts had gone, Lucifer opened his hand, which had been empty a moment ago, but now held a necklace with a blue gemstone, the exact same color as Michael's eyes.

"Gabriel gave this to me," Lucifer explained. "He told me I should be the one to give it back to you. Do you accept my gift?"

Michael could tell Lucifer was asking about more than just the necklace. He nodded and let Lucifer tie the clasp beneath his hair.

"Cough, cough." The voice came from the next room and Michael recognized Gabriel's humorous tone. "Are you both decent?"

Michael laughed. "Not a stitch of clothing between us," he said right as Gabriel strolled in the door, the warning coming too late.

Gabriel ground to a halt and gaped at Lucifer.

Michael smiled at Gabriel's reaction, knowing Lucifer's nakedness wasn't causing the archangel to stare so blatantly. To gaze upon Lucifer in the form he had been born to was to see something so pure and beautiful that even Michael had forgotten how the sight could take a man's breath away.

Gabriel sank to one knee before Lucifer and bowed his head, deferring to an angel who outranked even him.

"Oh get up," Lucifer muttered. "I've had enough beings kneeling before me. That's no longer what I want."

Gabriel rose and continued to stare at Lucifer, clearly at a loss for words.

"The archangels will wish to see him," Michael said.

Gabriel nodded. "And you too."

Michael and Lucifer dressed and the three of them left the cells. This time Lucifer carried Michael as they flew to the main concourse and the archangels' chamber.

From the moment Lucifer landed, depositing Michael gently on the ground beside him, they drew stares from everyone. Lucifer may have been able to hide amongst the angels before, but not any longer. The son of the morning could never be passed over.

Michael took Lucifer's hand and he could feel him shaking. "Don't be nervous," he said.

Lucifer smiled and together they walked away from the crowd and into the chamber of the archangels.

It didn't take long for the rest of the archangels to arrive and each of them appeared equally awed by Lucifer's presence.

"I don't think this will take long," Gabriel said as he took his seat.

Michael and Lucifer stood in the middle of the room and waited.

"Lucifer has been restored to us," Gabriel continued. "And Michael was the one to bring him back to the light. I therefore petition for Michael to be restored to his former status as archangel, and our leader."

"Agreed," Raphael declared, and one by one the rest of the archangels — even Raguel — voiced their support.

Power surged through Michael's body and he spread his wings for the first time in more than ninety years.

Gabriel gestured to the empty seat and Michael nodded. He didn't move from Lucifer's side to take his place, though, simply because he didn't want to release Lucifer's hand quite yet.

"Welcome home, Lucifer," Gabriel said. "I think I speak for everyone here when I say this is an unexpected pleasure."

Lucifer accepted his words with a small smile. Michael tried to stifle his own grin of delight, but it wouldn't be contained. This morning he had been so conflicted, and now he had everything he had ever wanted. He barely registered what Gabriel and the others said, but he heard just enough to understand the general gist of things. Lucifer would be performing his former duties, while at the same time he would be doing whatever he could to restore peace to the world, most specifically by encouraging the other fallen angels to follow his example and return to the light.

Michael felt sure he was up to the task, and he intended to help him in any way he could.

Gabriel called the meeting to an end, making one final comment that they would have to find another chair for Lucifer, so he might take his rightful place amongst them.

Lucifer laughed and sat in Michael's seat, pulling Michael onto his lap as he made himself comfortable. "Don't hurry on my account," he said. "I'm sure we can make do for a while."

Gabriel laughed and shook his head as he left the room.

Michael waited until the room had cleared before he wrapped his arms round Lucifer's neck and kissed him. "We have a lot of lost time to make up for, don't we?"

"We do indeed," Lucifer replied between kisses. "I think we should start immediately."

Michael settled into Lucifer's embrace. "I couldn't agree more."

* * * *

Michael and Lucifer had been home for nearly three months. Lucifer had moved in with Michael, declaring his home more modern and homely, unlike his own cold residence, far removed from the rest of the populace.

They were very much in a honeymoon period of their relationship, and although Michael knew it wouldn't last forever, he intended to enjoy the bliss for as long as he could.

Michael had visited all his friends, as well as his recruits, resuming his duties as though he had never left. He also spent some time on Earth, reconnecting with his daughter. Throughout it all, he kept Lucifer at his side, encouraging him to socialize, and not cut himself off from the rest of the angels, as he had before his fall. Michael explained to Lucifer that it wasn't because he feared he might fall again, he just wanted to ensure he knew how much he was loved, not just by Michael, but by the rest of the angels too.

"Our first day with no duties for either of us since I came home," Lucifer said as he attempted to tug Michael from the comfort of his bed.

Michael mock glared at his lover. "I take it we aren't sleeping in this morning?"

Lucifer shook his head and grinned. "Your guess is correct."

"It's still dark," Michael complained.

Lucifer laughed and whipped the covers from Michael. "Come on, hurry up, or we'll be late."

Michael grumbled as Lucifer prodded him in the ribs until he got out of bed. "Are you going to tell me what's so important I have to get up at this ridiculous hour of the morning?"

"No," Lucifer teased. "Besides, you used to wake this early on a regular basis, if I recall."

Michael slipped into his robes and shook his head. "That was when I had added incentive."

"And spending this glorious day with me isn't incentive?" Lucifer stuck out his lower lip but couldn't hold his pout for longer than a second or two before his easy smile reappeared.

"It's still night," Michael pointed out.

Lucifer ignored his complaining. "I'll make it worth your while," he whispered into Michael's ear.

Wide awake now, Michael let Lucifer lead him out of the house and up into the clear skies.

Michael wasn't sure where Lucifer was taking him at first, but as the trees opened up into a clearing, he recognized a place he hadn't been to in years. Lucifer's pool of jewels was still as beautiful as it had always been.

The colored gemstones glittered in the water and on the walls of the cliff, sparkling in the light of the new dawn, casting rainbows in the pool.

Lucifer stripped off his robes and dived into the water, surfacing for air a few moments later.

Michael sat on the grass, a sack of peaches Lucifer had

brought with them beside him.

"Are you enjoying watching me?" Lucifer asked from where he trod water in the middle of the pool.

Michael picked up a peach and took a bite. "Very much," he called back, grinning widely.

"Why don't you come join me?" Lucifer suggested. He floated on his back, the morning sun casting a warm glow over his perfectly sculpted body.

Michael didn't need any further invitation. He set aside his half-eaten fruit, slipped off his robes, and joined Lucifer in the water. Lucifer met him in the middle of the pool, and when Michael swam into his arms, he knew they had finally come home.

My Boyfriend's an Alien

Excerpt

Chapter One

Zakrynious tapped his foot impatiently as he waited for his turn to appear before the elders of his people. The queue to the transformation chamber — the only one on the entire planet of Trimmeron — stretched as far as the eye could see. He'd been standing there for hours and he still couldn't see the doorway at the front of the queue. At least this would probably be the last time he'd have to go through the ritual of transformation. Then again, he'd thought that before.

"What are you hoping for, Zak?" Strathryn, the young Camyl'on directly ahead of him, asked. Zak hadn't met him before today, but they'd been waiting so long Zak felt as though they were old friends. "I want to see what life's like on Marinatia."

Zak laughed loudly, prompting a few glares and admonishments from the others in the queue. "Rather you than me."

"What's wrong with Marinatia?"

Zak shook his head. "Everyone who goes there comes back smelling of fish. Once you've turned mer, there's no way to ever get rid of the stink."

Strathryn snorted back his laughter as the line moved on a few more inches.

Zak had not expected this latest transformation. Already close to maturity when he'd last been brought before the elders, it had been something of a shock to find himself back here once again. He had frequently wondered during the last few days what he would end up as this time. He could discount his own race and those he had already changed into during his puberty, but there were still incalculable possibilities.

As one of a race of chameleon-like beings, each of their kind took on several new appearances during their years of puberty up until adulthood. They remained in their new guises until whatever powers causing the transformations determined them ready to change again.

Zak had spent his last transformation on the icy mountains of Gr'chn and although he had enjoyed his time amongst the hospitable mountain people, he had been eager to rid himself of the coarse, furry hide they had developed so as to more easily endure the harsh climate. He much preferred his own softer furred body.

When Zak had reverted back to his natural state on the previous world, he had expected to have full control over his body and the ability to change appearance at will. When he'd realised he didn't, he had rushed to catch the next spacecraft back to Trimmeron so he could take the potion the elders provided to trigger and ease the next transformation. Luckily Gr'chn was an Alliance world and the locals didn't think anything of the fact that he was suddenly a different species.

He had once asked his father why they had to go through with the transformations. His father had told him the story of one of their youths who had refused to drink the potion to trigger the change to a new form. The transition had come anyway, and had been extremely painful for the youth, so much so that he'd had to be cared for by their healers for several days afterwards. The healers were still working on a way for their healing waters to help anyone else who dug their heels in about taking the potion. Unfortunately, the transformation ritual was shrouded in secrecy and the elders refused to reveal the contents of the potion to anyone. Without the knowledge of the ingredients, the healers were working blindly as they searched for answers.

Finally, after another two hours of waiting, Zak reached the doorway. At least now he could watch those transforming before him, which would help to pass the time.

Zak could see his parents, Aristania and Cor'shi, sitting in the chamber along with family members of some of the other youngsters. He gave them a small wave and they looked back at him proudly. He had barely seen them for more than a few days together since his first transformation. Such was the way things had always been for those of his kind. To enable the youngsters to learn about each form they took, it was customary for each young man and woman to be fostered out to a family on the world native to their new body.

The line crept forward and Zak's turn to stand before the elders finally arrived. He didn't have a great deal to say. The elders had already received their report from his foster parents on Gr'chn, which told them all they needed to know. They had also extracted from him copies of his own memories of his time on Gr'chn, adding his experiences and knowledge to their collective database.

All Zak had to do now was drink the vile concoction that would trigger his next transformation. He prayed it would be the last time he'd have to drink the revolting substance. When he reached maturity, around the age of forty, he would revert back to his natural form without being in control of the transformation for the last time. If he ever needed or wished to take on one of his other forms, that being any of those he had taken during the years of his puberty, he would be able to do so at will, and without the need of potions.

"Drink up, Zakrynious," the elder said as he passed him the heavy goblet. "Many others await their turn after you."

Zak gulped the lukewarm liquid down as fast as he could and waited for the potion to take effect.

The transformation never hurt, it simply happened. His first clue that the change had occurred was the realisation that he stood shorter than he had been a few moments before. Not a great deal shorter, just enough for him to notice he no longer stood eye to eye with the elder before him.

He looked down at his hands and frowned as he observed their new and strange colour. Pale ecru and smaller than he had been used to, they also had two more fingers on each hand than his natural form had. He wriggled the extra digits, already anticipating them being a nuisance until he became used to them.

"Well, this is quite unusual," the elder commented. He coughed nervously and looked behind him to the other elders. "I've never seen anything quite like this before."

Zak glanced towards his parents in the audience. They stared at him with expressions of surprise and perhaps a little curiosity. He turned back to the elder and waited for him to tell him where he would be living for the duration of his transformation. Until he knew which galaxy he would be residing in, he had no idea which spacecraft to go to.

One of the other elders stepped forward and peered at him closely. "Most irregular," he mumbled.

"What is it?" Zak asked. "What's the matter?"

"Why, we don't know what you are," the first elder replied. "I don't recall seeing one of those before."

"I thought we always took the forms of races who would play a large part in our lives." Zak looked from one elder to the other, waiting for one of them to explain what had happened.

The elder patted him on the arm kindly. "That's true. Now we just need to figure out what you are, so we can make arrangements for you to be fostered."

Zak nervously shifted on his feet.

More books from
L.M. Brown

Book one in the Heavenly Sins serial

*When an angel and a demon fall for the same mortal man
there is only one solution…share him.*

Book two in the Heavenly Sins serial

Is it possible for a demon to be a good man, or are all who have fallen for temptation evil at the core?

Book three in the Heavenly Sins serial

*With one of his lovers imprisoned in the Underworld, Mac
has no choice except to go where most angels fear to tread.*

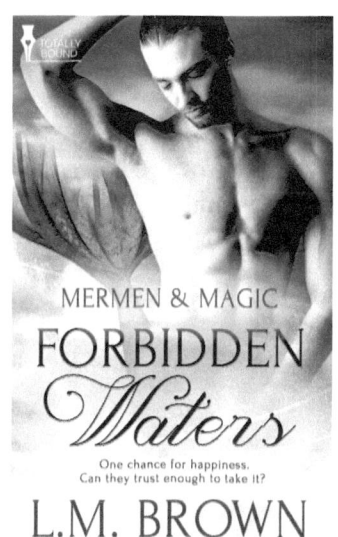

MERMEN & MAGIC

FORBIDDEN
Waters

One chance for happiness.
Can they trust enough to take it?

L.M. BROWN

Book one in the Mermen & Magic series

For the dying race of mer people, homosexual relationships
are prohibited. When Kyle falls for Prince Finn he knows
he is navigating forbidden waters.

About the Author

L.M. Brown

L.M. Brown is an English writer of gay romances. She believes that there is nothing hotter or sweeter than two men in love with each other… unless it is three.

When L.M. Brown isn't bribing her fur babies for control of the laptop, she can usually be found with her nose in a book.

L.M. Brown loves to hear from readers. You can find contact information, website details and an author profile page at https://www.pride-publishing.com/